CN00894730

Praise for tl
Award Winning

THE ALIEN SKILL SERIES

Reader's Favorite Book Awards 2021
GOLD MEDAL WINNER - Category Preteen.

Wishing Shelf Book Awards 2019-2020
SILVER MEDAL WINNER - Category Teenagers.

Feathered Quill Book Awards 2021
FINALIST - Category Young Readers.

IAN Book of the Year Awards 2020
FINALIST - Category Juvenile.

Reviews:

"An extremely timely message for today's readers."

"Solid aliens-crash-to-earth tale."

"Great new series for young and old alike!"

"One of the best series I have read."

BOOKS BY RAE KNIGHTLY

Prequel

The Great War of the Kins

Subscribe at: www.raeknightly.com

THE ALIEN SKILL SERIES

Ben Archer and the Cosmic Fall, Book 1

https://www.amazon.com/dp/1989605192

Ben Archer and the Alien Skill, Book 2

https://www.amazon.com/dp/1989605095

Ben Archer and the Moon Paradox, Book 3

https://www.amazon.com/dp/1989605141

Ben Archer and the World Beyond, Book 4

https://www.amazon.com/dp/1989605044

Ben Archer and the Star Rider, Book 5

https://www.amazon.com/dp/1989605176

Ben Archer and the Toreq Son, Book 6

https://www.amazon.com/dp/1989605214

The Knowledge Seeker

https://www.amazon.com/dp/B09HL252JQ

BEN ARCHER

THE ALIEN SKILL SERIES (BOOKS 1-3)

A boy with an alien power.

Rae Knightly

BEN ARCHER

THE ALIEN SKILL SERIES, BOOK 1-3

For information, go to :

www.raeknightly.com

Cover design by PINTADO

Book Formatting by Derek Murphy @Creativindie

Published by PoCo Publishers

ISBN E-book: 978-1-989605-02-8

First Edition: June 2019

For my husband,
the real superhero.

For Elianne and Diego,
who were born of two cultures.

For my parents,
Pierre and Nicole.

CONTENTS

BEN ARCHER AND THE ALIEN SKILL

BEN ARCHER AND THE MOON PARADOX

BEN ARCHER

and

THE COSMIC FALL

A boy with an alien power.

Rae Knightly

CHAPTER 1 *Missing*

Ben Archer knew that something bad had happened to him on the night of *The Cosmic Fall.* He knew this because, precisely one month after the event, he was still waking up every morning from the same nightmare. He would sit up straight on his bed, a scream stuck at the back of his throat. It was always the same. One minute he would be reliving that fateful night on his closed eyelids, the next he would be wide awake, sweat pearling his forehead, his mind grasping for the fading images.

Wednesday morning, September 27th, was no different. The alarm clock yanked the boy out of his turbulent slumber, sending the dark threads of his nightmare scattering to the back of his mind where he could no longer reach them.

A Jack Russell Terrier jumped onto Ben's bed to check on his master.

"'Morning, Tike," Ben mumbled, patting his faithful dog before sinking back into the bed. Gathering his thoughts, he searched his mind for the smallest hint of a memory. But it was already too late; whatever he had been dreaming about was already lost to his conscious mind.

The family doctor had explained that it was normal to

experience temporary amnesia after having been bedridden for almost three weeks. High fever could distort one's memory and provoke terrible nightmares. Seven days ago, when the doctor declared Ben healthy again, he recommended the boy take it slow but try to get back to his normal life as soon as possible.

Whatever normal means...

Tike wagged his tail, then nudged Ben in the neck with his wet nose.

"Okay, okay, I'm up already!" Ben grumbled.

He dragged himself out of bed, and pulled on the jeans and t-shirt that lay in a heap on the floor of his messy room. He headed for the bathroom where he checked his reflection in the mirror. His cheeks hadn't fully recovered their colour, and there were dark pockets under his brown eyes. His auburn hair stuck out all over the place, as though someone had tried to vacuum it during the night. He gave his head a quick brush but had to abandon a mesh of hair that poked out from the back of his head.

Tike waited impatiently by the front door.

Ben opened it. "Hurry up, Tike. I gotta go in fifteen minutes."

The white-and-brown dog scurried down the stairs of the apartment block, then headed to the yard to do his morning business.

In the meantime, Ben filled Tike's bowls with crackers and fresh water. He poured out his cereal and milk before sinking into the couch to gulp down his breakfast in front of the TV. He flipped through the channels as he munched on the crispy cereal. 8:00 a.m. meant the morning news came on.

"...tensions between China and the US have once again escalated due to the event social media has dubbed *The Cosmic Fall*," a news anchor with a serious air reported on Channel 2. "A source from the US Defense Ministry has claimed off-the-record that the American satellite which was destroyed in space four weeks ago, was in fact, designed to spy on Chinese territory. The head of the FBI has denied these allegations and continues to accuse China of destroying its communications satellite. On a more reconciliatory note, the President of the United States has once again urged the Canadian government to grant access to the crash site to both Chinese and US investigators to help them determine the exact cause of..."

Ben switched channels.

A morning talk show came on, showing a cheerful man who held up a palm-sized rock. "...it is so compact it weighs six pounds! But wait until you hear its price tag! One pound of this meteor debris is worth over a million dollars!"

The show host squealed while the audience watching the live show gasped.

"I can picture folks frantically overturning their yards to find meteor nuggets!" the show host laughed.

Ben pressed the control again.

This time an old black-and-white image of hills covered in torn-up pine trees appeared on the screen while a soothing voice explained in the background, "Thousands of hectares of trees were crushed to the ground like toothpicks by the shockwave of the exploding meteorite in Siberia in the 1970's..."

Ben turned off the TV in a hurry. His hand shook over the control.

I should know by now not to watch the news!

He jumped when he heard a scratching on the door, his cereal spilling over the edge of the bowl.

"Darn!" he muttered.

He opened the door to let Tike in, leaving a trail of milk all the way from the living room to the kitchen. Having lost his appetite, Ben placed the half-eaten bowl of cereal in the kitchen sink. He tore off a paper towel, then roughly soaked up the milk drops on the carpet. Tike watched him curiously with his head cocked.

"Think it's funny, huh?" Ben uttered, as he scrubbed the floor.

Not a sound left the dog's throat. Ben observed the terrier sitting patiently before him.

How come you never bark anymore?

Ben picked himself up from the ground and threw the paper towel away. He put on his jacket, then flung a water bottle, banana, energy bar and a wrapped-up ham sandwich loosely into his backpack before heaving it onto his right shoulder. While struggling to zip his jacket, he headed down the hall to his mother's room, his backpack scraping against the wall. The door stood ajar so he peeked inside.

Tike joined him and peered through the crack below him.

Laura Archer lay on her bed, fast asleep. She had recently begun working night shifts at restaurants and bars after losing her day job. Her former boss had not appreciated her spending week after week watching over her ailing son.

Ben hesitated to leave his sleeping mother, half hoping she would open her eyes. He wanted to tell her he'd had another nightmare. But when she didn't stir, he whispered, "Bye, Mom," before tiptoeing away.

He put on his runners. "I'm outta here, Tike. I'll see you in a bit." His eyes fell on his dog. Tike gave him a forlorn look that dug deep into the boy's heart.

Ben bit his lip. "Oh, come on, Tike! Don't do this to me again! I have to go to school. You know that!" He knelt to hug his four-legged friend. As he rubbed Tike's back, he felt the warmth of the fur and the beating heart inside the dog's chest.

We share the same fear.

Ben stood hastily, bothered by the thought.

Out loud, he said, "Take care of Mom, okay?" He quickly closed the door to avoid glimpsing Tike's eyes again.

* * *

At the doctor's recommendation, the twelve-year-old had reluctantly gone back to school, which was a drag because he had missed the first two introductory weeks of September. One of Ben's closest pals had been placed in another classroom where he had already made firm friends with a new boy. Ben's other classmates had formed tight-knit groups; they had prepared their first homework and knew which teacher taught what. Ben felt like an outsider disrupting a well-established order.

It didn't help that he spent the first week in a daze. He had a hard time concentrating on the lessons and felt exhausted by the time he got home. His mother told him to be patient, his body had experienced a great shock and was still pulling itself together. Young people recover quickly, she would say. You will be fine in no time.

I don't think so...

As he let himself out of the three-story building, Ben took out a plastic bag to pick up his dog's poop before the downstairs neighbour could complain. He threw the waste in public garbage, then jogged down the street towards school.

Not so long ago, he would have run down the three blocks of houses without a second thought. Yet although four weeks had passed since Ben fell ill, he ran out of breath as soon as he reached the first pedestrian crossing. He slowed to a fast pace as he hugged the walls of the houses, hunching over to fend off a sprinkling rain, and made it in time for the school bell. He weaved his way through the groups of students, intent on reaching the main door so he could get away from the outdoors and the crowds.

Something ripped. The weight of his backpack fell away from his shoulder. Catching his breath, he glanced down to find the strap had torn off. In his haste that morning, he had neglected to zip the backpack all the way. Its contents spilled onto the ground, his pens rolling over the playground, his notebook falling into a patch of mud, and his water bottle emptying itself on a library book.

Students burst into laughter around him while others pushed past in their haste to get inside. No one offered to help. Ben was left to fend for himself as he painstakingly recovered the pieces strewn around him. By the time he was done, the last couple of giggling students ran by, their shoes thumping on the asphalt.

Ben lifted his backpack with both arms to avoid any further embarrassing fabric tears. But as soon as he stood, he became fully aware of the empty playground and the immense sky above. He was alone, at the complete mercy of the emptiness, unprotected and vulnerable. His head swam dizzyingly and his vision blurred. Ben clung to his backpack for dear life. His heart raced, and his breath came in gasps as he experienced the burden of a full panic attack. As soon as he shut his eyes, the nightmare erupted without pity: a dark mass falling from the night sky, his Grampa shouting in warning, twisted eyes, the shadow of a man with white hair reflected in the fire, a whisper...

Mesmo.

Tike's snout on his cheek.

"Ben!" someone shouted, shaking him by the shoulders.

"Wake up! Ben!"

He opened his eyes. Tike's paws were on his chest, the dog's face close to his own. Above him, his mother called to him anxiously. He blinked and found himself lying in the middle of the playground, surrounded by Tike, Laura, and a couple of teachers.

A school assistant ran up to them, a cellphone in her hand. "I'm calling an ambulance," she announced, holding the phone to her ear.

"No!" Laura objected. "Please don't! I'll take Ben to our family doctor. He's familiar with Ben's condition."

The assistant hesitated, then put the phone away.

"Are you okay?" Laura asked Ben, eyebrows knitted.

Ben nodded to reassure her.

She helped him up carefully. "The school called me and said you were standing by yourself in the middle of the playground. I hurried over with Tike. You were completely paralyzed." She accepted Ben's backpack from one of the teachers.

Ben became excruciatingly aware of the adults staring at him strangely. From inside the school, students pressed their noses against the windows, pointing in his direction.

Oh, great! Nice way to blend in...

CHAPTER 2 *The Dugout*

Agent Theodore Connelly entered the office of High Inspector George Tremblay, deep in one of the Canadian Security Intelligence Service's best-kept secret underground facilities, hidden in northwestern Ontario. Although only thirty-seven years old, early loss of hair had pushed the agent to shave his head completely. This gave him a handsome, clean look which went well with the job.

The High Inspector sat behind his desk, legs crossed, ankle over knee, the tips of his fingers drumming together as he conversed with a man sitting opposite him. Several files lay open on the High Inspector's desk and he closed a couple of them before standing up to greet Connelly.

The assistant in a tidy suit and skirt who had led Connelly in, gestured elegantly towards the imposing man in his early sixties. "High Inspector George Tremblay, Head of the National Aerial Phenomenon Division of the CSIS," she said, before presenting Connelly. "Agent Theodore Edmond Connelly, Chilliwack RCMP, British Columbia." She then left the office gracefully.

Connelly said nothing as he offered his hand to greet the

High Inspector. The latter gestured towards the seated man with stern-looking straits. "This is Inspector James Hao. He is leading the investigation you have been assigned to. You will report to him at all times and he, in turn, will report to me."

Hao stood and shook Connelly's hand while they held each other's gaze.

Connelly took in the man's black hair streaked with grey above the ears.

The High Inspector invited both men to sit as he went through his thick files, one of which clearly contained information about Connelly. The High Inspector made direct eye contact with the bald man, saying firmly as if reading from a textbook, "Anything that is said regarding the current investigation is classified and divulging any or all information will be penalized immediately and without revoke in accordance to the law on treason to national security."

Connelly automatically responded, "Yes, Sir."

The High Inspector scanned some documents, nodding satisfactorily.

"You have made quite a stellar career, Agent Connelly," he began. "From patrolling the streets of Chilliwack for ten years, to leading investigations at the CSIS Headquarters in the past month. Your colleagues are already saying you're a wonder boy." He glanced at Connelly and said meaningfully, "The question is whether you know what is at stake..."

Connelly replied in a well-oiled manner, "I do, Sir. I witnessed *The Cosmic Fall* four weeks ago. I was the first on site. It has become my life's mission to investigate this event in order to protect my fellow citizens and my country. I will do anything in my power to achieve this."

The High Inspector clearly wasn't impressed. "Agent Connelly, you are well aware that tensions between China and the US remain high. The US is accusing China of shooting down one of its communication satellites, while China holds the US accountable for secretly spying on them. Canada, on the other hand, is maintaining its story that the satellite was accidentally destroyed by a passing meteor, which then broke into two pieces, both of which crashed on the outskirts of Chilliwack on the night of August 26. As you know, we have been feeding this story to the news media for weeks."

He let his fingers run down the sides of his tie. The tone of his voice became serious. "But we know better, of course. We know the true nature of *The Cosmic Fall* and the threat that it may be posing to our planet. The Canadian Minister of Defense is holding a confidential meeting of the highest order next week. Both Chinese and US military officials have been invited to the table to discuss what little we know." He bent forward on his chair again, jabbing his index finger at Connelly. "*You* will be briefing this meeting."

After pausing for effect, he continued. "The fact that you witnessed *The Cosmic Fall* and that you hold a US passport through your mother has acted in your favor. The FBI has endorsed you. Inspector James Hao, here, also has dual citizenship. He was born on mainland China and is highly regarded by the Chinese Ministry of State Security. It is imperative that you work together. After this meeting takes place, the CSIS will no longer be the only Agency watching you like hawks. Do you understand?"

Connelly confirmed, "Yes, Sir."

The High Inspector straightened the files on his desk. "Your file is impeccable..." he said, before adding slowly, "Except for one thing..."

Connelly's mouth twitched.

The High Inspector removed a folder from Connelly's

thick file.

"Your wife..." the High Inspector began, as he slid the folder across the desk.

Connelly took the folder and opened it. Clipped to the left side was a photograph of a smiling young woman. She had curly hair around a youthful, dark-skinned face. Her eyes were grey and her teeth a perfect white. She looked like someone straight out of a magazine. The name on the descriptive form on the right side of the folder read Tamara Connelly.

Ignoring Connelly's discomfort, the High Inspector proceeded. "You haven't returned home once since *The Cosmic Fall*. I'm not a marriage counsellor, Agent Connelly, but we've had countless calls from your wife since you arrived. She's starting to think that you abandoned her and your kid. She's threatening to take you to court to divorce you and demand full custody of your son. You say you have become obsessed with *The Cosmic Fall*, but we can't afford to have a civilian court nosing into your business here. So either you quietly make amends with her or the next time you're in my office you'll be signing divorce papers. Either way is fine, but keep her out of the loop!"

He leaned back into his office chair, observing the Chilliwack police officer. "Any comments, Agent Connelly?"

Connelly held the High Inspector's gaze before replying through gritted teeth, "Tell me where to sign."

Taken slightly aback, the High Inspector stared at the bald man. Then he broke into a loud guffaw, his belly shaking under his impeccable suit. A palpable weight lifted in the room. The High Inspector wagged a finger at Connelly. "I like you!" he chuckled. "Forget the wife, Theodore. You're married to the job now." They were suddenly on first-name terms.

James Hao joined in. "Good thing you're getting a raise,

Connelly. Child support is brutal!"

In no time, Connelly was given the necessary clearances to enter what was known as the Dugout. James Hao drove him to a plain, concrete building surrounded by lonely hills. They scanned their badges at the entrance and signed a form that a soldier handed over as he scrutinized them. They took an impressive steel elevator down seven floors. When the elevator stopped, the doors remained closed.

Hao studied Connelly intensely. "Behind these doors lies the truth of *The Cosmic Fall.* Once you walk through, there is no turning back. Do you understand?"

Connelly nodded impatiently.

Hao scanned his badge once more so the elevator doors could slide open, revealing a cavernous hangar made of concrete. Connelly stepped through onto a corridor overlooking this huge space where men and women, most wearing white coats, bustled around, working at desks full of computer screens or entering offices with glass walls bordering the left side of the hall. In the very centre, a sleek, unusual-looking craft hovered silently a few feet above the ground.

"This," Hao said dramatically, "is the intact alien spaceship we recovered from the Chilliwack crash site."

After giving Connelly a minute to take in the extraterrestrial vessel, they headed down concrete stairs to the floor of the hangar. As they circled the spacecraft, Hao explained, "We have not been able to access the vessel so far. We are using an electron beam to bore a hole into it, yet its material is so consistent that we have only been able to dent it two points of an inch. It's going to take time before we get any real results. But mark my words, we will get in eventually."

Connelly's mouth twitched. He examined the closed hangar.

Hao smiled proudly. "Impressive, isn't it?" he asked. "The craft was flown in from Chilliwack. It happened on the night of *The Cosmic Fall* under citizens' very noses. We were lucky your local police contacted the CSIS immediately. We sent in a heavyweight helicopter to pull it out in the dark before the media arrived. Then we loaded it onto a cargo aircraft Boeing C-17 and flew it over. The next feat was to lower it into this old underground bunker before building several floors above it to seal it in. We have no idea how this vessel works or what's inside, so we had to make sure it couldn't fly away on its own through some sort of remote command." Hao continued, "Bringing over the other two spacecraft was trickier, though, since they had broken into several pieces. You will be able to examine them later."

As he spoke, he gestured for Connelly to follow him down another set of stairs to the eighth and last floor. "As you know, we completed the cover-up by inserting meteor debris from Nunavut into the Chilliwack crash site to show to the media. No one was the wiser. One of the CSIS' finest moments, if you ask me."

Hao passed protective clothing and a helmet to Connelly. When they were both fully covered, he led the way into a cold, high-security chamber where three incubators lay side by side.

"And here, we have the spacecrafts' occupants," Hao breathed, as they stared at the three beings who lay in the incubators. Hao spoke in awe. "We recovered these extraterrestrials from the crash site. As you can see, they could easily pass as humans, though they are slightly taller than us. They have strong features, olive-coloured skin and high cheekbones. Their most unusual feature is their white hair. The one furthest from us is a female specimen with long, straight hair and faerie-like features. Next to her is a male of about the same age with short hair. The third being is an older male who may have been their leader."

Hao stared at Connelly to check his reaction, but he seemed unmoved by the fact that he was in the presence of creatures from outer space.

A man in a lab coat appeared behind a tall window. He gestured to Hao that he wanted to speak to him.

Nodding, he said, "I'll give you a minute to get to know our three prime 'suspects'. Too bad none of them are alive to tell us their story. Right?" He clapped Connelly on the back as he walked away.

Stiff and silent, Connelly towered over the incubators. All of a sudden his brow creased above his determined eyes and he gritted his teeth. He leaned onto the incubator closest to him with both hands and bent his head in pain. The muscles at the back of his neck twitched. Something odd was happening to his face, for it began to tremble abnormally fast behind the helmet, as if his skin had turned into rippling water.

His eyes went from green to honey-brown, his nose shrank, his face lengthened and, out of his bald head, white, spikey hair appeared. When the transformation was complete, Connelly had been replaced by an entirely different being.

He glared intensely at the lifeless aliens. Then, in the reflection of a windowpane, he noticed Hao taking leave of the man in the doctor's coat. Hao would be joining him again in no time. The being's jaw clenched in concentration. His face trembled again, his breath coming in fast gasps and sweat pearling his front. It took all of his willpower to regain his former aspect, yet by the time Hao joined him by the incubators, Connelly's head was bald and his eyes were green again.

* * *

The family doctor blamed Ben's panic attack on his slow recovery from his illness and recommended resting for another couple of days. Ben didn't think resting would magically rid him of his nightmares and panic attacks, but Laura reminded him they had no choice but to follow the doctor's advice. After all, how was the doctor supposed to provide Ben with a decent treatment if they had not revealed the real trigger of the boy's illness?

"We can't tell the doctor the whole truth, Ben," Laura said gently, as she tucked him under a blanket on the couch. Tike lay down next to him contentedly.

Ben toyed with the TV control, pursing his lips.

"You do understand why, don't you?" Laura insisted. She brushed his fringe away with her hand.

Ben sighed.

I do.

He went over the reasons in his mind: his mother had found him unconscious, lying between the roots of a tree on the outskirts of Chilliwack, his hair covered in dirt and pieces of corn leaves, his face black with soot. By the time they had made it out of Chilliwack, military helicopters were crisscrossing the sky and reporters were flocking in to cover *The Cosmic Fall.* A heavy plume of smoke billowed off the hillside next to Grampa's house...

Laura interrupted his thoughts. "If the doctor discovers you were in Chilliwack that night, we'll find a herd of reporters and investigators swarming our apartment. I need you to recover your health, but that won't happen if there are cameras stuck to your face."

Ben groaned. "I know, I know, Mom. You told me before. I

don't really care about the reporters. It's Grampa I'm worried about."

Laura knelt beside him. "I'm worried, too, honey," she said softly.

Ben asked, "Did you call him today?"

Laura looked down at her hands. "I call his house every day, Ben. I've called him a hundred times since *The Fall...*" She broke off.

Ben swallowed. "...and, still no answer?"

Laura's brows creased as she shook her head. "Still no answer."

* * *

By the next week, Ben headed back to school, but it wasn't long before he got himself noticed again, because Tike had somehow managed to escape the apartment and was found sitting politely in front of the school entrance. After the Principal realized that suspending Ben would not have any effect on the dog, and after most of the students voiced their excitement at having a cute dog "guard" their school, he decided to turn a blind eye on the problem.

From then on, Tike always accompanied Ben and waited for him patiently by the school entrance. Ben found this to be a huge relief. Knowing that his faithful friend was close-by brought him a sense of calm, and he was able to concentrate on his lessons again.

Unfortunately, the sympathy that Tike received from the students did not rub off on Ben, for he never felt the need to hang around with boys and girls from his class to talk about which movie they were going to see that weekend, or how to best handle Mr. Taylor's Math assignment.

When the school bell rang, Ben left in a hurry, hiding his dark brown eyes under his side fringe, hugging the brick wall of the school building, then crossing into a side street which fewer students used. He was barely across the road when he noticed two older boys hanging around behind a van. He swore under his breath for not having noticed them sooner, but it was too late. One of them, the tallest, shouted, "Hey! Oddball! Where ya goin'?"

Ben knew the bully's name was Peter. He hunched over, quickening his pace, but Peter called again, "Hey, wait up, Oddball. You have to meet my new friend, Mason."

Mason yelled in a sing-song voice, "Hi, Oddball!" Both boys sniggered as they followed him down the road.

Ben took off, his new backpack bouncing against his side, Tike following close behind. He was passing a chain link fence when, out of the corner of his eye, dark shadows approached him. He jumped and found three fierce-looking dogs cross a small yard to examine him up close. Ben's hair prickled at the back of his neck as the huge animals shadowed him from behind the fence. He was so mesmerized by the silent creatures that a car almost hit him as it emerged from the parking lot of an adjacent building. The man honked angrily, blocking Ben's passage.

Ben turned to face the bullies. They were just about to catch up with him when the three beasts threw themselves at the fence, barking wildly and growling menacingly. The two boys yelled, backing away in fright.

Ben stared at the scene in amazement while Tike tugged at his trouser leg as if telling him to get moving. Ben didn't need convincing. He sprinted off, heading into busier streets where he caught a bus to the coast.

* * *

Stanley Park was considered one of the most beautiful city parks in the world, nestled on a semi-island surrounded by Vancouver Harbour and English Bay. It was covered in lush, dark-green western red cedars, bigleaf maples and Douglas firs, while circled by the coveted Seawall where city dwellers and tourists alike could hike, jog, stroll, cycle or rollerblade while they enjoyed the view of the city skyline and the North Shore Mountains.

For Ben, it meant freedom to roam along forest trails or the beach while throwing a stick for Tike to fetch. When both boy and dog had had enough, they sat on boulders in front of the Seawall, close to the empty outdoor pool, which only functioned in the summer months.

The mid-autumn afternoon ticked by. Ben's backpack lay dumped aside, forgotten, as he threw pebbles into the water. Tike tilted his head at the sight of a small crab skittering among the rocks.

"Hey, you! Kid!" someone yelled. Ben whirled, startled. A young man on a bicycle wearing high-tech cycling garments and unplugging headphones from his ears, nodded. "Yes, you!" Then he pointed towards the parking lot behind the swimming pool. "Is that your Mom?"

A car honked and several pedestrians turned disapprovingly to see who could be making such a racket. A woman waved her arm energetically through the window of the car, which Ben recognized as being his Mom's old Toyota.

"Yes, thank you," he told the cyclist, flustered. He picked up his backpack, then jogged to the car with his head down. He had barely slid into the passenger seat before she scolded him. "What's the matter with you? I've been waiting for you all afternoon! You can't go off on your own like that! What if you'd had another panic attack?"

"Mom! I'm fine!" Ben retorted. "You don't need to be on my back all the time!" He braced himself for her answer while he put on his seat belt. He was reminded of how they had always been bickering at one another before his illness. They were both stubborn that way. But this time his mother remained silent.

Ben was startled to see Laura's chin quiver as a tear rolled down her cheek. She bowed her head to let her loose hair fall to the side of her face like a curtain so he couldn't see her cry. Her breath came in short gasps, accompanied by a wheezing sound.

Asthma attack!

The anger left Ben as soon as he recognized the sound. He reached for the asthma inhaler in her handbag and gave it to her. After she had sucked in a few breaths from the medication dispenser and regained control of her breathing, he asked carefully, "Mom, what's wrong?"

She stared out the front windshield, then turned toward him. Her red-rimmed green eyes revealed that she had been crying for some time. "It's your Grampa," she said softly. "He's in the hospital."

CHAPTER 3 *Evidence*

Inspector James Hao grabbed the doorknob, then pushed the heavy wooden door into the elegant meeting room. He allowed High Inspector George Tremblay and Agent Theodore Connelly to enter first, before following them without delay. He absorbed the room's occupants with a sweeping glance: a dozen men and one woman in business suits sat around a smooth, grey-tinted table. He spotted a couple of men in military uniforms heavily covered with war decorations, while High Inspector shook hands with the woman as he made his way to the head of the table, where he invited everyone to sit down. Hao joined him, while Connelly placed himself in the shadows, close to the wall.

The High Inspector thanked everyone for making it to the emergency meeting on such short notice. "The Canadian Government," he explained, "has opted to bring China and the US to the table to discuss the true nature of *The Cosmic Fall*. The reason for this, is that the event has become an international problem. The Government is considering involving other countries but does not want to risk a breach of information to the media at this point. We will now proceed without further delay." He presented Inspector James Hao, who moved forward to take his place in front of the curious onlookers.

Hao cleared his throat, thanked the High Inspector, and began. "On August 26 at approximately 10:46 p.m., a US satellite was destroyed while in full orbit around the Earth. Less than a minute later, several witnesses on the ground reported seeing an object hurtling across the sky. It crashed on the outskirts of Chilliwack in the province of British Columbia. At 10:57 p.m., a second mass fell from the sky and exploded sixty feet from the first. You are already aware of these facts, which were reported by the media. What you do not know is that at approximately 11:23 p.m., a third object reached the same location. This one, however, did not crash." He paused for effect. "It landed." He checked his audience for their reaction and got a lot of confused stares.

The Inspector clicked the button of a remote control, triggering a projector to cast images on a blank screen behind him. A close-up of the alien spaceship appeared. He heard gasps of surprise.

"The three objects which arrived on Canadian territory on August 26 were not meteor debris, as we have led the media to believe. They were unidentified flying objects—UFOs," Hao stated. "This image is of the third spacecraft, which did not explode and which we recovered on location. It is intact but has so far proven impenetrable."

Those around the table erupted into loud talking. The High Inspector stood to silence the attendees.

Several other, less obvious pieces appeared on the screen, as Hao raised his voice over the buzz. "These are the remains of the other two vessels which exploded upon impact. After closer examination, they clearly comprise the same kind of spacecraft." The pieces on the screen danced around each other before latching together like the pieces of a three-dimensional puzzle.

Hao clicked on the remote control and the screen went blank. When an image of the three alien pilots appeared, the audience exclaimed loudly. Hao almost had to shout to make himself heard. "We recovered the remains of these three beings from the crash site." He stared seriously at the people seated before him. "As far as we know, you are looking at the first extraterrestrial visitors to Earth known to Humankind."

It took much longer, this time, for the room to quiet down. Some faces flushed with anger, others became pale and drawn, while some attendees flung a series of questions across the room. The High Inspector, Hao and Connelly waited for the excitement to die down.

"Please," the High Inspector said. "We wish to present the facts to you before taking questions." He invited Connelly to come forward. "This is Agent Theodore Connelly, a police officer from Chilliwack, currently working for the CSIS. He was the first officer on the site of the crash. He has studied the evidence and has come up with some disturbing conclusions."

As if he were giving a lecture on some tedious subject matter, Connelly began, "Three ships. Three aliens." He pointed to an image of the ships and their occupants. "We assumed there was one alien per spacecraft. However, recent evidence shows this may not be so. As you can see, there is enough room inside the vessels for several more occupants. In vessel number one, which was the first to crash, we recovered DNA from the young alien man in this area of the ship." Connelly indicated. "But we recently discovered a different, unknown DNA—here." He pointed next to the image of the young alien male, who had been placed virtually within the spacecraft.

The room went deathly quiet as the attendees digested this piece of news. One man wiped the sweat off his forehead with a cotton tissue.

The woman with graying hair and stark composure spoke the words they all were thinking. “Agent Connelly, are you telling us that we are missing an alien suspect? Possibly a live, alien suspect?”

For a second Connelly held his breath, then said clearly, “I am, Minister. One, or more than one, alien suspects, who could be halfway across the world by now.”

* * *

Inspector James Hao leaned back in his office chair, a cold, wet towel pressed against his eyes. He heard his office door open and peeked under the towel to watch Connelly enter the room and throw a file on his desk. The bald man sat heavily in the chair opposite Hao.

“Do we have to do this now?” Hao grumbled, as he massaged his temples. “We just left the meeting!”

“We do,” Connelly confirmed matter-of-factly.

Hao sighed. “This had better be good, wonder boy.”

“It is. This is new evidence.”

“What?” Hao exclaimed, the towel falling from his eyes.

“Our meeting attendees got more than they bargained for, so I opted to leave out this piece of information.”

Hao frowned in disapproval but said nothing as he opened the file. A photograph of four broken pieces of glass lay before him. “What’s this?”

“This evidence came from the crash site,” Connelly explained. “When you assemble these pieces, they form a lens. I believe it is from a telescope.”

Hao frowned, his interest piqued. “Telescope... telescope...” he mumbled. Then his eyes brightened and he got up to search through a box on the floor labelled WITNESSES. He went through several files before fishing one out. He flipped the file RYAN ARCHER on his desk. “Yeah,” he said slowly, as he scanned the notes inside. “This witness stated he was stargazing in a field near his house when *The Cosmic Fall* occurred. Must be from his telescope.” He shrugged as he closed the file. “Makes sense.”

“But it doesn’t,” Connelly corrected, piercing Hao with his green eyes. He removed another picture from the file he had brought. This time it was a close-up of the lens. There were distinct fingerprints all over it. “I had these fingerprints analyzed,” he explained. “Most belong to the witness, Ryan Archer. But these smaller ones didn’t come up with a match.”

Hao straightened in his chair to analyze the information. Slowly, he said, “Are you telling me that we have a missing witness?”

Connelly nodded. “Ryan Archer wasn’t alone on the night of *The Cosmic Fall*.”

“...and he failed to mention it,” Hao finished, a million thoughts crossing his mind. “One missing alien. One missing witness,” he began slowly. “I don’t believe in coincidences. Get a team together and find out who was with Ryan Archer that night!”

He watched as Connelly picked up the file and stood with a smug smile. Just before turning to leave the office, Hao thought the Agent’s eyes flickered to honey-brown. He raised an eyebrow, then shook his head. “Trick of the light,” he thought, as he placed the wet towel over his face again.

* * *

By the time Ben and Laura reached Highway 1 Eastbound,

it was after five o'clock, which meant they were stuck in rush hour. Ben fell asleep as the sun set behind them in a myriad of yellow and orange streaks, while Laura navigated from one busy lane to another. They had travelled half the distance to Chilliwack when Ben woke up. He stared at the cloudy night, his mind wandering. A sudden thought crossed his mind.

"Mom?" he began, irritated by his own trembling voice. "Are we staying at Grampa's house?"

Laura glanced at him. "If we can't stay at the hospital, then yes, of course we'll stay at the house."

"Really?"

Laura sighed. "I can't afford to go to a hotel, Ben, you know that. And even if I could, I wouldn't. There's more than enough room at Grampa's house." He shot her an angry glance, so she added, "It's still our family home! What happened in the fields next to it doesn't change that."

Ben slumped back, scowling.

Laura's eyes softened. "You love that house, Ben. You remember that, don't you?"

He shrugged, saying nothing.

Yes, of course I remember. But that was before...

"You know, you're going to have to talk to Grampa." Laura interrupted his thoughts. Ben pretended to ignore her. She continued in a tender voice, "He's in intensive care, honey. He had a pretty big heart attack; he couldn't even remember his name. The nurse said the only thing they found on him was my cellphone number, which is how they got hold of me." Her voice wavered. "The thing is, I'm not sure how long he's got... You and he need to have a serious talk about what happened on the night you disappeared." She paused for a moment. "I need to have serious talk with him."

Ben turned to her, showing interest in the conversation for

the first time. "Are you still angry with him?"

Laura fell silent for a moment, then replied, "Grampa has always been there for us when we've needed him. I was so proud of him for helping us out after your Dad died. Remember when I told Grampa you had the measles when you were four years old? He jumped on the first bus over! And every time a school break started, you couldn't wait for me to drive you to Chilliwack! You were having so much fun with him over the summer holidays! I could tell from our phone calls!"

She broke off, then chose her words carefully. "But what happened on the night of *The Fall* is beyond me! Why did Grampa abandon you? What were you doing miles away from the house? How did you get there? And where has Grampa been all this time? All I got from him was a single phone call in the early morning after *The Fall* letting me know that he was fine but urging me to come and pick you up in Chilliwack. Since then, not a word to find out how you were doing, or to let us know where he's been. If Tike hadn't found me that day and led me to that tree you were lying under, who knows what could have happened!" She stopped herself as she shifted in her seat. "So, yes, I am still angry!"

Ben read his mother's face like an open book.

Not to mention out-of-your-mind with worry!

Ben turned his attention to the starry sky, mulling over what she had said, wondering whether, he, too, was angry. But he found he had a hard time grasping the feelings he had for his grandfather. Although he had excellent memories with his Grampa, his feelings for him tended to become entangled with the murky nightmare he kept having. And that was not something he wanted to linger on.

* * *

Over an hour and a half later, Ben followed his mother into the Chilliwack General Hospital with a heavy heart. He barely listened as a nurse explained that Ryan Archer was in a stable condition, and had been resting all afternoon in the Coronary Care Unit. However, he was not out of danger yet, she said. She also mentioned something about filling in some forms at the reception desk, as they were missing key information on their patient. But that could wait until later. First, she would take them to see Grampa.

Finally!

Ben saw Laura nod through the whole thing, though she seemed too shook up to reply.

When they entered Grampa's room, Laura placed a hand on Ben's shoulder to guide him to the hospital bed. Ben wasn't sure it was a gesture of comfort, rather, he guessed she needed someone to lean on, just as much as he did. And he understood why, because as soon as he saw his beloved Grampa, he had to swallow a huge lump in his throat.

Grampa was barely recognizable, tucked away in a hospital bed under crisp white sheets, his face covered by an oxygen mask, his chest hooked up to an intravenous pump and a heart monitor, beeping at the rhythm of his heart. Ben's vivid memory of a robust man, who stood tall as an oak, collided with the frail form that lay before him, and for an instant he thought they were facing the wrong patient. The old man's fading ash-blonde hair had almost turned completely white, while an unkempt beard dotted his chin.

Grampa wouldn't allow this!

Ben knew how much his Grampa railed against men who wore short stubbles, which, he declared, were neither clean shaven nor proper beards. Such laziness would not do, and he made a point to meticulously shave and comb his hair every morning. Ben held his breath as he remembered how his Grampa would affectionately attempt to paste down the lock of hair that always stuck out the back of his head.

Laura placed her hand on top of Grampa's. Ben fought against his tears as he noticed the bones under the long, thin fingers.

"Daddy?" his mother whispered.

There was no response.

They stayed beside Grampa for several hours, both crying silently, yet neither able to express their sadness.

When another nurse came by to check on Grampa, she told them they were welcome to spend the night in the waiting room. Or if they preferred, they could go home and rest: the hospital would call them if Grampa's condition changed.

Laura gave Ben a concerned glance. He took it he didn't look too great—and he didn't feel it, either.

"I'm going to fill in the forms at the reception desk," she said. "Why don't you get us something from the cafeteria? Then we'll head over to Grampa's house."

"But..." Ben objected.

"We can't leave Tike outside the hospital all night, Ben. He'll be safer at the house. There isn't much we can do right now, anyway." She spoke without much conviction.

Ben knew she wanted to stay, but decided against it for his sake. Yet he was too exhausted to argue, and the idea of his four-legged friend waiting outside the hospital was enough to make him agree.

Ben scouted for something to eat. The cafeteria had closed, so he settled for two rather dry-looking cheese sandwiches from a vending machine. He wrinkled his nose, but fed the coins into the machine anyway.

After getting the nurse to promise again that she would call if Grampa's situation changed, Laura and Ben headed to the house, which lay twenty minutes away on the outskirts of Chilliwack, surrounded by corn fields. It was almost two o'clock in the morning. The house loomed under a cloudy sky without a moon or star in sight.

Ben cowered in the car while his mother stood before the front door, illuminated by the headlights, searching for the keys in her handbag. She entered, switching on the corridor lights that splashed into the driveway. Ben reluctantly picked up their suitcases, dragging his feet inside, as Tike followed closely with his ears back and his tail between his legs.

They headed straight upstairs to the two guest rooms they had always occupied when they had vacationed at the house. Laura checked on Ben to make sure he had a warm quilt on his bed.

"Do you think Grampa will be okay?" Ben whispered from under the covers.

"I'm sure he'll be fine," she replied, before pecking his forehead to bid him goodnight. He could not read his mother's face in the dim light.

Ben closed his eyes as soon as she was gone, but his grandfather's face haunted him. He rolled around in bed and stared at the high ceiling. The room was a decent size. Grampa had painted the walls a soft blue after his grandson's birth. Two large windows looked out over the fields. An old carpet, a sturdy bed next to a nightstand, a cupboard with three drawers displaying a couple of photographs of baby Ben and Grampa, a sofa and several shelves with wooden toys and books Ben had played with for as long as he could remember filled the familiar room.

Ben was about to close his eyes again when something

caught his attention. He sat, suddenly alert. On a shelf on the opposite wall perched a sleek, white telescope. He had never seen it before. He got out of bed, pushed the sofa closer to the wall and clambered onto it before carefully removing the beautiful object. It still had the store tag attached to it.

It's brand new!

As he hopped off the sofa, something clanked inside it. He unwound the lens, then tilted the telescope to release the item that had come loose.

A silver watch slipped into his lap, followed by a piece of paper.

Ben stared at the unexpected items, then unfolded the note. It read, "Dear Ben, I believe this jewel is yours. I found it under the kitchen sink. Remember me when you look at the stars. Love, Grampa."

Ben stared at the note, then at the watch. At the centre of it glimmered a beautiful gem that might have been a diamond, though he didn't think diamonds shone this much. He wondered if Grampa had had it placed in the watch on purpose. One thing was certain, he had no recollection of it.

He sat on the edge of the bed for a long moment, sniffing and wiping his eyes with the back of his shirt as he stared at the items. When exhaustion gained on him, he let himself sink into bed. He covered his head with the bed sheets and fell into a deep sleep, the watch clasped tightly in his hand.

* * *

Tike lay next to a sleeping Ben, when a movement caught his attention. The dog lifted his head, his ears upright.

A tall man with white, wavy hair stood in the bedroom beside one of the windows. Tike sniffed the air and stared at the strange man from a few feet away. Then the form turned his head, distracted by something happening outside.

Tike jumped off the bed and stood on his hind legs to peek out the other window. Deer had materialized onto the fields, their antlers rising proudly over the cold mist. The animals remained in front of the house for a long time.

Then, as suddenly as he had appeared, the white-haired man vanished, leaving Tike staring curiously at the room.

* * *

In a bright, white office on the third floor of the Dugout, a CSIS fax machine clicked on, releasing a sheet of paper. A police report appeared bearing a picture of Ryan Archer's face. A red, handwritten note read, "Location: Chilliwack General Hospital."

CHAPTER 4 *Tiwanaku*

A tall man sat on the large steps of the Kalasasaya temple—an ancient monument that belonged to the ruins of Tiwanaku, a city built many centuries ago by pre-Inca people of South America. A cold breeze blew through the visitor's white, wavy hair, as he gazed at a stunning sunrise over the dry Andes mountain range which crossed eastern Bolivia. Behind him towered an impressive door built of perfectly carved stones, leading to an open courtyard guarded by a ten-foot monolith representing some forgotten deity.

In spite of his unusual hair, the man's strong features belonged to someone in his mid-thirties. He wore a crimson poncho over his long-sleeved shirt, protecting him from the early morning temperature. Closing his honey-coloured eyes, he let the sun warm his olive-tanned face. He did not immediately turn to greet the old Aymara native who had walked up behind him. After enjoying his fill of high altitude sunlight, the visitor stood and joined the older man, who offered him a broad smile.

"*Suma urukiya*[1], Observer," the old Aymara greeted.

The visitor's eyes softened as he answered, "*Buenos días*[2], Amaru."

"We have been waiting for you for a long time," Amaru said, before noticing that the visitor's attention had turned to the monolith placed centrally behind the gateway. Understanding his attraction to it, Amaru nodded. "It represents our shaman ancestor. A great shapeshifter. A rare skill, indeed, as you well know..." He trailed off.

They stared at it for a moment, before Amaru ventured, "You barely made it here alive. And yet I have been told that you wish to return to the crash site! Are you sure that is a wise decision?"

The visitor's gaze was lost in the distance as he replied, "Last night I had a vision. A spirit portal called me back to the crash site. Only one of my own could have sent me such a powerful message. It has to be my daughter! I must return to find out if she is still alive!"

Amaru sized up the white-haired stranger, before sighing and reaching inside his poncho. He produced a dark blue Canadian passport which he presented to the tall man. The stranger flipped through the pages until he found the identity and photograph of the passport's original owner. The name read Jack Anderson from Ottawa, Ontario. The face of a young man stared back at him with determination.

"Our scouts found Jack Anderson's body along the Inca Trail," Amaru explained. "He was reported missing two days ago after he went trekking on his own. Our scouts found his remains at the bottom of the mountainside. We have not yet informed

[1] *Suma urukiya* = 'Good day' in Aymara.

[2] *Buenos dlas* = 'Good morning' in Spanish

authorities that we have found him. Therefore, his passport will serve you for the next twenty-four hours. That is enough to get you back to Canada. But by tomorrow afternoon, we will be returning this poor man's body to his family."

The visitor nodded. "Yes, of course. I understand." He stared at Amaru, then said with sincerity, "*Gracias*[3], Amaru."

Amaru dismissed his thanks, continuing, "With luck, you will pass as Jack Anderson when you reach airport security." The old man dug into his poncho again and pulled out a beige fur hat with ear flaps so that the visitor could cover his unnaturally white hair. "Let us hope that this will do."

The visitor stared at his Aymara friend, sensing that he was not happy with the situation. "Amaru, my friend, rest assured that when the time comes, I will speak a good word for you."

Amaru glanced away hastily, clearly uncomfortable with the visitor's words.

"What is it?" the white-haired man asked, frowning.

Taking courage, Amaru said, "You are the Observer. Your mission is to be neutral and report the facts." He paused. "But dark forces are at work. Your companions have perished. Your daughter is lost, and you barely survived yourself. We fear that you are no longer neutral, that your judgment has been clouded."

The visitor put up a hand. "You said 'we'..."

Amaru stared at him unhappily, knowing that he had to finish now that he had started speaking his mind. "Yes. I speak for all the Wise Ones." He paused before adding carefully, "We have given you the information you came for, as is customary. It is not our place to judge. But word is spreading that you have already made up your mind about your mission. The word is

[3] *Gracias* = 'Thank you' in Spanish.

that your loss has blinded you."

The visitor replied sternly, "You cannot know my mind. I have made no decision, and I have yet to meet two Wise Ones."

Amaru bowed respectfully. "We understand. There is time yet." He led the visitor down the perfectly polished steps of the temple, away from a group of tourists who had appeared on the archeological site. "No matter," he continued. "What I meant to say is that I do not need you to put in a good word for me. I do not wish to leave this place. I have a wife, many children and grandchildren. We have wood for the fire, our llamas for warm fur and the most beautiful sunrises and sunsets on this planet. We could ask for nothing more."

The tall visitor stared at the old man in disbelief as they walked along the temple walls. After a long silence, he placed a firm hand on Amaru's shoulder, saying, "Perhaps you are wiser than the wisest, Amaru. Thank you for speaking your mind. I do not understand your wish, but I will respect it. When the time comes, rest assured that your name will not be mentioned. You will remain on this planet." He paused, before adding explicitly, "For better or for worse."

Relief washed over Amaru's face. He offered a wide smile. "Come, then, now that that is settled, we must get you on your way."

Before them lay the Akapana pyramid, where a group of Aymara men dressed in red ponchos and colourfully knitted caps with earflaps were waiting for them. When they approached, the group of men bowed their heads, saying in greeting, "*Suma urukiya*, Mesmo."

* * *

When Ben got up the next morning, he showered

hurriedly and glanced out his bedroom window while dressing. Next to his grandfather's house lay a field of browning corn crops, bordered by a line of trees and shrubs. Beyond that lay the famous field where *The Cosmic Fall* had occurred. Even though branches hampered the view, he could tell that the area was still sealed off by yellow tape to warn trespassers, though some of it had come loose and was flapping in the wind.

Higher up the hillside and overlooking part of the field, was Mr. Victor Hayward's modern, West-Coast-styled dwelling. Grampa's neighbour was a wealthy man who owned his own airline company, and this house was only one of his many different properties across the country. People in town said he was a big player in the Alberta oil sands, which meant he was away often.

Ben sighed and stroked Tike's back. He could hear his mother bustling in the kitchen, so he clambered down the stairs to join her. Tike did not follow him, preferring to sniff intently at a spot by the window.

The boy found his mother throwing out smelly items from the fridge. She had opened the kitchen door wide to let in fresh air.

"Morning, Ben. I guess we'll head out right away. The fridge and the pantry are empty. We'll find some breakfast at the hospital."

Ben nodded as he finished putting on his hoodie sweater. "I wonder where Grampa has been all this time," he said, noticing how the house had an abandoned feeling to it.

"Yes," Laura agreed, clearly unhappy and worried. "Let's hope we get some answers soon."

They argued about whether to leave Tike out in the backyard while they were at the hospital. Ben refused to leave his four-legged friend behind, but Laura convinced him that

Tike would be more comfortable at the house since the hospital did not allow pets inside. Ben reluctantly agreed, then hurriedly left so he wouldn't have to look at Tike's pleading eyes.

* * *

Twenty minutes later they had reached the hospital again, where they found things unchanged. Grampa remained stable and unresponsive. They hung around in his room; Laura sat by his bed and stroked his hand, Ben read magazines and switched through TV channels without really paying much attention. Looking for a distraction, Ben ended up going down to the gift shop while Laura fell asleep on a chair in the waiting area.

No sooner had she dozed off, when a nurse touched her shoulder. "He's awake," she announced.

Laura sprang up and hurried to the room, where she found her father with his eyes open.

She rushed to his side. "Dad!"

The nurse removed his oxygen mask before checking his vital signs. "Take it easy on him," she advised before leaving.

Laura took her father's hand. "Dad? It's Laura."

Her father's eyes focused, creasing into a smile. "Honeybee..." he began, his voice frail.

Laura's chin wavered at hearing her nickname, but she pulled herself together and shushed him. "Stay calm, Daddy. You suffered a heart attack. You're at the Chilliwack General Hospital"

She saw him frown worriedly for the briefest moment. Then he closed his eyes as if needing time to accept the news. When he opened them again, he asked unexpectedly, "How come you're not angry at me?"

Laura suppressed a nervous burst of laughter. She

recognized her Dad's sense of humour. "Oh, Daddy," she said with fake anger. “I'm *furious* at you!”

Ryan relaxed, forcing a small smile. “Oh, good,” he breathed. “You confused me there for a minute.”

Laura couldn't keep up the pretense. Her face crumpled. “I missed you so much!”

Ryan's smile faded. “Me, too, Honeybee.” He tapped her hand reassuringly. He scanned the room with his eyes. “Where's Ben?”

“He'll be up in a minute. I sent him to the gift shop to keep his mind busy. He becomes restless when Tike's not with him.”

“Huh!” Ryan said weakly. “So he's still got that yapping scoundrel?”

Laura didn't answer. Instead, she said, “He's missed you, too, you know.”

Ryan frowned, then responded with a twinkle in his eye, “The yapping scoundrel misses me?”

Laura smiled a watery smile. “No, silly, I meant Ben. He's missed you so much. We've been worried sick about you! I couldn't find you anywhere!” She broke off, her words caught in her throat. “Now is not the time, but when you feel up to it, we need to talk about what happened.”

Ryan had become serious, the cheeky twinkle in his eye fading as he spoke. “I need to talk to you, too, Honeybee.”

“Not now, Daddy. You need to get better first. The nurse said you need to rest. It can wait until you feel stronger.”

Ryan shook his head and wanted to speak, but a hissing cough left his cracked lips instead. Laura helped him drink sips of water from a plastic cup. “Listen to me now,” he began again. “Remember that notary on Knight Road?” When she nodded, he said, “He has my will.”

Laura opened her mouth to protest, but he silenced her.

"I'm leaving the house to Benjamin." Laura gaped, so he went on quickly. "No, listen! I know you don't want to live out there, but you can rent the place. You'll get good money from it. It will keep you afloat while you live in Vancouver. You will be the custodian of the house until Ben turns eighteen. Then he will decide what to do with it. He can sell it or live in it. I don't care. He will decide."

"Dad," Laura jumped in. "I had to drag Ben to the house last night. He's refused to go back in all these weeks because..." She stopped.

"...he's afraid," Ryan finished.

Laura nodded, glad they were on the same page. "He's terrified," she confirmed. She hesitated, but the burning question left her lips before she could help herself. "Why is he terrified, Dad?"

He would not meet her eyes. There was a long silence before he asked, "Do you two still fight?"

She sighed, looking away, frustrated that he was changing the subject.

Ryan pushed on. "You shouldn't take it out on him, you know, just because he has his father's looks." Laura glared at him, but Ryan continued. "He's a lot more like you than you know. All you see in him are his father's handsome face, brown hair and eyes, but inside... inside he's just like you, strong and stubborn and witty all at the same time. You should spend more time with him. He can be a lot of fun, believe me!" He let his words sink in, before adding, "I want you to take the boy on a long vacation, somewhere far away. Don't fuss about expenses! I'm leaving you a good sum of money, too."

"Dad!" she exclaimed, truly offended this time.

"Don't interrupt me, young lady!" Ryan snapped. "You get that boy away from here! And don't give me that excuse again that you have to work. You'll manage to make ends meet, I promise you. Take that boy on a trip and get to know him. He needs you!"

Laura couldn't face him. Too much anger boiled inside. She was the one who had planned on giving him a piece of her mind, yet somehow the tables had turned, and now he was the one lecturing her. "He needs you, too, you know!" she retorted. "You have no idea what we've been through! The nightmares, the long nights watching over him while he shook with fever! I had no idea how to deal with it because I had no idea what had happened! Yes, I understand that some freakish meteorite landed in your backyard and that it's a crazy thing to wrap your head around, but what was I supposed to do? How the heck was I supposed to talk to him about a thing like that?"

She was sobbing again, and it took all her willpower to whisper, "Where were you? Why didn't you call?" She barely realized he was squeezing her hand, inviting her to look at the door.

She found Ben standing there awkwardly.

Laura, caught off guard, raised her hand to her mouth. Her breath started coming in short gasps. Nervously, she reached for her handbag and took a couple of deep breaths from the asthma inhaler.

"I'm sorry," she whispered sincerely, before walking out.

* * *

Ben felt awkward being in the room alone with his grandfather, perhaps because he barely recognized the man who, not so long ago, had seemed like a sturdy oak, with his booming voice and roars of laughter. Now he was pale and thin, a shadow of who he had once been. Or perhaps it was the invisible wall of silence that had built up between them since his absence.

It was Ryan who spoke first. "I see your Mom found you okay..."

Ben knew he was referring to the day after *The Cosmic Fall*, when his mother had found him unconscious under a tree. He nodded.

Ryan's face relaxed. "Good, good," he said half to himself. The old man cleared his throat.

He's as uncomfortable as I am! Ben felt a pang of emotion at this realization.

"Are you studying hard, boy? Are you keeping up your grades?"

Ben nodded again briefly.

I don't want to talk about school grades.

Ryan repeated, "Good, good. Your mother tells me you're staying at the house?"

Once more, Ben nodded, staring down at his feet.

"Look at me, Potatohead," his Grampa ordered, using the nickname he had for his grandson. "She says you don't like it there anymore..." Since Ben continued to study the patterns on the floor, Grampa added softly, "...because of the nightmares."

This time Ben's head shot up, his eyes wide.

"Yeah..." Grampa acquiesced, before adding quietly, "I get them, too."

Ben went to stand by his grandfather's bedside. "You... you get them, too?" he asked shakily. "What do they mean? The nightmares? I can't remember anything. The doctor says I have amnesia."

Grampa studied the twelve-year-old intently. "Do you know what amnesia is, son? It's the brain's ability to protect you from disturbing memories. It keeps you sane. Have you ever thought that, perhaps, it was a good thing you have amnesia, and that, for your own sanity, it should stay that way?"

Ben stared at him, stunned. Whatever he had expected from his grandfather, this was not it. Somehow he had hoped for an explanation. He felt terribly deceived. "How can you say such a thing, Grampa? You're supposed to help me remember! So I can heal!"

To his bewilderment, his grandfather's lower lip began to tremble. The words came out with difficulty as he sobbed. "I'm sorry this happened to you, Ben."

"What do you mean, Grampa?" Ben asked quickly. "Sorry... *what...* happened?"

Grampa wheezed, "I'm sorry I wasn't there for you when you needed me."

Ben didn't know what his grandfather was apologizing for, but he was only too aware of the heart monitor that beeped unevenly. He took his grandfather's hand firmly. "It's okay, Grampa. It wasn't your fault."

Ryan nodded, a heavy weight visibly lifting from his heart. His hand clenched painfully around Ben's own as he gasped for air.

Two nurses appeared and rushed around the bed.

"You'll have to wait outside, son," one of them said urgently.

"Ben!" Grampa gasped. He struggled to speak now. A nurse put a firm hand on Ben's shoulder, but he shook her off. He bent down and put his ear close to Grampa's mouth.

Grampa breathed, "If... danger... find... Mesmo!"

Mesmo.

The name echoed in Ben's mind.

Ryan Archer sank into the pillows as a nurse placed the oxygen mask on his face again. Ben held onto his grandfather's hand, his eyes streaming with tears. “I love you, Grampa!” He could see Grampa's watery eyes returning the words as the nurse led him away.

Laura ran down the corridor, closely followed by a doctor who rushed into the room without saying a word, leaving them both stranded and huddling together.

CHAPTER 5 *Twisted Eyes*

Ben paced the corridor, throwing sideway glances at his mother. Laura's brow creased over her empty gaze as she bit her nails. He couldn't bear to watch her anguished face, so instead he followed the hands of the clock on the wall as they ticked away the minutes.

At last, the doctor came out to tell them that Mr. Archer was stable again. From what he understood, he said, the family had not seen each other in a while, so he cautioned them not to bring up too many strong emotions at this stage. He would reevaluate the patient's health in the morning.

Ben drew a deep breath, yet felt helpless as to what to do next. Waiting and doing nothing was nerve wracking, so his mother took him for dinner at the hospital cafeteria. He wasn't hungry, but it took his mind off things for a while.

They hung around for several more hours in the waiting room, until a nurse went to check on Grampa and informed them that nothing had changed.

By then it was one o'clock in the morning. Most of the hospital was dark and the corridors empty. When Laura suggested they get some rest at the house, Ben didn't even protest. He felt like he had spent the entire day on an emotional roller-coaster. Laura put her arm around his shoulder as they slowly headed for the exit.

A bald doctor in a white coat brushed past them. Ben caught the man's honey-brown eyes briefly as he moved away to let the doctor through.

Twisted eyes...

Something unpleasant tugged at the back of Ben's mind. But the moment vanished as soon as they stepped through the hospital doors into fresh air and he remembered that Tike was waiting for him.

When they reached Grampa's house, Ben hugged his four-legged friend happily. Tike licked the boy's face and wagged his tail excitedly. As boy and dog headed upstairs, Ben realized he had left the watch Grampa had given him on his bedside table. He vowed to put it on again as soon as he went to bed.

* * *

The bald doctor in the white coat followed the directions to the Coronary Care Unit. Once there, he picked up a clipboard containing patient information that was placed on top of the reception desk, without addressing the two nurses who chatted at the far end. He saw several screens behind the desk, some showing images from cameras laid out in the hospital corridors, while others monitored patients' status. He made sure the nurses were still talking before reaching over to touch the screens, which immediately turned to static. Satisfied, the bald man headed down the corridor and entered a room.

Ryan Archer rested in the dim light, his heart beating regularly.

The doctor closed the door, then locked it.

Ryan's voice sounded frail in the silence. "Who's there?"

The doctor walked to the heart monitor, then followed the IV line from the intravenous pump to Ryan's arm with the tip of his fingers.

Ryan asked, "Why did you lock the door?"

The doctor appeared in his field of vision. He wore a grey business suit, light blue shirt and tie under the doctor's white coat as if he had attended a business meeting before coming to the hospital. He studied Ryan with emotionless eyes. "You are Mr. Archer, yes?"

Ryan rolled his eyes, resigned. "I know who you are. You all look the same with your dainty suits." He stared back at the doctor before adding, "CSIS? FBI? What do you want now? I already told your buddies everything. Can't you see I'm on my deathbed? Give a man some peace!"

The fake doctor replied coldly, "Yes, I read your witness file. Quite interesting. But many gaps. Your story may have made sense to my 'buddies'. But not to me." He sat down on the edge of Ryan's bed, saying purposefully, "You see, you forgot to mention Mesmo."

Ryan stared at him in stunned silence, a veil of fear passing before his eyes. He glanced away, but too late, the man had captured his reaction. "Who are you?" Ryan whispered strenuously, trying to hide his discomfort.

The man quoted matter-of-factly, "I am Theodore Edmond Connelly, agent with the Canadian Security Intelligence Service..." He stopped, before adding darkly, "Though Mesmo would know me by another name." He sighed, seeming bored. "Nothing that concerns you, though."

Ryan stared at him in disgust. "What do you want?" His breath quickened behind the oxygen mask.

Connelly bent over until he was face to face with Ryan, his

voice coming in a slow, intense growl. "I want Mesmo! Where is he?"

Cold sweat dampened Ryan's forehead. Something odd was happening with the fake doctor's eyes. They were switching from green to honey-brown, then back to green.

Connelly continued, "You know who I am talking about. I want Mesmo! And you're going to tell me where he is!"

Ryan gritted his teeth. "How can you know Mesmo? No one at the CSIS knows Mesmo. You're lying! Who are you, really?"

Connelly smiled at him coldly, pleased that Ryan was coming to his own conclusions. Whereas the fake doctor had been bald a minute ago, now white, prickly hair stuck out of his head. He looked away into the distance, seeming to remember something pleasant. "Let's just say," he began, "that I am the one who made sure Mesmo's spacecraft crashed into a million pieces in your fields on the night of *The Cosmic Fall*." He turned to Ryan again, waiting for his words to sink in. His eyes became honey-brown again, and the muscle on the side of his neck twitched abnormally.

Ryan fought to keep a straight face, but his speeding heartbeat on the monitor gave him away. He understood. And he was afraid.

Connelly's smile faded. "Too bad Mesmo made it out alive. My mission would have ended all those weeks ago. Instead, I have had to endure this repulsive human face for weeks. I am tired and impatient. And when I am impatient, my anger tends to run out of control." He glared menacingly. "I am running out of patience now, Mr. Archer. Tell me where I can find Mesmo!"

Ryan whimpered. With a trembling arm, he tried to reach for the red call button on the wall behind his bed, but it was too far away.

Connelly grabbed Ryan's arm, pushing it down onto the bed. "Tell me!" he threatened.

The heart monitor beeped wildly as Ryan's breath became ragged, but his eyes hardened as he gasped. "You are a murderer! You won't get anything out of me!"

The alien put his mouth very close to Ryan's ear, making his skin crawl. "Maybe," he snarled, "I should ask your grandson!"

* * *

That night, the nightmares returned.

Twisted eyes!

Ben woke up screaming. He opened his eyes dizzily, trying to catch his bearings. When he recognized where he was, he tumbled back into bed, breathing heavily.

In an instant, Laura rushed to his side, shushing him and rubbing his back, until drowsiness carried him away again.

The next time his eyelids flew open, it was still dark and Laura had fallen asleep by his side. He caught sight of the watch he had left under the bedside lamp and reached for it in the dark. He put it on his wrist and covered his head with the bedsheet. Holding on tightly to the watch with his other hand, he calmed down and fell into an uneasy slumber once more.

* * *

In the room, by the window, a tall man with white, wavy hair appeared. Though his eyes were lost in the shadows, he observed the woman and Ben's form lying under the bedsheets.

He took a step forward.

The shrill sound of a phone echoed through the dark house. From somewhere in his deep slumber, Ben heard his mother gasp for air. He vaguely registered Laura leaving the bed, then heard her bare feet patter down the stairs.

The high-pitched sound persisted, finally pulling Ben from his sleep. He scanned the empty room, confused, then heard Laura's muffled voice turn to grief.

Grampa!

He sat upright in bed, fully awake.

Ben and his mother rushed to the Chilliwack General Hospital where they found a lot of commotion on Grampa's floor: hospital staff rushed around semi-dark hallways, talking intensely in low voices. They found a doctor and two nurses bathed in a ghostly, red glow from the emergency lights as they stood in the hallway before Grampa's room. The doctor broke the news: Grampa had passed away thirty minutes earlier.

Ben listened in disbelief as the doctor explained that Grampa had fallen out of bed, where the nurses had found him in cardiac arrest. Despite their best efforts, they had not been able to revive him.

Ben stepped away, his mind in turmoil, unable to conceive the news. He watched from a distance as the doctor talked quietly with his distraught mother. Then the doctor excused himself, saying that he needed to check in on his other patients because the hospital had experienced a brief outage.

One of the nurses asked Laura if she wanted to see her father one last time before they took him away.

Ben watched his mother nod.

Then, in a grief-filled voice, Laura asked, "Did he say anything, before...?" A sob stopped her from finishing the sentence.

"Well, he did, actually," The nurse replied. "But I'm afraid it didn't make much sense."

Laura waited expectantly.

"He said 'Find Mesmo.' Well, that's what I could make of it, anyway." The nurse shrugged apologetically. "Do you have any idea what that might mean?"

Laura lowered her eyes and shook her head.

Behind her, Ben's face turned ghostly pale.

* * *

The immigration officer eyed the tall man in the fur hat, then glanced at the dark blue passport he held in his hand. Before him, a crowd of tired but patient travellers chatted while waiting to be cleared through Customs and Immigration of the bustling Toronto Airport.

"What's with the hat?" the officer asked.

The man straightened the beige hat with ear flaps, so that the officer could get a better look at his face without removing it from his head. "A souvenir from South America," he explained. "From a guide who trekked with me through the Andes Mountains."

The officer eyed him without showing the slightest emotion. He checked something on his screen for an annoying amount of time, then reached for a stamp on his desk.

His phone rang. The officer picked up the receiver and listened silently. "Yes, Sir," was all he said, before hanging up. He stared at his screen thoughtfully, picked up the stamp again and pressed it onto Jack Anderson's passport, leaving a circular ink mark, allowing the man entry.

"Welcome back to Canada, Mr. Anderson," the officer said, offering the passport back to the man.

Mesmo reached out, but the officer held on to it. He

pointed behind him at the different line-ups leading to baggage reclaim. "Your connecting Victory Air flight to Vancouver is the first exit to the left. You don't have much time. Your luggage will follow automatically," he explained.

Mesmo nodded. The officer let go of the passport.

The tall alien, travelling under the name Jack Anderson, headed away from the cumbersome immigration officer and let out a low sigh of relief. He strode down the large hall and noticed an exit with a paper sign that read, "Victory Air 217, Vancouver."

Mesmo plunged through the automatic doors, briefly noting that he was the only traveller heading to that destination.

Five men in business suits waited on the other side.

"It's him," one imposing man said into a tiny speaker attached to his ear, as the doors slid shut behind Mesmo.

The other four men lunged at the alien, pinning him to the ground. Swiftly, the imposing man injected something into Mesmo's neck. The alien felt his muscles go weak and his sight blurred.

"We have him, boss," the man announced quietly into the speaker, as Mesmo lost consciousness.

CHAPTER 6 *Mesmo*

Two days later, Laura and Ben stood in the rain before Grampa's grave, dressed in black raincoats covering a black dress and a dark grey suit, respectively. They had trouble concentrating on the priest's eulogy, as they were taken aback by the number of people who had shown up at the funeral.

"I placed a small announcement with the date and time of the funeral in the Chilliwack Times obituary," Laura whispered to Ben with an emotional voice. "But I hadn't expected anyone else to come."

When the ceremony was over, people streamed away after paying their respects. Ben edged away, too overcome with sadness to be able to handle a conversation with the locals, who, he remembered, had known his mother and grandparents for years.

Tike had wandered off, giving the boy an excuse to search the green graveyard. He found his dog sitting alert next to a thick tree surrounded by shrubs. Glad to have something else to think about, Ben walked over to his faithful companion to see what had caught his attention.

"Tike?" Ben called, before realizing a man was standing

unmoving next to the tree. Tike gazed up at the stranger, his tail wagging uncertainly.

Ben stopped in surprise, glancing at the tall man who wore jeans, a brown jacket and a curious fur hat with ear flaps. The outfit looked utterly out of place for a funeral, yet there was something vaguely familiar about him. "Hi," Ben said timidly, encouraged by Tike's trusting attitude. The man stared at him without replying. "Er... did you know my grandfather?"

The man's face was drawn as if he had not slept in a long time or was fighting off an illness. "Yes," he replied without further explanation.

"Oh," was all Ben could say in return, noticing the stranger's unhealthy grey-tinted skin. The man gazed intently at Ben's arm. Ben lifted it up, confused, then remembered the watch that Grampa had given him. He tentatively turned his arm towards the stranger, the words slipping from his mouth. "It was my Grampa's before..." he broke off, nodding in the direction of the ceremony.

The man stared at the funeral procession, then up and down at Ben. He suddenly swayed and reached for the bark of the tree to steady himself.

"Are you okay?" Ben asked worriedly.

The man tilted his chin and winced. "Yes," he said forcefully as he straightened himself.

Ben opened his mouth to say something when Laura walked up beside him. "Oh, hello," she said to the stranger. "It's nice to see you again." Ben blinked at her in astonishment, as she continued, "I'm Laura, Ryan's daughter. Do you remember?" She held out her hand to greet him. "I'm sorry, but I don't remember your name?"

To their surprise the man stepped back, avoiding her touch by putting his hands in his pockets. Laura dropped her hand awkwardly. "Jack Anderson," the man said briefly as a manner of greeting.

Ben glared at his mother, waiting for an explanation.

"I met Jack a few weeks ago," she told him, her face flushed. "After you were well enough to go back to school, I drove out to Chilliwack, in the hopes your grandfather had returned from wherever it was he had disappeared to..." She waved her hand vaguely. "Instead, I found Jack here taking care of Grampa's place." She shook her head, remembering. "I never did get to see Grampa that time," she said sadly, before turning to Jack and adding, "Thank you for checking up on the house, by the way."

Jack nodded in acknowledgment. "Your father helped me through some difficult times."

"He seems to have helped a lot of people," she agreed, pointing to the dwindling crowd. Two elderly ladies under an umbrella waved her over. "Oh, I have to go," she said, sounding disappointed. "Er... why don't you come over to the house later? It looks like we're having an unplanned reception. We can talk further there, away from the rain."

When Jack didn't answer, Laura waved at him shyly before heading over to the two women who wanted to pay their respects.

Ben stared at Jack with new curiosity. "Will you come? To the house, I mean?" he was eager to talk to someone who had seen his grandfather in the past weeks.

The man shook his head. "I came here hoping to find someone." He gazed intensely at Ben, then added slowly, "But now I know I won't find her here." He took a deep breath, then turned around, saying, "Goodbye, Benjamin."

How do you know my name?

Ben felt an urge to hold the man back. "Wait!" he blurted.

"Have we met before?"

Jack glanced back before replying, "Yes." When he saw Ben staring at him hopefully, he added, "Your grandfather told me you couldn't remember." He paused. "It's probably better that way." He turned around again and strode off.

"That's what Grampa said!" Ben called after him. "That it was best I didn't remember. But I want to remember!"

Still, Jack kept on walking.

Ben's heart thumped desperately. He felt a pull towards this stranger. A small lock of white hair sticking out from under the fur hat triggered something in his mind.

Mesmo.

"Mesmo!" Ben yelled.

The man froze in his tracks, then slowly turned. Man and boy stared at each other.

"Grampa told me, just before he died, to find Mesmo," Ben said in awe. "You're Mesmo!"

I know it!

Though the man's eyes softened, he replied sadly, "I'm sorry, Benjamin. I can't help you." This time he didn't stop walking as he disappeared into the trees.

"Wait!" Ben ran after him. The branches swayed gently in the wind while the rain pattered on the yellowing leaves. Mesmo was gone. Ben and Tike found themselves at the edge of the forest, alone. Ben gazed back towards Grampa's grave; his eyes filled with tears.

His mom waited for him by the car. She opened the door as he trudged sadly over to her. Silently, they headed back to the house, leaving the soggy graveyard behind.

* * *

Not far off, a plume of smoke came out of the exhaust pipe of a white, unmarked van. Inside, two men in business suits typed on computer keyboards as they spoke through headsets. Inspector James Hao hovered behind them, surveilling the information on the various screens as he sipped on a cup of coffee. One of the men pulled up photographs of the funeral so he could review them.

"Send this off for processing immediately. I want a name for every face on these pictures," Hao ordered.

Fifteen minutes later, the van door slid open, and Connelly appeared in the rain behind them. He climbed in and pulled the door closed before taking off his dripping coat.

Hao cornered him, hissing, "Agent Connelly. You missed the whole thing! Where have you been?"

Connelly held his gaze before replying coldly, "Investigating."

Hao retorted in a menacing low voice, "You may have impressed the big guys at the Dugout, wonder boy! But remember who's in charge here! You do not go off on your own without prior authorization. I want a report on your current investigations on my desk by tomorrow. Do you understand?"

Connelly's mouth twitched, and it was only after a pause that bordered on insubordination, that he answered, "Yes, Sir."

Hao backed away, satisfied. "Good!" He grabbed his coat before opening the van door. "I'll take over from here." He shut the door with a bang, walked to a silver Nissan and slid inside. He drove off, the white van following closely.

* * *

It didn't take long for the house to fill up with people from Chilliwack. Laura suspected they had called each other, agreeing to meet. She didn't even have to worry about food or drinks; they appeared magically in the kitchen and living room with every person that arrived. She felt overwhelmed by so much attention. One person after another told her about how Grampa had helped them in one way or another. She even found herself talking for several minutes with a man in ragged clothes, long, unkempt beard, and weird knitted beanie hat. She suspected he was a homeless man everyone in Chilliwack referred to as Wayne the Bagman because he always trudged around town with his few possessions packed in a garbage bag. Laura wouldn't have been surprised if her Dad had met him while helping at the local shelter.

People lined up to talk to her. They wanted to tell her their stories of how they remembered Laura as a small girl or how her sick mother had passed away prematurely. Naturally, the conversation always tended to switch to *The Cosmic Fall*, and how the fallen meteors had affected every Chilliwack resident in one way or another.

From the corner of her eye, Laura caught Ben sneaking between people's backs, a ham sandwich in his mouth. She excused herself from a woman who asked her where her father had been the past six weeks. She took Ben by the arm, pulling him away until they found themselves in the large pantry next to the kitchen. She shut the door, switched on the light and leaned back.

She stood there for a moment, her ears ringing from so much chatter, staring at Ben in disbelief. They both burst into a nervous giggle.

"Who *are* all these people?" Ben asked, wide-eyed.

"I think half of Chilliwack is here! Grampa was some Chilliwack hero, by the looks of it," Laura said.

She stifled laughter at the thought. It felt good to release their emotions like this, even though it seemed highly inappropriate to be laughing at a funeral reception. Somehow, though, Laura knew her father would have approved.

Once the ringing in her ears had eased, Laura glanced at Ben worriedly. "How are you holding up?"

He shrugged, but answered bravely, "I'm okay."

Laura hesitated for a moment. "I spoke to Mrs. Gallagher. She and her husband run an accounting business downtown. Anyway, she's heading for Vancouver later to visit her daughter." She paused, before adding. "She has offered to take you with her. I think you should go."

"What? No way! Why? What about you?"

"I need to stay here to take care of things. I got a call from the notary in Chilliwack. He wants me to come in tomorrow for Grampa's will. I think you, on the other hand, might be better off at home. You've had nightmares ever since we got here. You were right; this place isn't doing you any good," she admitted. "Anyway, tomorrow is a school day. It might take your mind off things."

Ben groaned.

"Think about it, Ben. I'm going to be dealing with funeral companies, notaries, and bankers. You'd find yourself on your own while I dealt with this administrative mess. I'd feel better if you were back home with some routine. It might help with the nightmares."

She saw Ben open his mouth, then close it again in resignation. He nodded reluctantly.

"I'll only be a couple of days at the most," she said apologetically.

"It's okay, Mom," Ben said gruffly.

Laura's heart bulged. She hugged him and said. "I'm sorry you and Grampa didn't get a chance to talk."

She heard him swallow a sob as he hid his face in her sweater. She thought he was going to tell her something, but instead he said, "Can I ask you something?"

Laura stroked the side fringe out of his eyes. "Of course, honey. Anything!"

Ben spoke slowly. "Why do I have Grampa's last name? I mean, Dad's name was Robert Manfield, wasn't it? So why am I called Benjamin *Archer*? Shouldn't I be called Benjamin *Manfield*, like him?"

Laura rubbed his shoulders, thinking about her answer. "Well, your Dad was gone so soon. You were just a baby. I knew you wouldn't remember him at all, whereas Grampa took such good care of you... I don't know. I guess it made sense to call you Benjamin Archer." She paused before asking worriedly, "Does that bother you?"

Ben shook his head. "No, not really. I was curious, that's all." She frowned at him, unconvinced. He added quickly, "It's okay, really! I prefer the name Archer; it reminds me of Grampa."

She hugged him again, so he could not see her biting her lip as she rolled her eyes towards the ceiling. She said gently, "You'd better pack your bags." They glanced at each other. Then she asked, "Are you ready?"

He nodded.

She sighed before opening the door. A wave of human heat and chatter enveloped them as they headed back into the crowd.

* * *

Ben made his way from the kitchen to the stairs, ignoring someone who tapped him on the shoulder. He sprinted up the steps, headed for his bedroom, then froze at the doorway.

A man with short, black hair streaked with grey and wearing a tidy business suit stood near the shelves at the other end of the room, holding a cup of coffee in one hand and Grampa's white telescope in the other. When he realized Ben had arrived, he broke into a toothy grin. "Ah! Here's the boy I was looking for! You must be Benjamin Archer!"

Ben didn't reply.

"She's a beauty, isn't she?" the man continued, admiring the telescope, while almost splashing coffee on it. "Here, hold this for a minute, would you?" he said, handing the cup to Ben, who had to grab it with both hands as hot liquid dripped onto his arm. Fortunately, the man returned the telescope to its place, still speaking. "Your grandfather and I shared the same passion for the stars. They tell me you do, too." He turned to face Ben. With a smile he put out his hand, presenting himself, "James Hao."

The man's eyes bore into Ben's as he shook it limply, the cup dangerously wavering in his other hand. Hao ignored the cup, saying thoughtfully, "Hm, I'm surprised your grandfather never mentioned me. We go way back, him and me."

Ben scowled. "Were you looking for something?"

Hao's face lit up. "Ah, yes, actually. I spilled coffee on my tie. I was looking for the washroom when I walked by and spotted this beauty." He pointed to the telescope.

"The bathroom is on the other side," Ben said blandly.

Hao straightened. "Indeed!" But instead of leaving, he strolled to the window. "Quite amazing, isn't it, to think meteors crashed into these very fields? I'm sure only a handful of people in the whole world could claim the same. Your grandfather shunned the limelight, yet in a way, he became quite famous in spite of himself. He'll be making the headlines this weekend, too, though obviously for a very unfortunate reason..." Hao walked back over to Ben. "Why, you must have been on vacation when *The Cosmic Fall* occurred! Wouldn't you have loved to be here and witness something like that?" He gazed down at Ben, showing his neat row of teeth.

Ben stared back at him, then returned the cup. Hao carefully took it, holding it at the edges, as if Ben had dirtied it. "Well, you and I must have a chat soon... about the stars," Hao said as he moved towards the door. "See you later, then," he added as he left with a satisfied air.

Yeah, you wish!

Ben shut his bedroom door. He could still hear the man whistling down the corridor.

* * *

On the opposite side, Inspector James Hao locked himself in the bathroom. He stood before the mirror, whistling softly as he emptied the remaining coffee into the sink. He took a plastic bag from an inside pocket, and carefully placed the cup within it. He washed his hands and took his time to plaster down his hair. Still whistling, he tucked the cup in his inside pocket before stepping out. It bulged weirdly, so he glided down the stairs and left the house, walking with large strides to his car. He briefly noted that, although the rain had stopped, it had become very cold. Once inside the vehicle, he placed the cup in the passenger seat before driving away, tires screeching.

CHAPTER 7 *Crystals*

The house emptied slowly. Letting out a sigh of relief, Laura busied herself in the kitchen and noticed the garbage bag was overflowing. She carried it to the kitchen door leading to the backyard. The door squeaked on its old hinges as she pushed it open, cold air taking her by surprise. She went back inside to grab her mother's knitted shawl that always hung on a couch in the living room. She didn't remember it being this cold during the funeral. Although it was early October, it was too early for such a temperature drop.

She left the garbage at the bottom of the four steps outside the kitchen and was heading back inside, when she spotted a tall man in jeans and brown jacket standing with his back to her at the end of the yard, gazing over the fields. She recognized Jack Anderson with his weird fur hat at once.

She wrapped the shawl around her shoulders, took a step forward, then stopped as something crunched under her shoes. She glanced down and found the grass covered in delicate frost crystals. She bent to pick up a fragile, star-shaped crystal that fit in the palm of her hand before joining Jack.

"I hadn't seen one of these in years. It's so beautiful!" she began, before noticing the breathtaking scenery of golden cornfields tumbling down the hillside into the valley below. In the distance, the autumn sun peeked under menacing dark clouds, just above the mountain range. The effect was a mesmerizing, brightly golden sunset in a cold and dark world—a strange sign of summer still clinging in the face of the ever-looming winter.

"My father would have loved this," she said softly.

"I know," Jack replied after a while.

She looked up at him curiously. "You miss him, too, don't you?"

After a short silence, he replied, "Yes."

She studied his handsome features and high cheekbones. She noticed the small strand of white hair under his fur hat. He stared down at her with deep, honey-brown eyes that reflected pain and exhaustion. "I lost someone, too," he began. "My daughter..." he trailed away as he gazed out at the fields again. "She would have loved this, too."

A dozen raindrops fell on them, accompanied by a handful of very light snowflakes. Laura found herself crying silently, freely and without shame, giving in to her grief almost with relief. She cried for her father and for all the hurtful things they had said to each other. But most of all she cried for the things left unsaid between them. Yet somehow she knew everything was going to be all right, that he forgave her. Just as she forgave him now.

Standing very close to the fur hat man somehow made the cold air more bearable. Her misty breath mingled between the snowflakes and she found herself resisting the urge to take his hand, as natural as it might have seemed in their shared grief, for somehow she knew that if she did so the magic moment between them would evaporate. He had, after all, backed away from her when she had tried to greet him in the graveyard.

Once the sun had sunk behind the mountains, the cornfields became dark, leaving the way for the cold to penetrate through her shawl. Laura gazed into the distance as if hoping to hold back the last ray of sunlight. "I'm glad you came..." she began, turning to Jack, only to find him gone!

She stared in bewilderment at the space where, a moment ago, this mysterious man had been talking to her about his daughter.

"Jack?" she shouted, a chill rippling down her back as the wind picked up and large raindrops spattered on the ground.

But Jack Anderson had gone.

* * *

It didn't take Inspector James Hao long to get to the rendezvous point at a crossroad that led to Chilliwack. He found the white, unmarked van parked under some trees by the side of a lonely road.

Hao knocked on the van door to be let in by one of his men. He placed the cup in the agent's hands, ordering, "Get the fingerprints on this cup analyzed pronto and have them compared to the ones we found on the broken glass we recovered from the crash site."

The agent nodded.

Connelly and a second agent were in deep discussion, poring over the computer screens, only pausing when Hao came up behind them.

"What is it?" Hao asked.

The second agent looked up at him. "We may be onto something. Watch this."

He pulled up a photograph of the funeral from that

morning. It depicted a general picture of the graveyard, with autumn trees and lush grass, while in the distance a group of mourners gathered around Ryan Archer's grave. Some people strolled away, while others lined up to pay their respects to Laura Archer. At this distance, people's faces appeared small and blurry. Zooming in was the only way to get a better idea of people's identities.

"Agent Connelly noticed this in the corner," the agent explained as he zoomed into the left side of the picture, away from the crowd, slowly bringing Hao's attention to a dog standing by a tree. The agent zoomed out again so that a boy appeared next to the dog.

"That's Archer's grandson," Hao stated.

The agent nodded. "Yes, but look at this."

He moved the angle of the picture slightly so that Hao could make out the face of a man with a fur hat between the branches of surrounding shrubs. The boy seemed to be conversing with him.

"Who's that?" Hao asked swiftly.

Connelly spoke. "We've identified most of the people who attended the funeral. They are regular Chilliwack folk. But not this guy, though."

Hao snapped, "Are you telling me we don't have him in the system?"

"We're still searching."

"I want to know who that is! Find me a name!" Hao ordered. "We'll go back to the motel and work on this all night if we have to!" He pointed to Connelly. "And you! You're keeping watch. Report to me immediately if the Archer woman or her son leave the house!"

* * *

Connelly settled in the Nissan as the other men took off in the van. He sat back, crossed his arms and kept his eyes on the road before him. The rain thinned, making it easier for him to make out the people who passed in their cars. On a typical day there would have been very little traffic coming to and from the country road where Ryan Archer's house stood, as there were few neighbours, but on this late afternoon, the last of the reception visitors headed back to Chilliwack. Connelly watched as a man, covered in a large plastic bag and wearing a beanie hat, cycled by, glancing at him briefly. Connelly glared at him, unmoving, until he was far gone. Because of this, he almost missed the red Dodge Grand Caravan that slowed as it reached the stop sign of the crossroad.

Connelly could barely make out the woman driver and, next to her, a boy. A small dog's face stared out at him from the rear window. Connelly straightened, fully alert. It was the same dog as in the graveyard picture. He switched on the engine and followed the Dodge as it turned onto the highway heading to Vancouver, without informing his superior.

* * *

Laura Archer woke up to a grey morning, feeling refreshed and rested. She realized she hadn't had a regular night's sleep in a long time and the funeral had left her completely drained.

She showered, then put on some black slacks, a white top, a large, grey sweater with a V-neck, black ballerina flats and a pendant she had inherited from her mother. She brushed her shoulder-length hair, pinning it back into a ponytail, then headed downstairs, half expecting to hear her father's loud roar of laughter as she entered the kitchen. She swallowed hard when only silence greeted her. Still, it felt good to be in her childhood home with its full windows and wooden beams in the white ceiling. While she brewed some coffee, she wandered around the living room, stroking the furniture with the tips of her fingers, gazing at old photographs. She was struck by how quiet it was. Once upon a time, she would have rejected the lack of sound, she would have yearned for the bustling of the city, yet now found the calm strangely relaxing.

She headed back to the kitchen to pour herself a cup of the black brew. While sipping on the hot liquid, she leaned against the wall, then stared out the window towards the empty yard, catching herself thinking of Jack Anderson again and wondering how he could have disappeared so suddenly. Shaking her head to get him out of her mind, Laura washed the cup before leaving it to dry, then checked her handbag to make sure she had her wallet, identity cards, keys, some makeup and, most importantly, her asthma inhaler. After putting on her coat and a light shawl, she locked the door, then headed out into the chilly morning.

By 9:25 a.m., Laura had parked on Knight Road in downtown Chilliwack. She crossed the road, only to realize the notary's office was further up than she expected. She picked up the pace when a homeless man with his face hiding behind a thick scarf made her slow down. He jingled coins in a plastic cup at her. Automatically, she reached into her purse, and dropped some coins into the cup as she walked by—as her father had taught her to do since childhood.

As the homeless man with the beany hat saluted her with his hand covered in fingerless gloves, she heard him say, "You're like your daddy, you are."

She turned in surprise, then stopped as she recognized Wayne the Bagman—the homeless man who had spoken to her the day before at the funeral reception. "Hi," she said awkwardly, walking away more slowly.

He looked at her intently. "Where's that boy of yours? You shouldn't leave him alone, you know?"

"What do you mean?"

"It's not safe," he said as she distanced herself from him. "You need to take him away. Far away!"

Laura glared at him, then decided to ignore him. She had reached the notary's office and pushed the commercial glass doors inward.

"I wouldn't go in there if I were you!" Wayne shouted after her.

Laura frowned at him angrily, stepping inside.

She chose the stairs over the elevator to go up to the first floor, where she entered the reception office that had a sign on the front: CHARLES BOYLE, NOTARY PUBLIC. A couple sat in the waiting area, reading magazines.

A thirty-something-year-old assistant with short, brown hair stopped typing on her computer and smiled at her.

"Good morning," Laura said, smiling back. "I have an appointment with Mr. Boyle at 9:30. My name is Laura Archer."

The woman's smile evaporated, her face turning to panic. She stuttered, "Oh... but you're not supposed to be here..."

Laura stared at her in bewilderment. "Excuse me?" She recognized the woman's voice. "You called me a couple of days ago, after my father passed away, asking me to come in today!"

The assistant, who had been calmly working a minute ago, now seemed totally at a loss as to what to do. "I... er... you must have misunderstood. The notary is not in today," she stammered.

Laura stood with her mouth open in disbelief. She pointed to the couple sitting in the waiting room. "What about them?

Who are they waiting for?" The couple stared back at them curiously.

The assistant's eyes widened as she searched for an answer, but then muffled laughter came from the notary's office.

"Who's in there?" Laura asked angrily.

As the assistant opened her mouth to reply, Laura strode to the office door while the woman struggled to get out of her chair. "Wait!" she warned, but already Laura had opened the door to peek inside.

Two men, one of them with neat, graying hair, the other with thick glasses and a big belly, stood beside the notary's desk, laughing at a joke.

"We must plan another round of golf..." the man with the graying hair said, before stopping to find out who had interrupted the meeting. For a brief moment his eyes narrowed, before creasing into a smile. "Ms. Archer, what a pleasant surprise!" he said nimbly, nodding towards the assistant who stood behind Laura. He reached out his hand. "I'm Charles Boyle," he presented himself.

Laura shook the man's hand unhappily.

Boyle gestured to the chair before his desk, inviting her to sit. Then he turned to the plump man, leading him politely but firmly out the door. "I'm sorry, Mr. Smith, my assistant is reminding me of an urgent meeting I must attend. She will go over my agenda with you so we can finalize the paperwork as soon as possible. It was a pleasure catching up with you, as always."

They shook hands, then, as the client turned away, Laura saw the notary giving his assistant instructions which implied making a phone call, to which she hastily nodded in understanding. He closed the door, calmly returned to his desk, sat and crossed the fingers of his hands on the table in front of him in a business-like manner. "Ms. Archer," he said gravely. "We don't have much time."

"What's going on here?" Laura said in bewilderment.

Boyle inspected her curiously. "You did not bring your son along?" he asked.

Laura shook her head. "No, I sent him home. His grandfather's passing has not been easy on him."

Boyle nodded in approval. "Good," he said slowly, lost in thought. "Still, out of respect for your late father—may he rest in peace—I must warn you that my assistant is calling the police."

"What?" Laura exclaimed, perplexed. "Why?"

"Have you heard of the CSIS, Ms. Archer?" Boyle asked.

Laura blinked at him, racking her brain. "You mean, the Canadian version of the FBI?"

"Yes," Boyle acknowledged. "Well, you see, a couple of their agents barged into my office yesterday, waving a lot of official documents at my face." He gazed at her intently. "I intended to read your father's will to you this morning, as he had instructed me to do at his passing, but yesterday's unexpected visitors changed everything. You see, your father's assets have been frozen. The CSIS has taken hold of your father's will as well as his inheritance."

"What?" Laura burst, incredulous. "But why? Is that even legal?"

"Last week I would have said 'no.' I have never experienced anything similar," he said. "But, as it turns out, I was wrong. They did this in all legality. I'm afraid, Ms. Archer, that I am unable to read your father's will to you today."

Laura stared at him, her mind unable to grasp what he was saying.

Boyle continued apologetically, "To be honest, my assistant and I did not expect you in today. We... er... I guess we expected the CSIS to have made you aware of the situation by now. It was our error… we should have contacted you immediately.” He pulled open a side drawer and dug out a medium-sized envelope. “Nevertheless,” he continued. “I am glad you came, as they did not get their hands on this.” He handed the brown envelope to Laura, who took it with a look of total confusion. He said gently, “Don’t think I approve of what is happening, Ms. Archer. Your father’s passing is a loss to us all. The community greatly appreciated him, myself included.” His voice lowered to a hush. “This envelope was not part of the will. Your father entrusted it to me, as one friend to another, and made me promise to give it to you should you ever face any trouble. Please, do not mention this envelope to anyone. It is the only thing of your father’s that I was able to… how shall I say… omit from yesterday’s investigation.”

Laura sat like a statue, gaping at the envelope dazedly.

The notary stood, saying gravely, “However, I can’t ignore the arrest warrant that came in this morning. That is why it is my duty to call the police, Ms. Archer. So I beg you: leave quickly!”

Laura’s handbag tumbled to the ground as she shoved back her chair. “An arrest warrant? Why?” she asked, fumbling to pick up the handbag. “I’ve done nothing wrong!”

Boyle stared at her in surprise. “No, not for you!” he said. “It’s for your son. The arrest warrant is for your son!”

Laura gaped at him in horror.

CHAPTER 8 *The First Witness*

At dawn that morning, Inspector Hao had received new information from the Dugout about the fur hat man in the funeral photograph. Surveillance cameras at the Toronto airport showed him arriving a week ago from South America, travelling with a Canadian passport that identified him as Jack Anderson. However, as it turned out, the Bolivian Embassy had informed Canadian authorities two days ago that the real Jack Anderson had fallen to his death attempting to walk the dangerous Inca Trail. His remains were being flown back to Canada that same day. Meaning that the CSIS had no clue as to the real identity of the fur hat man, nor how he had managed to travel across the country from Toronto to Chilliwack without leaving a trace.

On the other hand, the fingerprints that Hao had gotten from Benjamin Archer at the funeral reception matched those on the pieces of glass recovered from the crash site, officially turning the boy into a previously unknown witness of *The Cosmic Fall*. Not to mention that Ben was the last person to have spoken to the fur hat man. It was high time they interrogated Benjamin Archer.

Hao had rushed to Ryan Archer's house, only to find it

empty. Quite conveniently, though, they had received a call from the local RCMP informing them that Laura Archer was currently at the notary on Knight Road.

"Has Connelly reported back yet?" Hao fumed, as one of the agents parked the white van.

"Not yet," the other agent replied, checking his phone for messages.

Hao swore as they searched the other side of the road with their eyes.

"There she is!" the agent who was driving the van said. They watched as Laura Archer left the notary's building.

"The boy's not with her!" Hao exclaimed.

The three men got out of the van. They swiftly crossed the road, closing in on Ben's mother.

* * *

Laura saw them at once, running towards her in their dark grey suits. One of them flashed a badge at her. "Laura Archer? I'm Inspector James Hao with the CSIS. We need to talk to you."

She glanced around desperately.

"In here!" someone shouted urgently. Startled, Laura turned around to find a man peeking out at her from a narrow back alley. It was Wayne the Bagman urging her to come to him. Following a wild, baffling hunch, Laura ran to the homeless man.

"Hold it!" Hao yelled. But already she had slipped into the back alley after Wayne who was holding a metal door open for her. She dove into darkness and heard the door shut behind her.

"This way!" Wayne urged. Laura realized they were in a dimly lit corridor. The sound of thumping fists hastened her on.

The homeless man turned out to be much fitter than he

seemed, for with a swift stride he led her up several flights of stairs to a closed emergency exit. Wayne pushed it open, and Laura found herself on a small, rusty bridge structure between two brick buildings above another back alley. A key materialized in Wayne's hand from under his rags and in no time the door to the next building opened. He ushered her through it so that, again, they were faced with corridors and stairways. Laura's head swam as she lost all sense of direction, while they ran up and down flights of stairs until Wayne led her to a garage with a yellowish Buick stationed there. He ran to the garage door to pull it open, then unlocked the car door on the driver's side before taking his place behind the wheel. "Get in!" he ordered.

Laura froze to the spot, fear gripping her heart. "Wait!" she urged. "I can't do this! What am I doing? This is insane! I'm running away from the police. I've done nothing wrong."

"It's not you they're after!" Wayne said impatiently. "They're after your son. You have to get to him before they do." Since she continued to hesitate, he barked, "Get into the car!"

Automatically, she obeyed, her breath coming in short gasps. He put the key in the ignition, the car spurted to life, and before long Laura found herself heading out of town, racing down the highway.

Once they were satisfied that no one was following them, she turned to Wayne. "What do they want Ben for?"

He glanced at her, saying nothing.

"And what about you? What have you got to do with any of this? Why are you helping me?" she insisted.

The man did not reply, concentrating on his driving.

"I'm talking to you!" Laura yelled. She was on the verge of a full-blown asthma attack.

Wayne did not seem affected by her outburst. "I always knew your father had made a mistake by not involving you. He was hoping to protect you from all this, but they were bound to find out about you sooner or later." He shook his head disapprovingly. "He should have known better."

Laura stared at him angrily, not appreciating his comments. She grabbed the wheel, veering it sharply to the right. He hit the brakes so hard the tires screeched.

"What's the matter with you?" he yelled through his thick, unkempt beard.

"I'm not letting go until you tell me what's going on!" she seethed, still grasping the wheel. Cars honked as they sped past on the highway.

"Yeah, all right!" he growled. "Now let go!"

Laura did as he asked, and he carefully wove his way back into the fast lane, muttering furiously under his breath.

"What's your name?" she demanded firmly.

"Wayne McGuillen. Professional homeless man, at your service!"

Laura glared at him. He didn't appear to be joking.

"Why are these people after my son?"

Wayne looked at her curiously again. "You don't know, do you?" She frowned at him to get on with it. "It's because of *The Cosmic Fall,* of course."

"The Cosmic Fall?" she said, incredulous. "What does that have to do with anything?"

He replied slowly, "Well, your son was there, on the night of *The Fall.* He witnessed everything."

Laura felt goosebumps on her skin. She remained silent, trying not to show that she was embarrassed not to know more about her son's involvement on that fateful night. She said, "Yes, I'm aware my son witnessed the fall of some pretty big meteors next to my father's property. I understand that this was a terrifying ordeal for him, but that doesn't explain why the police are after him."

Wayne stared at her before saying slowly, "The thing is, it wasn't meteors that fell into the woods that night. It was alien spacecraft."

Laura felt her breath shortening again. She closed her eyes to fend off the asthma crisis threatening to take over. She did not want to show any signs of weakness by reaching for her inhaler, so she forced herself to take long, deep breaths to calm down. "You're making that up. Everybody knows those were meteors. The news showed how they recovered the meteor debris from the fields. Why would you make up such a story?"

He answered slowly, "Because I was there, too. I saw them: the UFOs and the aliens. I saw all of it. As did your father, your son, and two others. There were five witnesses in all..." he trailed off, remembering. "Five civil witnesses, yet only four of us were picked up by the CSIS. Somehow they missed your son. Your father managed to hide him from them. A good thing, too! They brought us in for questioning. We thought they only needed us to file a witness report. Instead, they kept us locked away for weeks! They used the excuse that we might have been exposed to alien viruses and were dangerous to the public. In fact, they were afraid we would talk to the press. They went to great lengths to cover up the truth, which is why we were considered a menace." Laura could hear the hurt in his voice. "All I wanted was to be left alone for a quiet night's sleep in the woods. Instead, I found myself locked up for weeks, prodded like a guinea pig as if I were the alien."

Laura listened to him without moving, unsure what to make of his words. She couldn't tell if this man in ragged clothes had completely lost it, which was all the more alarming as he sounded so sincere. "Yet, here you are, safe and sound..." she said carefully.

Wayne didn't seem to mind her statement. "Somehow your father got word to the Canadian Human Rights Commission, and they were forced to release us in great secrecy, with tons of signed papers saying we would not reveal anything to any living soul. That's what they did officially, though behind closed doors, they bugged our houses and followed us day in and day out. That's when your father stepped in again. He helped us disappear from the police radar by finding us places to hide. He provided us with a new life so they would leave us alone.

"I went into the Yukon for a while. Couldn't take the cold. Came back to my hometown where I continued living rough. Kept an eye on your Dad. I knew he came into town incognito once in a while to sort things out for his family and the other witnesses."

He glanced at Laura again before adding, "Good thing I did, too. Found him by his car when he had his heart attack. Dropped him off at the hospital along with your phone number. But I guess I was too late..."

Laura stared at him sadly. His story made sense, yet at the same time sounded completely crazy. Part of her was very reluctant to accept anything he said because admitting it meant a huge weight falling on her shoulders. It was much easier to brush him off as mad. And yet he had helped her dad...

Suddenly, Wayne veered off the highway into a small dirt road leading through fields. Not long after, he turned into a lot filled with shrubs and a low, run-down house where white paint still showed through the cracked and peeling walls. In a swift movement, he pulled into a dusty garage before turning off the engine.

"What are you doing?" Laura asked, her suspicion growing tenfold.

"This is my stop," Wayne said.

Laura stared at him in bewilderment.

He threw the car key into her lap before getting out.

"Wait! What...?"

"This is as far as I go," he interrupted. "I did my part, paid my debt to your father. Go and get your son, Laura. Take the car. It was your father's anyway."

Laura slid into the driver's seat, then mechanically tried to get the key into the ignition. Her hands shook. "Wait a minute! Is that it? What am I supposed to do now? Where am I supposed to go?" She had so many questions, but at the same time, she wanted to get away as fast as possible.

"Don't trust anyone," he said, echoing her very thoughts.

She barely had time to back nervously out of the garage when he started pulling down the garage door.

"Hide! Like me," she heard him say, as the door shut firmly, obscuring her view of him. And just like that, he was gone.

Laura stared at the silent house. She was in a cold sweat, her foot trembling on the pedal. She remembered the Inspector's face as he lunged at her. He was real. The arrest warrant for her son was real. Ben's face flickered before her eyes and she strengthened her grip on the wheel. He was all she had, all that mattered. She did not want those CSIS men to come anywhere near her son. Feeling a wave of urgency wash over her, she pushed down on the pedal, and sped off, leaving the lonely man to his wild imagination.

* * *

After an unproductive search for Laura Archer and her mysterious saviour, Inspector James Hao entered the notary's office with his notebook in hand. As he drilled Charles Boyle about Laura and her son's whereabouts, he spotted something jutting out from under the notary's desk. It turned out to be an asthma inhaler with Laura Archer's name on it. He knew it required a doctor's prescription. Hao gazed out the window thoughtfully before putting the asthma inhaler safely in his pocket.

CHAPTER 9 *The Trap*

Almost sixty miles away, Ben stared out his classroom window, daydreaming. Concentrating on the lessons proved an impossible task.

He had made it to school on time that morning, thanks to the very obliging Mrs. Ghallagher from Chilliwack. Not only had she driven him back to Vancouver, she had also insisted he spend the night at her daughter's house, as she would not hear of him staying on his own after losing his grandfather so recently. He had found himself in an elegant family home on a tree-lined avenue in a well-to-do neighbourhood, with Mrs. Ghallagher's daughter, husband and three-year-old daughter. He had reluctantly joined their joyful, bustling family dinner before settling in a cozy guest room all to himself. However, they would not hear of Tike sleeping in the bedroom with him. This thorny issue had almost turned into a nasty conversation until Ben had unwillingly relented. Then, as soon as everyone was sleeping soundly, the boy had silently opened the kitchen door for his happy four-legged friend. They had huddled up close before falling fast asleep.

The next morning, Tike had scuttled under the bed before

Mrs. Ghallagher came to wake Ben up. After a hasty breakfast, she had ushered him into the car again so she could take him to school.

While Mrs. Ghallager was distracted by her granddaughter crying in the back seat, Ben was able to convince her that his mom was picking him up that afternoon; therefore, he did not need to spend another night at the daughter's house. She dropped him off at the main school entrance with his dog, backpack and a small suitcase, and watched until he entered the school building. Only then had he been able to breathe.

Fortunately, most teachers left him alone that day, though Ben's science teacher offered his condolences. Still, it turned out to be one of the slowest school days he could remember, worsening when he was in a classroom that allowed him to catch a glimpse of Tike waiting patiently outside in the rain. More than anything else, Ben longed to be with his dog, who offered him his only solace.

On one occasion he found himself staring outside again while his companions listened resolutely to the teacher when he noticed Tike standing still as stone, ears alert, one paw off the ground, like a hunting dog sensing its prey. Then slowly his tail lowered between his legs, indicating fear as if the prey had turned out to be a predator. Ben sat up, feeling alert for the first time that day. He followed the direction of Tike's gaze, immediately spotting what had caught the dog's attention.

A bald man was posted by the gates at the end of the playground, observing the school. Ben could not make out his features from this far, yet he broke into a cold sweat. He glanced around the classroom to see if anyone else sensed danger, but the other students worked placidly on their assignments. By the time he looked back, Tike was sitting again, though straight and alert, and the man was gone.

If he had not been able to concentrate before, it now became near to impossible. Earlier he had been in a sad, dreamy state, now he was alert and nervous, checking on Tike every two minutes. Ben was so focused on what was happening outside that he jumped when someone knocked on the classroom door. An assistant from the school reception came in. She whispered something to the teacher before turning to find Ben.

"Benjamin?" she said. "Could you come with me, please? And, bring your backpack with you."

Ben stood so fast his chair almost fell over. He crammed his books into his backpack, asking, as he followed her out, "What's going on?"

"There's a phone call for you. You can take it in the Principal's office," the woman said as she led him to the reception area.

The Principal's assistant glanced up as she spoke over the phone. "Yes, Ms. Archer, he's here. Please accept my condolences for the loss of your father." She nodded into the receiver before adding, "Yes, goodbye." She handed the receiver to Ben, saying, "It's your mother."

Ben took it from her, relieved. "Mom?"

His mother answered hurriedly on the other end. "I'm here to pick you up. Can you come right away? I'm on the side street to the right of the school."

"Ok. Hold on," he replied, eyeing the stern assistant. "My mom is here to pick me up. Is it okay if..." he began.

The assistant said, "Yes, yes, she told me."

"I'll be right there, Mom," Ben said into the receiver before hanging up. "Thank you," he said to the assistant, who ushered him out with a wave of her hand. "Make sure to let us know when you'll be back at school, Benjamin."

Ben nodded, already halfway out the door. He ran outside

with his backpack thumping at his side. He whistled to Tike who joined him with his tongue lolling and tail wagging. Suddenly, Ben stopped in his tracks.

My suitcase!

He had forgotten his suitcase with his clothes and toothbrush upstairs. He wondered briefly whether he should go back for it, but rapidly decided against it. He wanted to see his Mom.

I wonder why she's in such a hurry to pick me up?

He sped along the school wall, then out the side gate into the short street he had taken not so long ago to escape the two bullies. He walked at a fast pace, searching for his mother's car, then jumped when he passed a chain link fence. He had completely forgotten about the three guard dogs who prowled up and down the yard as if they had been waiting for him all afternoon. He tried not to pay attention to them but couldn't avoid feeling their dark eyes fixated on his every step. So much so, that he did not notice the bald man heading across the street straight towards him. It was only because Tike bounced back into him with his tail between his legs that he suddenly realized what was happening.

The man was almost on top of him, reaching out to grab him.

"Wha...?" Ben exclaimed, stepping back in fright. He didn't have time to finish his sentence, as he lost his balance and fell backwards into the sloping parking entrance next to the guard dogs' house.

The three beasts barked ferociously, throwing themselves at the fence.

Ben's breath was knocked out of him as he hit the ground. Fortunately, his backpack broke most of the impact, though he scraped his elbows.

Already the man reached out for him again. Tike tugged at the assailant's pants, but the man kicked him aside nonchalantly.

Ben blinked the stars from his eyes and rolled over swiftly. He dropped his backpack and slid further down into the dark, public parking structure. He ran down to the second and last level, splashing through the large rain puddle that had trickled down the ramp and accumulated at the bottom. Only a couple of cars were parked there with no one in sight who could help. Ben ran to the end of the parking lot, knowing full well it was useless, for there was no other way out.

Behind him the man followed more slowly, knowing he had Ben cornered. The guard dogs' hysterical barking echoed into the parking lot.

Tike hid behind Ben's legs. Ben had his back against the concrete wall, facing the man in the grey suit. It was the same man he had spotted from his classroom window that afternoon.

"Leave me alone!" Ben shouted at him.

The man continued to approach until he was a couple of strides away. He gazed, bemused, at the terrier who bared his teeth in an attempt to protect Ben, though not a bark or growl left his throat.

Ben thought it was a trick of the light, but he was sure he had just seen the man's eyes switch colour. He caught his breath.

Twisted eyes!

Then, to Ben's horror, the being's whole face began to tremble at an alarming speed, as if two identities struggled to take control of his features. When the unnatural shaking stopped, instead of the bald man with green eyes who had been there before, there now stood a taller man with spiky, white hair and honey-brown eyes. The being clenched his teeth, as if he were angry with his own transformation.

Ben yelled urgently, "Mom! Mom!"

The being turned his face away, a smile on the corner of his mouth, and Ben heard his mother say, "I'm right here, honey!" Then the being looked at Ben again as his mother's voice left his lips, "I told you I'd pick you up."

Ben's heart dropped like a stone, his skin crawling as if a hundred tiny spiders were skittering up and down his body. He stared at the abnormal man with dread. The being had spoken with Laura Archer's voice, the same one that he had heard in the receiver in the school office.

"Where... where's my mother? What did you do to her?" Ben's voice came out thick with fear.

The being didn't seem amused anymore. "I'm not here to talk about your mother, Benjamin Archer."

How does he know my name?

He stared intently at the boy, then said, "I'm here to talk about Mesmo."

Ben caught his breath. "I don't know what you're talking about," he croaked, his voice sounding weak and unconvincing.

The being was unsmiling. "Of course you do. You see, your grandfather and I talked about you four days ago."

Ben's eyes widened, his mind whirling back as something clicked in his memory. He had bumped into this man in the hospital after visiting Grampa that night, though back then he had been wearing a doctor's coat.

The night Grampa passed away...

Ben stared at the unnatural man with new fear in his eyes. "Who are you?" he breathed. Somewhere far away, the guard dogs barked incessantly.

"I am Bordock, also known as the Shapeshifter. That is my skill," the being said enigmatically. "I have been playing a hide-and-seek game with Mesmo for almost two months, and my patience is running out." His dark eyes bored into Ben's. "You spoke to Mesmo yesterday, in the graveyard, during the funeral. Why?"

Ben swallowed hard.

How can he know that?

Why did he feel smaller and smaller while Bordock loomed ever larger over him? Ben unconsciously reached for Grampa's watch, silently praying it would magically make him disappear.

"I don't understand what you want," Ben said helplessly. "Leave me alone!"

The Shapeshifter grabbed him by the shirt, glaring down at him. His eyes were deep, brown pools that stirred another memory in Ben's mind, one that was terrifying: something that had triggered many nightmares and which he had tucked far away into his unconscious.

"I want Mesmo," the Shapeshifter said menacingly. "And you're going to tell me where he is!"

"I'm right here, Bordock," a voice boomed from behind them.

Ben peeked from behind the Shapeshifter's shoulder as he turned around slowly.

Mesmo stood at the bottom of the ramp, his tall body reflected in the large puddle of rain.

The Shapeshifter let go of Ben's shirt, then placed himself before him, so that Ben had to stretch his neck to see what was going on.

The two men glared at each other with palpable hate.

"Finally!" Bordock said. "What took you so long?"

"Leave the boy alone, Bordock," Mesmo said. "He has nothing to do with this."

Bordock observed Ben curiously for a second, before jeering, "What would you care about an Earthling boy, Mesmo?

Have you lost track of your mission?"

"That's enough! You've done enough harm already!" Mesmo retorted.

"Not quite enough," Bordock said darkly, before adding slowly, "You're still here." He braced himself as the air filled with static, which drew to him like a magnet. An invisible force gathered around the Shapeshifter. His hands and arms began to glow.

In that instant, a car screeched into the parking entrance before coming to an abrupt stop. The car door opened and a woman stepped out. She bent to pick up Ben's backpack.

"Ben?" Laura called.

"Mom!" Ben cried back frantically.

The Shapeshifter launched a powerful ball of blue light straight at Mesmo who dropped down, placed his hands in the giant puddle then turned it into a solid, transparent shield that blew into a thousand fragments as it was hit straight on. The air fizzled and cracked, transforming into a fine mixture of mist and smoke.

Mesmo picked himself up.

Bordock grinned as he gathered energy; blue light emanating from his hands and arms again. But he froze suddenly when vicious barking boomed into the parking lot. The three massive dogs from next door dashed down the ramp and emerged out of the mist. They headed straight for Bordock and the boy. In seconds they would be upon Ben. His mother cried out in alarm. Ben put up his arms to protect his face, shouting, "Stop!"

Incredibly, they did.

The three beasts froze in their tracks right in front of Bordock, growling at him menacingly, searching for the slightest movement. They circled him, shaking with anticipation, barely containing their urge to pounce.

Ben remained stuck to the concrete wall, afraid to move an inch for fear they would turn their attention to him.

The mist dissipated, while everyone waited cautiously, mesmerized by the deep growling creatures circling the being in the grey suit.

When nothing happened, Bordock let out a hissing breath. He frowned angrily, saying through gritted teeth, "What is this? How is this possible?"

Mesmo, joined by Laura, seemed equally perplexed.

"This is not your doing! It cannot be!" Bordock snarled. "And your daughter's skill died with her! Unless..." he stiffened abruptly. Then, as if a silent message had passed between them, both Bordock and Mesmo turned their attention to Ben at the same time, a look of utter disbelief in their eyes.

Ben swallowed, shaking his head in confusion.

Bordock's eyes narrowed as if he were seeing Ben for the first time; the boy could see his mind was trying to comprehend the incomprehensible.

"Ben!" his mother called anxiously.

Her voice came through to him. Carefully, Ben extracted himself from between the wall and the man. He distanced himself from the Shapeshifter slowly, afraid he would lunge. But all he did was glare fiercely.

The air was static, the few dim lights flickered, as Mesmo urged, "Hurry!"

Laura grabbed Ben's shoulders in a kind of urgent hug, then pushed him ahead of her. The three sprinted up the ramp. Ben opened the back door of the car, jumped in, and was closely followed by Mesmo and Tike. Laura pushed their door shut as she got in. In an instant, the motor came to life. The car screeched backwards into the street, leaving Bordock to his fate.

CHAPTER 10 *Lighthouse Park*

They drove through the city, making it out before the start of rush hour, then crossed Lion's Gate Bridge to the north shore, which joined the Sea-to-Sky Highway going west. Laura checked her rear-view mirror constantly to make sure nobody was following them. Instead, she caught Jack Anderson staring intently at Ben.

When Ben put a hand to his forehead, saying, "Mom, I feel dizzy!" she veered sharply into a driveway leading to the forested coast, which soon turned into a dirt road surrounded by old, majestic red cedars with a sign that read Lighthouse Park. She stopped the car in the visitor parking lot in the middle of a lush forest, which was almost empty of tourists at this time of the season, then got out of the car hurriedly.

"What are you doing, Mom?" Ben asked.

She opened the back door, ordering, "You! Get out!" She pointed to Jack. He obeyed. She then closed and locked the doors by clicking on her car keys to keep Ben safe inside.

"Mom!" he objected, knocking on the window.

She took no notice of him as she faced Jack. "You!" she repeated. "Jack... or whatever your name is... You'd better tell me what's going on or I'm leaving without you this instant!"

Ben thumped on the car window.

"Stay right there, Ben, until I've sorted this out!" she ordered. She glared at Jack, both angry and afraid at the same time. "I've been chased around all morning by the police and now... this! Whatever this was!" She waved her hand in the general direction of the city, shaking her head, then continued without waiting for an answer. "Wayne was right. I'm taking Ben far away from here!"

"Bordock will look for you," Jack warned. "He will never stop. Not after what just happened."

Laura grimaced, "Don't you dare make this about us! We don't have anything to do with this Bordock—nor with you for that matter. Both of you leave us alone!" She reached for the car door.

Jack bent to the ground.

"What are you doing?" she asked fearfully.

He touched a small puddle with his index finger. The water crackled and turned into a beautiful ice crystal with intricate designs, like the ones she had seen at her father's house after his funeral.

She stared at the crystal, taken back to that beautiful, golden sunset over the fields, the grass crunching with fresh, delicate ice... She felt a calm wash over her instantly.

After a silence, she breathed, "Who are you?"

Ben banged on the door again. "Mom," his voice sounded muffled. Still staring at the ice crystal, Laura opened the door for him as if in a trance. Ben stepped out before she could change her mind. "Before Grampa died, he told me to find Mesmo if we were ever in trouble." He pointed up at the tall man, and added, "This is Mesmo."

Laura and Ben both stared at the stranger with his out-of-place fur hat until Laura ventured, "Then who is Jack Anderson?"

Mesmo shook his head sadly. "The real Jack Anderson died in a mountain climbing accident in Bolivia last week. I borrowed his name." He turned his attention to Ben. "Something happened in the parking lot—something I can't quite explain." He paused before continuing, "I'm going to need you to recover your memory about the night of *The Cosmic Fall*."

Ben gasped. "But you said you didn't want me to."

"Today changed everything. Your grandfather wanted you to forget—to protect you—but after what happened today, that is no longer possible. Bordock was after me. Now he is going to go after you, too."

"Hold on a minute!" Laura interjected. "What would you know about *The Cosmic Fall*?"

Mesmo held her gaze before answering, "I was the one who crashed that night."

Laura pointed a stern finger at him. "Hold it right there, Mister! Don't come to me with some crazy story about crashed UFO's. I heard that one already..." She caught her breath as her eyes fell on the ice crystal.

Mesmo explained. "Bordock shot down our spacecraft. My daughter and two of my companions perished. Somehow I survived. Your father found me and saved me by carrying me to his house. But the police picked him up after he went back to help my companions. I took Ben and escaped."

Laura gasped, something clicking in her mind. "Are you saying you carried Ben from my father's house all the way to Chilliwack that night?"

"Yes," Mesmo replied.

Laura stared at him with a mixture of awe and fear.

Ben grabbed his mother's arm and pleaded, "Mom, I need

to remember!"

Laura shook her head. "I don't know if that's a good idea, Ben. Besides, I wouldn't know how to do that. You know we've tried."

Ben turned to Mesmo. "Can you help me?"

"Yes."

* * *

The three of them sat on a small beach surrounded by boulders topped with fir trees. Way above, the white and red lighthouse illuminated the bay, while in the distance the lights of Vancouver glittered under the night sky.

Laura had had the presence of mind to check the trunk of her father's car, which contained two ragged blankets, some camping gear, a first aid kit, some cans of food, and instant coffee. Amazed at her father's foresight, she thanked him silently for having taught her how to start a fire when she was a girl. She warmed up a can of beans, which she and Ben devoured, though Mesmo would not touch it. They had found a plastic bottle in a garbage bin, then filled it with water from a tap placed at the park entrance for tourists visiting the site. The water was beginning to boil in the bean can. She would mix some instant coffee in it.

The stars became brighter, while a soft wind blew as they stared at the embers, thinking of the events of the day.

Mesmo interrupted their thoughts. "It is time."

Ben and Laura glanced at him expectantly.

Then, before they could do anything, Mesmo plunged his whole hand into the boiling water. "No!" Laura yelled in horror. Ben stood up in haste.

Mesmo did not flinch. Before their very eyes, the water

bulged out of the can until it formed a perfectly flat, elliptical shape, quite like a mirror, except that you could see through it. Ben and Laura stared with their mouths open.

"How did you do that?" Laura asked in awe.

"My skill is *water*," Mesmo said, as if that explained everything. "Come," he said to Ben, motioning for him to sit behind the floating mirror. "Touch the water with the tips of your fingers," Mesmo instructed. "It will not hurt."

Ben did as he was told, half expecting to be burnt, but all he felt was the cool liquid under his fingertips.

"Close your eyes and go back as far as you can to the night of *The Cosmic Fall*," Mesmo said. "Try to picture it in your mind."

Ben shifted uneasily, trying to remember something from before, but as usual everything from that time was a dark haze in his mind. Tike, with his tail wagging slowly, placed his paw on Ben's leg. Immediately an image of a baby dog yapping excitedly appeared behind Ben's eyelids. He heard his mother gasp. He snapped his eyes open to find the same image of a barking Tike emerging like a reflection on the water mirror, as though it was a strange TV screen reflecting his thoughts. The image wavered. Mesmo urged him to keep concentrating.

Ben focused on baby Tike, remembering when Grampa had let him into his room one summer when he was six years old. It was a beautiful memory, one that made him smile, but then the image wavered as his grandfather's face lingered in his mind. He opened his eyes again, noticing that his mother's lips were pressed together. He shifted uneasily. Mesmo encouraged him to continue. But Ben could not get past that one memory, as it played over and over in his mind. He looked at Mesmo helplessly.

Mesmo reached out to the transparent screen, touching it

with the tip of his finger. It came to life at once.

The alien man sat in an unusual vehicle with soft lights and smooth walls. Outside, everything was dark until the craft glided to the right. The Earth appeared, vast and majestic. He was following another identical craft with which he exchanged strange words. The soft, disciplined voice that came back belonged to a girl. They gently navigated their spacecraft ever closer to the Blue Planet. Then a sharp flash of light zoomed from behind them, almost hitting the first vessel.

The girl's voice burst in warning. Mesmo exchanged urgent words with her as he steered the craft around to see from where the shot had come. No sooner had he done that, when two more shots were fired from a dark spacecraft behind them. One shot flew past, crashing into the American communication satellite, which exploded. The other hit Mesmo's ship with full force, making it shudder as it spun out of control. Mesmo heard the girl call his name frantically as he sped towards the Earth. Everything went black until Mesmo recovered his senses. He saw city lights racing towards him. He tried to veer the spacecraft to the right, only to face a dangerous slope he could not escape.

On the watery screen, Ben and Laura watched as Grampa's house whizzed by, the neon lights from the kitchen, Mr. Hayward's house, the fields and the dark island of trees. Then they saw the explosion as Mesmo's ship hit the ground.

The screen became transparent again. Mesmo let out a gasp of breath as if he had been holding it the whole time. Ben and Laura stared at the alien, speechless.

Ben shivered as Mesmo held his gaze. "Go on," the alien urged.

CHAPTER 11 *The Cosmic Fall*

Reluctantly, Ben touched the liquid mirror again with a trembling hand. In his mind's eye, he was taken back to the field near his grandfather's house.

"There's the Big Dipper," Grampa said, making Ben jump.

Ryan Archer squinted through the eyepiece of an old telescope, which he had directed across the Chilliwack valley and its distant mountains. Grampa and Ben had placed the telescope on top of a blanket in the middle of a nearby field on this starlit August night. A warm breeze brought scents of corn and earth to their nostrils. Trees and shrubs bordered both sides of the field, though to their right they could glimpse the ugly neon light which Grampa had forgotten to switch off when they had set out on their stargazing expedition.

"This was your mother's once, you know?" Grampa said slowly, while he concentrated on getting the image focused. "I made it for her when she was little. Too bad it ended up forgotten in the attic after the lens broke. I'm so glad you found it again!"

He stood to stretch his back, then shook his head. "I can't believe how easy it was to get a new lens delivered to my doorstep! Great job, kiddo!" He patted Ben on the back. "There's a pretty smart brain hiding behind that potatohead of yours!" He chuckled, inviting Ben to check out the stars through the telescope. "I look forward to some more internet surfing classes on your next vacation, eh?"

Ben stuffed the remainder of a biscuit in his mouth, then wiped his hand on his jeans before glancing through the eyepiece. Tike scampered around his feet, bumping into the legs of the telescope.

"Tike!" Ben scolded, his mouth full. His dog kept running around them, barking excitedly.

They followed the dog with their eyes, then noticed what had caught his attention. On the road at the end of the field behind them, Thomas Nombeko, the friendly town mailman, cycled by on his way home. Thomas waved at them in the dark, shouting something they didn't quite catch.

"'Night, Thomas!" Grampa bellowed, waving back, as the cyclist disappeared into the night. Grampa frowned. "Strange..." he said half to himself. "There's a light on in Mr. Hayward's living room. I thought he was away on business?"

"Grampa! What's that?" Ben shouted, interrupting.

Grampa straightened again, following Ben's pointed finger.

There was a brief, horizontal streak, way up in space, followed by an expanding light as if something had exploded. Then a long, white line descended towards the Earth. It kept falling for what seemed like a long time, its trajectory taking it straight to the lights of Chilliwack.

"Whoa!" Ben gasped in wonder.

But then the falling object did something it wasn't supposed to do; it changed course! What had been a perfectly elliptical line across the black sky, became a soft 90-degree angle, so that without warning, the object was suddenly heading straight towards them.

Shooting stars don't change trajectory! What the heck is going on?

Ben broke into a cold sweat. "Grampa?" his voice wavered.

Grampa gripped the boy's shoulder to pull him away. Instead, they found themselves frozen to the spot. There was nowhere to run, no time to think.

They could hear the burning object whistling through the air as it raced towards them at frightening speed.

"Grampa!" Ben screamed.

Chaos descended upon them with a horrible, screeching noise that went on and on as the object fought its last battle with gravity. They were struck by a deafening explosion, a blinding light, a wave of heat. The ground heaved beneath them.

Tike let out a death howl that pierced Ben's heart. The boy barely registered hitting the ground; the air sucked out of his lungs. Ben and his grandfather lay in a heap, their bodies pelted by dirt bullets.

A heavy silence followed.

The boy extracted his hand from Grampa's tight grip. His brain was rattled. Grampa coughed up dust.

The ball of fire had missed them, landing in the woods nearby. Flames flared behind the dark trees where the object had dragged itself to its terrible end.

Boy and man helped each other stand. Ben found his legs were like jelly. He picked up a silent, shivering Tike in his arms.

"Ben, are you all right?" Grampa asked. He scanned the boy from head to foot, then brushed off some of the dirt on the boy's face.

Ben stared at him with dazed eyes, then nodded slowly.

An object at the edge of the patch of forest caught their

eye. They walked towards it slowly, Ben clinging tightly to Grampa's arm. A broken piece had been blown sky-high and had landed on the ground not far from them. It was about the size of a car door, and it had the smooth, silver colour of metal.

"An airplane!" Ben breathed.

That's why it changed course in the middle of the sky!

The poor pilot had managed to veer the ailing aircraft away from a direct crash with the town of Chilliwack in the hopes of finding a place to land. Instead, he had only found a wall of trees in his path.

Grampa took Ben firmly by the arm, pulling him away. They both half-ran, half-trotted across the field in the direction of Grampa's house. They ignored the blanket and telescope. They crossed through the few shrubs and trees separating the two fields and viewed Grampa's house with relief. Ben didn't think the neon kitchen lights could ever look so welcoming. He tugged at his grandfather to get going. Grampa held him back.

"Listen to me very carefully, Benjamin," he said sternly.

Ben listened.

You never call me Benjamin...

"I have to go and help the people who crashed back there."

Ben's mouth opened in a terrified objection.

Grampa held up his hand.

"Boy, time is crucial! I need you to run to the house, pick up the phone and dial 911. Tell the police a plane fell next to my house. We need the fire department and ambulances. Do you understand?"

"No way, Grampa! You're not going back there!" Ben gasped.

"There's no time to argue! Do it, now!" he ordered, his eyes ablaze.

Grampa's words worked like a trigger. A sense of extreme

urgency propelled Ben forward. All he could think of were the people who had crashed in the plane.

Ambulance! Fire department!

The words repeated in his mind with each step. His shoes thumped on the dry ground. His eyes fixed on the kitchen light, as it beckoned him. The wide field stretched away from his small frame as he gasped for air. He had almost made it across when something horrifying happened; the lights inside the house went out!

Ben froze. Darkness crashed around him. He could barely make out Grampa's house, now a black, empty giant.

No electricity, no phone...

The realization struck Ben with full force. He picked up Tike in his arms for comfort. The dog shivered uncontrollably.

Drat! Why doesn't Grampa have a cellphone?

The fire in the woods illuminated the sky behind him.

If I hurry, I'll catch up with Grampa.

Ben knew he wasn't thinking straight, but he needed to do something. He couldn't just stand there. The boy bolted away from the house, back across the field, a stitch nagging at his side.

Maybe I can help...

He was too set on finding his grandfather to notice a small burst of light in the night sky, followed by an elliptical line streaking towards the Earth.

Ben was sobbing by the time he reached the blanket and telescope in the middle of the second field. It was a comforting island at the centre of a danger zone. Yet, once there, it was still as cold and lonely, offering no protection. The tears made it impossible to search for Grampa. Everything was a blur.

He sagged down onto the blanket, exhausted and frightened. He wiped away his tears and sniffled.

Stop being a wuss! Grampa needs help.

Feeling ashamed, he blinked several times to clear his eyesight and paid more attention to the wall of dark trees. He took a deep breath, picked up his dog again, then left the blanket and telescope on stiff legs. His whole body ached. The air felt cold and humid, in spite of the crackling fire coming from within the woods.

Ben had nearly reached the edge of the trees when he heard the familiar whistling in the air and caught sight of the fireball out of the corner of his eye. He turned to face it, though he might as well have been a lonely tree about to be swallowed by a tornado. The fiery bullet was already almost on top of him. He barely had time to shut his eyes and brace himself for the impact.

For a second time that night, there was a deafening crash. Ben was knocked to the ground. A heat wave followed, then a grinding hiss that came nearer and nearer. Chunks of earth and metal whizzed by, narrowly missing him. He covered his head with his arms to protect himself and Tike. Heat from the object warmed Ben's face as it came to a stop right before him.

When he opened his eyes, the field resembled a war zone. Huge, twisted pieces of metal surrounded him, burning. A long, fiery runway indicated the distance the object had travelled since its impact. And before him was the craft, or rather what remained of it, for it was almost entirely buried in the ground.

Ben stayed rooted to the spot; his voice stuck in his throat.

The flames licked at the wreckage, minding their own business. Ben stood there, shaking like a leaf before the billowing black smoke. He didn't think the smooth wreckage that jutted out of the ground looked like an airplane at all, though he noticed a hole near the front, indicating it was hollow. Carefully, he took a few steps closer to the opening and glanced inside. He came face to face with a girl. Her big eyes bored into him from deep inside the wreckage. They both froze and stared at each other fearfully.

She had a pale, delicate face and long, white hair. He noticed her eyes were a deep honey-brown before she shut them tightly. She was like a delicate fawn in great pain. Ben knelt on the ground and bent over the opening in the wreckage so he could get a better look. It was dark inside, but the nearby firelight illuminated the girl's face. The rest of her body was stuck under debris.

"Are you hurt?" he asked shakily.

It took a while for her to open her eyes again. When she did, they reflected an immense weariness. Her skin had turned slightly gray.

Ben reached out a hand to her, feeling an urgent need to help. She stared at it suspiciously, showing no intention of taking it. Ben frowned, then suddenly realized his hand was bleeding. He wiped it hastily on his trouser leg, before holding it out to her again. She stared back at his hand, hesitant. At that moment Tike peeked over the edge. As soon as she saw the dog, her expression softened. She turned her face away and he heard her gasp in pain. She looked at him again, with determination this time, as she extended her pale hand to him.

Ben was puzzled to see her palm was bleeding, too. But before he could say anything, her hand clamped onto his, and instead of bracing herself to get pulled out, she mumbled some unintelligible words while staring at him with an intensity so frightening Ben's heart almost stopped. He tried to pull away, but she had him in an iron grasp. Their eyes locked, their blood smears mingled, and a sudden, powerful surge of energy flowed into Ben's body. His mind exploded in a myriad of sensations as if every stem cell in his brain had been activated.

Then, as suddenly as it had begun, it was over, and she let

him go. Ben's arm hung limply over the side of the craft, as he stared down at her in shock. His whole body tingled. Slowly he retrieved his numb arm and found his hand balled into a tight fist. He carefully unwound the fingers of his hand, only to discover a tiny, sparkling gem in its centre.

The diamond in the watch!

Another part of his mind nudged at him, but all he could think of was the girl who gazed at him with a worried look on her face. There was a brief silence as if an electrical storm passed between them. She let herself sink back into the wreckage, her face becoming a deeper gray, her eyes reflecting an inner peace.

"Mesmo," she murmured.

He thought he saw her smile before she closed her eyes.

"No!" Ben shouted, reaching for her as her body slipped out of reach.

Ben's eyes fluttered open. He was back on the beach, sitting before the fire, surrounded by Laura and Mesmo. Before him, the liquid screen had lost its consistency and had splashed to the ground. The embers sizzled. A wind had picked up, while a couple of raindrops fell unnoticed onto the thick sand.

Mesmo breathed heavily, his hand still raised as if he had not yet realized that the watery mirror had disappeared. Ben stared at him with wide eyes.

Laura was the first to come out of her trance. She approached Ben on her knees, taking her son in her arms. "Now I know," she said softly, hugging him.

He squeezed her back, feeling tired and empty, yet also strangely lightheaded, for a great weight had been lifted from his shoulders. Something that had burdened him had suddenly been extracted and was no longer only his to carry. He felt strangely relieved.

Mesmo stood and walked to the edge of the water. Tiny

waves lapped the shore peacefully, though raindrops fell more insistently.

Ben let go of his mother, and walked over to him.

After staring out at the dark waters for a long, silent moment, Mesmo gazed down at Ben quizzically. In a startled voice, he said, “She gave you her skill!”

“What do you mean?” Ben asked as rain splattered down his face.

Mesmo ignored him. He spoke into the night with a broken voice, “Then my daughter truly is dead...”

Laura came up behind them and led Ben away from Mesmo, as the alien continued to stare, motionless, at the black sea. “That’s enough for now,” she said softly when Ben wanted to object.

Reluctantly, he followed her, sneezing hard. They collected the blankets and empty cans before heading up the steep slope next to the lighthouse. By the time they reached the car, they were worn out. Laura switched on the car heater for a while as they snuggled up as best they could in the car seats, Laura in front and Ben at the back, then covered themselves with their damp jackets. Ben barely recollected his mother switching off the car before he fell into a deep, dreamless sleep.

CHAPTER 12 *The List*

Laura woke to the sound of pounding rain. It washed over the windshield like a waterfall so that she could barely see outside.

She put the key into the ignition without starting the car, revealing the time on the dashboard. Almost 10:30 p.m. Ben stirred in the back seat, so she switched on the radio and tried to make out what the reporter said over the drumming noise outside.

"...Coast Guard has had to call off the rescue mission due to the bad weather conditions and will make another attempt to save the crew of the drifting ship at dawn tomorrow."

A woman took over. "Yes, Ronald, this freak storm will wreak havoc on traffic if it continues tomorrow morning. We urge drivers to be extremely cautious in this treacherous weather, as roads are slippery, with limited visibility..."

Ben stretched and yawned. He glanced around. "Where's Mesmo?"

"I've been wondering the same thing," Laura said. She put on her coat. "I'm going to look for him." She opened the car door, getting soaked as soon as she stepped out.

Ben came up behind her in a hurry. "I'm coming with

you!"

You're not closing the door on me again!

They grabbed a blanket, thinking to hold it above their heads. It drenched instantly and stuck like glue to their hair and faces. In the end, they left it, then advanced carefully on the muddy path. They would not have been able to get very far if it hadn't been for the lighthouse that served as a beacon indicating the way.

Soon they saw Mesmo standing upright with his back to them on a flat, rocky ledge, illuminated by the sweeping beam, his elbows close to his body, his hands outstretched, his body glowing faintly from an inner source of energy. As they approached, they saw that not a drop of rain had touched him; he was completely dry and unaffected by the storm raging around him.

Ben and Laura held on to each other to keep from slipping, their hair plastered to their faces, their shoes pools of water.

"Jack!" Laura yelled over the sound of rain. The alien man did not budge. "Mesmo!" she called. "You have to stop this! It won't bring your daughter back. She's gone, Mesmo. There was nothing you could have done. I'm sorry about that. But if you're responsible for this storm, you have to stop immediately! You're putting people in danger. Look around you! We're drowning here!"

She let go of Ben, then reached out to touch Mesmo's shoulder, only to find that there was nothing there! Gasping in surprise, she lost her footing and passed *right through him*!

Ben yelled in fear.

Laura hit the ground, then slid down the smooth, rocky ledge. Only a jutting bush saved her from toppling all the way down into the sea.

"Mom!" Ben cried in horror, rushing to help. On his stomach, he crawled towards her. He stretched out his hand, but she was just out of reach. He looked up at Mesmo's projected image, which stood still, unmoving. The alien's head turned towards them.

"Mesmo!" Ben pleaded. "Help her! Please!"

Ben watched as the solid-looking Mesmo bent to touch the ground. Immediately the rain moved away from them like a curtain. The surface dried up while icy spikes spurted out of the rock all the way down to Laura. She used them to pull herself up. Ben grabbed her, and heaved her up to safety.

They toppled to the ground, breathing heavily, their eyes on Mesmo. The drape of rain fell over them again, though with less intensity.

Woman and child stared at the tall man, unable to comprehend how he could look so real to them. He gazed back, his eyes emitting a million unreadable thoughts. He looked haggard and weak. His skin had turned a light grey.

Then he vanished.

Laura gasped.

She and Ben crawled backwards in fright and stared at the empty spot. The rain continued to fall and the beam from the lighthouse swept by them. Yet they had to accept the unacceptable. Mesmo had disappeared into thin air.

Ben sneezed. Laura helped him up. They trudged back to the car, grasping onto each other as if they might disappear, too. They regularly checked over their shoulders without speaking. Ben sneezed again. They entered the car, soaking wet, and, after a few unsuccessful attempts, Laura started the car. She backed out of the parking space, switched on the lights, and carefully drove away from the haunted lighthouse park.

Ben secretly checked on his mother while she drove.

I can hear you wheezing!

They arrived in North Vancouver where Laura stopped at a Comfort Inn in the hopes of getting a room to shower and rest for the night. There, she found that her credit card was no longer working.

They drove on, shivering with cold. Laura eyed the gas meter nervously. It was dangerously low. It was not easy to find anything open at such a late hour—the streets were empty, especially after such a downpour. They crossed over Highway One and came to an all-night diner called The Bearded Bear. Relieved, they sat down at a table away from late-night truck drivers, and ordered as much food as they could with what little cash Laura managed to fish out of her pocket. While they waited, she insisted on Ben going to the men's room to dry himself off as much as possible. She didn't want him falling sick. She suggested he use the hand dryer on his t-shirt.

I wish I'd brought my suitcase along!

Ben remembered he had left it at school. There was nothing he could do about it now. By the time he came back he felt somewhat refreshed, though his clothes were still damp. The hot food on the table lifted his spirits. A big hamburger awaited, while his mother had ordered chicken soup. He hadn't realized how hungry he was and barely noticed when his mother excused herself to go and clean herself up as well.

He was busy digging into his fries when she came back, but she did not touch her food. He noticed her breath coming out in short bursts. Laura searched through her belongings, telling Ben he could have her soup if he was still hungry.

"Are you sure?" he asked, seriously tempted.

She nodded absentmindedly, going through her things.

"I'll eat your bread roll. But you should have the soup," Ben suggested.

Laura slumped into the high restaurant seat, looking crestfallen. Ben forgot the bread roll he had brought to his mouth. He saw her flushed face.

"What is it, Mom?" he asked, although he had already recognized the signs.

"It's my inhaler," she said with short gasps. She opened her handbag for the third time. "I can't find it! I'm certain I had one, but it's not there anymore."

Ben swallowed the piece of bread which stuck in his throat as he looked at her worriedly.

She tried a small, reassuring smile. "Don't worry, I'll be fine. It's the least of our concerns. Just finish the soup."

"No, Mom, you should eat. You'll feel much better," he insisted.

Laura made an effort to eat, while Ben watched carefully, but soon she put the spoon down and said, "I'm drained, Ben. Could you take care of the bill? There should be enough..." She indicated the money on the table. "I think I'll go and lie down in the car for a bit."

She walked away slowly, while he asked the waitress to pack up the remaining soup and bread to go. By the time he had plopped the coins on the table, counting them twice, his mother was already fast asleep in the back seat. He covered her with the blanket and was going to settle down under her jacket when he noticed an envelope sticking out of its inside pocket.

He opened it and found a small piece of paper that had been torn out of a standard notebook. He recognized his grandfather's handwriting right away. On it, were five names with a phone number under each one.

1. Ryan Archer
   604-721-883

2. Wayne McGuillen
   604-347-222
3. Thomas Nombeko
   250-981-310
4. Susan Pickering
   778-919-832
5. Bob M.
   416-627-003

CHAPTER 13 *The Island*

Ben dozed off while studying the list. He started awake when Tike nuzzled him in the neck. He waved the dog away with his hand, then rested his head uncomfortably against the cold windowpane. The dog jumped onto his lap, placing his two paws on his chest, trying to catch his attention. Ben blinked several times. The lights of the all-night diner were out and the parking lot was empty. Only a couple street lamps produced modest islands of lights, while everything seemed peaceful.

"Go to sleep, Tike," Ben whispered, pushing him away from his face as the dog licked him.

His mother moaned from the back seat. Ben snapped his head in her direction.

Laura tossed in her sleep, the blanket slipping off onto the floor. Ben bent over the car seat to move the locks of hair that were plastered to her cheeks. He touched her hand. It felt cold as ice. She was drenched in sweat and shivering uncontrollably.

She's burning up!

"Mom!" he gasped worriedly.

He covered her with the blanket again, and rolled up his jacket under her head before emptying her purse on the driver's seat in the hopes of finding some analgesic to bring down the fever. He found none. An hour went by and she was worsening. Her breath wheezed again as she twisted on the uncomfortable back seat.

Ben got out of the car and jogged towards the street, searching for a passerby or car. There was no one in sight. He thumped on the door of the diner, knowing full well its occupants had gone. He raked his hands through his hair in despair.

"Mesmo!" he called hesitantly, searching the empty parking lot with his eyes. Only a soft breeze answered.

Tike jumped up to lick his hand encouragingly. They headed back to the car. Ben slipped into the driver's seat. The time on the dashboard said 2:55 a.m. He would have to wait many hours before anybody came along. He glanced at Tike helplessly. The dog sat in the passenger seat, his tongue lolling to one side, with a paw on the sheet of paper that Ben had found in his mother's jacket. Ben fondled the dog's ears while he studied the list of names again.

He knew the first name, Ryan Archer. That was his grandfather. He did not know any of the others. As he stared at the phone numbers again, he realized that the one belonging to Wayne McGuillen started with 604, like his grandfather's, which meant he lived in the same area. He was not familiar with the zone numbers 250 or 416, but he pondered the number that started with 778. That was a local number, he was sure of it. It belonged to someone named Susan Pickering.

He delved into his mother's handbag and pulled out her cellphone, only to realize the battery had died. Desperately, he glanced around and spotted a public phone booth attached to the side of the diner.

I didn't know they still made those!

He had never actually used one before. After going through his jeans pockets, he found he had sufficient coins to make a phone call. He stared into the dark, wondering if this would lead him anywhere.

Tike placed a paw on his arm as if encouraging him to follow his instincts.

"C'mon, Tike," Ben whispered, as he got out of the car and headed for the phone.

He punched the numbers, then listened to the ringing on the other end. It went on and on for some time. He almost gave up, when someone picked up the receiver, and a woman's voice barked, "What?"

Ben was taken aback, then remembered it was three in the morning; decent folk were fast asleep at this time. "Er... hello," he began hesitantly. "Is this Susan Pickering?"

There was a silence. Ben thought she might hang up.

Then the woman said more slowly, "Who wants to know?"

"I... well... my name is Benjamin Archer. I'm Ryan Archer's grandson. I think you knew each other?"

Further silence.

"I'm sorry to bother you, but my mom's very sick, and we need help," he pressed on.

After a while, she said, "Where's Ryan?"

That confirms that they knew each other.

"Grampa died last week. He wrote your name and phone number on a piece of paper. I thought maybe... well, maybe..." he stammered.

"Where are you?" she interrupted.

Ben glanced around.

I have no idea!

"I don't know exactly... I'm in the parking lot of a place called The Bearded Bear Diner..."

"I know where that is," she said abruptly. "Stay right there! Don't talk to anyone! Don't contact anyone! I'm coming to you." Then she hung up before Ben could say anything else.

The boy stared at the receiver, a million thoughts going through his head. Tike gazed up at him with his tail wagging slowly.

* * *

The waiting was the worst. Ben would sometimes doze off to the strangest of dreams; then he would wake with a start, check on his shivering mother and his surroundings worriedly. It felt like forever before a red car screeched into the parking lot around 5:30 a.m. It came to a stop beside them.

Immediately, a bulky woman with light brown hair worn in a hasty bun on top of her head stepped out, then hurried over to open the driver's door before Ben had time to react. Without a word of greeting, she stared at him with determined, blue eyes. When she noticed Laura lying on the back seat, she checked her vital signs.

"She's running a fever," the woman stated, business-like.

Tell me something I don't know!

She opened the back door of her own car before waving Ben over. "Come on, help me here," she ordered as she began to pull Laura out of the car.

"Wait a minute," Ben protested. "What are you doing? Where are you taking her?"

The woman in her early sixties shot him a stern glance. "You in trouble, boy?"

Ben, taken aback, stared down at his sneakers uncomfortably.

The woman grunted. "Huh! Just what I figured. I'm taking

you somewhere safe. You can't very well take her to the hospital, can you?"

Ben silently agreed, though he wished his mother had been conscious enough to approve of what was happening. Reluctantly, he helped the woman carry his mother to the other car.

"Grab your things," Susan urged. She was clearly in a hurry.

Ben did what he was told, though their belongings were reduced to his mother's handbag, his grandfather's list, and their jackets.

He went to sit beside his mother on the back seat, placing her head to rest on his lap. Tike sat at his feet, trembling with anticipation.

"What about our car?" Ben asked.

Susan Pickering revved up her own red car, speeding away from the parking lot.

"You won't be needing it anymore."

Ben watched as their vehicle disappeared behind the bend.

They drove for about half an hour onto a winding road bordered by sparse houses and areas heavily populated with deep green Douglas firs, until they reached the small town of Deep Cove, nestled at the foot of Mount Seymour and the Burrard Inlet. Rows of sailboats and motorboats were anchored in the marina. As dawn approached, Ben could make out the outline of the mountains on the other side of the inlet and dark, sporadic islands jutting from the water.

Susan Pickering turned left off the marina, driving until the houses became less frequent. Then she abruptly took a small dirt road to the right, which soon led to a run-down shed and small, wooden pier by the water. She got out of the car, then busied herself opening the shed door and foraged inside.

Ben stepped out of the car as well, taking in his surroundings. The calm waters turned a lighter shade of blues and pinks as the sun began to rise, contrasting with last night's storm.

Susan Pickering had found some blankets in the shed, which she carried to a small motorboat tied to the end of the pier.

"Are we taking the boat?" Ben asked nervously.

"Sure are," the woman answered. "Give me a minute."

She disappeared back into the shed, leaving Ben with his stomach churning. He did not like the idea of open water. He wrapped his arms around his shoulders as if to warm himself, feeling his grandfather's watch close to his cheek. Suddenly Tike ran behind Ben excitedly. The boy whirled, and jumped at the sight of Mesmo standing only a few feet away. Ben stepped back, unsure what to expect, as he stared at the imposing man.

"What happened?" Mesmo asked, seeing the shed, the boat, then Laura, lying in the back seat of the car.

"She's very sick," Ben said weakly, wondering which direction he should run if it became necessary. But the alien cut off any escape to the winding road they had used, while the open waters trapped him from behind.

I can't leave Mom behind!

Mesmo had not moved since he had magically appeared, so Ben mustered up enough courage to approach him. He reached out his hand. Mesmo understood his gesture and did the same. Ben waved his hand up and down, each time going right through Mesmo's own.

Ben stepped back, asking with a shaky voice, "Are you a ghost?"

Mesmo's eyes twinkled as if he found the question funny. "A ghost is a spirit belonging to someone whose body has died," he began. "I am not a ghost. My body is not dead. It is just not... here right now." He paused, before adding, "But my spirit is free to roam."

Behind them, Susan Pickering, who had emerged from the shed, stopped in her tracks. "What...!" she began. "Who's that?" Her face flushed with anger.

Ben held up his hands to calm her down. "It's okay! He's a friend!"

She stepped closer to take a better look at the stranger. The fact that a lock of white hair stuck out from under Mesmo's fur hat made him look quite out of place.

"He's a friend," Ben repeated, trying to sound reassuring. "His name is Mes... er... his name is Jack Anderson. He's..."

Susan Pickering interrupted him. "I know who he is," she snorted. She had her hands on her hips, inspecting the man up and down like he was some curious object. After a while, she said sternly, "You've caused a lot of harm, Mister. A lot of harm." She shook her head disapprovingly. "How did you find us anyway?"

Ben cleared his throat to come to the rescue. "Er... he was following us. Didn't you notice?"

Susan Pickering frowned at him angrily. "Was he now?" Then she sighed, adding, "Well, I don't want to know. But since you're here, might as well prove yourself useful. Help me carry this sick lady into the boat, would you?"

Ben and Mesmo shot a glance at each other. The boy ran to Susan's side, blurting, "I can help!"

Ben and Susan struggled to pull a very weak Laura out of the car, then the three of them stumbled down to the pier while Mesmo watched from a distance. With some difficulty, they managed to place Laura on the back seat of the motorboat. Susan went back to her car to drive it into the shed, then closed and locked the door with a padlock.

They all took a seat in the boat. Susan, who saw that Mesmo was not helping her by uncoupling the rope that held the boat to the pier, grumbled, “Men!” under her breath, before bringing the motorboat to life. Ben had to bite his lip to stop himself from grinning, while Mesmo stared at him in bewilderment.

They headed off into the inlet, a bright, cold sun chasing away the night and the remaining clouds from last night’s storm. In spite of the low temperature, it was going to be a beautiful day. Susan had provided some thick blankets to keep Laura warm, which Ben struggled to keep in place as the wind tried to blow them away. All the while he couldn’t help gawking at Mesmo.

Jeepers! This guy is some kind of phantom from outer space!

He fought off the urge to laugh crazily and forgot that the sky had been weighing down on his shoulders only moments ago.

They sped past one of the small islands, then approached another. Ben made sure he was out of earshot before mustering up the courage to sit near the alien, making sure not to touch him. He asked, “What is it like, where you come from?”

Mesmo didn’t seem to mind the question. “It’s not that much different from this place,” he replied as he indicated the calm waters and surrounding mountains. “What I mean is, you’d have to fly at a very low altitude to realize that there was a whole city spread out under the forests, hills and snowy mountains. It is a very beautiful and... balanced... place. We have many laws to maintain this balance, we grow up with the deepest respect for them. Which is also why we do not have wars or hunger or suffering because we do not allow ourselves to experience strong, conflicting emotions like people on your planet.”

He blinked as if realizing that Ben was wondering where all this was going. He cleared his throat, then continued, "Our lifespans are longer than Earth humans by about forty years. We have three suns and four moons. Our days last thirty-two hours. We have cities on the moons and in the oceans. We live where our skills are most useful. Our skills give us purpose in life."

Intrigued, Ben wanted to ask more questions, but Susan had turned around, gesturing for him to grab onto the rope. They were already slowing to a stop next to the wooden pier of a tree-filled island in the middle of the inlet.

The chubby woman deftly maneuvered the motorboat next to another rustier one, which also lay docked there. A large patch of grass led to a fringe of tall fir trees. Ben could make out the shape of a log cabin tucked between them. It was quaint and inconspicuous.

The perfect hiding place!

"Where are we?" Ben asked.

"Home," Susan replied.

"Oh..." Ben nodded, understanding why it had taken her so long to pick them up from The Bearded Bear Diner.

With some effort, Susan and Ben managed to help Laura out of the boat. They dragged her to the cabin, with Susan muttering under her breath the whole way because Mesmo deliberately lagged behind. Ben had to suppress a nervous giggle again. If this woman found out that Mesmo wasn't really there, but was some illusion or projected image, she would kick them into the inlet in a heartbeat!

The cabin was surprisingly cozy. On the left was a small, functional kitchen with a white, countertop island, while on the right, a snug living room with an open fireplace. The walls and roof were made of logs, the floor was planked with wooden boards. Some sustaining logs crisscrossed the ceiling. Practically everything Ben laid his eyes on was made of wood, which gave the whole place a warm, camping-out-in-the-forest sort of feeling.

Further in, Ben glimpsed a wooden dining table with four chairs, as Susan directed him through a door at the end of the living room which led to a bedroom with a large, thick mattress on an old bed frame. They placed Laura on top of it, and she moaned as she sank into the soft, plush duvet.

No sooner was this done than Susan shooed Ben out of the room, ordering him to get the rest of the things from the boat. She did, however, allow Tike to stay quietly on the bed next to Laura. Ben did as he was told, then found he had nothing more to do but sit restlessly in the living room with Mesmo. An old cuckoo clock ticked loudly while they waited.

Ben was glad to get another chance to interrogate the alien. "Where did you go last night?" he asked.

Mesmo did not reply right away, as if pondering how much he should say. "Spirit travelling takes a lot of energy and concentration. Sometimes it is necessary for me to return to my physical body to regain strength."

Ben could tell that there was more to it than that, but since Mesmo offered no further explanation, he asked, "What about what you did with the rain puddle in the parking lot? And the boiling water? And the ice spikes on the rock? Those were real!" Ben insisted.

Mesmo nodded. "My skill is not connected to my body. It is connected to my spirit. I take my skill with me when my spirit travels."

"You keep on talking about your skill. And last night you said 'She gave you her skill.' What did you mean by that?" Ben asked.

Mesmo stared at him intently.

"My skill is *water*," he began carefully. "I can manipulate it in any way I choose. It's a very useful tool on this planet and one of the reasons I was chosen for this mission. Bordock's skill is *shapeshifting*. He can take on the shape of any being, though at a great cost in energy. Kaia—my daughter—her skill was... how would you say..." He searched for the word. "My daughter's skill was *translation*. I was against her coming, but she knew how important she was to the mission. She would not back down." His voice trailed off as he remembered.

"Translation...?" Ben asked carefully, eager for an explanation.

Mesmo ignored him and continued. "Bordock wanted to exterminate us, along with our skills, so we would not be able to complete our mission." He stopped. "I don't think he counted on my daughter leaving her skill with you."

Ben felt a chill run down his spine.

I don't want to talk about Bordock!

"Wait a minute. You said your daughter's skill was translation. What does that mean?"

Mesmo searched for his words again. "Well, it's when you understand different languages and can pass on meaning from one language to another so that different beings can communicate with each other."

Ben was utterly perplexed. "That doesn't make sense. I don't speak French or understand Japanese or anything like that."

Mesmo looked at him, amused, before answering. "Maybe not human languages. But languages from different species."

Ben continued to stare at him, confused.

Mesmo added, "Those dogs who attacked Bordock in the parking lot—they understood you, didn't they?"

CHAPTER 14 *Spirit Portal*

Ben sat opposite Mesmo in Susan Pickering's living room, his mind bubbling with questions. Unfortunately, he did not get a chance to interrogate the alien further, as Susan appeared in the bedroom doorway. She glanced at them before busying herself in the kitchen. Within minutes she produced a peanut butter sandwich, which Ben accepted gratefully, although at this point he was having a hard time keeping his eyes open.

"How is she?" Mesmo asked. Through a yawn, Ben still couldn't understand how the alien could look so real.

"Her fever is high," Susan stated, as she poured water into a kettle, then placed it on the stove. "I've given her something to bring down the temperature. All we can do is make her comfortable and wait for her immune system to kick in. Could be a couple of days."

"What about her asthma?" Ben blurted, his brain functioning in a haze.

Susan glanced at him hastily. "Asthma?" When he nodded, she said, "What are you talking about, son?"

"Last night," he began, searching his memory, "she was looking for her asthma pump and couldn't find it."

Out of the corner of his eye, Ben caught the worried look that crossed Susan's face.

"What?" he asked fearfully. "We can get another one from the pharmacy, right?"

Susan answered carefully. "We'll see what we can do. Right now, young man, you're going to take a hot shower and change out of those smelly clothes so I can give them a good wash." She motioned for Ben to follow her up the stairs, where there was another big bedroom and bathroom across the narrow hall.

"But," Ben objected, following her. "I don't have anything else to wear."

"Here," she said, throwing a large, light blue shirt at him. It was obviously hers, so Ben blushed. Susan saw the look on his face, then scolded, "Come, there's no one else here. You think he cares?" She gestured down at Mesmo who was still in the kitchen observing the boiling water in the kettle. "Towels are in the bathroom," she added, heading down again.

"Wait!" Ben called after her. She stopped midstride. "I still don't know who you are! I mean, why are you helping us?"

She turned back to face him. "I'm a witness, like you." She said, staring meaningfully at him. "I had a small cabin in the woods in Chilliwack, not far from your grandfather's house. Used to go there whenever I could, to clear my mind. I was a nurse at the Children's Hospital, you see. Tough place." She paused. "I was in my cabin, on the night of *The Cosmic Fall.* I heard the explosions in the forest, called 911, then ran with my first aid kit to see if anyone was injured."

She looked down at Mesmo, "That's when I saw you, your... 'companion'... and the spaceships... I knew instinctively I wasn't supposed to be there. Ran back to my cabin as though the hounds of hell were after me! I was terrified, I don't mind saying. Didn't take long for the helicopters and police to arrive.

Then later the military. The area turned into a war zone! They brought me in for questioning, along with other witnesses, including your grandfather."

She stayed lost in thought for a while. "I guess they thought we might have been in collusion with the aliens, or infected with some extraterrestrial disease, or, worse still, that we were actually little green men in disguise..." Her voice raised in anger as she spoke, so she sucked in air to calm down, then added, "Let's just say your grandfather was a very resourceful man. He managed to contact the Human Rights Commission, and suddenly we were released, a full three weeks later, when the news had died down at last! We thought we were free, but the police watched our every move like hawks. They bugged our phones. I even found hidden cameras in my elder son's home. They were so afraid we would talk. It was because of the Chinese and the Americans, you see. They're all involved in this, they all want to know the truth..."

She glared down at Mesmo. "Anyway, to make a long story short, Ryan Archer offered me a chance to slip away and lay low for a while, away from prying eyes. So I took it, even though it meant not seeing my sons again." After a silence, she finished, "I've been living here ever since."

She headed down the stairs. "I know you were there, too, Ben. Fortunately for you, they never found out. Your grandfather made sure of that. He made me promise, if you were ever in trouble, to help you. So that's what I'm doing."

* * *

Ben couldn't remember falling asleep. When he opened his eyes, he was snug in bed in the upstairs room. After listening for sounds and not hearing anything, he tiptoed downstairs. He checked in with his mother, finding her fast asleep, with Tike stretched out next to her, guarding her. The dog opened a sleepy eye, then hopped off the bed excitedly. He rolled on the living-room floor happily, expecting a tummy rub, which Ben obliged to. Tike then pulled at Susan's large t-shirt playfully.

"Are you laughing at me?" Ben teased, chasing after the dog. He headed to the kitchen, grabbed an apple and was taking a bite when he saw the note. "Getting groceries. Your clothes are in the dryer. Susan."

Ben peeked outside, realizing it was still light. While munching on the apple, he found the dryer with his and his mother's clothes clean and warm inside. He pulled on his jeans, the apple caught between his teeth, then folded his mother's clothes as best he could before placing them on her bed. He stood by her side for a while, noticing that her breathing was short. He wiped her face gently with a cold, wet cloth, then stroked her hand. She did not wake up. He roamed in and out of the house looking for Mesmo, Tike at his heels, but the alien was nowhere to be seen.

Susan came back around 4 p.m., the motorboat full of groceries. She put him to work, carrying bags, putting away food in the fridge, boiling water in the kettle, making tea, cutting vegetables and setting the table. Although the woman was bossy, Ben was happy for the distraction.

Soon the house smelled of hot vegetable soup and oven-baked chicken with mushrooms. Ben's stomach rumbled. Susan made a tray with fresh bread, soup, some chicken and tea, which she brought to Laura's bedside. With difficulty, they managed to prop up her head on a thick pillow so she could take a couple sips. She was so frail that she could not handle the bread or chicken. She tried to give Ben a reassuring smile, though the dark circles around her eyes told another story.

Susan and Ben sat down for supper silently. Digging hungrily into his food, Ben asked, "Were you able to get her inhaler? I couldn't find it in the grocery bags."

Susan glanced at him. "No, son. Asthma inhalers require a doctor's prescription, which we can't get at the moment."

Ben's shoulders drooped as he stared at his soup.

"She'll be fine," Susan said sternly. "Let her fight this. She's strong enough." She must have noticed he wasn't convinced, because she added, "Asthma inhalers aren't a cure for influenza, son." She gestured towards his plate. "Eat! It won't do her any good if you fall sick too."

Her words stuck in his mind, so he forced himself to eat, even though his throat was tight. He noted that she did not ask about Mesmo or why he wasn't around anymore.

* * *

On the third day, Laura's fever still had not broken and her skin was whiter than the bedsheets. Susan watched her until deep into the night. Ben took over during the day while Susan tried to catch up on sleep, but the truth was Ben was not sleeping much either. He was beside himself with worry. He had already tried to convince Susan several times to take his mother to the doctor. She tried to reassure him, telling him that she was monitoring Laura's temperature closely, and reminding him that going to a doctor or hospital was too risky.

Ben sulked at the edge of the water where he sat down, staring dismally at his feet as they dangled from the pier. He touched his watch unconsciously.

Grampa, I wish you were here...

He was so deep in thought that he did not notice Mesmo poised on the lawn, gazing out at sea, his face turned towards the sunshine, like a flower that had been placed in the shadow for too long. Tike went to greet him, inviting him down to the pier. The tall man followed the dog, then bent down next to Ben. The boy sniffled and wiped his eyes as he turned away. Then he said angrily, "Where have you been?"

Mesmo rested his arms on his knees. “I told you,” he began carefully. “I can’t be away from my physical body for too long.”

“Well, why don’t you bring your body over here next time?” Ben snapped.

“It’s not that simple,” Mesmo said.

“I don’t get it,” Ben insisted. “Why are you here sometimes, and sometimes you’re not?”

Mesmo replied gently, “That kind of depends on you.”

Ben stared at him, confused, then saw that Mesmo was pointing at his wristwatch. “Do you remember when Kaia gave this to you?” Mesmo asked, indicating the tiny, glittering gem at the centre of the watch. “I guess your grandfather had it placed in this watch for you. You used it unknowingly for the first time a couple of weeks ago. I was in South America then. I felt it call me. I thought it was Kaia! I immediately boarded a plane to Toronto by using the identity of Jack Anderson.” He paused, gazing into the distance. “I had hoped that, somehow, Kaia had survived and was calling to me. That was the only logical explanation. Then I reached your grandfather’s funeral, and found out it was you, all along...”

He fell silent, so Ben had to push him on. “Me, all along, who did... what?”

Mesmo looked at him with his honey-coloured eyes, “...you, who was calling me...” He pointed at the watch again. “...with this.”

They both stared at the shimmering diamond-like stone.

Mesmo explained, “You could call it a spirit portal. It’s a

device that, when activated, allows my spirit to travel to it. When you touch the device and call me with your mind, I will hear the call and can then decide whether or not I wish to travel to you in spirit. A human from Earth could not activate it, but I guess you are more than a normal Earth human now..."

Ben decided to ignore a quiver in the pit of his stomach and studied the shiny gem instead. "I'm glad you're here," he said. "My mom's not getting any better. I know she needs her asthma pump. I'm sure she has a spare one at home. All we need to do is sneak into the apartment. I know where she would have kept it..."

Mesmo held up his hand. "Ben, listen to me." His eyes were unreadable as he said slowly, "I came to tell you that I can help you no further."

Ben shook his head as if to get rid of his words. "No, it's okay. I've got it all figured out. You see all we have to do is..."

"Ben!" Mesmo interrupted. The boy stopped in mid-sentence with his mouth open. Mesmo repeated more insistently, "I only came to make sure that you were safe. But I can't help you any longer."

Ben stared at him, incredulous. "Yes, you can! Of course, you can. You've got all those powers. You've helped before. Why wouldn't you help us now?"

When the white-haired man answered by remaining silent, Ben stood up hastily, casting him a furious look. "Well, go on then!" he yelled, tears flowing down his cheeks. "Do your disappearing trick! You're so good at that! See if I care! My mom and I, we've gotten by fine without you before. It's not like we need you now!"

He ran to the cabin, Tike close at his heels, ignoring Susan who had been observing them from afar. She dried her hands on her apron, glaring at Mesmo, before heading back inside.

* * *

That night Ben snuck into bed early without talking to anyone.

Susan finished cleaning up the kitchen when she noticed Mesmo in the doorway, looking out. She joined him, then stopped in her tracks, for she quickly realized what had attracted his attention.

Like a ghost in the moonlight, a huge, white moose stood quite still, close by the water. The skin from this proud, adult male glittered from the long swim it had just taken. Its large antlers crowned its head while steam came from his nostrils. Susan stared in awe as she stood silently beside Mesmo. "I'd heard of them—these albino moose. They are extremely rare," she breathed, afraid to startle the animal. "I never thought I'd see one up close." She glanced at the white-haired alien beside her, taken aback by the meaning of her own words. They observed the beast until it faded away into the nearby trees.

Susan Pickering stared up at Mesmo giddily, her voice coming in a whisper, "Did you make it come?"

Mesmo shook his head, "No. It wasn't me. It was the boy."

Susan started. "Ben? How? I thought he was..."

"...human?" Mesmo finished for her. "Yes, he is human. But my daughter passed on her skill to him. She passed on her ability to communicate with other species. He just isn't aware he's doing it. The moose must have sensed something, and couldn't figure out what it was."

Susan remained silent, pondering this information. After a while, she asked carefully, "What are you doing here, Jack?"

"Mesmo," he corrected. "My name is Mesmo."

"All right, Mesmo," she repeated. "What are you doing

here, exactly?"

He stared at her for a moment, before answering, "Why do you ask, Susan Pickering? The less you know, the less trouble you will attract to yourself. I know you know that." He let his comment hang, before offering, "My task is to be an observer. My companions were going to help me complete this mission, but now that they are dead, I am not sure I will make it..."

Susan shook her head to indicate she did not want to hear any more. "No, no," she argued. "That's not what I meant. I wasn't asking you what you're doing here, on Earth. I don't want to know about those things. I'm asking what you're doing here, on my island, in my cabin."

Mesmo shifted, showing unease at her question. Then he reached out a hand towards her. "Take my hand."

She frowned suspiciously, wondering where this was going, then hesitantly lifted her hand to take his. Instead of touching real, solid flesh and bone, her hand slid right through his, as though it were made of thin air. She jumped back, holding on to her hand as if it had been burnt.

Mesmo gave her a small smile. Before she could find her voice, he said, "No. I am not a ghost."

He gazed out at the night while Susan remained stuck to the wall, afraid to move an inch. "I can disconnect my spirit from my body and travel great distances in the blink of an eye. However, to do so, I must have access to a portal which will allow me to appear as you see me now." He paused. "The boy has that portal."

He turned to face her again, his eyes hidden under the shadows of his brow. "You see, I fell into a trap at the Toronto Airport. I was lured into a corridor away from other travellers. Several men attacked me, knocking me unconscious. When I woke up, I was strapped to a bed in a white room surrounded by machines and men in doctor's coats. I do not know who is holding me or why. But they know who I am and that I am not from this planet."

He spoke with a strain in his voice, "My people respect freedom above all. We do not do well in confined spaces. Being shut away from the outside kills us. If the boy had not activated the spirit portal, thus offering me a means of escape—even though it is only an illusion of sorts—my situation would have become unbearable. I would have died long ago." He stared at Susan before finishing, "I am here, on your island, Susan Pickering, because the boy is keeping me alive..."

Susan regained her composure, the fear in her eyes slowly replaced by displeasure as he spoke. "So it's exactly as I thought," she muttered.

Mesmo stared at her blankly.

She approached him, pointing an accusing finger, though from a safe distance to avoid touching his non-essence. "You're not here *for* the boy; you're here *because* of him," she hissed.

Mesmo shook his head, not understanding. "Is there a difference?"

"There's a huge difference," she said sternly. "The boy thinks you care about him, that you're here for him. You're not, you're only using him to survive." Since he didn't react, she continued, "You're torturing that boy! He's forming a bond with you; he looks up to you. The longer you stay, the harder it will be for him to see you go. Because, one day, you will go. Or am I wrong?"

When Mesmo still didn't reply, she sighed, exasperated at his seeming lack of understanding. "Don't you see? If his mother dies, he'll be on his own..."

They heard a clatter as someone closed the upstairs bedroom window. Susan glared at Mesmo angrily. She knew

Ben had overheard their whole conversation.

The alien's eyes were shrouded in the dark, his face expressionless. "Yes, Susan Pickering, I am using the boy to stay alive, as you say, and, yes, I will leave when I am done here. Where I come from, we do not give in to strong emotions the way humans do. I must remain neutral and impartial if I am to complete my mission..."

"Neutral and impartial!" Susan snorted. "You stopped being neutral and impartial the minute you fell from the sky! The minute you lost your daughter and met them." She pointed indoors to show she was referring to Ben and Laura. She stepped into the cabin, away from the cold. "You call yourself an observer. Well, my alien friend, I think it's time you opened your eyes."

* * *

Mesmo gazed at the stars for a long moment, thinking of Susan's words, for they resonated in his mind like an echo. Had his friend Amaru not said something very similar recently, on the high Andes Mountains of Bolivia? Something about having lost his ability to be the Observer? He struggled with this thought before Kaia's beautiful face emerged in his memories, and he knew he must continue, no matter what. For her sake.

He stepped inside, then headed to the bedroom where Laura was fighting for her life. Her body was shivering. Her forehead glistened with sweat. Though he could not physically touch her, he could sense the water imbalance in her body as his hand hovered over her shoulder. He concentrated for a moment, sending a warm flow of energy from his palms into her body until the balance had somewhat been restored. She stopped shivering and rested more peacefully. He could not heal her, but at least she would be calm for a while.

Mesmo noticed how her hair had turned a dull, lifeless colour. It was a sharp contrast with the subtle halo of light that had formed around the contour of her head as the setting sun had shone through her ash blonde hair back on the fields of Chilliwack. Her green eyes had stood out against the early autumn pallet of ginger, apricot and maroon-coloured leaves. He traced her fine features into his mind, closed his eyes, then let himself glide back to his physical body, which lay almost three thousand miles away.

As usual, he first recovered his hearing, which captured the low beeping of machines, then he opened his eyes to blurry, artificial light, and, lastly, he felt the pain. It always hit him like a brick wall, making him groan. Even though he knew to expect it, he could not get used to it.

Immediately, he heard the muffled voices of several men who rushed into the room in their pale green antiviral, protective suits and mouth covers.

One of them waved a bright light into Mesmo's eyes, confirming, "He's back." While another ordered, "Check his vital signs." A third one was pulling at the straps that pinned his arms and legs to the hospital bed.

"He's good," the second one said, after analyzing a heart monitor.

"Call the boss," the first voice ordered through the only doorway leading out of the white, bleached room. "Tell him he's back. Vital signs have returned to normal."

The third man injected something into Mesmo's arm, muttering, "Where'd our Martian go this time, I wonder?"

CHAPTER 15 *The Crossing*

Inspector James Hao and Agent Theodore Connelly met in the hallway of the Vancouver Police Department.

Hao quizzed, "Well?" As they entered an elevator going up to the fifth floor.

Connelly reported, "Still nothing. All we have is Laura Archer's attempt to register at the Comfort Inn in North Vancouver and the abandoned car at The Bearded Bear Diner. We've interrogated all possible witnesses. We've gone through all local traffic video cameras. We've found nothing. Not a trace of them."

The elevator pinged when they arrived. They stepped out, headed down the corridor, then into an office with a desk strewn with documents. Hao searched through the papers, before pulling out a file.

Connelly said, "We have no reports from any units placed in the area. That guy you saw with Laura Archer outside the notary office in Chilliwack might still be helping them. We don't know who he was."

Hao growled, "Well, if you had actually been there instead of running off on your own wild-goose-chase, maybe we wouldn't be asking ourselves that question!" He licked the tip of his finger to flip through the file as he glared at his partner.

Connelly's mouth twitched.

Turning his attention to the file again, Hao said thoughtfully, "We know they are running out of money since we froze Laura Archer's accounts. Plus the waitress from the diner said the boy paid for their food with change. We also know they no longer have a car. So they can't be far. We have units controlling all major exits. They will have to come out in the open sometime." He pointed at the report. "The waitress said Laura Archer didn't eat, then left the boy alone to pay. Why did she do that?"

Connelly shrugged. "How should I know? What do we do now? We have no other leads... "

Hao put down the report, smiling. "Oh, I think we do. It's only a matter of time."

* * *

Ben tiptoed down the stairs in the dark. He was fully dressed. It was not yet dawn, and a chill made it through his sweatshirt. He borrowed a plaid blanket which he put over his shoulders to ward off the cold. Silently, he peeked into the bedroom where his mother lay.

Ben took his mother's hand, whispering, "Hang in there, Mom. I'll be back soon."

He gestured to Tike, who jumped happily into his arms, then the boy grabbed the boat key that hung next to the front door. The two of them ran swiftly to the pier where they hopped into one of the motorboats. Although fog clung to the water, Ben could make out the lights from Deep Cove and the outline of the mountains, as dawn neared.

The boy released the boat from the pier, then took an oar to maneuver it away from the shore. Once he was at a safe distance, he put the key into the ignition, then, his heart beating fast, switched the motor to life. It made a huge racket in the silent night. He looked around fearfully, certain he would wake up half the inlet. Everything remained peaceful, so he moved the motorboat forward slowly, his hands trembling as he learned to control it. He had to stretch his neck to get a good view over the front of the vessel, though in the end, it turned out to be quite manageable.

He was making good way when the mist cleared slightly, revealing a navy blue sky with some twinkling stars above. The pitch dark waters surrounded him, while the night sky went on and on into the void overhead. Although he had left the island several minutes ago, his heart still beat fast. He wiped his forehead with the back of his hand and found it glistening with sweat in spite of the cold air. His breath came in gasps.

What's wrong with me?

With dread, he recognized the symptoms, but it was too late. The sky collapsed on him from all sides. His vision blurred. In a desperate move, he switched off the motorboat before dropping to his knees with his hands to his head. The vast, empty night swallowed him up, crushing him to the floor of the swaying boat.

He had a clear vision of himself standing in the field next to his grandfather, listening to the hissing noise just before the spaceship came crashing to Earth. Everything swayed, making him feel physically sick.

"Grampa! Grampa!" Ben begged.

Tike jumped up and down before him with his ears laid back, trying to pull the boy out of the panic attack that had grasped his mind.

"Ben!" Grampa called, as he stood silhouetted against the burning wreck.

"Ben!"

The boy heard his name loud and clear, except it wasn't coming from his mind, but rather from the boat he was crouching in. He opened his eyes carefully, trying to comprehend how Grampa could have materialized onto the boat with him.

Mesmo stared at him from the back of the boat. The alien called his name; his hand plunged into the water as if he were testing its temperature.

Ben slowly uncurled his arms from his head. He noticed the boat was no longer rocking about aimlessly, instead, it felt stable as it advanced at a slow pace. He stood up carefully, his mind clearing. Behind Mesmo, the town of Deep Cove slowly receded. He turned to face the front of the boat. His eyes widened as he realized it was heading back towards the island at a steady pace.

"No! Stop that! You're going the wrong way!"

Mesmo scolded, "It's too dangerous! You can't do this on your own!"

Ben's eyes welled with tears. "What am I supposed to do then, huh? Who's going to go with me?" He glared at Mesmo. "Are you?"

Mesmo stared at him intently without answering.

"Exactly!" Ben continued. "You're not going to do anything about it! So go away! Mind your own business!"

"Benjamin!" Mesmo said sternly. "I need your help." He lifted his hand out of the water. Immediately the boat began to rock softly to-and-fro.

Ben's jaw dropped. "*You* need *my* help?" He stared, incredulous. "Is that supposed to be a joke?" He turned his head away, not wanting Mesmo to see the hurt on his face. Before he thought better of it, he snapped, "Why didn't you say anything before? About being kidnapped?"

Mesmo answered, "My problems did not concern you. I had expected to get out of this mess already. But I have no access to water, so I can't defend myself." He wrung his hands together, saying in defeat, "I don't think I can get out."

Ben stared at the sea, a mixture of emotions bubbling inside him. "So, am I supposed to feel sorry for you now?" he snapped.

"No." Mesmo answered matter-of-factly. "But I want you to understand why I said I am no longer able to help you. My abilities are limited. If you cross this inlet to try to get your mother's medication on your own, I can't guarantee that I will be there to help you. You need to go back to the island and find a solution with the Pickering woman."

"I don't have time to sit around and chat with Susan!" Ben retorted. "I might be too late already!" He sat down heavily, pulling the plaid blanket around him. He hung his head between his knees, sulking.

After a long silence, Ben peeked over his arm, suddenly afraid that Mesmo was gone. But the alien had his head turned towards the stars, as though he were drinking in the fading night with his whole being. He closed his eyes as the first ray of sunlight cut through the horizon.

Ben couldn't help noticing how Mesmo's skin tone went from a light grey to a darker, healthier tan. "Why didn't you tell me I was keeping you alive?" he muttered.

He didn't think Mesmo had heard him, but the alien opened his dark eyes. "It wasn't your burden to carry."

Alien and boy stared at each other as a bright sun emerged between patches of thick clouds.

Ben said, "Look. You need me. I need you. Help me get my mother's inhaler. Then we will help you out from wherever you are. Once we've freed you, you can go on with your precious mission, and my mom and I can go home."

The white-haired man gazed thoughtfully at the boy, before stating carefully, "I don't think..." He suddenly grimaced and bent over in pain, surprising Ben.

"What's the matter?" Ben said quickly, but only the soft morning breeze blew over the boat in answer. Mesmo was already gone. Ben sat down again, disheartened. "Come back," he begged to the wind.

* * *

After waiting in vain for Mesmo to return, Ben sighed, then said to his terrier, "It's just you and me, Tike."

He pondered the island for a while.

Should I go back?

Tike placed a paw on his leg encouragingly.

"I can't face Mom with empty hands, can I?" He took a deep breath, turned on the motor, and navigated the boat towards Deep Cove again. He had enough worries on his mind this time to remember he was actually supposed to be afraid of the open skies. Somehow Mesmo's presence had pushed away all thoughts of panic attacks. As he attached the boat to the pier of the quaint harbour, he breathed in deeply with renewed energy.

He and Tike jogged to the nearest bus stop where they took the first bus to the Lonsdale Quay in North Vancouver. There, they hopped onto the Seabus that crossed the short sea arm to the City of Vancouver. Ben and Tike hopped onto the Skytrain heading to Burnaby, where he reached his apartment block. It felt like an eternity since he had last seen the low-lying, three-story building with twelve apartments.

The boy hesitated, knowing there could be danger. He hid behind some bushes on the other side of the street, carefully scanning the area. Five minutes later a police officer walked out of the building, got into a police car, and drove away.

"We're in luck!" Ben whispered to Tike. He ran across the road to the back of the building, carefully making his way to the end until he was right below his own bedroom window.

"Wait here, Tike," he ordered. The dog sat down obediently.

Nimbly, Ben grabbed onto the drainpipe, climbed onto the windowsill of the downstairs neighbour, and checked no one was inside. He pulled himself up until he reached his window. It opened smoothly as the lock had broken many years ago and had never been fixed. Swiftly, he dropped into his bedroom and looked out the window, making sure no one had seen him. Only Tike stared up at him, tail wagging and tongue lolling.

Ben scanned his messy bedroom. He hopped across the room, avoiding a dirty plate, his Xbox controller, a bicycle helmet, and comic books. He failed to notice a football hiding under the hanging sheets of his bed. He kicked it accidentally with his foot. It rolled across the room and struck the door with a thud. Ben froze and listened for any noise coming from the apartment. All he heard was his thumping heart. He let out his breath in relief.

He grabbed an old backpack and stuffed underwear, socks, trousers and shirts into it. Next, he crept across the hallway into his mother's room, scanned it for any danger, and packed some clothing for her as well. He opened all the drawers hurriedly, searching for an extra asthma inhaler his mother might have kept tucked away. He found nothing.

Once the backpack couldn't hold another thing, he closed the zip, placed it on his shoulders, and left the bedroom to continue his search. A movement at the end of his mother's bedroom made him jump before he realized it was only his reflection in a mirror. He wanted to kick himself.

Pull yourself together!

He stepped into the corridor.

The man with black hair streaked with grey stood at the other end of it, waiting for him. He held up an asthma inhaler. "Looking for this?" the man taunted.

Ben's heart sank like a stone. He recognized the neatly dressed man from the funeral reception he had found handling his grandfather's telescope.

The man took out a badge with a picture ID. "James Hao," he said, presenting himself again. "*Inspector* James Hao, from the Canadian Security Intelligence Service. I thought you might be needing this at some point." He waved the inhaler at Ben before putting it into his trouser pocket. "I think you and I need to have that chat now."

Not on your life!

Ben rushed into the bathroom, shut the door, and locked it. Not a split moment later Hao banged against it, shouting, "Open up!"

Ben heard him call for reinforcements. He opened the bathroom window and threw the backpack out, narrowly missing Tike below. Ben had a leg out the window when he looked back, struck by a sudden idea. He jumped back into the bathroom and opened the drawers, frantically searching through the brushes, toothpaste, hair dryer and makeup.

At the very back, in a corner, he found something he hadn't expected to find but took anyway. It was his mother's engagement ring—the one Ben's dad had given her before he died and which she never wanted to wear. He shoved it far into his jeans pocket, then kept on searching. Ben was shocked to hear a banging on the apartment's front door. He heard Hao open it and several voices flooded the apartment. He searched the drawer desperately, one last time. At the last minute, his fingers curled around something familiar.

Got it!

He pulled out his mother's spare inhaler, feeling exhilarated. Holding on to it tightly, he dashed to the window and began to climb out. But all his hopes crumbled when the door crashed open. Hao rushed in, followed by another police officer.

Desperately, Ben threw the inhaler out the window just before they grabbed his arms. He shouted, "Fetch, Tike! Find Mom! Hurry!"

The two men pulled him back, Hao yelling down the corridor to another police officer, "Follow that dog!"

* * *

Down below, Tike bounced around wildly in circles. As soon as he saw a police officer appear from behind the building, he grabbed the inhaler between his teeth and darted back in the direction they had come.

The nimble Jack Russell ran as fast as his little legs would carry him. Even though he quickly lost the police officer, he charged on as if he was being pursued by hungry hounds. Being a smart dog, he did not have any trouble finding his way back to the Skytrain that he had taken with Ben over an hour ago. This took him back to the Waterfront Station where he zigzagged past commuters down to the pier of the Seabus. He slipped into the ferry that crossed the Burrard Inlet back to North

Vancouver, then waited for the bus to Deep Cove to open its doors to let in passengers. When a little girl pointed out the dog to her mom, Tike scurried to the back of the bus where he lay down under a seat, shivering uncontrollably, his mouth painfully wrapped around the inhaler.

By the time Tike got off the bus at Deep Cove, he was no longer running. He stooped low with his head down. He only stopped once to drink thirstily from a dripping water fountain before heading slowly to the marina where he found the motorboat safely tied up to the pier. The dog hopped into the boat, then sat down on the driver's chair. He looked around expectantly. When no one showed up, he dropped the inhaler at his feet, his tongue lolling.

The faithful terrier waited patiently for his master to appear until exhaustion took over. Then he curled up on the seat, his legs carefully wrapped around the precious inhaler as he closed his tired eyes.

CHAPTER 16 *Black Carpenters*

On the first floor of the Vancouver Police Department, in a small, windowless room with one table and two chairs, Ben waited. Although his heart fluttered with worry, he found himself distracted by a movement at the edge of the table. A carpenter ant crawled along its metal surface before heading down a table leg. Ben watched as it made its way to the floor before scurrying on towards the door.

If only I were your size...

In his mind's eye, Ben became the insect that darted over the gigantic floor, reaching the slit under the door, the brightly lit corridor, the elevator, the way out...

The door whipped open, and Inspector James Hao entered. With one colossal foot, he crushed the ant, making Ben jump as his vision of freedom went dark. The inspector sat down opposite Ben in his neatly pressed suit and perfectly trimmed hair. He dropped a file on the desk while scrutinizing Ben as he flipped through the pages. He picked out a couple of pictures which he slid across the table.

Ben stared at them, puzzled. One picture showed pieces of glass, while the other had an enlargement of a fingerprint.

"Seven weeks ago," Hao began, "We recovered all evidence from the crash site that took place near your grandfather's property. At first, we couldn't figure out what these pieces of glass were doing in the middle of the field. When we put the pieces together, however, we realized it was the lens of a telescope with the faint trace of a fingerprint on it." He pointed to the picture on the left. "The fingerprint turned out to be yours."

He studied the boy for a while before continuing. "We believe you were there, on the night of *The Cosmic Fall.* We believe you witnessed everything, yet you did not come forward with Ryan Archer, to provide your version of facts and, perhaps, invaluable information to national security."

Ben fidgeted in his chair, distracted by an ant that was tickling him on the leg. He was at a loss as to what to reply.

"This isn't a game, boy," Hao growled. "Our country, our very lives may be at stake. It's imperative we find out if the culprits behind *The Cosmic Fall* are a risk to our nation, to our planet! I don't know what game Ryan Archer was playing when he failed to mention your involvement. Were he alive today, he would have been arrested for interfering with an ongoing national investigation. So if he told you to keep silent, you had better think twice about that!"

A heavy silence followed. Ben cleared his throat. "The thing is, I can't remember anything. The doctor says I have amnesia..." he lied weakly.

Hao didn't look impressed. He took out another picture. Ben gasped as he saw the image of himself talking to Mesmo at his grandfather's funeral.

"I see your memory is already improving," Hao said bitterly.

Ben stared from the picture to the inspector, then back

again, his face drained.

"I want to know who that is," Hao said. "And you're going to tell me."

Someone knocked loudly on the door. Before Hao could respond, a bald man with an authoritative look stepped in.

Twisted eyes!

Ben turned white as a bedsheet and shrank into his chair in shock.

Connelly did not heed him as he turned to Hao, saying, "I need to talk to you outside."

"Not now," Hao replied impatiently.

"This is urgent. It can't wait."

Hao tapped a pen against the table impatiently, then got up, gazing down at Ben as he closed the button of his suit jacket. He gestured towards Bordock, presenting him to Ben. "This is Agent Theodore Connelly. He's been an invaluable asset on *The Cosmic Fall* case. While I step out, I suggest you work on recovering your memory, kid. You wouldn't want to get into more trouble than you already are in." Hao left the room, oblivious to the long, cold glare that Bordock threw at the boy.

The door closed, leaving Ben on his own again. His skin crawled, and his head exploded with questions.

What is Bordock doing here?

If he was frightened before, now Ben was terrified.

* * *

"What is it?" Hao hissed impatiently at Connelly, as they moved down the hall to avoid being overheard by the police officer placed in front of the room where Ben was being held.

"The Representative for the Children and Youth office is sending a lawyer to defend the kid," Connelly said in a low, urgent voice.

"A lawyer?" Hao exclaimed through gritted teeth. "I don't have time to deal with lawyers! How did they catch wind of this so quickly?"

"The office is automatically flagged when youth under the age of eighteen are arrested," Connelly explained.

"We can't have a lawyer poking around!" Hao said angrily. "We need to get a clearance from High Inspector George Tremblay and transfer the kid to the Dugout ASAP!"

Connelly insisted, "The local police are talking. They think we're drilling an underaged witness without giving him proper representation."

"The local police can say anything they want," Hao retorted. "This is a matter of national security! They have no idea what we're up against! No, the CSIS has precedence in this matter! I'll set all hounds loose on anyone who so much as approaches the boy." He pointed his index finger at Connelly. "I'll have Tremblay sign the transfer papers. That will allow us to override any questions from meddling lawyers or the RCMP. In the meantime, you keep an eye out. Make sure no one enters that room!"

"Wait!" Connelly cut in urgently as Hao walked away.

"What now?" Hao snapped.

"I have an idea that might convince Tremblay to speed things up."

Hao blinked at him. "What are you talking about?"

Connelly opened one side of his suit jacket, revealing a transparent vial that jutted out of his inside pocket. It contained a syringe and blood collection tube.

"We need to take a blood sample from the boy and have it analyzed," Connelly said.

Hao held up his hands to hide the contents of Connelly's

pocket, glancing around to make sure no one had seen them. "Are you crazy?" he growled. "Not here, not now! There will be time for that later."

"No, hear me out!" Connelly urged. "I read in the files that the other witnesses had abnormal levels of lead in their blood after *The Cosmic Fall*. If the boy's blood matches that of the other witnesses, we'll have more undeniable proof that he was present. Besides, who knows what else we might find. Are we even sure he is who he says he is?"

Hao shook his head. "You're jumping to a lot of conclusions. A blood sample at this stage is out of the question. If the boy talks to anyone..."

"He won't talk." Connelly interrupted in a convincing tone.

"That's beside the point," Hao continued. "If something like this were to get out we'd lose our jobs faster than you can blink."

"*I'd* lose my job," Connelly corrected. "I'll take the sample. If word should ever get out, I'll take the fall. I'm acting on my own. You're not aware of anything."

Hao stared at him, unconvinced.

Connelly insisted. "All I need is five minutes. Just think, if the blood reveals anything out of the ordinary, we'll be able to get all the clearances we need."

Hao looked around nervously. "All right," he said finally. "You have five minutes."

Connelly nodded, then turned away.

Hao called him back, "For the record, I don't like your methods. They've proven effective so far, but you're on your own on this one. This conversation never took place."

Connelly nodded before heading to the interrogation room, while Hao took the elevator to the fifth floor where he began making phone calls from his makeshift office.

* * *

Ben ignored a second ant that crawled slowly across the table. Instead, he had his hand clamped feverishly onto his wristwatch, praying silently for Mesmo to appear. To his dismay, the door opened, and Bordock stepped in.

The boy and the bald man glared at each other. Fine sweat pearled Ben's forehead as he cowered deep in his chair, feeling like a trapped animal.

Without a word, Bordock shoved aside the second chair with his foot, then took out the transparent recipient, which he placed on the table. The ant scurried away. Carefully, Bordock opened the vial to take out the syringe and blood collection tube.

Ben's eyes widened. "What are you doing?" he asked fearfully.

Bordock removed the plastic wrapping from the syringe, answering, "Taking a blood sample."

Ben shook his head in protest, unable to speak.

Then, the alien pulled up the sleeve of his own, grey suit jacket and, still looking at Ben, pricked his own arm with the needle. Slowly, dark alien blood filled the syringe. Once he had filled it up, he pulled out the syringe, inserted the needle into the blood collection tube and transferred the thick liquid. He then stuck a small label onto the tube, writing on it with a black pen. BLOOD SAMPLE-BENJAMIN ARCHER.

"That's not my blood!" Ben croaked. "Why did you do that?"

Bordock finished wrapping everything up again. "To make sure they have a reason to keep you," he stated coldly.

"Why?" Ben whispered, barely able to speak from fear.

Bordock placed the recipient back in the inside pocket of his jacket. He squinted at Ben with his unnatural eyes, which changed from green to honey-brown. "For some reason," he said, "wherever I find you, I find Mesmo. So, as long as you are here, I am confident he will be joining us at some point." He straightened the front of his jacket, and added, "And if he doesn't, then the CSIS will find him for me."

Outside, in the corridor, they could hear Hao arguing loudly with a woman. Bordock's eyes narrowed threateningly. "You know what I'm capable of," he hissed. "I wouldn't say anything if I were you."

In that instant the door flew open, revealing a woman with blond, curly hair and modern, black glasses. She stared up and down at Connelly in a condescending way. "You! Out! I won't have anyone talking to my client."

Ben was glad she didn't notice the lethal look Bordock gave her as she placed a briefcase on the table. Addressing Ben in a business-like manner, she said, "You have the right to remain silent, Benjamin. You don't have to answer any of these men's questions. I'll be doing the talking for you from now on. My name is Barbara Jones. I've been assigned by the Representative for Children and Youth to represent you." As she clicked open the briefcase, she added, "In other words, I'm your lawyer."

She turned to face Connelly and Hao. The latter was seething at her from the corridor. "That will be all, gentlemen. You'll be hearing from my office when I'm done."

She closed the door on them. Both men walked away with quick strides.

"Did you get the blood sample?" Hao asked angrily.

"Yes," Connelly answered.

"Get it analyzed ASAP! We need to put a stop to this right

away," Hao barked.

* * *

Barbara Jones sat down. "It's Benjamin Archer, right?"

Ben nodded, taken aback by this sudden shift of power.

She flipped through some documents in a very thin file, then pursed her lips, dissatisfied. "Well, they didn't leave me much to work with. I only have a home address and that you avoided questioning by law enforcement."

She closed the file before staring at Ben over the rim of her glasses.

"So," she began, showing interest in him for the first time. "Let's hear it."

Ben stared at her with his mouth open, "I... er... what do you mean?" He was excruciatingly aware of Bordock's proximity.

Barbara Jones moved forward in her chair, accidentally crushing a carpenter ant with her arm as she leaned on the table. "Look, honey, my office had me move my schedule around just for you because you are a minor. I'm here to defend you, okay? That means that whatever you did, you can tell me. My job is to get you out of here as soon as possible."

She waved her hand at him, inviting him to speak. One large ant was climbing up the sleeve of her white shirt while another one was crawling across her closed file.

"So, let's have it," she repeated.

Ben was distracted by the ants.

How did so many get in here?

"I... " he began, his mouth dry as parchment.

Bordock could be listening right behind the door!

Ms. Jones became impatient. "Honey, I have thirty minutes

to listen to your story before they kick me out of here. Let's see, how about we start with something easy, okay? For example, you can give me your dad's phone number. I promise I'll call him up as soon as I leave. How about that?"

Ben stared at her helplessly, "I... don't have a dad. He died in an accident after I was born."

The lawyer closed her eyes for a second, as an ant crawled up her cheek. She brushed it away with a motion of the hand as she arranged a strand of curly hair behind her ear.

"All right," she said a bit more gently. "How about your moth... Ouch!" she yelled, brushing at her arm. "Something bit me!" she gasped, her face flushed. She shrieked and bolted out of her chair, massaging her leg. She noticed the carpenter ants scurrying over the table, on her arms, on her legs, up her neck. She yelled again as they bit her. She brushed at them frantically, bobbing up and down like a ragged doll on a spring.

The police officer who had been standing guard in front of the room rushed in. "What's going on?" he demanded.

"Let me out of here!" she yelled, bouncing around. "Ouch!" She gestured towards Ben. "Get that boy out. This room's infested with ants... eek! Get him to a washroom! And call pest exterminators or something." She darted down the hall, distraught.

The policeman noticed the ants crawling all over Ben, and hurriedly led him down a couple of doors to the men's toilets. "Get in there and clean yourself up," he ordered, yelling as he was bitten in the neck.

Ben did as he was told, suddenly finding himself all alone in the washroom of the Police Department.

As he stood there, gathering his senses, the carpenter ants that had been crawling all over him scurried to the floor, then vanished into the cracks in the wall. Ben checked his clothes, then stared in the mirror. All the ants were gone, leaving him without a single bite mark.

Jeepers!

Breathing fast, he turned his attention to the door which he locked in an automatic gesture. He leaned his head against it, closing his eyes dizzily. When he looked up again, Mesmo stood by the sinks, his face ashen. Ben let out a sob of relief.

"Ben," Mesmo said softly yet urgently. "I don't have much time! Turn on the taps."

Ben sniffed and nodded hurriedly. He opened all the taps to let water flow into the four sinks.

Mesmo indicated that the boy should move away from the door. The alien placed his hands in the stream of water, which immediately obeyed the energy that emanated from them. The liquid flowed horizontally against the wall then dripped to the floor. It spread out swiftly, covering the main door and doorknob before racing across the tiles. Ben had to move back until he was against the wall next to a toilet. Even there, the water flowed along the wall up to a window located right above Ben's head. The whole washroom was covered in water that danced to a silent song, obeying the mysterious force that came forth from Mesmo like a magnet.

In an instant, the swirling motion stopped, then the water froze. The door became white, the doorknob crackled under the weight of the ice and the floor glistened with a slippery sheen.

Above him, Ben heard the bars in front of the window snap from the cold.

"Go on!" Mesmo encouraged him.

Ben clambered onto the closed toilet bowl, then shoved open the window. The metal bars which had snapped from the cold easily slid away before falling to the ground below. He pulled himself up, saw that he would be able to fit through and that the ground wasn't too far down. He turned to Mesmo, only to find him gone. "Mesmo!" he whispered.

Someone banged on the door, calling him to open up.

Ben wasn't going to wait around this time.

CHAPTER 17 *Granville*

Hao rushed past the frantic lawyer, saw the empty interrogation room, then joined the policeman who was trying to force open the door of the washroom.

"What's going on? Where's the boy?" he yelled angrily.

"He's in there. Locked himself up." The policeman grunted as he shoved his weight against the door.

Hao pushed him aside to grab the doorknob, then yelled as his hand burned from the freezing temperature of the metal.

"I don't care how you do it, you get this door open pronto!" he barked.

Another large policeman joined them. After three attempts at throwing themselves with full force at the door, it gave, and they crashed in a heap inside.

Hao clambered over them, then fell heavily to the ground as he slipped on the sheet of thin ice that covered the floor. Groaning, he got back up. After several slippery attempts, he reached the open window.

"He's out!" Hao yelled as he peeked through the window into the street. "Go! Go! Go!" he ordered the policemen, who were slipping and sliding over the frozen floor.

* * *

Ben raced down the street. As he was about to turn a corner, he risked a glance back, only to find Hao and a couple of police officers barging out of the Vancouver Police Department after him. Turning the corner, he had to stop and lean against a wall. Dizziness had grasped his mind, and he swayed. Was he having a panic attack? He shut his eyes tight, forcing his breathing to slow.

Not now!

He ignored the stitch in his side and thudded on. As his lonely footsteps hit the pavement, Tike's absence weighed heavily on him. He crossed a busy road to the Skytrain station, then froze when a police car rounded a corner, placing itself at the very entrance. He backtracked hurriedly across the street. Hao appeared only a block away.

Ben slapped desperately on the door of a bus that was about to drive away. The driver frowned disapprovingly but let him in anyway. Ben hopped on, catching his breath as he saw Hao pointing in his direction. To his dismay, the bus headed southwest instead of north. His mind raced.

Granville Island!

If he could make it to the small peninsula that was a hotspot for tourists, he could get lost in the crowds and find another transport north. Ben glanced around fearfully. He spotted a police car with its lights whirling in the distance, as it zigzagged through traffic. It caught up with the bus a short distance from Granville Island. Ben hit the emergency button, and the doors swung open. Hao was getting out of the police car, when a throng of sports cyclists whizzed by, giving Ben the opportunity to dash down to the well-stocked public market. He pushed through groups of people strolling around the small, quaint streets strewn with art galleries, restaurants and artisan shops.

If only I could reach the marina!

He knew there was an Aquabus that could take him across to the City of Vancouver, with its skyscrapers, a short distance across the river. Too late, he glimpsed a police officer checking things out in the direction he was headed. Ben's heart raced as he felt his options of escape narrowing. He ducked into the large indoor market, making his way through the crowd of tourists who were picking out perfectly formed fruits and vegetables. The tourists gasped as Ben ran into them, making them accidentally knock over a pyramid of neatly arranged oranges which tumbled to the ground. Ben didn't have time to apologize. He dove out of the market and faced the other side of the marina, which was cluttered with pleasure boats and ferries.

Behind him, Hao pushed his way through the crowds inside the market.

Ben ran down a pier, bumping into people taking pictures of the scenery. At the end of it, tourists donned bright, orange fishermen waders and matching waterproof jackets with large hoods. Ben squeezed into this group. A stack of the orange garments lay on the floor, placed there for the tourists who were getting ready for a trip out to sea.

Without hesitating, Ben grabbed a large pair of pants and a jacket, putting them on in a hurry, copying what the other men and women were doing. Not a moment too soon, as a police officer, closely followed by Hao, appeared above the pier. They scanned the area with their eyes.

A tourist wearing the bright fisherman combination stood up, leaving a corner of a bench unoccupied, so Ben slipped onto the seat, trying to blend in with the crowd.

"It's almost time!" the woman next to Ben said excitedly.

He turned in surprise. An old woman with wrinkled cheeks and sunken eyes stared at him with a big, false-teeth smile.

"Is this your first trip, son?" she asked.

Ben checked his surroundings anxiously. Hao approached the entrance to the pier. Hastily, the boy turned to the old woman, who looked like she might be eighty, or closer to ninety. "Er... yes," he said vaguely.

"This is my forty-fifth trip!" she said proudly. "I met my late husband, Harold, on a trip like this, forty-five years ago! We would celebrate our wedding anniversary every year by making the same trip again." Her voice faltered only slightly, immediately replaced by her smile again. "You might think I'm a silly old lady, but I know Harold's spirit is watching over me today. I remember my first contact with the giants... oh, my! What a sight...!"

She chatted on. Ben no longer listened. Hao had jogged up behind the group of tourists and was asking them questions.

In the same instant, the orange-clad men and women trooped in front of a ferry which they began to board. Ben followed the flow with the old woman not far behind. A young, strong-built sailor who was asking for boarding tickets caught him by the arm. "Hey! Ticket, please!" he said with a strong accent.

Ben pointed to the people lining up behind him. "Uh... my Gran has them." He pushed on swiftly behind the other tourists, heading straight to the back of the ferry and several rows of outdoor benches. He hunched down as far away as possible from the ferry ramp, next to enthusiastic tourists who chatted in an array of different languages.

There was a bit of commotion on the ramp as the muscular sailor with a tight, black T-shirt requested tickets from the old lady.

"Oh, dear," she said worriedly. "Oh, where did I put that ticket?"

An imposing man with broad shoulders and a captain's hat emerged from the bridge to inquire about the delay. When he noticed the old woman, he said with a thick, Australian accent, "Mrs. Stenner! Welcome aboard! I hadn't realized it was that time of the year already."

"Oh, Captain, I feel so foolish, I don't know where I put my ticket," she answered, dismayed.

"Two tickets." The stern-faced sailor corrected behind them. "She's also missing her grandson's ticket."

"Grandson?" the woman asked, confused.

The Captain waved a hand at the sailor, dismissing him, then, smiling, gently led the old lady to a front seat. "Come, I'm sure everything is fine. After all, you're our most faithful customer, aren't you, Mrs. Stenner? How many years has it been, exactly?"

"Forty-five!" the woman replied, returning his smile.

"Forty-five!" the Captain exclaimed, "Crikey! How about that! And you brought your grandson along this time? What a wonderful idea!"

Mrs. Stenner stared at him, at a loss for a few seconds, before her eyes brightened suddenly and she giggled, "Yes... er... of course! My grandson! Lovely lad!"

"Good. Well, enjoy your trip, Mrs. Stenner. I must get up to the bridge as we are leaving in a couple of minutes," the Captain said, saluting her by lightly lifting his hat.

No sooner had the groups of families and friends of different nationalities settled on the benches, than the ferry moved away from the pier, heading out the harbour entrance into the open sea.

The Captain's voice boomed over the loudspeakers. "Ladies and gentlemen. This is Captain Oliver Andrew speaking. Welcome aboard the Haida Gwai II. The weather is looking fair as we head across the Strait of Georgia for our four-hour whale watching trip. We are happy to announce that several orca pods have been spotted in the past weeks. We should be in for quite a show..."

Four hours!

At the back of the ferry, hunched on the edge of a bench, Ben's face had gone pale as they moved away from Granville Island, away from the shore and further away from his mother.

At the edge of the pier, Hao paced up and down the marina, giving orders over the phone to spread out the search.

* * *

Susan Pickering sat by Laura's side as she finished taking her temperature. When she saw the number on the thermometer, she pursed her lips as she stared out the window. Laura's fever still had not broken. Being a nurse with experience, she knew that was not a good sign. She stroked the sick woman's arm, saying in a low voice, "Come on, Laura, you have to fight this!"

To her surprise, the young woman opened her eyes a crack. Through pale, dry lips she managed to ask, "Ben?"

Susan had to look away so that Laura wouldn't notice the worry on her face. Then she smiled reassuringly. "He's fine. He's resting—as should you."

Laura seemed satisfied with the answer because she closed her eyes again.

Susan stayed next to her for a long moment, staring out the window—biting her lip as she wondered what had happened to the boy.

* * *

The room was large and impeccably white. Two men in green protective suits talked together quietly, analyzing the data on their computer screens behind a glass window, as Mesmo lay inside a full-body CT scan machine. He had been tranquillized and was unaware of what was going on.

Until now.

"He's waking up," one of the men said.

"Ok, let's pull him out," the other one replied after a while. "It's no use anyway."

He pressed a red button, releasing the motorized examination table which hummed slowly out of the machine.

A third man entered the room behind them. The two radiographers recognized him immediately in spite of his green protective suit and mouth cover. He was slightly shorter and heavier built than the other two.

"Boss," they said in a manner of greeting, straightening in their seats.

The man nodded briefly, before entering the examination room. He bent over Mesmo, who blinked as he tried to regain focus. The alien's eyes focused on the thick black and grey eyebrows overshadowing small, green eyes behind the man's black glasses.

"Well?" the third man asked with authority, directing his question to the two radiographers.

"Still nothing, Sir," the younger of them answered. "Even after using the tranquillizer, we are getting the same interference."

"Show me!" the man ordered.

The two men sitting behind the window glanced at each other, uncertain. "Going through the procedure again could put a strain on his heart, Sir," the younger man ventured.

"Do it!" the boss insisted, joining them with determined strides.

Immediately the younger man obeyed. He pressed the red button again so that the examination table rolled slowly back into the tunnel-shaped machine.

Mesmo struggled against the straps holding his arms as he entered the claustrophobic hole of the CT scan.

CHAPTER 18 *Humpback*

As Susan Pickering's motorboat bobbed up and down in the bay of Deep Cove, Tike woke to the sound of two men laughing loudly as they trudged along the pier with buckets, fishing rods and a picnic box. The terrier lifted his head to watch them curiously.

The men chatted and laughed as they loaded their motorboat which lay further down the pier. One of them pointed to the other side of the inlet, in the general direction of the island that was the Pickering woman's home.

Tike pricked his ears, alert. He picked up the asthma inhaler between his teeth before jumping onto the pier. He slowed down until he saw that the men were busy placing their gear near the front of the motorboat, then hopped nimbly on board, scurrying under a bench at the back. He glanced out nervously. The men had not seen him.

Not long after, the motor rumbled to life. Then they were off, zipping away over the waters straight to the opposite side of the inlet.

Tike waited patiently before emerging from his hiding spot. He peeked out to watch the approaching piece of jutting land on which Susan lived. As soon as the boat was close enough to the island, Tike emerged from under the bench. He grasped the asthma pump tightly with his jaws, then leapt into the air before falling full force into the swirling, cold water.

The impact came as a shock. The dog almost lost his grip on the inhaler as he spun round under the water. He moved his paws frantically, trying to reach the surface again.

Tike's head emerged between the waves. He swam feverishly with his ears back and the white of his eyes showing. The small waves lapped at his face; the salt stung his eyes, the cold was numbing. No matter how hard he paddled, his short legs didn't seem to be bringing him any closer to the shore. Water entered his throat. His jaw hurt from holding the inhaler and exhaustion took over. Soon only his snout stuck out from the water.

Tike stopped swimming, surrendering to the flow of the tides. The dog sank down into the water...

...and his paws touched sand.

In a last effort, the valiant canine began swimming again, pushing against the sand to move forward, until his head was completely out of the water. He reached smooth rocks which lay close to the surface. They allowed him to cover the last meters to the shore, where he stepped out onto the beach next to the short pier that he and Ben had left that very morning.

* * *

Inspector James Hao contacted his men as he paced the walkway in front of Granville Market. The reports were fruitless: the boy was nowhere to be found. He scanned the river and harbour opening as he spoke over the phone, excruciatingly aware of how many small sailing ships and motorboats were coming and going. It was going to take a lot of manpower to check every boat stationed within the small harbour, one by one.

He had barely hung up when his phone rang. It was Connelly.

Hao filled him in on what had happened at the Police Department, including the ant incident, followed by the boy's escape from the frozen bathroom. When he finished, there was silence at the other end of the line.

"What is it?" Hao asked, fully expecting Connelly to accuse him of making the whole thing up.

Instead, Connelly replied slowly, "Well, that makes sense."

"What do you mean?" Hao asked.

"The preliminary results from the boy's blood test have arrived. They need further research, but the evidence is already pretty conclusive."

"Well?" Hao urged.

"The blood sample does not match that of the other witnesses," Connelly said. "Rather, it matches that of the aliens."

Hao put his hand through his black hair streaked with grey above the ears, pacing from one end of the walkway to the other, as Connelly's words slowly sank into his mind. "What are you saying?"

The agent's voice came clearly over the phone. "What I'm saying, is that the boy's blood is not human." He paused for effect, before adding, "It looks like we've found ourselves another alien."

* * *

On the island in the middle of the Burrard Inlet, Susan Pickering finished filling a basket with wood for the fire.

She walked back to her cabin, only to find the door ajar. She stepped inside carefully, noticing small, wet prints on the kitchen floor. The area around the dog's bowls was littered with crumbs of dog food and splashes of water. The paw prints went towards Laura's bedroom.

"Ben?" Susan called urgently.

She dropped the basket, then rushed to the back, pushing open the bedroom door. She found a very ruffled Tike rolled up in a ball on the bed, fast asleep.

Laura's head was propped up on a pillow with her eyes open. In one hand she was grasping an asthma inhaler. She showed it to Susan, saying with a frail voice, "Where's Ben?"

* * *

The Haida Gwaii II sped onwards across the Strait of Georgia, heading further and further away from Granville Island.

Ben lay hunched over his knees, his feet resting on the edge of the bench in front of him, his head down between his arms. Around him groups of people chatted away excitedly over the loud humming of the motors, making funny faces as they took each other's pictures in their fancy orange suits and life jackets.

Others were reading the whale watching company pamphlet, trying to memorize the names of the different types of whales they might encounter. The list was quite impressive, as it included Killer, Humpback, Minke and Blue whales, as well as Pacific white-sided dolphins.

Someone patted Ben on the back. He glanced up hurriedly.

"Have some chocolate," Mrs. Stenner, the old widow from

the pier, said gently, offering him a chocolate bar. "You'll see, it will help with the seasickness." She waved the bar at him. He took it gratefully. "Harold's pockets were always full of them," she chatted amiably. "He didn't eat them himself, mind you. He was always careful about his diet, poor dear. No, he did it for me. He knew I would always ask him for one, my Harold did." She stared into the distance, remembering.

Munching hungrily on the chocolate, Ben said with a full mouth, "I'm sorry I got you into trouble."

Mrs. Stenner clicked her tongue. "Tut, tut! I won't hear of it. My Harold always paid for two tickets, and so I shall, too, this year!" She patted him on the leg, before adding, "You relax, dear, enjoy the trip. You'll see, when you get back, everything will be all right." She got up, humming to herself as she strolled around the boat.

Ben sighed, then decided to explore the boat as well. It was made of three decks: the bridge deck with the cockpit, the main deck with outer and inner rows of benches to accommodate the tourists, and the lower deck with machinery and the captain's quarters. Thick, white clouds rolled across the sky, once in a while letting some sunshine through, while seagulls swooped around them, squawking. Ben wasn't invested in the scenery around him. The fact that he had had a panic attack on Susan's motorboat that morning crossed his mind, yet all he could think of was his mom and Tike. How was his dog ever going to make it all the way to Susan's island?

I miss you!

With a heavy heart, he settled down near the front of the boat, below a jutting window from the indoor tourist area. Great exhaustion came over him. It had been a long day, full of intense emotions. The boat's engines ran smoothly, carrying the craft evenly over the water. The sound lulled him. The occasional sunshine warmed him as he huddled from the sea breeze. Before long his head bobbed until it rested against the wall, and he fell into a deep sleep.

* * *

About two and a half hours later, up in the cockpit of the Haida Gwaii II, Captain Oliver Andrew was sipping on a cup of hot coffee, when a crewman turned and stretched out the speaker from the marine VHF radio to him, "Captain, it's the Coast Guard. They want to speak to you directly."

The broad-faced Captain picked up the receiver, speaking with a distinctly Australian accent. "Captain Andrew here, over." He listened for several minutes, before saying, "That seems highly unlikely, Sir. But send over the report: I'll have it checked out by my crew. Over and out."

He hung up, drummed his fingers on the dashboard impatiently, then turned as the fax machine came to life. A crewman picked up the printed document and handed it to him. The Captain read it with curiosity.

"J-Pod, three miles northwest," a crewman announced, pulling the Captain out of his thoughts.

Captain Andrew placed the arrest warrant with Ben Archer's face on it on the table, then took his binoculars to inspect the area of interest.

A family of about twenty orca—also called an orca pod—frolicked in the open waters some distance ahead.

"That oughta keep Mrs. Stenner happy," the Captain muttered half to himself, though the crewman overheard him and chuckled.

Behind them, the young sailor who had been checking the boarding tickets entered. He searched his jacket hanging from a hook in the wall, pulled out a sandwich wrapped in aluminum foil and sat down at the small table in the middle of the cockpit. He was about to take a big bite when the Captain noticed him. "Better hurry with that, Egor. I'm announcing a J-Pod in two minutes."

The tanned sailor with tattoos on his muscled arms pulled the sandwich away from his mouth. "Yes, Captain." As he lifted the sandwich again, he spotted the upside-down arrest warrant. He gasped. "That's that old widow's grandson!" He said as he picked up the paper, turning it the right way up.

Captain Andrew let go of his binoculars in a hurry. "What did you say?"

Egor was still holding his sandwich in one hand and the paper in the other. He nodded towards Ben's face. "Yes, that's him, the boy who's travelling with that woman... What's her name again?" He frowned as he tried to remember.

"Mrs. Stenner?" the Captain offered.

"Yes, that's it! She couldn't find the boarding tickets for her grandson and herself, remember?"

The Captain and the sailor exchanged a glance as they began to grasp the situation.

"Get Mrs. Stenner up here, would you?" the Australian ordered.

"Yes, Captain!" Egor answered, rising quickly, the sandwich now forgotten on the table.

The engines stopped close to the orca pod as the young man left the table in search of Mrs. Stenner. Over the loudspeaker, the Captain invited the tourists to watch the black and white animals from the rear end of the deck, which they did in an instant, clicking their cameras as the animals played in the water.

In the cockpit, Captain Andrew could hear Mrs. Stenner's

voice long before she reached the top of the stairs. As soon as Egor opened the door for her, she exclaimed excitedly. "Thank you so much for inviting me up here, Captain! I..."

"Mrs. Stenner!" the Captain interrupted, holding up his hand to silence her. "Please, Mrs. Stenner, didn't you say you were travelling with your grandson? I was hoping you might have brought him up here with you."

The old widow stared at him blankly. "Grandson? What grandson?"

Captain Andrew scowled as he waved the arrest warrant in her face. "This grandson?"

She squinted to see the image better, then giggled. "Oh! That boy! This is his first trip, you know? But that's not my grandson, by the way. I have six granddaughters and only one grandson! Can you imagine? He just turned three..."

"Mrs. Stenner!" Captain Andrew scolded. "Are you telling me you lied to me? And that I have a stowaway kid on board my ship?"

"Ooh!" Mrs. Stenner quipped, wide-eyed. "A stowaway! Well, how about that..." She stopped as Captain Andrew held up his hand again. He stared down at his feet with gritted teeth, fighting to remain calm.

"Blimey," he swore under his breath.

* * *

Ben woke up to excited shouting. He blinked and searched the boat with his eyes, then realized the tourists had flocked to the back of the ship to observe the group of orca that was apparently putting on quite a show. The ship's Captain spoke over the loudspeakers, explaining the nature of the orca family, where they came from, how old they were, what they ate, and even named some of the individuals, recognizing them by the shape of their tails and dorsal fins.

Ben didn't have the energy to participate in the excitement. He was still tired and hoped to catch some more sleep. At least that way he wouldn't have to listen to his worried thoughts or his grumbling stomach. He closed his eyes again but could not find any peace this time. He had an eerie feeling of being watched. When he realized there was no one else there, he settled down again.

That's when he saw a great humpback whale basking at the surface of the water right in front of him. Ben blinked, thinking at first it might be a large rock. Then he saw the big, black eye staring at him silently, as the beast swam along, accompanying the soft swaying of the boat.

Ben glanced around, discovering he was the only one who had noticed the huge mammal. He slid from his comfortable spot and approached the edge carefully, afraid any sudden movement might frighten the great beast away. It remained there, motionless, captivating him with its one huge eye. Boy and whale gazed at each other with curiosity. Ben felt an awe towards the animal that he had never before thought possible. In his mind, he could hear the muffled silence of the deep sea, while the immensity of the ocean reflected in the whale's eye. There was a sense of great freedom in the vastness of the open waters, away from the sounds of humming motorboats, of wind and rain, drifting at will for miles and miles.

"What are you looking at?" Ben said softly, as the whale swam level with him. "Are you going to keep me out of trouble?" he asked.

As if in answer, the whale spewed out a loud stream of air and water through its blow hole before sinking slowly beneath the surface like a ghost.

Beware...

"Hey, kid!" someone barked behind Ben. "Free ride's over now."

Ben whirled to face the sailor in his black t-shirt and jeans, suddenly feeling overwhelmingly nauseous, though he couldn't tell if it was from motion sickness from the boat or something brought on by the whale.

"You'd better come with me," the sailor said. "The Captain wants to speak to you."

He was standing very close to Ben to show he meant business. It crossed Ben's mind to make a run for it, but he had to give in to the obvious: there was nowhere to run to.

CHAPTER 19 *Haida Gwaii II*

When Ben entered the cockpit, closely followed by Egor, the Captain was waiting for him with his hands on his hips. The Australian was about to say something to the young sailor, when he wrinkled his nose. "Ugh, what's that smell?"

Egor fidgeted as he remained by the door. "Sorry, Captain. The kid threw up on my shoes on the deck."

The Captain glowered. "Well, what are you waiting for? Get cleaned up! And take care of that deck, too. I don't want anyone slipping and hurting themselves."

The sailor opened his mouth to object, but the Australian glared at him in warning. Egor straightened. "Yes, Sir!" he said hastily, exiting the cockpit.

Ben concentrated on remaining standing; his legs were like jelly. He felt terribly awkward standing before the Captain with his huge orange waders and jacket. The Captain waved him to the table so he could sit. The smell from Egor's abandoned roast beef sandwich left Ben's stomach churning, though, curiously, he couldn't tell whether it was from seasickness or extreme hunger.

"I'm Oliver Andrew, Captain of the Haida Gwaii II," the Australian introduced himself.

Ben glanced at him shyly. "I'm sorry I threw up on the deck," he said apologetically. "...and that I didn't pay for my ticket."

The Captain crossed his arms. "Do you think this is about an unpaid ticket, son?" he asked. "Tell me, do you know how many people are on board this ship?"

When Ben shrugged, the Captain explained, "There are forty-seven tourists and six crewmembers, me included. That's fifty-three in total. Fifty-three! Not one more, not one less. And I'm responsible for all of them. In case you hadn't noticed, we're way out in the middle of the Strait. Should we run into any trouble, we'd be on our own here."

He paused to make sure he had the boy's attention. "So," he continued, "If we were to have problems, I'd be looking to save fifty-three people. Not fifty-four. If you were to slip and fall into the water, no one would know to look for you, because no one would have known you had snuck onto the boat." He turned to look out at the vast sea—Ben's eyes following his. "Do you see why you did a very irresponsible and dangerous thing?"

Ben stared at the floor.

I understand full well.

"Now," the Captain said. "For the safety of my passengers and crew, I want to know what's going on. Why are you here and what did you do, son?" He waved a finger at him.

Ben glanced up at him angrily. "I didn't do anything!"

Captain Andrew shoved the arrest warrant towards him. "That's not what it says here, mate. This CSIS guy seems to think otherwise."

Ben sat back, his heart sinking.

The Captain waited for him to respond. Since Ben didn't reply, he said, "Fine, have it your way." He took the paper from the table, then picked up the speaker from the marine VHF radio. "I'm sorry, son, whatever trouble you're in, you'll have to face the consequences. You're too young to be dragging arrest warrants behind you."

He said into the speaker. "Charlie Bravo One, Charlie Bravo One. This is Alpha Foxtrot. Come in. Over."

"Alpha Foxtrot. This is Charlie Bravo One. You are speaking to the Coast Guard. Go ahead. Over," a woman answered.

The Captain kept his eyes on Ben the whole time. "This is Captain Andrew Oliver from the Haida Gwaii II. Patch me through to Inspector James Hao from the CSIS. Tell him I have his suspect in custody. Over."

"Copy. Over."

There was a long silence, then a man's voice answered, "This is Inspector James Hao. Who is this? Over."

Ben's face paled as the Captain presented himself and explained the situation.

"Excellent work, Captain," Hao said. "Give me your location. I will dispatch an amphibious helicopter to pick up the suspect. Over."

The Captain stared at the receiver, somewhat taken aback, before replying, "Negative, Inspector. I will not have any disruptions to my trip, nor will I cause panic among my passengers with unusual maneuvers. We will head back to port immediately. We will arrive in less than an hour. Over."

The Captain listened expectantly. Then the radio crackled back to life.

Hao said, "Understood. You are not to let the boy out of your sight. He already escaped from the Vancouver Police Department this morning. Over."

The Captain glanced at Ben in surprise, then said, "I need to know what I'm up against. The arrest warrant is vague. Please elaborate. Over."

There was another silence before Hao replied icily, "This is a confidential matter relating to national security, Captain. I am not authorized to elaborate. We expect you here in one hour. Over and out."

The Captain bit his lip, unhappy with the answer, but said, "Roger that. Over and out."

He put down the speaker, inspecting Ben, who looked like he was about to throw up again. The Captain headed to the back of the cockpit, where he opened a cooler and fished out a Coke. He handed it to Ben, who gulped it down thirstily.

"Blimey!" Captain Andrew said. "Slow down, mate! The Coke will settle your stomach but don't overdo it!"

Ben put down the can, and eyed the sandwich hungrily. The Captain noticed. "Go on, eat it, if you think your stomach can handle it. You'll need a clear head when we arrive."

Ben didn't wait to be told twice: he chomped down on the sandwich as if he hadn't eaten in days. In the meantime, Captain Andrew gave orders to turn the boat around and head back to Granville Island. Ben was swallowing the last piece of bread when Egor returned. The sailor's eyes immediately fell on the empty aluminum foil. He glowered at Ben without saying anything.

Captain Andrew turned his attention to Ben again. "Shouldn't you be calling someone? Your mom? Your dad? To let them know you're safe?"

Ben bit his lip, then shook his head.

"There has to be someone," the Captain insisted.

"There is," Ben replied with great effort. "My mom. But she's very sick." He gazed pleadingly at the Captain, before blurting, "I don't want her to die! That's why I went to get her inhaler! I thought if I could treat her asthma, maybe she would get better..."

The Captain frowned as he lifted his hat to scratch his forehead. He sighed. "Listen, son, talk openly to that inspector. Explain things to him. I'm sure he will be reasonable."

Ben sank his head into his hands, mumbling, "I don't think so."

When he didn't elaborate, the Captain said, "Egor, take him down to my quarters." He turned to Ben again. "Go on, son, and don't try anything funny. I want to bring everyone back safe and sound. All fifty-four of us. Is that clear?"

Ben nodded, resigned. He followed Egor who had opened another door that led to stairs to the lower deck.

* * *

"What happened?" the man asked with a deep voice, as he drummed his fingers on the long, polished table, his thick golden ring shining. He stared out the window at the Toronto skyline without really seeing it.

Another man's voice answered over the phone. "It's just like we thought: it was his heart. The CT scan machine proved too much for him. We almost lost him."

The man adjusted his black-rimmed glasses while he sat in the elegant meeting room in a high-backed chair. His thick black and grey brows pulled together in a frown. "Is he awake yet?"

The voice at the other end said, "Not yet. Might be a while."

"I don't have a while!" the gold-ringed man said impatiently. "I need answers! And I need them soon!"

The other man said calmly, "If we keep on pushing, you may never get any answers at all."

The man in the meeting room drummed his fingers even harder, mulling things through.

His contact continued, "We have an idea as to why we 'lose' him so often. We think he uses a mechanism that puts him in survival mode, like bears when they go into hibernation. He's capable of shutting down organs. He crawls into a shell to save energy. What happened in the CT scan, however, was different. He went into shock this time. He must not have been expecting it. He panicked and didn't have time to go into that hibernating state."

The man in the meeting room stood up and walked over to the window. In an agitated voice, he exclaimed, "I don't care what shell he crawls into. You find a way to prod that alien out! I was supposed to have results. Now everything is delayed!" He paced before the window, staring down twenty-four floors to the street below. "My flight leaves tomorrow. I'll be gone for three months to oversee the site. Let's hope our business partners don't lose patience. Our Martian fellow had better be ready to talk by the time I get back."

The man at the other end of the line said, "I'll make sure that he is."

* * *

Ben tried the doorknob several times, though he already knew it was locked. He turned to scan the Captain's quarters. On the left was a closet, and near the windows was a small sofa attached to the wall. On the right, he noticed a desk with a neat pile of documents, a sextant, and a picture of the Captain with his arm around a smiling woman and two children: a boy about Ben's age, and a smaller girl. Ben stared at the picture for a while.

They seem so happy.

On his way to look out the window, Ben struggled to move. The waders and jacket were cumbersome in this cramped room, so he removed his life jacket and both orange attires, then left them on the floor. He kneeled on the sofa, pulled the one side of the window that could slide open, and stuck out his head. A cold wind and ocean spray hit his face, making him squint. His hair blew in all directions.

He could make out the entrance of the sea arm that led to Granville Island in the distance, yet, what caught his attention, was that they were travelling past the red and white lighthouse where, some nights back, Laura and he had seen Mesmo disappear before their eyes.

Ben automatically reached for his watch. He rubbed it, wondering if Mesmo might come, but nothing happened. Ben glanced out the window again.

Should I jump?

The boat was moving fast, the waves lapping at the sides, while the lighthouse was quite a distance away. Even with a life jacket on, he wasn't sure he could make it. The Captain's words rang in his mind, "If you were to slip and fall into the water, no one would know to look for you."

Ben pulled back, closed the window, and gazed around helplessly.

* * *

Inspector James Hao was joined by Agent Theodore Connelly and a police officer on the pier where the Haida Gwaii II had docked moments ago. The tourists were asked to descend one at a time. They threw curious glances at the officers as they headed back to the tourist stand of the company that had sent them on the whale watching trip.

Captain Oliver Andrew stood by, thanking the passengers as they left, while Mrs. Stenner approached him to say goodbye. "A memorable trip, as usual, Captain!" she gushed. "Though for the life of me, I could not find that boy again. He seems to have vanished into thin air!"

The Captain smiled gently. "Don't worry, Mrs. Stenner, we found him. He's in good hands."

"Oh, well then, I'm sure he is!" the old woman replied. "Don't be too hard on him, poor lad. Why, at his age, I would be skipping school to go swimming at the lake all day! Those are the memories that last. This boy is no different. He needs adventure and freedom. Don't squash that spirit in him!"

The Captain took her hands in both of his. "You are a wise woman, Mrs. Stenner. And you are right, as always." He winked at her.

"Goodbye, then, see you next year!" she smiled, waving at him.

She was one of the last passengers to disembark. She cast a vexed expression as Hao and Connelly pushed by without waiting for her to step onto the pier.

Hao presented himself and Connelly to the Captain, as they shook hands. The Captain invited them to follow him to the lower deck. On their heels was another police officer and Egor, the young sailor. When they stood before the Captain's quarters, Egor took out a key, turned it in the lock, and pushed the door.

It wouldn't budge.

Hao and Connelly exchanged a quick look before pushing Egor aside. They tried to shove open the door, only managing to do so with some effort. The Captain's desk blocked the way. They had to work to push it aside to gain access. As soon as Hao and Connelly were inside, they noticed the open window.

Connelly inspected the marina, with its many small boats and sail ships. "There!" he exclaimed. Hao followed his index finger as he pointed out to sea.

In the distance, they could make out a spot of orange from Ben's waders and life jacket drifting on the water, close to a pier on the opposite side of the small harbor.

Hao turned to face the Captain angrily. "I told you to keep an eye on him at all times! Weren't you listening when I told you he escaped once already?"

Captain Andrew looked embarrassed as he stuttered, "I... er... I didn't expect..."

Hao ignored him, turning to Connelly instead. "Let's go! Hurry, before the kid reaches the other side!"

Hao shoved past Captain Andrew and Egor, though not before saying menacingly, "This won't go without consequences, Captain!"

Captain Andrew shrugged helplessly, then watched as the inspector, the agent and the police officer rushed away.

* * *

All kinds of small sea vessels dotted the piers of Granville Island, some old and rusted, others gleaming and slick. It was a maze of pleasure boats. Hao and Connelly had a hard time finding their way to the correct pier from which they could fish Ben out of the water.

After a couple of wrong turns, they made it to the end of a pier from which they spotted the orange waterproof jacket floating on the lapping waves.

The police officer who was accompanying them clambered down a short ladder to the water level. He reached out to catch Ben as he drifted past, but all he found was an empty, rolled up jacket which bulged with a pocket of air.

The three men glanced in surprise at the piece of clothing. They searched all around for the missing boy who was supposed to be wearing it. He was nowhere to be found.

Connelly swore. "He tricked us!"

Hao exclaimed, "The ship! He never left the ship!"

CHAPTER 20 *Paddleboard*

Laura sat carefully on the edge of the bed, her feet dangling a few inches above the wooden floor, as she drank a creamy soup that Susan had served her. The hot liquid that slid down her throat felt terrific. For the first time in many days, her strength was returning.

She patted Tike on the head, praising him. "Good dog!"

Tike's tongue lolled happily.

"Where's Ben, Tike?" she asked softly. The Terrier jumped off the bed, then rushed out into the kitchen with his tail wagging.

Laura tried to get to her feet to follow him when Susan entered. "Whoa, girl! Back into bed with you. This is no time to go for a jog."

She ushered Ben's mother back under the bedsheets. Laura opened her mouth to object, but her face had already drained of energy. Although she was no longer hungry, she accepted some toast with cream cheese and forced herself to continue eating, determined to get well as soon as possible.

Tike peeked back into the room to check whether Laura was following him. When he saw that she had gone back to bed, he trotted out of the house, over the grass, then down to the short pier. Once he had reached the end of it, he sat down, staring out over the water, waiting for his master to return.

* * *

In the Captain's quarters in the hull of the Haida Gwaii II, a soft breeze entered through the open window. Below it, a couple of seals rolled playfully in the water. A door squeaked open, and Ben stepped out of the Captain's closet. He had to push the desk, as it was blocking his way. Soon he stood in the middle of the room, listening for sounds.

When satisfied he was alone, he carefully stepped into the corridor, up the stairs and into the cockpit. Since there was no one there, he gathered courage, opened the door leading out, and hurried down the exterior stairs, at the end of which he could see the ramp connecting the ship to shore.

As Ben hopped down the last step, Captain Andrew appeared from the back of the ship, which had been out of Ben's range of vision.

The boy froze. He watched the Australian, who only had to take one large stride to block Ben's access off the ship.

"Smart bloke, aren't you?" the Captain said, observing him with his arms crossed. "That's what I'd figured."

Ben found his voice. "What are you going to do?"

Captain Andrew sighed, "I don't know. I guess that depends on you."

Ben swallowed hard. "What do you mean?"

Egor came running up behind the Captain. He spotted Ben and wanted to grab him. The Captain held up his arm, indicating he should stand back. Egor stared at his boss in surprise.

"I have a son, you see," the Captain said, concentrating on Ben. "He's about your age. And if he were in trouble, I'd want to be sure he came to his mother or me for help."

"I told you," Ben said desperately. "That's exactly what I'm trying to do. I'm trying to reach my mother!"

Egor turned away from them, then said hurriedly, "Captain, those policemen are heading this way again."

Ben was stricken as he stared at the Captain.

Slowly, the Captain stepped back. With a movement of his head, he said, "Go on then. I choose to believe you. Go help your mom."

Ben rushed forward, but the Captain stopped him again. "Wait," he said, as he handed him a life jacket. "Take this and wear it. I don't want to be fishing you from the bottom of the harbour."

Ben took it. "Thank you," he said earnestly. The Captain got out of the way so that Ben could escape down the ramp.

"Don't make me regret this!" was the last thing he heard the Captain shout behind him.

* * *

Tike sat at the end of the pier, observing the inlet and the mountains. Suddenly he stood, his body weight rolled forward, his tail lifted and his ears pricked. He remained like that, listening attentively. On the surface, the lapping waves and a soft breeze blowing through the fir trees could be heard.

Only the most trained ear or high-end underwater hydrophones would have been able to capture the sound that was travelling deep below the surface of the inlet. The ethereal vocalizations of the humpback whale went from low to high-pitched clicks, echoing far and wide until they reached Tike's ears.

The dog froze, fully alert, one paw lifted from the ground, until he could take it no longer. He darted up and down the pier in excitement.

Realizing there was nothing he could do to respond, Tike sprinted back to the cottage like a bouncing ball.

* * *

Ben ran away from the Haida Gwaii II. The only way off the pier was blocked by the approaching police officers. He had no choice but to find another way to escape.

He bent over, hiding between two ships, when a movement in the water caught his eye. He glanced down, noticing another, lower pier, almost at water level. Beside it, two seals swam playfully. But it wasn't the seals that had caught his attention. Instead, on the edge of this pier, lay a lime green paddleboard and black paddle, ready for use.

Ben looked around, wondering who it might belong to. There was no one else in sight. He bit his lip, trying to decide what to do, as he did not like the idea of stealing. What convinced him, however, was the image of the lighthouse he had seen from the Haida Gwaii II when they first motored into the Burrard Inlet. The idea of boarding to a safe place won out over his fears. Relieved at having some sort of plan to distance himself from the searching men, Ben hurriedly put on the life jacket, placed the paddleboard in the water, and began paddling between the boats until he was close to the harbour exit. Full of determination, he left the harbour, Granville Island, the Inspector, and Bordock behind.

* * *

Tike scurried into Laura's bedroom excitedly.

She sat in a chair by the window, looking out to the bay and biting her fingernail. "What is it, Tike?" she asked.

The terrier sprinted to the door, running back-and-forth to catch her attention.

Laura did not doubt the dog's intelligence. She found her slacks, shirt, and sweater, and followed Tike out of the house. She was halfway across the lawn when Susan called out, "Laura! What are you doing? You're in no shape to be wandering around like that!"

Laura said with full determination, "Ben needs me. I can't wait any longer. I'm going to find my son and I won't let you stop me!"

There were dark patches under her eyes, and she swayed slightly. Susan held on to her arm.

"All right!" the woman answered reluctantly. "All right! We'll both go. But we have to be smart." She frowned, thinking hard. "You go on to the boat," she decided. "I'll get jackets, your inhaler, the car keys, and some other things. Do you think you can make it?"

Laura nodded, though she seemed terribly frail.

The two women split ways. Laura cautiously made her way to Susan's second motorboat, following Tike, who was already waiting for her at the pier.

Before long, both women and the dog were speeding across the inlet towards Deep Cove.

* * *

Sailboats dotted the bay, their owners enjoying what was probably going to be one of the last mild days before the coming winter. Further out, huge container ships were anchored, waiting for their turn to unload their cargo at the Vancouver Harbour. Behind them were the shores of North Vancouver bordered by the North Shore Mountains. Following this coastline westward with his eyes, Ben spotted the lighthouse he was heading for.

Jeepers! It's miles away!

Somehow, looking out from the hull of the Haida Gwaii II a couple of hours ago, the distance from the lighthouse to Granville Island had seemed very short. Of course, he had been on a sturdy, fast-moving boat. Now, he was a tiny speck on the bay with the City of Vancouver and Stanley Park slowly moving away from him as he paddled furiously.

He had been so eager to get away from Granville Island! He wasn't ready to admit yet that trying to reach the lighthouse was a big mistake.

I won't make it...

CHAPTER 21 *The Breach*

Once they had docked the motorboat and recovered Susan's car from the shed, both women and Tike drove off towards Deep Cove. Laura assumed Ben would have headed to their apartment. She clung to the faint hope that he might still be there. She wouldn't hear of Susan contradicting her, even though she knew it was a dangerous decision to go there.

Susan headed to the bridge that would take them into Burnaby, driving well over the speed limit. Suddenly, Tike went crazy in the back seat. He jumped frantically onto Laura's lap, almost causing Susan to crash.

Susan yelled in surprise. "What's wrong with that dog? Make him stop!"

Laura replied quickly, "No! We should pay attention to him. I think he knows where Ben is. He'll take us to him." She held the terrier gently, urging him, "Go on, Tike, find Ben. Find him!"

Tike pricked his ears. He gazed determinedly out the window to Laura's right.

"Turn back! We need to head further west," she ordered Susan.

"But..." Susan began.

"Susan! Please!" Laura begged.

Susan stared at Laura and shook her head in disapproval but did as she was told.

* * *

Ben was only halfway across the bay by the time the sun had descended on the horizon. When he realized he was almost at a standstill, he sat on the board, his head dropping, his legs dangling in the cold water. His arms were numb with the effort of constant paddling. He shut his eyes tight, shivering under the weight of the infinite firmament above and the cold water below. A small plane flew overhead. Ben forced himself to wave at it—even though he knew it was futile; there was no way they would notice him from up there.

Mesmo! Where are you?

He wished the alien would magically appear to save him again, but Mesmo's words echoed in his mind. "If you cross this inlet, I can't guarantee that I will be there to help you."

Ben lay down on the paddleboard, exhausted. His dog's absence from his side weighed heavily on his heart.

Mom! Tike!

Something thumped at the back of the paddleboard. Ben gasped in fear and pulled up his legs as he turned to see what had hit him.

The head of a brown seal popped out of the water, observed him curiously, then disappeared again under the board. Before him, another seal appeared. Ben watched as both animals flipped and pirouetted at great speed.

"You're the ones from the harbour!" he exclaimed.

He relaxed, realizing that they were not out to harm him.

Instead, the big, black eyes of the good-natured mammals invited him to join them in their underwater game.

Play! They seemed to say.

Their whiskers glistened with droplets as they waited for him to react. All Ben could do was shiver with cold.

"Help me!" he begged through shivering lips.

Immediately, one of the seals grabbed onto a rope that was tied to the front of the board, tugging at it briefly. The rope disappeared into the water, as did the seals, but a moment later, Ben felt another tug. The paddleboard moved forward slightly, and suddenly Ben found himself being pulled across the bay.

Ben was dumbfounded at his luck, though he had to lie down as he began to feel dizzy. Drops of water sprayed into his face. He closed his eyes. He tried to stay awake, but the constant up-and-down movement of the board lulled him.

The seals surfaced, then dove again in a kind of dance-like movement. Ben didn't know whether he was awake or dreaming. He felt as though he was dancing with them below the surface, twirling gracefully in a weightless world. He forgot about the heavy burden of the sky. He felt liberated. Nothing could touch him. His mind was free to wander and whirl below the waves. His heart leapt with excitement as he tried to keep up with his playful companions.

Then, suddenly, the marine mammals disappeared into the depths with one swift movement.

"Play!" Ben heard himself plead, longing for the seals to keep him company. He blinked awake at hearing his own voice and found himself floating under the shadow of the mountains, not far from shore. He could make out small beaches separated by big, grey boulders topped with fir trees and, a short distance to the left, the towering lighthouse. The seals were gone.

Ben tried to stand on the paddleboard. His brain was

strangely lightheaded as if he were suffering from seasickness again. How long he had been unconscious, he couldn't tell. The sky had become a soft pink reflecting on the calm waters. Gentle wisps of clouds were turning a brighter red while the mountains threw black shadows into the water.

So close!

He was only about ten yards from shore. He knew he had to put his mind and effort into reaching land, even though he ached as if he had been swimming for hours. His soaking wet clothes stuck to his body under the life jacket and he trembled uncontrollably.

After trying unsuccessfully to put some weight into his paddling, he glanced up at the imposing rock formation from which his mother had almost slipped and fallen some nights before. It seemed to taunt him to come closer.

That's when Ben spotted Mesmo.

The alien man was standing tall and proud on the ledge, roughly at the same place where Ben and his mother had found him on the night of the downpour.

The silhouette of a woman came running up beside him, followed by a small dog.

Ben's heart leapt into his throat. "Mom!" he yelled, exhilarated.

She saw him, waved, and yelled back, "Ben!"

Tike ran back and forth before her.

Ben's energy returned in an instant. He paddled as fast as he could.

Susan joined the others on the ledge. She and Laura searched for a way down to the small beach where Mesmo had helped Ben recover his memory. Laura headed down when she realized Mesmo had not budged. She followed his gaze out to sea—not towards Ben—but further away into the horizon.

Ben saw Mesmo raise his arm to point into the distance. He turned to see what had caught the alien's attention. He noticed the dot of a ship far away.

"Ben!" he heard his mother yell again, only this time the tone of her voice had changed. She was desperate.

He saw her point in the same direction as Mesmo. "Hurry!" she shouted.

When Ben looked behind him again, he was startled to see how quickly the ship had turned from a dot on the horizon to a fast approaching speedboat heading straight towards him. Ben's heart leapt into his throat.

I know who's on that boat!

He wanted to get to shore and safety, but his hands were frozen. He lost his grasp on the paddle in panic. It slipped into the water and began to drift away. Ben dropped to his stomach, frantically trying to reach for it. He could hear the motorboat roaring towards him. He spotted Mesmo, Laura, Susan, and Tike disappearing into the trees as they began clambering down the hill to reach the beach. Ben gave up on the paddle, resorting to his hands to move forward in the water, like a surfer.

It was useless.

In no time, the large motorboat passed him by, cutting off his path to the beach. Ben hung onto the paddleboard for dear life as the waves almost toppled him into the water. The motorboat went quiet after it maneuvered as close as possible to Ben. The boy's fingers curled tightly around the paddleboard even after the surface of the water had gone still. The dark blue metal of the ship pinged with static while the paddleboard thumped against its side.

After a moment, a rope ladder bounced down.

Hao called out, "Benjamin Archer!"

The boy lifted his head. The inspector stared down at him

grimly. Next to him stood Bordock. Ben spotted a couple of police officers. The white letters on the side of the boat confirmed that it belonged to the Vancouver Police.

"Climb aboard!" Hao ordered.

Ben searched around with his eyes: his mother and Mesmo were nowhere to be seen. Overwhelmed with despair, he stood slowly on the paddleboard and stared helplessly at the rope ladder.

"We could wait here all night." Hao said impatiently. "You wouldn't last long. The temperature is dropping fast. So make a wise choice and get up here!"

Ben bit his blue, shivering lips. He knew the inspector was right.

I'll freeze if I stay out here much longer!

With a sinking heart, Ben grabbed onto the ladder, and put a foot on the first step.

Don't!

He stopped. Something in his mind was urging him not to take another step upwards. He glanced down at the space between the paddleboard and motorboat. It was very dark. Eerily dark. He stared at the water, transfixed.

Hao's voice was icy cold. "Benjamin Archer! Hiding is useless; I already know what you are."

What's he talking about?

Ben cast a look at Hao, then at Bordock, gritting his teeth. For a split second their eyes locked in a silent battle. Ben took his foot off the ladder and pushed himself away from the boat as hard as he could. Not that it mattered, as he only floated a couple of inches away. Hao lifted his arms in frustration.

Ben bent down on his knees, and slowly paddled away from the boat with his hands.

Hao shouted, "What do you think you're doing? Get back

h..." He broke off in mid-sentence, his mouth wide open.

The massive humpback whale breached the surface. It soared like a huge mountain between the paddleboard and the motorboat as if in slow motion, reaching way up above their heads. For a split second, it remained transfixed in time, towering over them, its massive grey body glimmering in gold and red in the setting sun, majestically poised like a statue. Then it plummeted back, shattering the illusion.

Ben grabbed onto his paddleboard with all his might, bracing for impact.

Hao yelled in shock.

There was a colossal splash and the paddleboard somersaulted in the air before falling back into the water, ejecting Ben far below the surface, but closer to shore. For a moment he was lost in a silent, dark world of air bubbles and churning seawater before his life jacket pulled him upwards. He spluttered, gasping for breath.

There were cries for help as the motorboat groaned and tilted sideways dangerously. Already the whale breached for a second time, soaring above the ailing ship. A new shockwave sent them tumbling in all directions, submerging Ben again, while causing the motorboat to dangerously take in water.

Ben struggled to reach the surface. He had gulped in a good amount of water this time. His arms flailed desperately, while he tried to find his bearings. His hand fell on something soft. He blinked, trying to make out what it was.

It was Tike. The dog had come to his rescue.

Ben grabbed the dog's collar and let himself be pulled to the shore.

Laura and Mesmo ran up to him as the waves tossed him against the beach. "Ben!" his mother yelled, wading into the water to pull him out.

Susan joined them, then helped Laura drag Ben onto the shore. Laura sobbed and kissed his forehead as he hugged her back weakly. In the distance, the police motorboat lay on its side with half a dozen agents splashing in the water.

As Laura stroked her son's hair, Ben stared dazedly into the bay. He watched as the humpback whale slowly retreated into the distance, its tail sticking out of the water as if bidding him farewell.

Ben turned his attention to Mesmo, who stood nearby, gazing at him intently. Just before losing consciousness, he saw the alien break into a discreet smile.

He's proud of me!

CHAPTER 22 *The Shapeshifter*

After resting for two full days following Ben's escape at the lighthouse, both he and his mother made speedy recoveries in the cozy island cottage. Laura's appetite returned, while Ben was thrilled to find Tike again. He covered his dog in praise after hearing how his faithful companion had made it all the way back to Laura with the asthma inhaler clamped in his mouth.

That evening, Ben was heading out with a bucket and fishing rod when he caught sight of Mesmo's tall form on the pier. He had not seen the alien man since he had been pulled out of the water beneath the lighthouse. Ben ran over to him, Tike close at his heels.

"Mesmo!" Ben gasped, catching his breath. "You're back!"

Mesmo smiled. "Yes," he said. "And I see you are feeling better."

Ben nodded. "If it hadn't been for that whale, I don't know what would have happened. Did you see that? How could it have known I needed help?" He spoke in wonder.

"Because you asked for help," Mesmo said matter-of-factly.

Ben frowned at his words. "Really?" he asked. "How? I

don't remember doing that."

Mesmo smiled. "You don't realize your power yet. Your skill is barely beginning to take hold."

That smile again!

Mesmo's words made Ben feel uncomfortable. "You're proud of what happened, aren't you?" the boy quizzed.

"I am," Mesmo answered.

"Why?"

"Because I wasn't sure my daughter's skill would survive. But clearly, it has," he answered, still smiling.

He seems to think this is a good thing.

"What if..." Ben asked carefully, "...I don't want it?"

Mesmo's smile faded. "That question is irrelevant," he replied. "It is part of you now. You should be happy."

Ben walked to the end of the pier to avoid Mesmo noticing that he did not share the alien's enthusiasm. He attached the hook to the end of the fishing line while he carefully thought about his next question. "What if the skill is making me sick?"

Mesmo went to stand beside him with a look of confusion on his face. "Sick?"

Ben shrugged, already regretting his question. He attached the bait to the hook, ignoring Mesmo's stare. Then the boy leaned back and threw the line far out into the dark water. "I didn't know you could fish for trout in the dark, did you?" Ben commented casually.

Mesmo wasn't letting him get away with a shrug as an answer. "Ben, what do you mean: the skill is making you sick?"

Ben sat down at the edge of the pier and sighed.

"It's nothing, really. I felt nauseous after encountering the whale. And there were seals, too." He wound up the spool and threw the line into the water again. "It was strange. In my mind, I was swimming with them under water. All I wanted to do was play with them. I forgot where I was and lost track of time. But when I came to, I felt so dizzy!"

Mesmo smiled again. His face relaxed. "Well, of course! You'd been floating on the ocean for hours! I'm not surprised you felt seasick!"

Ben didn't answer.

I knew you'd say that!

He anchored the fishing rod between two wooden planks so he wouldn't have to hold it and scratched Tike's head as the dog lay down on his lap contentedly.

What about the ants? I wasn't on the ocean then!

Ben didn't want to talk about this supposedly fabulous skill anymore. The alien obviously had no idea how uncomfortable the subject made him. While Mesmo was totally relaxed about it, Ben realized that the more he thought about this alien skill, the more afraid he became. It had been shoved on him without his consent, and he did not understand it.

They both gazed at the starry night until the fishing rod suddenly tensed. Ben grabbed at it and expertly caught a decent sized trout, which he placed in the bucket. He wasn't smiling when he saw his prize, though. "I used to go fishing with Grampa," he said softly, remembering.

Mesmo observed the trout, then said, "Ryan was a good man."

"How do you know? You barely even met him!" Ben quizzed. He sat down on the edge of the pier again and pulled up the side of his jacket collar so that Mesmo wouldn't notice he had closed his eyes tight. A part of him regretted having caught the fish.

"Actually, I did," Mesmo replied. "I went back to his house a couple of times between my travels. We spoke about many things, including how to best protect you."

Ben remained silent, concentrating on Mesmo's words to ignore a wave of nausea. Instead, he pictured his grandfather and Mesmo making plans about him. Thinking about his grandfather suddenly reminded him of something. "I meant to tell you," he said. "Bordock was at the hospital on the night Grampa died."

Mesmo's eyes widened. "Are you sure?"

"Yes. He was also at the Police Department. Did you know he works for the CSIS? How is that possible? How can the police not know he's an imposter?"

Mesmo remained thoughtful for a while, then said, "He has shifted. He has taken on the appearance of another human." He looked at Ben. "I think this would be a good time to finish recovering your memories from the night of *The Cosmic Fall*."

Ben frowned. "What do you mean? I thought we had done that already."

Mesmo bent over the side of the pier and placed his hand in the water. A soft, blue light emanated from the palm of his hand. The water responded by streaming upwards from the surface until a round, flat screen of transparent liquid took shape in front of the pier.

Mesmo sat beside Ben again, his hand outstretched as he maintained the liquid screen before them. His voice sounded bleak as he said, "You need to go back to the night I crashed. We need to find out what happened after my daughter passed away."

Ben stared hesitantly from Mesmo to the floating screen. He bit his lip, then reached out to touch the water with the tip of his fingers. He closed his eyes and was thrust back to the night of *The Cosmic Fall*.

* * *

"Mesmo," the girl murmured as she closed her eyes for the last time.

"No!" Ben shouted, reaching for her, but her body had slipped out of reach.

Ben stumbled away from the wreckage, sobbing. He held his right hand up before his face, slowly uncurling his fist, and in the fire-lit sky, saw that he was no longer bleeding. Instead, in the middle of his palm lay a glimmering gem. It reminded him of his mother's pretty diamond ring, the one she never wanted to wear and kept at the very back of a bathroom drawer.

"Benjamin!" he heard his grandfather gasp behind him. Grampa ran up to him, terrified. "Oh, my gosh, are you all right?" He pulled Ben to his feet. "What are you doing here, Potatohead?" He usually used that name when he was joking. Not this time. His brow tightened as he said angrily, "I told you to go to the house!"

"The house went dark," Ben argued. "There's a blackout."

Grampa muttered something under his breath, lifted a silent Tike up from the ground and pulled Ben away from the remains of the craft.

"Wait!" Ben objected. His Grampa paid no heed.

"This isn't right," Ben heard his Grampa mutter. "Something's not right." He froze in his tracks.

Ben bumped into him and glanced around his grandfather to find out why they had stopped. He gasped.

A tall man stood before them, surrounded by burning debris. He was shrouded in darkness, so they could not see his face. He did not move but kept his shining eyes on them. He had wavy, white hair. It was Mesmo.

Grampa held on tightly to Ben, ready to run, alert for any sign of danger.

Mesmo swayed. His legs gave way, and he crashed to the ground.

Grampa didn't wait to find out more. He was already running, pulling at Ben's wrist to keep going.

"Grampa!" Ben yelled. "Wait, Grampa! We've gotta help him!"

Grampa stared at him in surprise, hesitated, then looked back at the fallen man. Slowly, he approached the stranger. Grampa shoved at him gently with his foot, so they could see his face. It was streaked with dirt, while his hair was pure white.

Grampa lifted Mesmo over his shoulder until the man's head and arms were dangling over his back. He groaned with effort, teetering under the weight. He stabilized himself, got a better grasp around the man's waist, and lumbered away from the scene of the accident; Ben following his every footstep with Tike safely tucked into his jacket.

After a long and tedious time, they arrived at the house. Grampa pushed through the kitchen door and headed for the living room. There, he dumped Mesmo onto the couch like an old potato sack, then sagged to his knees, panting.

Ben put a hand on his shoulder worriedly. Grampa nodded to say he was fine. When he had caught his breath, he stood, and both stared at the mysterious man on the couch.

Ben took his grandfather's arm.

"Grampa," he said softly. "There are others."

Grampa stared at his grandson in amazement. He nodded slowly, answering in a distant voice, "I know. I saw them."

"We must help them!" Ben stated. The boy squeezed his grandfather's arm. "It's okay. I'll stay here." Ben nodded reassuringly, "I'll be okay."

Grampa nodded back. Without a word, he headed outside again. His shoulders slumped as though he were still carrying a heavy weight.

Ben tried the phone, though he knew the line would be dead. He headed to the kitchen window to watch his grandfather cross the field once more. He watched even after he had disappeared into the trees, following him in his mind's eye as he would reach the first crash site.

Maybe he'll find the girl.

Ben absentmindedly rubbed the palm of his hand, suddenly remembering the small diamond he was still clasping in his other hand. Tiny sparkles of light emanated from it. He stared at it in awe as it began to glow.

The window panes rattled alarmingly, making Ben jump and drop the jewel, which rolled under the kitchen sink. Tike bared his teeth as he crouched low.

Something was happening outside, in the field right before the house. A dark spacecraft descended slowly to the ground, about twenty meters away. It was black as the night and had a sleek form. It hovered a meter above the earth, humming softly, each hum sending an invisible wave that rattled the windows.

Then it went silent.

Ben froze to the spot, his throat dry and the hairs on the back of his neck prickled. The night was silent, expectant, and he hardly dared to breathe.

From some invisible opening in the craft, the form of a man appeared. He had spiky, white hair. Judging by his strong build, he could not have been very old. He was too far away for Ben to distinguish anything else, but for some reason, he broke into a cold sweat. No matter how much he longed to hide, he was rooted to the spot. He was afraid the slightest movement would alert the man to his presence.

Then an unexpected sound caught the attention of them both. The sirens from a police car swiftly approached on the road from town.

The alien from the spacecraft stood alert for an instant, listening, then after confirming the siren was approaching, the being ran straight for the house.

The spikey-haired man reached the bushes below Ben's window just as the headlights from the police car illuminated the house. The car came to a stop on the gravel before the front door, the whirling red and blue lights on its roof splashing across the lawn.

Agent Theodore Edmond Connelly stepped out. He spoke into the radio, listened as a woman's voice gave him instructions, then shut the car door and jogged towards the house.

Ben could hear the police officer's footsteps on the gravel as he approached before he banged on the front door. The noise shook Ben to the bone. "This is the police. Open the door! Mr. Archer, are you there?"

Ben's heart pounded. He sensed the presence of the man lurking below, like a spider in a web waiting to catch its prey.

After a moment, the sounds of footsteps on the gravel told Ben the police officer was moving away from the front door. He stopped for an instant before breaking into a run over the lawn. Ben peeked and could see the police officer freezing as he took in the dark spaceship. His hand was on the gun at his side, but he was too dumbfounded by what he was seeing to remember his own safety.

In the distance, more sirens wailed. The police officer turned to head for his car when he noticed something in the bushes behind him.

Ben opened his mouth in warning, but his voice was paralyzed in his throat. He heard the police officer yell, "Hold it!" as he reached for his gun—too late. He was struck by a sudden ray of intense blue light. Ben heard him groan as he tumbled to the ground.

The dark form materialized from the bushes under the window, running toward the dead man. Hastily, the murderer placed his hand an inch above Connelly's face until a blue light emanated from it, enveloping them both. Before his very eyes, Ben saw the white-haired being's face transform and take on the bald police officer's traits. Ben could tell that the alien was in great pain as this was happening. His mouth twisted and the muscles of his body bulged abnormally beneath the clothes. As the transformation completed, the eerie blue light faded away. In a swift movement, the murderer heaved the dead man's body on his shoulder and carried him to the spaceship, where both disappeared. Shortly after, the fake Theodore Connelly reappeared in full police garments, his victim still inside the spacecraft. He ran to the middle of the field when a helicopter flew overhead, its powerful searchlight illuminating the ground. Ben saw the murderer with Connelly's face gaze up to the house with its eyes that were two pools of darkness that carved themselves into Ben's mind.

Twisted eyes!

Then several things happened at once. Mesmo, who, a moment ago, had been lying unconscious on Grampa's couch, placed a firm hand on Ben's mouth, pulling him down. The lights of the house sprang back to life. The helicopter hovered over the police officer who was shielding his eyes with his arm. Several police cars, ambulances and firefighters made a dramatic entrance onto the road next to the field, as the night came ablaze with noise and flashing lights.

* * *

The liquid screen lost its consistency and returned from where it had come with a splash.

Ben backed away, breathing heavily. He stared at Mesmo with wide eyes.

"You passed out," Mesmo explained. "I carried you out of the house and ran all night until we reached the town. I left you under a tree, close to some houses, and sent Tike to look for help. Then I left."

Alien and boy stared silently at the dark inlet, lost in thought.

Tike pricked his ears. They followed the dog's gaze and found Laura walking towards them, her hands stuffed deep into her jacket pockets to fend off the cold.

"Any luck?" she asked cheerfully.

Ben stood hastily and handed her the bucket with the trout's head sticking out of it. "I'm turning vegetarian," he said gloomily.

Laura laughed, then noticed her son's sunken eyes. "What's the matter?" she asked worriedly.

"Tired," he muttered. "Going to bed." He trudged off toward the cabin with the fishing rod.

Laura followed him with her eyes, then turned to Mesmo. "What happened?" She asked, holding the bucket tightly in her arms.

"He'll be fine," the alien replied grimly.

She studied the alien as they headed back to the cabin. She noticed the grayish tint on his skin. She stopped and said softly, "What about you? We haven't had a chance to talk. Are you all right?"

He turned his head towards her. "I am better, yes."

She pulled out a hand from her pocket and gently weaved it through his own. There was only empty air where her eyes saw a firm hand. She held her breath, then said, "Ben told me about your troubles. He said you are being held against your will." She looked up at him again. "What happened to you?"

He stared at her grimly as they began walking again. His voice sounded pained. "I was kidnapped at the Toronto Airport. The man who is responsible for holding me knows that I am not from this planet. He is the head of a powerful organization, I can tell."

"A government agency?" Laura ventured.

Mesmo shook his head. "No. I don't think so. This is something else. I have not been able to figure it out yet."

Laura said, "We will help you in any way we can."

Mesmo shook his head again. "That would not be a good idea. You are safe here. Leaving this island would be too risky."

She noticed the dark rings under his eyes. "You don't look well, Mesmo..." she said softly.

He grimaced. "They placed me in a confined space. It is the one thing my species dreads." He glanced at Laura. "I couldn't take it. My heart stopped. They were able to revive me, but I barely made it..."

Laura gaped at his words. "Mesmo!" she breathed, her eyes wide. She stood before him to get his full attention. "Don't give up!" she said determinedly. "We'll find you and get you out, I promise."

Mesmo smiled sadly. "What Ben is doing for me is enough already. His spirit portal allows me to escape my jail briefly, even if it is only part of me. The man who is holding me has gone away for several months. That will give me some time to recover and find a way to escape." He trailed off and looked up at the night sky.

Laura gazed up as well, then said, "I meant to thank you, for taking care of Ben. Ever since the events in Chilliwack, he's been so afraid, so fragile. But he's changing. I can see it. He's becoming more confident by the day. You do that to him. He trusts you." She smiled. "So for that, thank you."

The door to the cabin opened, and light splashed onto the lawn. Susan let them in and took the bucket from Laura. "Here, let me get that," she said. "You go on up and get some rest."

Laura nodded and smiled shyly at Mesmo. "Well, goodnight then," she said, her eyes on him, before turning away.

Susan dumped the fish into the kitchen sink. She washed it energetically before cutting it open, then removed its entrails, while Mesmo watched curiously. After a long silence, she said coolly, "Still playing with their hearts, are we?"

Mesmo straightened. "I need them, just as much as they need me."

Susan eyed him with displeasure. "Yes, but who's going to get their feelings trampled on in the end?" She shoved the fish into the freezer, then peeled off her latex gloves. "You?" she asked accusingly.

CHAPTER 23 *Flight*

Two weeks later Ben woke up to a misty morning. He found Susan bustling about in the kitchen, making breakfast. She had spent almost an entire day on the mainland the day before, returning with loads of fresh food. The whole house smelled of eggs and bacon. Ben checked in with his mother to see if she was ready to come and eat.

Laura awoke, stretching lazily. Ben grinned, noticing how much better she looked: her cheeks were rosy, she had put on some much-needed weight, and she looked rested.

She smiled at him. "'Morning, honey," she said as she patted the bed to invite him to sit beside her, noticing that his mood had significantly improved over the past weeks.

He did so reluctantly, his stomach grumbling. He leaned back and stared at the ceiling. "It's as if we were on vacation or something," Ben commented.

Laura turned to face him, saying cheekily, "Well, technically, it's the middle of the term. We need to find a way to get you back to school."

Ben stared at her in horror. "Are you serious?"

Laura poked him in the side. "Dead serious."

"Ouch! No way!" Ben objected, half giggling. In defense, he grabbed a pillow and hit her gently on the head as she poked him playfully in the side again. That only triggered more pillow fighting. They both giggled until Mesmo appeared in the doorway. They stopped midway in their fight, their hair in a mess, grinning sheepishly as the alien man stared at them with utter bewilderment.

"Well, don't just stand there!" Laura said as she threw a pillow at him, forgetting that he wasn't really there. The pillow went right through him, landing on the other side of the doorway. Ben fell backwards on the bed, laughing uncontrollably.

"Oops!" Laura said, putting a hand to her mouth.

Mesmo frowned. "What are you doing?"

Laura wiped away the tears at the corner of her eyes as she tried to control her laughter. "We're being foolish, is all. Don't you ever have laughing fits where you come from?"

"No, of course not," he said. "Why would you want to do something that makes you cry?"

Ben guffawed, placing a pillow over his face.

"That's enough, Ben," Laura warned, putting a hand on his shoulder with a smile still on her face. Addressing Mesmo, she said, "Sometimes people cry from happiness. It's very liberating. You should try it sometime."

Mesmo shook his head in disagreement. "We learned, long ago, that excessive emotions were the root of many wars. Strong displays of emotion are considered barbaric."

Laura's smile wavered. She gazed at Mesmo with renewed interest, then asked carefully, "Is there... family... waiting for you back home?"

Mesmo shook his head.

Ben, who recovered from his laughing fit, stared at him quizzically, blurting, "What? Don't you have a wife or something?"

"Ben!" Laura growled from the corner of her mouth, her face flushed.

Ben blushed immediately. "Sorry!" he mumbled, realizing that this conversation had taken an awkward turn.

The alien man answered, "If by 'wife,' you mean a life companion, then, yes, I had a 'wife.' She died not long ago."

Laura and Ben stared at him, suddenly silenced. "I'm sorry," Laura said earnestly, before adding slowly, "Perhaps one day you will remarry."

Mesmo frowned. "What is 'remarry'?"

"Er..." Laura struggled. "It means to take another wife. Find another... 'life companion.'"

Mesmo shook his head. "That is not possible! We are matched once in our life. There can be no other."

"Ugh!" Ben said, suddenly losing interest. "I smell waffles."

He leapt off the bed, then said, "Excuse me!" as he waited for Mesmo to move aside and let him through. Technically, Ben could have walked right through the alien, but for some reason, that seemed inappropriate.

"Are you coming?" the white-haired man asked Laura, who had fallen silent.

"Yes, yes," she said, waving him on. "I'll be right there."

He nodded, looking at her curiously, then followed Ben to the kitchen.

Laura stared at the floor, lost in thought. She was no longer smiling.

* * *

Breakfast lifted their spirits. Laura feasted her eyes on the well laid-out table full of fresh bread, eggs, bacon, waffles, jam and fruit.

"Thank you, Susan!" she exclaimed. "I don't know how we can ever repay you!"

"Sit down and eat a hearty breakfast. You'll be needing it." Susan ordered sternly.

Laura obeyed. "I'm going to have to find work. We can't go on like this. We've run out of money."

"Oh!" Ben exclaimed through a mouthful of waffle. "We still have some money. Well, sort of." He plunged his hand into his jeans pocket, fishing out something small and holding it up in the palm of his hand. Swallowing, he said, "Dad's ring."

Laura started, turning red. "What? How...?"

"I found it back home, in the bathroom drawer. I figured if you never wore it, maybe we could sell it."

Laura hastily took the engagement ring from him, throwing an embarrassed look at Susan and Mesmo.

Mesmo pointed at the ring in her hand. "Your... life companion?"

"I..." she began.

"Dad gave it to her so they could get married," Ben interrupted, munching on some grapes. "He died in a car crash when I was a baby." An awkward silence fell on the table, though Ben was in too good a mood to notice. "Show me the flower trick again, Mesmo! Please?" he begged as he helped himself to some more bacon.

Laura slipped the ring into her own pocket, relieved to change the subject, then filled her plate as she watched Mesmo touch the surface of a jug of water. The liquid obeyed his command, flowing into a complex bouquet of delicate, transparent flowers, the stems gently swaying to an invisible breeze, the thin petals turning a glistening silver as they froze.

Ben gasped in wonder, his eyes twinkling. Laura smiled gratefully at Mesmo, then glanced at Susan to see if she approved. The older woman was staring at her untouched plate with a sullen face.

"Susan?" Laura said, concerned. "What's the matter?"

The unsmiling woman lifted her eyes, then said darkly, "You are going to have to leave." She had spoken in a low voice, yet they all heard her loud and clear.

Laura coughed up the grape she was trying to swallow. Mesmo lost his concentration, and the watery flowers splashed onto the table. Ben stopped chatting, turning his attention to his mother questioningly. They stared at their host, wondering if they had heard her correctly. They waited for Susan to admit she was making a distasteful joke. Instead, she glanced at them and insisted, "You heard me. You're going to have to leave. Today!"

There was a long, uncomfortable silence. Laura cleared her throat. "Hum. Yes. Of course! We have long outstayed our visit. You have treated us so well, Susan, that we sort of lost track of the fact that we were invading your home and your privacy."

Susan rested her forehead in her hand, her elbow on the table. "That's not it," she began. She stared at them guiltily, before continuing, "I called both my sons yesterday afternoon, while I was in Deep Cove. I'd been resisting the urge to do so for quite some time. I think of my sons every single day, but having you around somehow reminded me how much I missed being able to touch them, to hear their voices, to hug them... They are both married. My youngest had his second baby last month." She broke down into tears. "I can't live like this anymore. I need to see them. I need to see them so bad it hurts," she sobbed.

Laura hurried to her side to hug her. Susan sniffled before

adding, "I'm meeting them in Deep Cove this afternoon."

Mesmo cautioned, "They won't be the only ones meeting you there, Susan."

"Don't you think I know that?" she retorted. "Don't you think I know my son's phones are bugged? That a hundred prying ears overheard every word we said?" She shook her head as she blew her nose on a napkin. "I don't care. I don't care anymore. They can arrest me, jail me, accuse me of god-knows-what. But I want to see my sons."

A new silence settled heavily among them, as each realized the consequences of Susan's action. Their hiding place was compromised. Danger loomed closer to their doorstep with every passing minute.

"You saved our lives, Susan. We will be forever grateful for that. But you must go and see your sons, no matter what," Laura said. For the first time, she dared look into Ben's wide eyes, then said determinedly, "We will pack our bags and leave. If you could drop us somewhere on the mainland, we'll disappear from your life."

Somewhere above the cabin, they heard the roaring of an airplane.

Susan sniffled again. "That won't be necessary."

* * *

Tike scampered outside, followed closely by Ben. They rushed out onto the grass to watch the small hydroplane as it descended onto the inlet. It broke through the last clinging mist as it landed, then headed straight for the island.

Laura and Mesmo caught up with them, anxiously trying to make out who was inside the plane. The motor spluttered as the pilot slowly maneuvered the craft next to the pier before coming to a final stop. The plane bobbed up and down. They could see the pilot moving about inside as he prepared to exit.

Susan stepped out of her wooden cabin. Smiling, she said, "Don't worry, he's a friend."

Laura relaxed while Ben ran after his dog, excited to study a hydroplane up close. Susan followed the boy towards the pier where a dark-skinned man with a very thick, knee-length, winter jacket, stepped out of the plane. Immediately, he proceeded to remove the cumbersome piece of clothing.

Laura and Mesmo watched from afar as their host greeted the middle-aged man who was wearing jeans and a black sweater. He hugged Susan. Then they talked for a moment before the man turned his attention to Ben and Tike. He shook the boy's hand, then patted the small terrier, whose tongue lolled in a canine laugh.

Ben sprinted back to his mother. Grinning, he said, "I know who he is!" Instead of explaining further, he ran into the house, leaving Laura and Mesmo clueless.

Susan and the newcomer walked slowly over to them, still chatting somberly until they came face to face. Susan introduced them. "This is Thomas Nombeko, originally from Chilliwack. Thomas, this is Laura Archer—Ryan Archer's daughter. And this is... er... Jack Anderson."

Thomas Nombeko shook Laura's hand while he eyed Mesmo with a touch of fear in his eyes. Nervously, he held out his hand to greet Mesmo the same way. Susan pulled it down, indicating he shouldn't insist.

Ben came rushing out again. Breathless, he said, "He's on Grampa's list!"

He proudly held out the small, brown envelope which he handed to his mother, who frowned as she peered inside, then took out the crumpled notebook page containing the list of five people in Grampa's handwriting.

"See?" Ben said, pointing to Susan's name. "This is how I contacted Susan. And here's Thomas Nombeko. They were all Grampa's contacts."

Laura recognized the names on the list: Ben Archer was her father, Susan Pickering was their host, Wayne McGuillen was the homeless man from Chilliwack, and Thomas Nombeko was standing before them. "You are all witnesses!" she exclaimed, suddenly connecting the dots.

Thomas Nombeko nodded. "Yes. I used to be a mailman in Chilliwack. I lived not too far from your father's house. I even saw your father and Ben on the night of *The Cosmic Fall.* I was cycling home that night and spotted them out on the field," he said. Then addressing Ben, he added, "You probably don't remember that."

Ben looked down at his feet.

I remember.

Not wanting to linger on the memory, he pointed to the last name on the list. "This Bob M. must be another witness."

Susan and Thomas both stared at the last name on the list, then shook their heads, confused.

"I've never heard of him," Susan pondered. "Come, let's go inside. There isn't much time. You must get packing. Thomas here has offered to take you to a safe place."

"Really?" Ben said excitedly. "Where are we going? Are we flying?" Ben had already taken a liking to the fourty-something-year-old man, who had a soft demeanour and a contagious laugh.

"We are flying, yes."

"Whoa!" Susan interrupted. "You promised, Thomas, not a word about where you're going. I don't want to know."

They stepped into the house, chatting happily.

* * *

Laura stayed behind. Her face had become drawn as she stared blankly at the names on the notebook page. She jumped when she realized Mesmo stood silently behind her. Guiltily, she folded the sheet three times so it would fit in her back pocket. "I'd better hang on to this," she said in a shaky voice. "Might come in handy." She smiled without meeting his eyes, then headed inside.

Soon they were packed and ready to go. Ben, Mesmo and Tike were already headed to the hydroplane with Thomas, who was diligently explaining how the craft functioned.

Laura checked the log cabin one last time to make sure they hadn't forgotten anything, though they were travelling light as they had become stranded without any belongings. Susan had managed to buy them some emergency clothing and toiletries, but that was about all they had.

Laura approached Susan, who waited by the doorway. "Will you be all right?" she asked.

The woman had become somber, yet she gazed at Laura with determined eyes. "You don't have to worry about me. I'm a survivor. Nothing could be worse than what I've already been through. Though this time I'll have my sons near me. I know they will defend me in any way they can." She paused before adding, "And anyway, it's not me they want..."

Laura said carefully, "Susan, if they catch you, I want you to tell them everything you know."

Susan stared at her in surprise.

"Listen to me," Laura urged, taking her hand. "Mesmo has many enemies. One, in particular, is extremely dangerous. He will do anything to get to Mesmo. He will know if you are lying or holding back information. So don't hold anything back. The main thing is that you don't know where Thomas Nombeko is taking us, so we will be safe."

Susan nodded. She checked to make sure the others were out of earshot, before saying, "I have something to tell you as well." She led Laura to the fireplace, where she picked up an envelope off its shelf. She handed it to Laura. "When the government agents released us, your father gave me this letter and asked me to give it to you, were we ever to meet."

It was Laura's turn to stare at Susan as she accepted the envelope.

Susan held onto Laura's hands. "Be careful, Laura. We don't know who this Mesmo is. Not really." She hesitated before adding, "Don't let him break your heart." She let go of Laura, then headed out before the other could object.

Once Susan was gone, Laura tore open the envelope. She carefully read the letter inside. For a long time, she stood in the middle of the living room, holding her father's letter close to her chest, her cheeks wet with tears. Finally, she dried her eyes, breathed deeply, threw the letter in the dying embers of the fireplace, and waited for it to catch fire. She stepped out of the cabin, closed the door for the last time, and went to join her son who had boarded the hydroplane with Mesmo, Thomas and Tike.

Before long they had taken flight, swooping over the tiny island, the shimmering inlet, and Susan Pickering who was waving goodbye from the pier. They soared up over the majestic, snow-capped mountain ranges that went on and on for as far as the eye could see, heading towards an unknown destination.

EPILOGUE

"My Dearest Honeybee,

(You are to destroy this letter as soon as you have read it.)

If you are reading these words, then it means I have failed you.

I have tried, by all means possible, to protect you and Ben from falling under the radar of some treacherous people so that you could lead a normal life. But if you have met Susan Pickering and she has given you this letter, then it means all my efforts were in vain. It means you and Ben are in grave danger and that, for whatever reason, I can be with you no longer.

Please understand, my Honeybee, that meeting with you would have meant drawing all kinds of prying eyes your way. I had to avoid that at all costs. No matter what, you must not let anyone lay their hands on Ben. I swear, Laura, if secret agents catch him they will never let him go. They all want the same thing: they want to know about the aliens that crashed in Chilliwack on the night of The Cosmic Fall. They want to know about their technology, their planet, their intentions, their WEAPONS...

You'd think it would be for scientific reasons and for the advancement of the human race. But no, they are power-hungry egoists intent on dominating their fellow human beings.

If you found Susan, then you will have gotten my list. You can trust all the names on that list. I insist: ALL of them. Even the last one. You know who I mean...

There is also another who you can trust. His name is Mesmo. He crashed in my backyard on the night of The Cosmic Fall and survived. I have spoken to him many times during his short visits. I know he will protect you because I saved his life. I pray he will have found his way to you. Beware, Laura, Mesmo's mission on Earth is greater than our understanding, and he will crush you if he feels you are standing in his way.

Yet, I know you, my angel, and even an otherworldly creature could not resist your kindness. You may be our only hope!

You have already met Mesmo. You met him on that fateful day when you came looking for me in Chilliwack. I was there, Laura. I was hiding from you. I could not let you in, no matter how much I ached to. But I swear, I was holding you in my arms the whole time you were talking to Mesmo on the doorstep, and I never wanted to let you go.

I hope you will find it in your heart to forgive me because I cannot forgive myself.

I love you, always,

Dad

BEN ARCHER

and

THE ALIEN SKILL

Human or alien?

Rae Knightly

CHAPTER 1 *The Spacecraft*

Once more, Inspector James Hao found himself staring at the final report containing the results of the blood sample. No matter how hard he tried to make sense of it, the evidence remained undeniable: the individual the sample had been extracted from was not a human being.

Hao couldn't believe that, a little over a month ago, he had been sitting opposite the subject in the interrogation room of the Vancouver Police Department. Never would the Inspector have suspected that, behind the innocent features of a twelve-year-old boy, lay a creature from another planet. Hao's stomach twisted at the thought.

A week ago, High Inspector George Tremblay, Head of the National Aerial Division of the CSIS, had tapped the file with the tips of his fingers. "This file remains between us," he had said, eyeing Hao and his collegue, Connelly. The three men had stood in the High Inspector's office, facing each other.

Tremblay had lifted an eyebrow at Connelly. "You took the sample without my prior authorization. I should fire you for acting in such an unprofessional manner. You can consider yourself lucky that your hunch about the subject was correct.

Nevertheless, this information will not enter the official investigation and is not to be mentioned beyond this office. The fact that this child, this Benjamin Archer, is an extraterrestrial must remain between us. Is that clear?"

Hao had observed Connelly out of the corner of his eye, secretly satisfied to watch his colleague being reprimanded by their chief. Even though he had taken a dislike to his colleague and had personally disapproved of the blood extraction, he had to hand it to Connelly for getting results. All in all, he had to admit that Connelly's methods of investigation were particularly efficient if not particularly legal.

The cell phone on Hao's desk buzzed, pulling him out of his thoughts. A message arrived, accompanied by a tiny image. Hao's forehead—creased in concentration a second ago—softened, and a chuckle escaped his lips. He pressed the image to enlarge it, and the huge, black nuzzle of an English Shephard appeared. The black dog was checking out the camera of whoever was taking the picture.

The message read: DID YOU FORGET ME?

Hao smiled and checked his watch. It was close to midnight at the Dugout, located in Eastern Canada, which meant it was nine pm where the message had originated.

What am I doing, still stuck at my desk at this hour? Hao brooded.

He hesitated for an instant, then pressed on the message to dial the number. The phone rang once before someone picked up, and a woman's voice answered in surprise, "Hello?"

"Hi, Lizzie," Hao said.

"Jimmy?" the woman said. There was shuffling in the background and Hao heard Lizzie's muffled voice, "Still! Sit still, Buddy!" Then her voice sounded clearer. "Oh my gosh! You should see that! He knows it's you! Yes, Buddy! It's your daddy!

Your long-lost daddy..."

Hao heard the English Shephard bark happily, and he was reminded people lived normal, tranquil lives out in the real world.

"Jimmy?" Lizzie began. "I can't believe it's you. I sent that picture of Buddy, but never thought you'd actually have time to call back. Must be my lucky day!"

Hao grinned. "How are you, Sis?"

Lizzie sighed in an exaggerated manner. "Do I really need to tell you? Buddy uprooted my rosebushes this afternoon. You know how we love him around here, but, honestly, I love my flowers more."

Hao could hear Buddy panting in the background.

Lizzie continued, "I haven't heard from you in ages! When are you coming home?"

Hao's mood darkened as his eyes slid back to the blood file on his desk. "Not anytime soon. I've got a big case on my hands. Probably the biggest I'll ever work on." He sighed. "I realize Buddy's a burden for you. Do you want me to contact the dog kennel we talked about?"

Lizzie remained silent for a moment, before answering earnestly, "Of course not. I love my roses, but if it helps you, then I'm happy to keep Buddy for a bit longer. You know Geoffrey and I wouldn't want to see him cooped up and miserable."

Hao let out a silent breath of relief. "Thanks. I owe you one. When this is over, we'll go pick out some rose-bushes together."

"You?" Lizzie scoffed. "In a plant nursery? Never gonna happen!"

They both laughed.

"Seriously, Jimmy," Lizzie said with a concerned voice.

"There's always a new case popping up. You make it sound as if you were the only one catching the bad guys. I know I'm repeating myself, but bad guys will be around with or without you. And, trust me, there's a dozen younger James Bonds out there longing to take your place."

Hao scoffed, "Take it easy, Sis, I'm not that old!"

Lizzie clicked her tongue which meant to him that she wasn't ready to crack jokes. She pushed on. "If you were still married, your wife would be the one scolding you instead of me. So brace yourself while I nag you for a bit!"

Hao stood with a knowing smile. He paced along the office window overlooking a cavernous hangar and let her have her moment.

"I know how important it is to you to put the criminals behind bars and I, more than anyone, appreciate how hard you work to keep we little citizens safe," Lizzie spoke. "But, you have to stop acting like you're the only one carrying the burden." Her voice sounded thick with worry as she added, "I just want to make sure you stop in time."

While he listened, Hao gazed at the impressive, alien spacecraft that hovered a few feet from the concrete floor at the center of the dim hangar. Everyone, except for security, had left for the night. Only a couple of emergency and forgotten office lights illuminated the area. He thought he saw a movement blend into the shadow cast by the spacecraft and leaned forward, forgetting the phone stuck to his ear.

Lizzie's concerned voice came through to him again. "I know you. You wouldn't call unless something was wrong. Is something the matter?"

Since nothing moved in the grey hangar, except for his own reflection in his office window, Hao's well-built frame relaxed, and he turned to head back to his desk.

"Jimmy? Are you listening?" she asked.

"Hm, yeah, I'm listening," he replied with a tired voice. He sat back in his office chair and rubbed his left temple as he shut his eyes. He needed to rest, but the case wouldn't let him go. And suddenly he realized why.

"It's weird," he said thoughtfully, speaking more to himself than his sister. "You know me: you know I'm an expert at telling good from bad, right? I mean, I understand the mind of a murderer; I know how to pick out a crook; I'm always a step ahead of elaborate thieves. I catch them and put them behind bars, where they belong." He broke off, picking up the file in front of him. "But these ones, Lizzie? Jeez, for all I know, they could start World War Three tomorrow, and I wouldn't even suspect." He shook his head, surprised at his own confession. "The thing is, for the first time in my career, I've been asked to chase down criminals I don't understand." He paused. "And that frightens me."

* * *

Agent Theodore Edmond Connelly paused in the shadow of the spacecraft until Hao disappeared from view. The bald, green-eyed man set his jaw: he had almost gotten caught by Hao as he snuck up to the hovering spaceship. Had Hao spotted him, it would have led to a load of unnecessary questions, something Connelly could not afford to answer right now.

He grimaced while he waited. As soon as Hao moved away from his office window, Connelly reached out to the sleek ship. At the touch of his fingers, an invisible door opened faster than the eye could see. Connelly jumped inside and the door slid shut behind him.

Without delay, the bald man approached the front of the

spacecraft where he pulled up hovering screens filled with undecipherable patterns and intricate symbols.

Behind these transparent screens, the ship's large window dominated the concrete hangar. Connelly was not worried about being caught. He knew that, while he could look out, no one could look in. He was safe.

After performing a couple of movements over the screens, he connected to the Dugout surveillance cameras. He made sure that they remained disabled and showed static, then worked remotely to activate them again. His mouth turned into a thin line of concentration.

He checked the time. It had been almost four minutes since he had cut the power to the cameras—thus allowing him safe access to the spacecraft. Way too long! If he didn't turn the system on again soon, security would notice—if they hadn't already.

This was all Hao's fault. What was his colleague doing in his office at this time of night? The man's diligence irritated him.

Sure, it served him well, but he had to constantly be on his toes to avoid Hao's scrutiny from focusing on him. For now, Connelly was satisfied to remain in Hao's shadow. It avoided him having to interact too much with others. Hao did all the talking, while Connelly watched and learned. Yet the man kept on intercepting his own progress. Connelly knew that, should Hao become a burden, he would have to silence the man permanently.

At the moment, though, he had more pressing matters. It only took him half a minute to bring the Dugout cameras back online, yet by the time he was finished, his brow creased in pain.

Connelly stood and staggered backwards into a cubicle to the side of the spacecraft. At a wave of his hand, a stream of energy washed over him in blue surges, and his face began to tremble with unnatural speed. He sagged against the back wall, breathing heavily, unable to stop the transformation from taking its course.

Out of his bald head grew spikey, white hair; his nose lengthened; his muscles tightened; and he stretched a few inches taller. He groaned, leaning his forehead into the cradle of his arm.

When the shaking stopped, he glanced up with empty, honey-brown eyes. Bordock stepped out of the cubicle, then stretched his neck and shoulders, exhaling slowly as he did so.

This shapeshifting business was proving harder than anticipated, yet he knew he had no choice but to hold up the pretence that he was Connelly if he was to find Mesmo and the boy. Time was not on his side. He should have been gone long ago. Yet all trails of the fugitives had gone up in smoke. His pulse elevated at the mere thought.

His eyes fell on six, large circles outlined on the back wall of the ship—three above at eye-level and three directly below. Small lights blinked at him, inviting him over. He couldn't resist the temptation and pressed a couple of buttons on the lowest circle to the right. A long tube ejected from the wall. It contained a form inside.

Bordock stared at the pale face with white lips and closed, sunken eyes of the man who lay in the tube before him. He noticed how a soft blue light reflected on the man's bald head.

"Enjoying the ride, Connelly?" Bordock smirked.

He noted with satisfaction that the features of the real Connelly were well preserved in the tube, meaning he would still be able to shapeshift into the agent. In fact, the man looked like he was sleeping peacefully. Bordock tapped on the small screen that should have indicated an extremely slow heartbeat brought on by induced sleep.

There was nothing.

"You'll have company soon enough," he promised the dead man.

Bordock let the real Connelly slide back into his unusual coffin, then tapped the other incubators for good measure. They would fit Mesmo and the boy, as well as Mesmo's other three companions, who lay on the last floor of the Dugout. Then, and only then, would he have the necessary proof that his task was complete and he could leave this repulsive planet behind.

With that in mind, he headed back to the front of the ship, where he called up an impressive amount of screens. He surveilled them with renewed determination. On one of these many screens, Mesmo's face appeared, while behind it an innumerable amount of live camera images from road surveillance cameras flickered with thousands of faces on them: the computer scrambled to find a match.

Below it, the same operation was happening with Benjamin Archer's face.

As the night wore on, the alien shapeshifter searched for the fugitives from within his spacecraft, while in the office a few feet away, he knew that Inspector Hao was doing precisely the same thing.

CHAPTER 2 *Poison*

Wake up!

Some part of Benjamin Archer's mind whispered to him, but the words did not match the intense dream he was having. In it, he was caught in the middle of a lightning storm. He was surrounded by bright sparks that gave off bluish, electric charges which shot into the darkness, in such a way that he did not have time to figure out where he was. Were his feet even touching the floor? He didn't think so.

He became extremely apprehensive as the storm intensified. It reminded him of a girl with long, white hair. She was grasping his hand, staring at him fiercely as she discharged a flow of energy into his body.

He squirmed in his sleep, trying to escape something he could not run from. But as he did so, he felt himself drop into darkness at an alarming speed. His arms flailed in a meek attempt to slow his fall, while a deep, repetitive sound reached his ears. Whatever it was, he was careening towards it.

Thud-thud, thud-thud it went, louder and louder.

A roaring sound reached his ears, and without warning, he was thrust into a thick liquid, surrounded by nasty, blue filaments.

Poison!

He writhed at the realization. The blue threads followed him into the dark-red rivers that were his own blood. His mind zoomed out and he saw the complex network of his veins, like a million tree-roots, all heading in the same direction.

Thud-thud, thud-thud.

In an instant, the poison would reach his heart and be pumped throughout his body.

He scrambled to stop this from happening, but it was as if he were swimming in dense water. His heart pounded like a drum, releasing the poison to every living cell, ingesting, expulsing, ingesting, expulsing.

Stop!

Wake up!

Two voices were fighting for attention, one internal, the other external.

How does that even make sense?

Wake up!

Ben's eyes fluttered open. He rolled to his side, breathing heavily. He reached out to his bedlamp, but just as he flicked on the switch, he thought he saw a bluish halo around his hand. He blinked several times, now wide awake. He shut off the light again and stared at his hand; of course, it was normal. He leaned back into his pillow, switched on the light again, and took in the normalcy of his bedroom: a desk with a chair, a window with dark-blue curtains, a beige carpet, a bed with a thick, dark-brown duvet which he had half kicked off.

And Tike, who was staring at him with his tongue lolling from his place beside the nightstand. The white-and-brown terrier placed his paws on the side of the bed to lick his face.

Ben scratched the dog's ears absentmindedly. Was he ever

going to have a normal nights' sleep again?

The blue filaments of his dream followed him as he got up, showered and dressed. A lump of fear grew in his throat, and he knew why: a second before waking, he had glimpsed the poison exiting his heart and spreading to the rest of his body.

It was too late, of course. The alien girl had infected him with the alien skill just over three months ago. Every cell of his body would have absorbed it by now.

Ben remembered Mesmo's words when he had asked him, "What if I don't want it?"

Mesmo had replied, "That question is irrelevant. It is part of you now. You should be happy."

Only, he wasn't.

Too much had happened for him to think about it much, but as soon as Mesmo confirmed the alien element was part of him, a terrifying thought dawned on him.

I am no longer entirely human.

Ben knew, with unspoken certainty, that with every passing day, the infection was making him less and less human, and more and more alien.

* * *

Tike didn't seem affected by Ben's mood. He scampered down the stairs and headed to the kitchen.

As Ben followed him, a man's voice reached his ears. He remembered that his mother had started a new job at a local Tim Horton's that morning, so the man was apparently talking on his cell phone. This was confirmed as soon as he entered the kitchen and found Thomas Nombeko sipping a cup of coffee with the phone stuck to his ear. The dark-skinned man thrust a couple of fingers in the air as a matter of greeting without letting go of the cup as he continued to speak.

Ben slipped into the chair of a small breakfast table and was about to reach for a slice of bread when he saw his mother's note: "Dear Ben, Enjoy your first day at school. Love, Mom."

He smiled, thanking his mother silently for her soothing words. They made him feel less alone. He grabbed the pen that she had used and wrote. "Thanks, Mom. Enjoy your first day at work. Love, B." She had left at dawn, so he knew she would be back before him and would read the message on her return.

By the time he had spread peanut butter on his bread, Thomas had hung up and grinned at him. "Hey, kiddo! How did you sleep?"

"Fine, thanks," Ben answered automatically, reacting to the man's contagious smile, then remembering the dream. He swallowed the piece of bread through the lump in his throat.

Thomas sighed, a worried look passing briefly through his eyes. "That was work," he said, waving the cell phone at him. "They're asking me to fly a doctor to a town up north. Some kind of medical emergency." He put the phone away in his back pocket as he shook his head. "I promised your mom I'd take you in on your first day of school. You know, to show you around and all that. But now this came up..."

Ben studied his host's genuinely concerned face and said hurriedly, "It's ok. I can manage. I know what a school looks like." He tried to sound sincere, but an image of his old school and the two bullies, Peter and Mason, flickered through his mind.

He could tell that Thomas wasn't convinced. "I don't know. I promised your mom. Plus, we want to be able to face any awkward questions together." He bit his inner lip while he thought. "You could start tomorrow instead."

Ben considered this for a moment. Facing a whole class of

new students did not sound particularly inviting, but spending a day alone with his thoughts was even less so. He breathed deeply to give himself courage.

Might as well get it over with.

"No, it's okay, really. You already took care of the administrative stuff, right?" When Thomas nodded, Ben continued, "So it's fine. I'm almost thirteen, you know? I'll find my way around. And if they ask anything, I'll tell them to contact you."

Thomas placed his empty cup in the dishwasher and beamed. "All right, kiddo. Gotta get those neurons working, eh?" He chuckled warmly as he headed out of the kitchen.

In the short week they had spent with the forty-three-year-old man, Ben had learned that their kind host was never one to worry for too long. He hoped the man's positive attitude would brush off on him. As a witness of *The Cosmic Fall*, who had had to give up his job as a postal worker in the town of Chilliwack and who had had to flee government intrusion by moving east to begin a new life, Ben considered that Thomas Nombeko had done quite well for himself.

After swooping Ben, Laura, Mesmo and Tike off Susan Pickering's island, Thomas had explained how he had been taking intensive flying lessons in Chilliwack before his life was turned upside down by the events that took place there. Yet, *The Cosmic Fall* had ultimately allowed him to fulfil his life-long dream of becoming a pilot. He had ended up in the small town of Canmore, on the edge of the Canadian Rocky Mountains in the Province of Alberta, where the local Canmore Air Company was swift to hire him after he proved his flying skills. Ben laughed inwardly as he remembered the panicked look on Mesmo's face at the words "flying skills" while the hydroplane took them low along the West Coast to escape radar detection.

Thomas appeared in the kitchen doorway, covered in a thick, knee-length winter jacket, gloves and knitted hat. “Are you done with that yet?” he said, pulling Ben out of his thoughts and indicating his half-eaten piece of bread. “We have to get going.”

Ben blinked, stuffing the rest in his mouth. “Wha’? A’ready?” He glanced at the clock on the wall. It was still early.

Thomas burst into laughter, showing his pearl-white teeth. “Have you looked outside yet, kiddo?”

Ben gulped down his milk and placed the cup in the dishwasher, glancing through the kitchen window as he did so. Everything was white.

“Oh!” he exclaimed, understanding Thomas’ hurry.

“Yes, ‘oh’ is right.” Thomas chuckled. “I’m going to need your help clearing the car out of the driveway. The sky dumped six inches of snow on us during the night. You’d better get used to it. They say we’re headed into an unusually cold winter.”

Ben opened the fridge door hurriedly. “Okay, give me a minute, I’ll be right out.” He’d forgotten he’d need to make his lunch. This going-back-to-school business was going to take some getting used to. He suddenly felt like he’d been thrown through a hurricane these past months and hadn’t quite landed on his feet yet.

Inside the fridge were several small plastic containers with food in them and a post-it with a smiley face drawn on it. Ben felt a rush of warmth as he took out the neatly packed lunch.

“Thanks, Mom,” he said to himself with a smile.

He placed everything in a backpack Thomas had lent him, then rushed to the front door before realizing he still had to put on his snow gear.

Sure, it snowed back west where he came from, but it only felt like yesterday since he had been spending his summer vacation at his grandfather's house. Now he was suddenly thrust into sub-zero temperatures and needed to think in terms of dark, gloomy days. He felt a pang of worry as he imagined himself sitting for hours in a new classroom while he tried not to think about everything that had happened to him, and everything that could still happen. He pushed the thought away and concentrated on pulling on his snow boots, warm jacket, scarf and gloves.

"C'mon, Tike," he said to the dog as he heaved his backpack on his shoulder. Leaving Tike behind did not even cross Ben's mind.

He opened the front door and was greeted with a street lined with townhouses, parked cars and snow-covered walkways. The snow removal trucks had already cleared most of the town, but Ben could tell that people were driving with care.

Thomas handed him a second snow shovel and both set to work clearing the driveway in front of the car. When they settled in it, Thomas exclaimed, "Hang on a minute! I can't take Tike to work with me."

"He's coming with me," Ben interjected, to which Thomas raised an eyebrow. Ben glared at him to show him that that was the end of the discussion.

Thomas shrugged. "Fine by me," he said as he moved the car into the street. "Just remember it's a twenty-minute walk if they send you home. There's a bus, too. It's line twenty-five. You can take it when school lets out. The school said it's only three bus stops to my place." He pointed out some street names and landmarks so Ben could find his way back.

Finally, Thomas parked opposite the Lawrence Grassi Middle School. It was a large, low-lying building with an extensive, snow-covered playground around it. Children made their way to the main door, often stopping to throw a snowball at their friends.

"This is it," Thomas said in a low voice.

Ben figured he was scanning the surroundings to make sure everything was safe. He felt a small shiver run down his spine.

Thomas turned to him with genuine concern in his eyes. "Will you be okay?"

Ben nodded bravely. He picked up his backpack and got out of the car, managing a small "Thanks."

"Hey, kiddo," Thomas said urgently as Tike jumped out of the car after the boy. Ben bent his head to look at the man in the driver's seat. "What's your name?" Thomas asked.

Ben frowned at the question. "Benjamin Arch..." He began, then froze, his eyes going wide. He bent his knees, not so much to be at eye-level with Thomas, but rather because his legs had gone weak.

I almost fell for it!

"It's Ben Anderson," he said with a strained voice.

CHAPTER 3 *The Declaration*

Ben gazed at Thomas, repeating to himself, "Ben Anderson, Ben Anderson..."

Thomas nodded tensely. "Ben Anderson. Not Benjamin Archer. This is important: it's the name I registered you under." He warned. "Don't forget."

Ben could tell Thomas was hesitating to let him go, so he nodded, stood back and closed the car door swiftly.

If I don't do this today, I'll never do it.

He crossed the road with Tike at his heels, feeling Thomas' gaze follow his every footstep. The lump in his throat magnified. How could he forget the story they had made up to cover their tracks and integrate into the town of Canmore?

He played the conversation he had had with Laura, Mesmo and Thomas over in his mind so he wouldn't forget any details.

Thomas had suggested that Mesmo—whom they would call Jack Anderson—was his former colleague from back west. He had been laid off, so Thomas had offered him a job at Canmore Air. When Jack had accepted, he had brought his wife and son—Laura and Ben Anderson—to Canmore. Thomas was offering them a place to stay in his three-bedroom townhouse until the family could get back on their feet and find their own place to rent.

Ben thought it was a brilliant plan. He couldn't understand why his mother had gone crimson as she stuttered to find an alternative story. Did it bother her that much to pretend to be married to the alien?

When Ben suggested Laura wear the ring his real father had given her before he was born, Thomas broke into a wide grin. "Excellent! That's it, then. It's settled Mr. and Mrs. Anderson."

It had seemed pretty straightforward at the time, yet now that he was faced with reality, things suddenly felt a lot more complicated. He would have to watch every word that came out of his mouth. He had no choice. He knew that, although his mother wouldn't admit it, they had run out of money. The secret services had frozen her accounts so all they had was whatever bills and coins they had on them. They would have to lay low until they could figure out the next step. With that in mind, Ben entered his new school and headed to the administration, though not before looking for a secluded spot behind the school where he settled Tike with a warm blanket and crackers.

The curly-haired school receptionist peered at him as Ben said dutifully, "Hi, I'm a new student. My name is Ben Anderson. I'm in grade seven."

The woman broke into a smile. "Oh, welcome, Ben! We've been expecting you." She glanced around behind him as if searching for someone. "Did you come on your own?"

Ben cleared his throat. "Yes, my mom had to go to work."

A look of sympathy crossed her face, though it was swiftly replaced by her smile. "Good on you, then, for taking the first step on your own. Now, let's see, you'll be in Ms. Amily Evans' class. That's in room 103. Let me get the Principal. She will want to take you there herself."

Ben opened his mouth to protest, but she disappeared into a side corridor, leaving him to wonder for the hundredth time whether he was ready for this.

The school bell rang and a throng of noisy students filled the entrance behind him.

The receptionist appeared several minutes later, followed by a petite woman with black, shoulder-length hair.

"This is Ben Anderson," the receptionist said, waving a hand at him. "He's the new student for Ms. Evans' class that Thomas helped register last week." She turned to Ben and said, "Ben, this is Mrs. Linda Nguyen, our school Principal."

The Principal smiled, studying him with small, black eyes behind modern, black-rimmed glasses. "Hello, Ben. Welcome to Lawrence Grassi Middle School. I was looking forward to meeting you. Thomas says you're a bright student." She shook his hand firmly, gazing at him with sincerity. Ben immediately felt bad about having lied about who he really was.

"Come on, I'll take you to your class. You'll be impatient to meet your new friends." She led him down corridors covered in lockers which were stacked with winter clothes, chatting amiably about the amenities and after-school activities he could join. He was relieved that she didn't ask him any questions about his background. He knew that Thomas had covered the details when he had registered Ben.

A handful of late students hurried to their classrooms, greeting the Principal awkwardly as they passed. Mrs. Nguyen stopped in front of room 103. Once Ben had removed his winter clothes, she knocked before entering.

Ben's heart did a double flip as she ushered him inside. Twenty-four pair of eyes turned to look at him. He fully expected to be greeted by cold stares and sneering whispers.

"Good morning, class," Mrs. Nguyen said. "This is Ben Anderson. He'll be joining you as of today. I trust you will make him feel at home." It wasn't a question, but a statement. She nodded towards the teacher. "I'll leave you to it, Amily." She patted Ben lightly on the shoulder, before closing the door behind her.

Ben's teacher stood up from her desk and headed towards him. She had short, brown hair and a youthful face. Her slim neck stuck out of a turtleneck sweater of a gray-blue colour. Ben liked her as soon as her mouth widened into a smile.

"Hi, Ben," she said. "I'm Ms. Amily Evans, your seventh-grade teacher. We're glad to see a new face around here, aren't we class?"

A wave of giggles reached Ben, though he found they weren't of a mocking kind. Some hands waved at him, and he heard a couple of *Hi, Bens.*

"Let's find you a seat," Ms. Evans said, searching the room. Multiple hands shot in the air as several students shouted, "Over here!" One chubby boy in particular waved his hand wildly above his head. There was a free seat next to him by the window, on the opposite side of the classroom.

Ms. Evans placed a soft hand with long fingers on Ben's shoulder, where the Principal had patted him reassuringly moments ago as if it was some kind of unspoken gesture of comfort used by the school personnel. "Hm, yes," she said. "How about you sit next to Max, by the window?"

Ben nodded. He didn't trust using his voice yet. He made his way to his new spot, noticing the wide eyes and shy smiles from the other students on the way.

They're as nervous as I am!

It was a surprising thought, and he felt a weight lift

partially from his shoulders.

They mustn't get many new students around here...

The realization struck him. He slid into his seat, feeling more relaxed by the minute. The bullying virus clearly hadn't affected this classroom because he didn't hear any jeering comments directed at him.

"So, Ben, where are you joining us from?" Ms. Evans asked.

Ben tensed in his seat.

Here we go with the questions.

"Um, Vancouver."

"Ah!" Ms. Evans exclaimed knowingly. "I bet it's not as snowy as it is here yet!"

Ben shook his head, smiling. It would be several weeks—even months—before snow reached the West Coast.

Ms. Evans addressed the class. "It's not easy changing schools in the middle of the year so I expect everyone to lend a hand if Ben needs it. Let's show him some Canmore hospitality, all right?"

There were many nods of agreement.

"Ben, we have to get on with the class. Follow as best you can and come and see me during the first break please," Ms. Evans instructed.

Ben nodded, exhaling silently.

This isn't too bad, after all.

* * *

By the time the last hour of class began, Ben felt as though the day had gone by in a blur. A considerable amount of information had been dumped on him, though everyone—teachers and students alike—had reassured him that he could ask questions or come to them for help anytime.

At lunch in the bright, roomy cafeteria, most of his classmates had hovered around him and fought about who would sit next to him. They had bombarded him with questions about his previous school and why he had moved to such a small town in the middle of the school year. Ben had fed them the story he had practiced with Thomas and Laura, though fortunately, they interrupted him so often that he hadn't gotten much of a chance to answer everything properly—which suited him fine.

Now, as he stared at the snowy landscape from his classroom window, he realized it had been strangely comforting to refer to Mesmo as his dad. He had never had the opportunity to call anyone *Dad* before since his own father had passed away in a car crash after his birth. Referring to someone as *Dad* stirred unknown feelings in him, even if the whole story was just pretence.

He blinked as he realized the teacher was already talking.

"...Declaration of Human Rights," Ms. Evans said, as she finished writing a website on the blackboard.

Ben straightened in his chair. It had been reassuring to find that he wasn't too far behind in most classes, which seemed to please his chubby neighbour greatly, as the boy regularly peeked at Ben's notes, whispering with wide eyes, "You've seen this already?" and "What did she say?" This material, however, was new to Ben, and he wondered where Ms. Evans was going with it.

She walked over to Ben's desk with a document in her hand as she spoke. "I'm sure you all consulted the United Nations' website, which I wrote on the blackboard, like I asked you to."

Many students scrambled to pull out the same-looking document from their backpacks.

Ms. Evans dropped the stapled pages on Ben's desk, saying quietly to him, "This is for civics class. Try and read up on it by next week, would you?"

Ben nodded and stared at the bold title on the first page: UNIVERSAL DECLARATION OF HUMAN RIGHTS. It was eight pages long and was printed off the UNITED NATIONS website. Ben scanned the pages curiously.

Ms. Evans leaned against the corner of her desk, locking her fingers before her. "So... who can refresh our memories and tell us what are the United Nations?"

A girl called Rachel shot her hand up in the air.

Ms. Evans waited for other hands to appear, but since none did, she pointed at the tall girl. Ben had already identified Rachel as the smart one in the class, yet was surprised to find she was not afraid to speak her mind. In his previous school, the bright students tended to avoid raising their hands, for fear of being reprimanded by less studious companions.

The dark-skinned girl answered with a clear voice, "It's an organization of countries that work together to bring peace to the world."

Ms. Evans smiled at her. "That's about right, Rachel. The United Nations is an international organization that promotes peace and co-operation throughout the world. Does anyone know where the headquarters are located?"

Someone shouted, "New York!"

"Right again," Ms. Evans said. "The United Nations was created in 1945, after the Second World War, to try and avoid such a terrible conflict from ever happening again. Now, what I wanted to talk about today is one of the most important documents that was signed at the United Nations by almost all the countries in the world." She waved the document at them.

"It is called the Universal Declaration of Human Rights. It

contains thirty articles, which apply to all human beings. Since I'm sure you've all read the articles like I asked you to, maybe we could help Ben here by sharing some of them with him?"

Some students fidgeted in their seats, while others glanced at the pages hurriedly. Rachel's hand shot in the air again.

"Yes, Rachel?"

"The thirty articles talk about how people's rights must be protected. Like the right to freedom or the right to life," Rachel explained proudly.

Ms. Evans agreed. "Yes. Each and every one of us has fundamental rights that must be protected at all costs. We take for granted that we can go to school, go home to our families, travel freely to other countries or feel safe in the presence of the law. Yet you should not take these rights for granted. Many generations passed and many conflicts occurred before these rights were finally written down. Now, let's talk about these thirty articles. What types of rights do you think need protection?"

Some hands went in the air.

"The right to vote?" a girl called Kimberly said from the front row.

"Very good." Ms. Evans approved. "We all have the right to elect people that we would like to represent us in our government. Did you know that women weren't allowed to vote until the 1920's? And that there are still countries where women are not allowed to vote?"

"Children aren't allowed to vote!" a boy called Tyler noted. Everyone laughed.

"Hold on a second!" Ms. Evans smiled. "That is actually an excellent point, Tyler. Do you think children should be allowed to vote?"

"Sure!" He grinned. More laughter.

"Then why do you think they are not allowed to vote?" Ms. Evans asked.

Tyler shrugged.

Rachel had her hand up and answered before Ms. Evans had time to pick her. "Because you have to be eighteen to vote. You have to be a responsible adult."

Ms. Evans agreed. "That's right. This is an interesting topic which we will talk about later. But let's get back to our fundamental rights. What types of things do you take for granted, but would be afraid of losing?"

Only Rachel's hand was in the air. Most other students pouted at the document on their desk.

"My family?" someone ventured.

Ms. Evans agreed. "Yes, we all have the fundamental right to form a family and to live with our parents, brothers and sisters, husband or wife. No one may threaten our family. No one has the right to impose marriage on you, either. There must be mutual consent: both must agree to marry."

Ben saw Tyler make a vomiting gesture. His friend Wes sniggered beside him.

"What else?" Ms. Evans asked.

There were hesitant faces, so Ms. Evans said, "What about the right to life and freedom that Rachel mentioned earlier? Let's read Article 1 of the Declaration. 'All human beings are born free and equal in dignity and rights.' Or listen to this one. 'No one shall be held a slave or tortured.' It took thousands of activists and hundreds of years to abolish slavery and protect freedom. The freedom to move around, to think freely, to choose your religion, to travel to another country without being afraid of imprisonment..." All eyes were fixated on their teacher.

"Here's another one related to freedom. 'No one shall be subjected to arbitrary arrest, detention or exile,' and, 'Everyone charged with a penal offence has the right to be presumed innocent until proved guilty.' I want you to think about this for a minute. Do you have any idea what this means?"

The students hung onto the teacher's every word.

"It means no one can be arrested and put into jail without proof of wrong-doing. The police need to find concrete proof that you did something very evil before they can arrest you. Unfortunately, there are countries where the opposite happens: first you are arrested and, while you are in jail, you must provide proof that you are innocent! In other words, you are presumed guilty until proved innocent! Can you imagine how scary that is? How can you defend yourself for something you didn't do, if you are already in prison?

"You see how important this document is? It protects all human beings from suffering unjustly. So let's see, what else should we be protected from?" She paused, but since no one spoke, she added, "What would you like to be protected from? What makes you afraid?"

Some students started chatting.

"War," one of them said.

"Losing my house."

"Starvation."

"Not being allowed to go to school." That was Rachel, of course.

"Monsters under my bed," Wes muttered.

Everyone burst out laughing.

"I hate spiders," Kimberly, who was playing with her long ponytail and munching on a piece of chewing-gum, told her two friends. Her comment carried over the laughter, triggering more guffaws and babbling, and suddenly the tenseness in the classroom evaporated.

Ben glanced at the teacher, thinking she would be upset at

having lost the students' attention. Instead, Ms. Evans watched with a small smile as conversation erupted through the room. Kimberly, Alice and Joelle were three tight-knit girlfriends who Ben took to be the reasonably well-behaved lot. They spent most of their time chatting about their impeccable braids and ponytails, trendy clothing and lightly visible make-up. He had already gathered that they were not usually amused by the two boys, Wes and Tyler's, comments, which they apparently thought were childish and annoying.

Ms. Evans clapped her hands. "Okay, kids! It sounds like we're going to have to create a new Declaration. The Lawrence Grassi Declaration of Human Rights." She wrote on the blackboard. ARTICLE 31. NO ONE SHALL BE SUBJECTED TO THE FEAR OF LIVING WITH A MONSTER UNDER THEIR BED.

Giggles.

Ms. Evans turned around. "So, who's next?"

Ben grinned. Max had told him over lunch that Ms. Evans was the favourite teacher in the school. He understood why and admired her ability to veer the babbling back to the subject at hand.

"No one shall be subjected to the fear of snakes," someone said.

"Very good." Ms. Evans smiled.

Ben's neighbour ventured, "No one shall be subjected to thunder and lightning."

"Everyone has the right to sleep in on Sundays," Tyler shouted gleefully, triggering hoots of laughter.

A voice broke through the noise. "No one shall be subject to the fear of abandonment."

The laughter died down, and everyone turned to see who had spoken.

Ben spotted a girl wearing black clothes and a black beanie hat sitting, motionless, with her arms crossed before her. Her eyes were hidden behind soblack bangs that reached down to her chin in such a way that it was hard to tell what she actually looked like. He hadn't noticed her before.

"Kimi? Were you sharing your article with us?" Ms. Evans asked.

A silence fell over the classroom.

The girl repeated, "No one shall be subject to the fear of abandonment."

Wes snorted at the heaviness of the comment.

Ms. Evans ignored the rude reaction. "That's pretty deep, Kimi," she spoke to the girl. "We often think fear comes from live or inert things around us—like spiders or lightning—but in fact, the worst and strongest fears come from immaterial things, including from our own minds. You'll notice that most of the articles of the Declaration are immaterial, such as freedom and life. Good one, Kimi."

Ben continued to stare curiously at the girl.

"What about you, Ben? Would you like to share an article for our Lawrence Grassi Declaration with us? What would you like to be protected from? What is your worst fear?"

Ben's heart dropped like a stone. He turned around slowly to face the front of the classroom, fully aware that he had suddenly become the center of attention. A million thoughts flashed before his eyes.

Burning objects falling from the sky. Twisted Eyes. Blue filaments coursing through his blood...

"Uh..." was all he could utter. He sweated profusely.

A handful of seconds passed, yet they felt like an eternity. Mocking smiles were creeping onto some faces.

Come up with something, you idiot!

"No one shall be subject to panic attacks," he blurted.

Scattered laughter.

He kept his hands under his desk to avoid anyone seeing them tremble.

"All right," Ms. Evans smiled acceptingly. "Speaking in front of a room full of unknown faces would trigger a bit of panic, I'd say! It sounds like you know what you're talking about!"

Some of Ben's tension ebbed away. Mentioning panic attacks had been the appropriate comment. His teacher obviously believed he was feeling shy about speaking in front of the class.

"Yeah, I used to have panic attacks," he admitted, glad to have found a safe subject and thinking she'd move on to the next student.

Instead, she said, "Really?"

Ben wrung his hands together under the table.

"You said *used to.* Does that mean you don't get them anymore?" she asked with genuine interest. She must have noticed his discomfort, because she added, "I'm sorry. I don't even know how we came to this theme. We're way off subject! Sneaky kids!" She wagged an accusing, yet playful finger at the class. "It just struck me that you named a fear that you don't seem to suffer from anymore. I was hoping you'd share how you did that with us... if you feel up to it, that is?"

Ben swallowed.

He realized he had expected most people to show indifference to his presence. Instead, it was the complete opposite in this classroom.

And then there was the panic attack thing. Ben hadn't really given it any thought, but the truth was that he hadn't had one in a long while. Had he really gotten rid of them?

Everyone waited for him to answer, so he cleared his throat. “Actually, I think it’s thanks to Mes... um... my dad. When he’s around, I feel safe. I guess he’s helped me put things into perspective.”

Ben listened to his own words in amazement. Did Mesmo really have that effect on him? He had to admit, he always felt safer when the alien was around. Mesmo made his fears seem less overwhelming.

“Thank you for sharing, Ben,” Ms. Evans smiled encouragingly. “Putting things into perspective is an excellent way to face your fears. I mean, seriously, how many of us are scared of spiders?”

Several hands went up in the air, including Ms. Evans’.

“Now think how big you are compared to a tiny spider,” she continued. “You could step on it without a second thought. It should be more afraid of you than you are of it! You see, when you truly understand the thing that you fear, you'll be able to put it into perspective, and you’ll realize that maybe your fear is unfounded.”

Ben tried to picture Bordock as a tiny spider. It didn’t work.

Ms. Evans rubbed her hands together. “Anyway, let’s get back to our Declaration. We’re talking about much bigger things than spiders. We’re talking about protecting the whole of humanity against serious threats such as war, loss of life, loss of freedom, slavery, etc. Pretty fearsome things, I would say.” She picked up a copy of the Declaration. “Let’s read article twenty-six.”

Ben sagged back into his chair, his mind buzzing.

CHAPTER 4 *Kimimela*

Not long after, the school bell rang. Ben jumped as several chairs screeched back, releasing students from their desks. He realized almost everyone had been paying close attention to the time and had slowly been feeding their backpacks so that, as soon as the bell chimed, they were ready to dart out of class.

Pull yourself together!

His first day back at school had been more of a roller-coaster ride than he had expected.

"Are you taking the bus?" Max asked.

Ben looked up in surprise. "Huh? Oh, yes. I'm taking the twenty-five."

Max heaved his backpack over his shoulder. "Yeah, most of us are. I can show you where it is."

Tike.

"Oh, um, that's ok. I need to sort out a couple of things before I leave."

"Oh, 'kay. See you, then," Max said, sounding disappointed.

"I'll catch up with you," Ben offered.

Max's face brightened. "'kay." He waved shyly and headed

out.

By the time Ben left the classroom, most of his companions had gone. He grumbled inwardly when he remembered he had to put on his winter gear again. While he struggled with his boots, he saw Kimi leaning her right foot against a low shoe cabinet, tying the laces of army boots. Observing her curiously out of the corner of his eye, he noticed that everything about her was black: boots, jeans, a knee-length jacket, long side bangs and beany hat.

What a gloomy girl.

He cleared his throat. "That was a pretty deep thing you said—you know—about fearing abandonment?" he ventured.

Her head shot up, and her black eyes pierced him accusingly. "Yeah! Look who's talking. The boy with the super dad. Aren't you lucky?" she snapped.

Before he could react, she placed her heavy boot on the floor and stomped off.

Ben stared at her with his mouth open.

What's up with her?

He shook his head in disbelief. At least that reaction was closer to what he had been expecting all day, so it didn't bother him too much. He wrapped his scarf around his neck, then followed the girl from a safe distance. He slipped to the side of the school where he had left Tike. His dog peeked at him from behind a wall, then rushed out to greet him. Ben knelt to rub his back.

"Hey there! What's that?" A voice burst out from behind him.

Ben whirled around to find a man in a basic coverall staring at him.

"Is that your dog?" the man asked.

Ben swallowed. It was no use denying it. "Yes," he said,

looking at the ground. To his surprise, the man bent to scratch Tike behind the ears.

"Hi, you! What's your name?" he said in a friendly voice. The dog grinned.

"His name is Tike," Ben offered.

"You're a good dog, aren't you?" the man said to the terrier.

Ben watched curiously.

The man stood, then offered his hand.

"I'm Joe, the school caretaker," he said.

"Ben Anderson," Ben answered, shaking the man's hand. "I'm new," he added as an afterthought as if that excused his dog being there.

"Well, Ben Anderson, I take it you know animals aren't allowed on the school grounds?"

Ben looked at his feet. He couldn't picture a day without Tike nearby.

Joe pursed his lips. "Come, I think I may have a solution." He gestured for Ben to follow him until they reached a utility door with a sign that read FURNACE ROOM. Joe opened it to reveal humming machines inside. A whiff of warm air escaped the room. "This isn't exactly ideal, but you could leave Tike here while you're in class. I can check up on him and give him a couple of breaks outside during the day. I don't mind. I have dogs of my own. And you can pick him up here. Just make sure you don't forget him, 'cause I lock up the school at 6 pm."

Ben grinned, unable to believe his luck. "Thanks!" he said earnestly.

This is perfect!

"That's it, then. Off you go. If you hurry, you might catch the bus." Joe ushered him out.

Ben waved, then he and Tike sprinted across the

playground. He could see busses filling up with school children. Max's red backpack stood out in the crowd. Ben headed in the same direction and made it just as the last students settled into their seats.

The back of the bus was rowdy. Tyler and Wes occupied the back seats, talking loudly. Max sat a few rows forward. The curly-haired boy waved and slid over into the empty seat by the window.

"I saved you a spot," Max said, fishing a big bag of cookies from the open backpack on his lap.

"Thanks!" Ben spoke out of breath as the bus departed. Tike jumped onto his lap.

"Whoa!" Max exclaimed, hugging his cookies.

Ben laughed. "Don't worry. Tike won't eat them." He scratched Tike's ears, noticing the forlorn look the dog was giving him.

Max shrugged and dug into the bag. "Wan' one?" he asked Ben while he stuffed his mouth.

Ben helped himself to a cookie and made sure some crumbs fell onto his lap as he bit into it. Tike was quick to notice. As he chatted with Max, Ben spotted a person dressed in black on the sidewalk. A blast of cold air hit him in the neck.

"Hey, Kimimela!" Tyler shouted out the back window. "My monsters won't abandon you. You want them?"

Ben whirled and caught Kimi making an obscene gesture at Tyler. Wes cried with laughter.

"Shut up, Tyler!" Ben yelled. The words were out of his mouth before he realized it.

Tyler pulled his head away from the window, startled. His face flushed, but not with anger. He shrugged sheepishly and closed the window, then flopped down next to Wes, eyeing Ben with a touch of respect. The noise in the bus died down a bit.

Ben settled into his seat again, his arms crossed across his chest. Hearing one kid making fun of another made his blood boil. It wasn't the girl's fault if she was an outsider. He, for one, knew exactly how that felt.

Max hadn't budged; he was still chomping away. He offered Ben the cookie bag. "Don't mind her," he said. "She wants to be alone."

Ben considered this as he took a bite. "What did Tyler call her? I thought her name was Kimi?"

"Kimimela," Max corrected.

"Kimimela? That's a strange name. I've never heard it before."

Max stuffed a cookie in his mouth. "Dats cuz' it's naydiv."

Ben stopped munching. "Naydiv?"

Max swallowed hard. "No, dummy. *Native*, like, Native American. You know...?"

Ben stopped bringing the cookie to his mouth, his eyes widening in understanding. "Oh, I see. She's First Nation, then."

"Only half," Max explained. "Her mom's from the Dakhona Reservation. I don't think she lives there anymore, though." A boy sitting behind them tapped Max on the shoulder and asked for a cookie. Max turned to chat with him.

Ben stared out the window, lost in thought. He recognized a shop window and suddenly remembered he lived only three bus stops away from the school.

"I gotta go!" he said, picking up his backpack. Tike slipped to the ground and caught the last of his cookie. "Bye." He waved at Max.

The back of the bus erupted, "Bye, Ben!"

Ben grinned at Wes and Tyler as they shouted their goodbyes gleefully.

"See you tomorrow!" Wes yelled in a sing-song voice,

waving his arm in the air like a ballerina. Just before reaching the door, Ben saw Tyler shove his friend into the window, so Wes' arm hung limp above his head. "Aargh!" the boy groaned with heavy exaggeration.

Ben shook his head. Those two clowns were rowdy but harmless.

He hopped down the steps, almost walking straight into Mesmo as he landed on the snowy walkway. He straightened to take in the tall alien standing before him.

The doors slid closed and the bus took off in a roar.

"Hi," Ben said through the sound of the motor.

"Hi," Mesmo replied.

Ben ignored Wes and Tyler as they sped by with their faces plastered against the bus window, their mouths open in crazy grins and their noses flattened against the windowpane.

"New friends?" Mesmo asked.

Ben snorted. "Not really," he said, then shrugged. "Maybe."

Facing Mesmo always stirred inscrutable feelings deep inside of him. Chatting about simple things such as a school day seemed trivial when faced with a being from a distant planet who had crossed the universe in a spaceship that far surpassed any human technology. It always took Ben a couple of giddy seconds to accept this information before he felt comfortable enough to speak with the alien.

"Should you be here?" he asked finally.

Mesmo checked his surroundings, frowning. "Do I look out of place?"

Ben considered the alien man who was wearing jeans, a brown jacket and a curious fur hat with ear flaps. Aside from his height and one strand of white hair peeking out from under the hat, he fit quite well among humans.

"It'll do," Ben said. "At least your hat is appropriate for this climate." He indicated the snowy city street. A few pedestrians wore different types of hats to fend off the cold. "I'm more worried that someone might step into you." He reached out and passed his hand through Mesmo's arm. He found it fascinating to observe the fabric of Mesmo's clothes, the details of his hands, the tiny hairs of his fur hat. Everything looked completely solid. Yet—he knew—the man who apparently stood before him was not really there. Not physically anyway.

"I don't remember calling you," Ben pondered, checking that his silver wristwatch with the spirit portal was still safely attached to his arm.

Mesmo gave him a small smile. "You don't need to. Our bond is growing stronger. The portal is now always open to me. I can come and go as I please."

Ben stared at the snow, wondering whether he liked that piece of information or not. "Let's go," he said, subdued.

They walked side by side towards Thomas' house.

Footprints.

The word formed in Ben's mind, making him glance back.

Tike stared at him, then sniffed at the snow.

"Oh!" Ben exclaimed. "You're not leaving any footprints!" Both he and Mesmo observed the ground behind them. There was only one set of footprints in the snow and they belonged to Ben. He stared at the alien quizzically.

Mesmo smiled. "Well now, that is something I can remedy." A soft glow appeared around his hands, and as he put one foot in front of the other, the snow under his feet melted.

Ben watched the patches of walkway appearing next to his own footprints.

Of course! Mesmo can manipulate water, and snow IS water!

He grinned and nodded approvingly. "Cool!"

CHAPTER 5 *The Crow*

The weeks would have gone by smoothly if it hadn't been for what happened on a Tuesday morning.

Ben got used to catching up on homework, helping Max understand assignments and the three girlfriends—Alice, Joelle and Kimberly—making annoyed comments when Tyler and Wes cracked rude jokes in class. The gloomy girl, Kimi, brooded at the back of the class and avoided contact with anyone. But all in all, Ben was quite content going about his normal school activities with his friendly classmates.

The problem, however, didn't come from school. It came from an entirely unexpected source. And that source was Tike.

Never in a million years would Ben have thought that he'd have any kind of issue with his four-legged friend, but that Tuesday morning, something that he had refused to accept so far was thrust into the light.

He was running late and hurriedly finished lacing his snow boots to his feet.

Drats! I forgot my gloves upstairs!

He considered untying the boots again so he wouldn't dirty the carpet but then decided against it. He'd have to do without gloves that day. He zipped his jacket, thrust his backpack on his shoulder and shoved the key into the front door to lock it.

"Tike!" he called, realizing the dog was still inside.

His terrier zipped through the door to join him outside and wagged his tail enthusiastically, Ben's gloves clamped in his mouth.

Ben stiffened. Had he spoken aloud when he remembered his gloves? He was pretty sure he hadn't. He reached out to take the gloves from Tike's mouth, but froze again. A blue halo of light surrounded his hand. He jumped back, staring at it in fright. He heard the blood rushing to his ears, and his heart began to thump harder.

Thud-thud, thud-thud.

He shut his eyes tight and shook his head—as if that would rid him of a reality he refused to accept.

He already knew that Tike was trying to use the alien skill to communicate with him. He had suspected it for quite some time, but no matter how wonderful the idea seemed, he would not, could not, accept it, for accepting it meant opening up to the alien poison in his blood. It meant accepting that he was becoming an anomaly, a mutated being that was neither human nor alien. Hadn't Inspector Hao glimpsed Ben's true self when he had said, "I know what you are!"

Not *who.* But *what.*

He was turning into a *thing.*

"Hey, kiddo! Time to go!" Thomas called from the driveway.

Ben held his glowing hands close to his body, nodding vaguely in Thomas' direction. He noticed that Tike was no longer wagging his tail, but stared at him curiously. Ben found he could not stare back at his own dog. He concentrated on putting on his gloves, his brain fighting to shut Tike out, and in so doing, shut out the skill.

I have to ignore it.

That was his only remedy. If he ignored the skill's existence, there was a chance it would weaken. Maybe it would even disappear altogether. The problem with that strategy was this: he would have to ignore Tike as well.

Ben didn't think about it further until he picked up Tike after school. The sight of his dog brought the incident back to his mind and he found himself reluctant to look at Tike's eyes. Instead, he said, "C'mon, let's hurry, or we'll miss the bus."

They left the school from the side door, but instead of heading for the bus stop, Tike suddenly darted away from Ben in the opposite direction.

"Tike!" Ben yelled. The terrier was already halfway across the football field, heading toward a row of trees.

"Tike! Come here!" Ben called again, annoyance creeping into his voice. He jogged after the dog, then slowed down when he realized a form was crouching in front of some bushes.

Ben frowned. "Tike?" he said more slowly.

The person's head turned to face the dog, and Ben recognized the long side bangs as they slipped before the girl's eyes. Kimi shoved the strand of hair behind her ear and made a gesture as if to block Tike from moving forward. When she noticed Ben approaching, she threw him an angry glare. "Hey! Is that your dog?" she shouted. "Call him off!"

Ben reached her side. "It's okay. He's friendly," he said reassuringly.

No need to overreact.

But she was no longer looking at him. Instead, Ben realized both the girl and his dog had spotted something low in the bushes. Branches rustled revealing a black crow that cawed loudly, thrashing around as it tried to free itself.

Ben's gloved hands warmed abnormally. Blood rushed to his ears, accompanied by a wave of intense fear. Stars swam before his eyes, and he almost retched as an overwhelming pain made his left arm go limp. He dropped to his knees in the snow, wincing.

Kimi, who pushed aside some branches, must have thought he had gasped in surprise, because she said, "Sh! Don't make a noise. I think it's hurt. And pull your dog away. He's scaring it."

Ben blinked tears from his eyes and tried to ignore the staggering pain that drowned his thoughts. He inhaled silently several times, almost drowning in the bird's fear as it coursed through his brain.

Don't be afraid.

He directed the thought at the crow, trying to counter the bird's panic. It eyed him with beady, black eyes, its wings spread at a strange angle, its beak half open. From a corner of his brain, Ben observed his huge self from the bird's eyes. His heart raced in combined rhythm with the crow's. The fear that grasped his mind was not his, yet he felt it to the core. He vaguely registered Kimi speaking next to him and tried to concentrate on what she was saying, though her words sounded foreign.

"I think its wing is broken," Kimi said. "I've tried to catch it, but it keeps flapping around and getting stuck further in."

It hurts!

Ben's head exploded with words that were not his. And searing pain throbbed through his own arm. His heart raced, *thud-thud, thud-thud* and for a second he lost himself completely in the crow's mind. Frantically, he sent soothing thoughts to the bird.

I'll help you.

The crow gave up flapping and regarded him with the eyes

of a trapped animal. They stared at each other, each assessing plausible dangers. The fear in Ben's mind subsided somewhat and he was able to think more clearly.

Don't be afraid. I'll help you.

He sent the thought to the crow again, more clearly this time, and it bowed its head in acceptance. Ben reached out to it.

"No!" Kimi pushed his arm away. "It'll peck at you!"

He heard her as if from somewhere far away. Removing his scarf, he held it from both ends and slowly approached the crow.

It's okay. Trust me.

He wrapped his hands carefully around the tense body, ignoring the searing pain in his arm. With the greatest care not to touch its broken wing, Ben lifted the bird and wrapped it in his scarf. By the time he stood again, his mind had cleared somewhat, and he realized that Kimi was staring at him with her mouth open.

"Wow!" she breathed. "How did you do that?"

Ben hoped his inner struggle wasn't showing on his face. He shrugged and replied, "I have a way with animals, I guess."

Kimi snorted, "Yeah, I'll say!" She frowned, considering him with worried eyes. "Are you okay? You look like you saw a ghost."

No, I'm not okay.

Cold sweat accumulated on his forehead. He felt sick, like his stomach was in his throat; his legs were weak. "I should take it to a vet," he said unsteadily. "Do you know any?"

An indefinite emotion flickered over the girl's eyes, but Ben couldn't tell what it was because her long strand of black hair hid half her face.

"Yes, I know one," she replied without much enthusiasm. She picked up her backpack and added, "Come on." She headed off with Ben following.

He found himself on the very sidewalk where Tyler had shouted at Kimi from the bus several days back.

As if reading his mind, Kimi slowed down so they were walking side by side. "I heard about what you said to Tyler on the bus the other day," she said. "You didn't have to do that."

Ben gave her a sideways smile. "Tyler's a jerk."

To his surprise, her laugh came out crystal clear and authentic. He liked it immediately. "Wes, too!" She agreed, grinning.

They chatted sporadically, Ben having to stop to catch his breath once in a while and to shift the bird's weight away from his aching arm.

Twenty minutes later, Kimi led him away from the street and into a back alley. They passed snow-covered yards and garden sheds until they reached a property with a brick structure that was detached from the main house. Kimi opened a low fence and let him through. Then she fished some keys from her jacket pocket, one of which she inserted in the door lock of the small building. When Ben glanced inside the dim room, he found a curious table in its center while cabinets lined the back wall. A couple of animal cages were stacked against the side.

Kimi switched on a bright, neon light, then hurried across the room to grab one of the cages, which she placed on the table.

"Here," she said. "You can put the crow in the cage for now."

Ben did so reluctantly, ignoring its caws. "So... uh... where are we exactly?" he asked.

She avoided his eyes. "I live here," she said, pointing vaguely at the house opposite the square building. When Ben continued to stare at her quizzically, she sighed and added, "My mom's a vet. She doesn't practice anymore, though. She's been... sick."

"Oh," Ben said, studying the room again. Suddenly the central table, the cabinets containing medical supplies, and the animal cages made sense.

Kimi headed to the door. Still without looking at him, she said, "Wait here. I'll get my mom."

He watched her leave, a slight frown above his brow.

It's as if she didn't want me here.

Pain!

Ben whirled to face the crow in the cage. The blood rushed to his ears again and he could not control it. The crow stared at him with its tiny, round eyes, oblivious to the boy's inner struggle. A cold ripple travelled up and down Ben's back. So, was this going to be his new reality? Was he going to feel every animal's pain and thoughts? He wanted to cry from despair. He could barely stand the feelings of one creature. How was he ever going to survive the burden of thought from the whole animal kingdom? And with each contact, he could sense the blue filaments in his blood multiplying, anchoring themselves into his very being. He still had his gloves on, but he could feel his hands warming with alien power. A wave of nausea washed over him and he had to hold on to the table for support.

The crow thrashed, causing searing pain to shoot up Ben's arm every time the bird hit the cage.

"Stop it!" Ben muttered through gritted teeth, before realizing he was no longer alone. He turned to find Kimi, followed by a woman.

The woman was slightly taller than him, had long, straight black hair to her waist, dark eyes, thin lips and elegant features. She must have been stunning at some point, but right now she wore an old sweater and she seemed very tired. Even with

Kimi's beanie hat and side bangs, the resemblance to her mother was striking.

"This is my mom, Maggie," Kimi explained, sounding as though she was trying to excuse the woman's unkempt appearance. "Mom, this is Ben Anderson."

Maggie stared at Ben with intelligent eyes, then turned her attention to the crow. She pulled the bird out of the cage, then carefully unwrapped it from its makeshift nest in Ben's scarf. Speaking to Kimi in a language he couldn't understand, she examined it.

"It has a broken wing," she stated finally in English, confirming Ben's diagnosis. She gently stretched out the bird's wings one at a time, revealing beautiful, shiny feathers that reflected a bluish tint under the artificial light.

Ben bent in for a closer look. He had never seen a crow up close before. "She's beautiful!" he exclaimed.

Maggie glanced at him. "She?"

He distanced himself from the table. Had he really said that?

Maggie concentrated on the bird but addressed him. "You know your birds," she said.

Ben bit his inner cheek nervously.

Maggie placed the crow back in its cage and busied herself in the medicine cabinets. "You say you brought this bird without getting a scratch?" she asked in English, eyeing Ben.

Kimi stepped in, "Yes, *Ina*[4]. It's as if the crow knew we wanted to help it. It didn't struggle at all."

"Hm..." Maggie said thoughtfully, before adding, "Not many would save a crow. They are not popular animals. Yet they are particularly clever and have a great memory. They live in

[4] *Ina*: 'mother' in the Dakhona language

large groups called a 'murder of crows'." She paused, throwing Ben a glance. "But then, you probably knew that already."

"Ugh! Mom!" Kimi interjected, clearly irritated.

Ben sensed the strain in Kimi and Maggie's relationship. He tried to steer the conversation away. "Can you help her?" he asked, rubbing at his arm.

Maggie pulled out some medical supplies and said, "Yes. I will reset her wing and feed her so she will survive the winter. We should be able to release her in a month." As she turned back to the table, she spotted Tike sitting by the door. "And who's this?" she asked.

"Oh, that's my dog, Tike," Ben answered. "He's a Jack Russell Terrier."

"Yes, I can see that. Six years old, I'd say. Though there's something unusual about him. He hasn't barked once at the bird..."

Kimi's eyes widened. "That's true! I've never heard him bark."

Ben shifted uncomfortably. This was not the way he wanted the conversation to go. He was extremely aware of the crow nearby, nagging at his mind. "Tike never barks," he said vaguely.

Maggie frowned and headed over to Tike. "I wonder why that is," she said, bending to scratch Tike's ears. "I could check him out..."

"No!" Ben interjected too quickly. Maggie glanced at him, frowning, so he added, "Thank you, but maybe some other time? Er... I actually have to go now. My mom will be wondering where I am."

I need air.

He nodded towards Kimi. "Sorry, I didn't realize how late it was. I'll see you tomorrow."

"Oh, okay," Kimi said, sounding disappointed.

Ben picked up his backpack a little too quickly, feeling their eyes burning into his back as he left. He hurried down the back alley and paused next to the side of a house. In his mind's eye, he was lying on the examination table. The woman with the black eyes stared at him. She applied a pressure on his arm that hurt so badly his eyes watered and he retched. He swore he could physically feel the alien venom spreading through his body. He shivered, though not because of the cold air. He was cold inside. Cold from fear.

"Ben?"

He jumped at Mesmo's voice. He held his jacket tightly around him, staring at the alien. "Jeez! You have to stop doing that!"

"Doing what?"

"Appearing out of nowhere like that. You startled me," Ben replied, catching his breath.

The man surveyed him, then frowned, "What's the matter? Are you sick?"

Turning away, Ben said, "It's nothing,"

Mesmo insisted. "Benjamin?"

"I told you! It's nothing!" Ben snapped. He strode off, his shoulders hunched, his hands deep in his pockets.

CHAPTER 6 *Enceladus*

Laura heard the front door open and close. She stepped out of the kitchen, her hands laden with dinner plates, just in time to see Ben rush up the stairs to his room. Laura dropped the dishes on the table and joined Mesmo by the door.

"What's the matter?" she asked. Not waiting for a reply, she climbed the steps and saw Ben shut his bedroom door, almost hitting Tike on the nose. Tike jumped back, his ears laid back, one paw off the ground.

Laura knocked on the door. "Ben? Are you all right?" When there was no reply, she knocked again. "Ben?"

His muffled voice came through. "Long day, Mom. I just want to lie down for a while."

Laura bit her lip, hesitating, then picked up Tike in her arms. Scratching his neck, she reassured him. "Don't worry, Tike. He'll get over it." She headed back down the stairs, adding, "Come on, let's go for a walk."

Tike hopped out of her arms, his tail wagging.

"Can I join you?" Mesmo asked.

Laura felt her cheeks flush, so she bent to put on her boots. "Yes, of course. Let's go out back. There's less chance we'll run into anyone."

Once she had on her winter gear, they headed out through the kitchen door, which led to a small, fenced yard, then open landscape for as far as the eye could see. She gazed at the snow-covered fields to the right, the low hill before them, and an impressive string of mountain ranges to the left. They were at the edge of the Canadian Rocky Mountains, which dramatically cut the skyline with their jagged peaks.

Tike scampered off in front, sticking his snout in snow mounds, no doubt searching for hidden rodents.

Laura glanced sideways at the alien, noticing his grayish skin. She felt a pang of worry. "Are you holding up?" she asked, drawing her eyebrows together.

He nodded but did not look at her.

"Tell me about today," she said. Laura knew he expected the question because she asked him the same one every day. He gazed into the distance, then answered mechanically, "Nothing new. Same, bare room: a hospital bed, a large mirror, cameras in the ceiling..."

"Any contact?" she pressed.

He shook his head. "They pushed the food tray through the slit at the bottom of the door—same as always. Hamburger, fries, apple slices, orange juice... No contact."

"Hm," Laura said half to herself. "Until their boss returns..." She stared at the ground as she walked, deep in thought, going over the details in her mind. They had already determined that Mesmo was being held closer to the East coast, though in Canada or the US was not yet clear. They had figured this out because of the regular times Mesmo was being fed, which was twice a day. Only, they had calculated that the evening for Mesmo was early afternoon for Laura, meaning he was two or three hours ahead of her.

She glanced at the tall alien again, noticing that his cheekbones were more pronounced. *He's losing weight*, she thought, picturing a diet of soggy hamburgers. Something clicked in her mind—something that Ben had said before their departure to Canmore. "I'm turning vegetarian," her son had said. His comment had seemed to have nothing to do with Mesmo, but for some reason, it made Laura stiffen. "Are you eating?"

He turned his head away.

"Mesmo!" she gasped, her hand covering her mouth as she guessed the answer. "You don't eat meat, do you?" The realization sent a shiver down her back.

He still did not face her. "I have no appetite," he said finally. "The food on this planet is strange to me."

Laura stared at him with wide eyes, realizing where his unhealthy appearance came from.

"Mesmo!" she said worriedly, "You have to tell them! You have to eat something! I'm serious! You have to keep up your strength to give us time to find you!"

"I am running out of time..." she heard him say.

"Don't give up!" Laura pleaded. "We'll get you out, I promise."

"That's not it," he said, turning to her at last. "I must complete my mission and reach Enceladus within four full Earth moons. After that, it will be too late."

Taken aback, Laura frowned. "What do you mean?"

"Every two hundred Earth years, the planets of your solar system align in such a way that their gravitational pull causes abnormal friction at a location near Enceladus. This opens a window between our galaxies, allowing us to travel from my home planet to Earth and back for a limited time. That window to my galaxy will close in four full moons or approximately one hundred and twenty Earth sunrises."

Laura sucked in a breath. She hadn't expected such a mind-boggling answer. Once again, she realized how little she knew about this man and where he came from. "You mean..." She swallowed. "...that if you don't make it to this Enceladus within four months, you'll be stuck here for two hundred years?"

His honey-coloured eyes fell on hers. "Yes," he replied.

Her heart dropped like a stone. "Mesmo," she said gently, not wanting to add more to his misery. "Aren't you forgetting something? Even if we free you from whoever is holding you, you don't have a spaceship."

He glanced sideways at her. "Bordock has a ship."

She fell silent, reeling from the task ahead. How were they ever going to free Mesmo, complete his mission—whatever it was—and find Bordock's ship in four months? She couldn't even begin to understand how long it would take him to reach this Enceladus, but anything located in outer space sounded impossibly far.

They headed back, walking in silence. She wished she could tell him something encouraging. About to push open the kitchen door, she had an idea. "What about the spirit portal? Couldn't you send your spirit to your planet? Send a message? Ask for help?"

She released the door and faced him. He stood close and she could see the details of his jacket and the fabric of his shirt. She caught herself longing to touch him. He smiled, and she noticed his teeth stood out pearl white in his olive-tanned skin. The walk in the open had done him good.

"Spirit portals have limited power. Their reach is only within your solar system. The signal would distort and dissipate within the contact point between our galaxies," he explained. "It may seem that my spirit is free to travel great distances, but the truth is it remains bound to the spirit portal. That is why I am always near Ben. I am caught in an invisible bubble of which the spirit portal—hence, Ben—is the center." He shook his head. "The spirit portal is not the answer."

"Fine," she said. "We'll find another way. But until then, you have to promise me something."

His brow lifted. "What?"

"Eat!" she ordered.

* * *

Laura knocked on Ben's door again but did not wait for an answer. This time she stepped into his room, followed by Tike who jumped onto the boy's bed.

Ben's head was propped against his pillow with a document in his hand and surrounded by school books.

"Thomas brought Chinese food. Want to come down?" she asked.

Without looking up from his reading, he answered, "Sure, I'll be right there."

Laura hesitated, then went to sit at the edge of his bed. She sifted through the books. "Lots of homework?"

Ben sighed and sat up, dropping the document beside him. "No, it's okay. I can handle it."

She hoped he would open up more, but since he didn't add anything, she said, "I know it's hard, starting over. Especially in a new school with new friends. Just hang in there while I get us back on our feet again, okay?"

He shrugged. "Actually, it's not too bad. They've been pretty friendly so far."

Laura nodded. "Same here. I'm beginning to like this town."

"Me, too." Ben's brief smile disappeared.

"Is something the matter?" she asked, reading his face like it was her own. She touched his left arm, but he pulled it away and she thought she saw him wince.

"I'm fine."

She noticed he wouldn't meet her eyes.

"It's just," he hesitated, searching for words. "I'm not sure where I belong."

"I know," Laura said, staring at the floor. "I feel the same." Their eyes finally met. "It's normal to feel like that, at your age," she added. "But our situation obviously doesn't help." She patted his leg. "I promise I'll find us a place where we can belong."

His eyes lowered.

"Look at me," she said. He did. "I promise you," she insisted. "Do you believe me?"

He nodded, but his eyes had drifted away again.

As she descended the stairs, Laura found Mesmo and Thomas bending towards each other, concentrated on a deep conversation. When they heard her approach, they distanced themselves, and the frown on Thomas' brow disappeared. He broke into a grin and he clapped his hands. "Come on, dinner is getting cold!"

CHAPTER 7 *Gift*

A week later, Ben found Ms. Evans with a smug smile on her face. He glanced around at the rest of the students as he organized his pens and books on his table. Several of them were grinning.

Did I miss something?

He figured they had been telling a joke before he arrived, so he ignored them and sat at his desk.

"'Morning, class," Ms. Evans greeted them.

"'Morning, Ms. Evans," the students chanted back.

Still smiling, Ms. Evans glanced in Ben's direction. "I don't think Ben knows our tradition yet. So how about we put some extra effort into it?"

Ben stared around the classroom in bewilderment.

What's going on?

"Ready? One, two, three! Happy birthday to you, happy birthday to you..."

They all chanted extra loudly, while Ben's face flushed in surprise.

When they finished singing, Ms. Evans handed a card to him, saying warmly, "Happy thirteenth birthday, Ben. Everyone signed a card for you. We always sing when it's someone's birthday so you'll be hearing this a lot this year."

Ben grinned as he accepted the card. He turned around to survey the back of the classroom, but Kimi wasn't there. She had been absent ever since the crow incident. He whispered to Max, "Is Kimi sick?"

The round-cheeked boy shrugged. "'Dunno." He glanced at Ben's backpack hopefully. "Did you bring cupcakes?"

Later, after school, Ben came home to a delicious smelling house.

His mom stepped out of the kitchen with a broad smile. "Happy birthday, Ben!" she said, hugging him. "Did you have a good day?"

He showed her the birthday card. He had never gotten this much attention from his classmates before, so this day had turned out to be quite special. He started telling her about it, but loud grumbling burst from the kitchen.

"Are you all right in there, Thomas?" Laura yelled from the living room.

Thomas appeared in the doorway. "Darn onions!" he said, wiping his eyes with a kitchen towel. Then he spotted Ben and his face brightened. "Hey, kiddo! Happy birthday!" He squeezed Ben, then lifted him up.

Ben squirmed. "Put me down!" he protested, laughing.

Thomas put him back on his feet and pretended to have a fist-fight with him. Ben copied him, dancing from one foot to the other, launching fake punches at the man, then ended up on the couch with Thomas tickling him in the ribs.

"Stop it!" Ben laughed until his eyes watered.

Laura grinned. "That's enough, kids! Our meal's going to burn!" She pointed her index finger at Ben. "You're not allowed in the kitchen, is that clear? Thomas is making a pot pie and I'm baking a cake." Her face twisted as she admitted, "At least, I'm trying to."

Thomas released Ben with a contagious laugh, then headed back to the kitchen.

Still grinning, Ben picked himself up and was heading upstairs when the doorbell rang. He opened the door, only to find there was no one there. A whiff of ice-cold air smacked him in the face. Tike scurried outside.

"Tike!" Ben called, grabbing his scarf and wrapping it around his ears and mouth as he followed the dog. Tike tailed a person who walked away hurriedly with hunched shoulders.

"Kimi!" Ben yelled, recognizing the long, black coat.

He ran after her, trying to ignore the biting cold. He reached her and touched her shoulder. "Kimi?" he said again.

Only then did she stop and look at him.

"Hi!" Ben said.

She hid her face behind her long bangs, seeming embarrassed at having been discovered. "Hi," she said shyly. "I didn't mean to disturb. I'll come by some other time."

"No, no, that's okay. Can we go inside, please? I'm freezing!" He stuffed his hands in his pockets.

She was obviously reluctant to accept, but she nodded and followed him back to the house. He took off his scarf, noticing that she didn't move from the front door even though he had closed it. She seemed to want to be able to head out again at the slightest chance.

"You weren't at school all week," Ben noted. "Have you been sick?"

She shook her head, her eyes hiding behind the strand of hair sticking out from under her black beanie. "I had to help my mom," she said vaguely. "She hasn't been feeling well."

"Oh, I'm sorry." An awkward silence fell over them, until

he ventured, "Er... is there something we can do to help?"

She shook her head. "No, it's fine. It's just that, I was wondering if I could borrow your notes."

Ben's face brightened, finally understanding the reason for her visit. "Of course!" he smiled encouragingly. "Do you want to hang your coat here?"

She started taking it off when she noticed the nicely laid table. Her eyes widened. "Oh! I didn't realize you were going to have dinner! Maybe I should go..."

At that moment, Laura stepped out of the kitchen. When she saw Kimi, she glanced at Ben in surprise.

He gestured towards the girl. "Mom, this is Kimi from my school..."

Laura's face broke into a smile. "Hi, Kimi. That's so sweet of you to come by for Ben's birthday!"

Ben and Kimi exchanged a lightning glance. Kimi's face went crimson. "I... I had no idea!" she stammered. "You should have told me it was your birthday," she scolded. "You obviously have plans. I'll come back another time..."

But Laura put her hands on her hips. "Now wait a minute! Ben hasn't had any school friends over since we arrived! Why don't you stay for dinner? We'd love to have you!"

"Mom!" Ben exclaimed, the blood rushing to his cheeks, then he refrained from saying anything more as he realized he didn't dislike the idea. He glanced at Kimi to see how she would react.

The girl resembled a small bird caught in a trap. Ben could see her brain scrambling for an excuse. "I don't know..." was all she came up with.

"I'll tell you what," Laura offered. "Why don't you guys head on up and start your homework. You can think about it and decide later, Kimi. How's that sound?"

Kimi replied in a small voice, “Um, okay.” She apparently liked the delayed decision better.

Ben smiled excitedly. “Yeah! Come on up! I need help with the literature assignment.”

Kimi hung up her jacket this time, though she kept her beanie hat on. “Why didn’t you tell me it was your birthday?” she hissed as they climbed the stairs.

“Because you weren’t at school, dummy!” he teased. Kimi punched him in the side and he laughed. When they reached the landing, he turned to her, saying, “Hey! How did you know where I lived?”

She shrugged. “Everybody knows where Thomas lives.”

* * *

Laura struggled with the icing pipe; the frosting she had made was too runny and oozed down her fingers instead of on the cake. She squealed when the doorbell rang again and stuffed the sweet goo into her mouth before it fell to the floor. As she opened the door with her sticky hands, she heard Kimi clambering down the stairs behind her.

A woman with waist-long, black hair stood in the dim light.

“Hi,” the woman said. “I’m Maggie, Kimi’s mother.”

“Hi, nice to meet you. I’m Laura,” she replied. “Sorry I can’t shake your hand; mine are full of icing.” She let Maggie in, suddenly realizing that there was a furious look on the woman’s face. It was directed at Kimi.

“Kimimela!” Maggie said sharply. “Where have you been? I’ve been looking all over for you!”

“I was doing homework!” Kimi snapped. “I missed school, *remember*?”

“What’s gotten into you? You don’t go to people’s houses

uninvited! These people obviously have things to do!" Maggie retorted.

"Fiiine!" Kimi said in exasperation as Ben joined the group. She grabbed her jacket, glaring at her mother. "Let's go, then!"

Thomas materialized out of the kitchen. "Maggie!" he bellowed. "Is that you? I don't believe it! It's been ages!" He rushed to the woman with his arms outstretched and a big smile, oblivious to the unfolding drama. He placed both hands gently on the woman's shoulders and kissed her on each cheek.

"This must be my lucky day!" he continued enthusiastically. "You won't believe what I'm making! I'm trying out your famous pot pie recipe and failing grandly at it! You're just the person I need! Please, please, help me. I need to know which herbs you use..." He chatted away, leading Maggie into the kitchen before she could object.

Laura, Ben and Kimi remained in the hallway, staring at each other uncomfortably.

Laura jumped into action. "Ben, grab an extra set of chairs. Kimi, could you add a couple of plates to the table, please? Dinner will be ready in five minutes, and we've got plenty of it!"

Everyone pretended nothing had happened only a moment earlier. Kimi hung up her jacket once more, then helped Laura with the dishes while Ben brought two chairs from the upstairs bedrooms.

Aware that Thomas was trying to lighten the mood, Laura noticed he gave Maggie and Kimi no chance to leave the house. He kept Maggie in a constant conversation until, unexpectedly, they were all sitting at the table, admiring Thomas' steaming pot pie and Laura's fresh spinach salad.

Only Mesmo's seat was empty. Laura figured it was best to set a plate for him, explaining that her husband, Jack, was working late. Maggie accused Thomas of making Ben's dad work too late on the boy's birthday, to which Thomas replied that Jack had no reason to complain: he was working in the warm Canmore Air hangar while he himself had just come from a three-day trip way up in the Inuvialuit Region.

Laura glanced at Thomas in surprise, wondering what Thomas had been doing so far North of the Arctic Circle. She had become used to Thomas' frequent absences, as he was hired as a pilot to fly to remote locations. She hadn't realized he had to fly that far away and made a mental note to question him later. She stood up, saying she would bring something to drink for this special occasion.

In the kitchen, she took a bottle of red wine from a cabinet, opened it, then found three wine glasses for herself, Thomas and Maggie. When she turned around, Thomas was standing right behind her.

"Oh!" she gasped, almost dropping the bottle.

Thomas had a bleak look on his face which caught her off guard. "Not that!" he whispered, taking the wine bottle away from her.

"Hey! What are you doing?" she objected.

Thomas put a finger to his lips, indicating she shouldn't speak so loudly.

Laura lowered her voice. "What going on?"

Thomas said in a quiet, serious voice, "Maggie can't handle alcohol."

Laura's eyes widened. Very slowly, she let out a long, "Oh!" Carefully, she placed the wine glasses back on the kitchen sink, then turned around to face him again. "I'm sorry," she breathed. "I had no idea."

Thomas nodded sadly. "Juice would be better," he said, then headed back to the dining room where she heard him say joyfully, "Who wants seconds?"

When Laura sat down again, Thomas was asking Maggie to tell them stories about the people of Canmore, most of whom she had known for years. Both Thomas and Maggie took turns telling funny stories about the neighbourhood, making them all laugh.

When it was time for dessert, Laura switched off the lights and brought in the cake she had baked for her son. They sang Happy Birthday, then Ben blew out the candles after Laura encouraged him to make a wish. When she switched on the lights again, Mesmo was standing in the kitchen doorway, startling them.

Recovering swiftly, Laura shouted, "Surprise!"

Ben said, "Hi, Dad!" with a crooked smile on his face.

Laura cleared her throat, then introduced him. "This is my husband, Jack." She turned to him, adding, "You made it home just in time for the cake, honey!" She moved a chair aside at the table so he could sit with them without having to shake Maggie and Kimi's hands. Laura presented the guests to him while she cut the cake.

Mesmo nodded to them, then turned his attention to Ben. "Happy birthday, Ben," he said, playing along. "There's a gift waiting for you in the yard."

Laura threw him a warning glance, but he ignored her.

"Really?" Ben said with genuine surprise.

Before Laura could react, Ben and Kimi were out of their chairs, dashing to the kitchen. The adults followed.

Laura heard Ben exclaim, "Wow!" as he opened the kitchen door and rushed out. Ignoring the freezing air, she spotted the gift immediately: a very well made, round igloo with a square opening.

"Terrific!" Kimi exclaimed.

Ben ran back, his eyes shining. Breathless with excitement,

he said, "Thanks, Dad. I love it!"

Mesmo nodded. "I thought you would."

A smile crept on to Laura's face. She caught Mesmo's eye and mouthed, "Thank you."

* * *

Later that evening, Thomas insisted on driving Kimi and Maggie home so they wouldn't have to walk in the cold. Laura was stacking dishes in the dishwasher by the time he returned.

"Where's Mesmo?" Thomas asked.

"He's still outside." He'd been outside ever since the children had discovered the igloo.

Thomas headed for the wine bottle, pulled out the cork and filled up two wine glasses. He passed one to Laura and they gently clanked their glasses together.

"Here's to a not-too-messed-up-cake," Thomas said, winking at her.

Laura laughed. "Here's to a scrumptious pot pie."

They each took a sip out of their glasses.

"I had a good evening, Thomas!" Laura said earnestly. "I'm glad Kimi and Maggie decided to stay. It made Ben really happy. He needed some sense of normalcy."

Thomas nodded. "I needed that, too. I mostly avoid town folk. They're too nosy. But Maggie's okay."

Laura glanced at her wine glass thoughtfully. "Thank you for stopping me earlier. I had no idea Maggie had a drinking problem."

Thomas placed his glass on the kitchen counter and began cleaning a pot in the sink. "I don't think she was always like that, you know? Apparently, before her husband abandoned her, you wouldn't have recognized her. She was a hard worker. Her veterinary practice was the place to go if you had a sick animal. She'd take on a lot more work than she could handle because her good-for-nothing husband spent his days on the couch. I don't know what she saw in him. They say he was never satisfied. He always expected more of her and she would try to keep him happy." Thomas handed her a pot, which she dried with a kitchen towel, absorbed by his tale.

"Then one day he packed his bags, went out the door, and never came back. Maggie couldn't get over it. She felt it was her fault he'd left. She's been on a downward spiral ever since. She gave up on her practice, she's given up on being a mother to Kimi..." He paused, thinking, then added sadly, "Basically, she's given up on herself."

Placing the dry pot on the kitchen counter, she observed Thomas while he spoke. With some surprise in her voice, she said, "You have feelings for her...!"

Thomas handed her another pot, looking her straight in the eyes. "I do," he admitted. "I'm not ashamed of it. She's a wonderful woman! She's just forgotten it." He scrubbed a pan mechanically, lost in thought. "If only she would remember who she was, maybe I wouldn't be so invisible to her..."

Laura stared at him sadly, trying to find something comforting to say. Before she could reply, Thomas said half-jokingly, "What a sad pair we make, you and me!"

She stopped wiping the pot and frowned. "What do you mean?"

He stared at her in surprise. "Come now! You read me like an open book, Laura. Don't think I haven't been reading you, too!" He rinsed the pan, shaking his head with half a smile on his face. "Me, in love with a woman who barely knows I exist. And you, in love with an extraterrestrial. For goodness sake!" he snorted. "It couldn't get more complicated than that!"

Laura stopped drying the pot altogether, her mouth open in protest, but when she realized he was onto her, her cheeks turned crimson, and she remained silent.

Thomas glanced at her and said gently, "There's nothing to be ashamed of. These aren't feelings you can control. They just kind of creep up on you until you can't shake them off again." He pulled the plug from the sink, then rested his hands against the side. "We've got to keep believing, Laura. Anything can happen. You never know..."

Laura stared at the window to an imaginary landscape outside. It was too dark to see anything, except for the light from the kitchen and her own reflection on the windowpane. "Mesmo has to leave within four months," she said in a haunted voice.

Thomas frowned. "Why?"

"He said he must return to a place called Enceladus. If he doesn't make it there within four months, he'll be stuck here. He won't be able to go home, ever."

"Enceladus, Enceladus..." Thomas repeated as if trying to remember something. He grabbed his iPad from the kitchen table and Googled ENCELADUS.

Laura watched over his shoulder as the results appeared on the screen. She scanned the articles, one which mentioned an Enceladus from Greek mythology. But what caught their attention were images on the right of the screen. They belonged to a ghostly, grey-white moon which, the description said, belonged to Saturn, the sixth planet of the solar system.

CHAPTER 8 *Northern Lights*

After insisting that Thomas head up to bed, Laura finished putting things back in place. She switched off the kitchen lights, then sipped on her wine, enjoying a calm moment to herself. As her eyes grew accustomed to the dark, she began making out the landscape through the window. To her surprise, she could see quite far, and it wasn't until she bent over the counter that she realized the full moon was shining, illuminating the snow-white hillsides. The glimmering globe rested on top of the distant mountain range, ready to dip behind them and leave Canmore in complete darkness. As she observed the tranquil scenery, she noticed movement on top of the nearest hill. She squinted and stuck her forehead to the frosty windowpane to get a better look.

Two figures were silhouetted against the skyline.

Laura grabbed some dusty binoculars from the top of the fridge and glued them to her eyes. Soon, Mesmo came into view, tall and straight, while before him stood a much shorter woman with a thick parka, snow boots and snow trousers. Although her head was covered by a warm fur-lined cap, her long, black braids flowed from both sides of her neck to her waist. She had a long, straight nose, high cheekbones and slanted eyes. Her skin was creased from being out in the weather for many years.

The pair looked sufficiently out-of-place to catch Laura's attention. She observed them for a long moment, attracted by their curious silhouettes and mysterious conversation.

Suddenly, both figures turned their faces in her direction and she was convinced they were looking straight at her. She shrank back, her heart beating fast. But then she straightened and frowned. *Why am I hiding?* She purposefully opened the kitchen door and glanced in their direction.

The woman bent and placed something on the snow, then turned and walked away in the opposite direction from the town. Mesmo remained where he was, standing still as a statue.

Laura went inside again, grabbed her jacket and snow boots, then headed out the back door. The cold was so intense she almost turned back. Yet Mesmo's simple brown jacket and relaxed stance played tricks on her mind, convincing her maybe it wasn't that cold after all. She plodded forward, struggling to put one foot before the other as she sank knee-deep in the snow.

She was half-way there when Mesmo bent and placed his hand above the snow. A soft, blue light emanated from it, seeping through the surface to Laura's feet. The snow melted before her eyes, forming a solid path all the way up the hill. She joined him easily, finding that it wasn't as cold as she had expected. They stood next to each other, taking in the rolling white landscape covered by the starlit sky.

Laura glanced at her feet and found what looked like a deformed treble clef from a music partition. She picked it up: smaller than the palm of her hand, made from a heavy metal she couldn't identify.

She held it up to Mesmo quizzically.

"Will you keep that safe for me?" he asked.

She stared at the object again. "What is it?"

"Information," he said.

She frowned. "Who was that? The old woman you were talking to just now?"

"She is *Angakkuq*[5], the Wise One from the North."

As usual, his answer left her with more questions, but something clicked in her mind. "From the North?" her mind whirled. "Did Thomas fly her over?"

Mesmo nodded. "Yes. I could not travel to meet her, so she agreed to come. Thomas picked her up at my request."

"Why?" Laura asked, bursting with curiosity. "Why did you need to meet with her? Why do you need this object? Does it have to do with your mission?"

Mesmo stared at her. "Yes."

Laura waited in vain for more, but since he remained silent, she insisted, "Will you tell me why you came to Earth?"

He gazed away and she thought he might not answer. But then he said, "I came to assess the planet. My people have been doing so since before the beginning of the Human era, every two hundred Earth years. Seven Wise Ones report to us from different parts of the planet, from places you currently call Bolivia, Australia, Kenya, Polynesia, Norway, China and Northern Canada. I have met with six of them now. My last stop after Bolivia was going to be China, but then I came back here instead and was waylaid..."

Laura's eyes widened in amazement. "You've been to all those places?"

Mesmo nodded. "I have."

Laura needed a moment to let this revelation sink in. An uneasy feeling seeped into her mind. He had said something

[5] *Angakkuq:* 'shaman' in Inuit.

about assessing the planet, and, even though his people had supposedly been visiting the Earth for millions of years, she had to ask, "Are you going to... invade us?" She had seen enough science-fiction movies to nourish her imagination.

He took in the view again with his head turned, so she wasn't sure he had heard her. But then she thought she heard him mutter, "We cannot invade what is already ours."

"Excuse m...?" she began, her voice freezing as she caught a movement in the sky out of the corner of her eye. Her head shot up in surprise.

The moon had dipped behind the mountains, leaving only the stars to light the white surroundings. But then the movement came again. It was a river of bluish-green light that illuminated the night sky, swaying in total silence like a kaleidoscope from one end of the firmament to the other. It transformed from a small stream to a wide mantle that covered them, flowing and twirling smoothly over their heads.

"Aurora borealis," Mesmo whispered.

Laura's voice was lost in her throat. When she found it again, she echoed his words. "Yes. It's the Northern Lights!"

They watched in awe as the solar wind, which hit the Earth's atmosphere, transformed into a swirling display of colours, ranging from green, to blue, to purple. Its magnificence left Laura speechless. She had never seen the Earth put on such an overwhelming show. She felt tiny before such celestial power. They stood side by side as though they were the only beings alive in this quiet world, and the sky celebrated their existence.

Her eyes slid back to Mesmo. "You know I love you, don't you?" she breathed, the words leaving her mouth in such a natural way, she did not even try to stop them.

He turned to face her. Although covered with shadows, his brows knit together slightly. Was it from sadness? Or disappointment? He opened his mouth to speak, but she interrupted before he could.

"Don't!" she said. Then, more gently, "You don't have to say anything. I've been fighting this feeling for the longest time. There's nothing I can do about it. It's the simple truth and I have to learn to live with it."

She studied his handsome face. "I don't expect anything from you, Mesmo. I know your people won't allow you to love again..." She sucked in air. "...which is something I will never understand... but I know you have to leave. And I promise I will do everything in my power to help you get back home." Her eyes clouded. She breathed deeply and turned to face the landscape so he wouldn't see her tears.

The Northern Lights faded away slowly, leaving place for the stars and distant, incoming clouds. A freezing wind picked up around them, seeping through their invisible cocoon.

"Laura," he said.

She struggled to look at him, not wanting him to see her so vulnerable. When she faced him, she noticed that his eyes were sparkling. Was he crying, too?

He stated in a clear voice, "I cannot love you."

They held each other's gaze for the longest moment, like an invisible bond drawing them together. Then, without warning, he closed his tired eyes and disappeared.

Laura gasped at the sudden, cold void before her. The wind whipped at her face, freezing her ears and nose. With a heavy heart, she abandoned the hilltop and trudged back to the house, holding the alien object tightly. And all the while, she pondered the hidden meaning behind Mesmo's words, when he had purposefully said, "I *cannot* love you," instead of "I *do not* love you."

* * *

In a high-rise of Phoenix City, sprawled in the Arizona desert, a stocky man typed a password on his laptop. The screen wavered before revealing black-and-white images. The camera that filmed the images was placed in the top corner of a bare room. A hospital bed was the only furniture. A tall man lay on it.

The stocky man adjusted his Gucci glasses before his small, green eyes before using the mouse on his laptop to zoom in on the sleeping man's face, then waited expectantly. Soon, the sleeping man's eyes fluttered open. He remained lying still for some time before pushing himself up into a sitting position with difficulty. Even on the black-and-white image, his white hair contrasted with his darker tan and eyes. After remaining that way for several minutes, the subject being watched so intently carefully got off the bed, then took a few paces around the room, rubbing his face with his hands.

He seemed to notice a food tray that had been shoved under the only door in the room and stared at it for some time, before reaching down to pick it up. He placed the tray on the bed and poked unenthusiastically at its contents. Finally, he picked up the hamburger and took a small bite.

A distant voice came through the computer. "Boss, are you watching this?"

The stocky man knitted his thick black and grey eyebrows, unhappy at the interruption. "Of course, I am!" he said icily. "The question is, what am I to make of it?"

The voice said neutrally, "He's getting better. Whatever it is he's doing during his blackouts is working. We held off the feeding tube as long as we could. The invasive procedure could have set his heart racing again. So this is a good sign."

"Is it?" The green-eyed man asked as the air conditioning

started blowing through his curly black and grey hair. “I don’t trust him,” he stated. “For all we know, these blackouts could be his way of reaching out for help. We don’t know what he’s capable of.”

There was a silence at the other end, then the contact said, “There’s not much we can do except monitor him until you return.” There was a pause, then the voice asked, “How’s it going on your end, Boss?”

The man sitting in the Phoenix office stretched out the fingers of his left hand which held a golden ring on the index finger. “We’re good for now,” he said. “Our partners will hold off. But I must get answers when I return or things will get ugly.”

The far away contact asked carefully, “What if he doesn’t have answers?”

The stocky man snapped, “Of course he has answers! You don’t cross half the universe without that type of knowledge! Mark my words: that alien has the information I need, and he will give it to me!”

CHAPTER 9 *Cold Friendships*

Wes and Tyler ambushed them on a Monday afternoon in early February. By the time Christmas break had come and gone, Ben and Kimi had forged a strong friendship and he had long since grown accustomed to walking home with her instead of taking the bus. Sometimes she would drop by Thomas' house so they could do their homework together, or they would take Tike for a long walk. Ben knew he was clinging on to Kimi, first and foremost because he enjoyed her company, but also because she kept both his feet on the ground. With her, Ben remembered to be a student, a friend, and, basically, an ordinary boy going about his normal teen business.

It happened just as they reached the school field bordered by a group of pine trees.

"Aargh!" Ben yelled when a freezing snowball smacked him in the back of his neck. He barely had time to turn to search for the culprit, when Kimi's backpack was struck by another snowball. They heard laughter and spotted Wes and Tyler peeking out from behind the trees.

"Take cover!" Kimi shouted as they were pelted by another batch of snowballs.

They searched for safety but found none, so they scooped up snow themselves and aimed at the two hidden boys. But their efforts were useless; Wes and Tyler had the advantage of cover and a stack of ammunition.

Kimi howled at the top of her voice and charged towards the attackers. The two boys threw their remaining snowballs at her until she fell headfirst into the snow. Then, they hooted with laughter.

"Whoa!" Tyler shouted when he saw Kimi getting up again.

"She's crazy! Run for it!" Wes yelled.

The boys made their escape, laughing loudly.

Ben caught up with Kimi. "Are you okay?" he asked, unable to wipe a big grin from his face when he saw her snow-covered face.

"What?" she retorted. "I scared them off, didn't I?" She grinned at him as he reached for her hand to pull her upright. She brushed the snow from her flushed cheeks.

They headed off again, checking their surroundings for another attack. Once they had made it safely to the street, Ben invited Kimi over for some hot chocolate, which she accepted gladly. She was much more at ease in Thomas' house since Ben's birthday dinner three months earlier, and clearly enjoyed his and Tike's company. She did not seem in a hurry to go home anymore.

They sipped on the hot liquid in Ben's room. He tapped a pen on his notebook, trying to figure out a math problem, while Kimi lay on her stomach, scratching Tike's head.

"Ben," she said. "How come Tike can't bark?"

Stiffening slightly, Ben answered, "He was in an accident. I think the shock damaged his vocal chords."

"Really?" Kimi exclaimed, placing her weight on her elbows to look at him better. "I wonder what type of accident it was. I've never heard of anything like it before."

Ben pretended to concentrate very hard on his math book. Staring at the numbers, he said deftly, "How come your mom calls you Kimimela?"

Kimi rolled on her back, staring at the ceiling. She blew the side bangs out of her eyes, then said, resigned, "It's a Native name. It means 'butterfly.'" After a pause, she added, "My mother's name is Magaskawee. She is of Dakhona First Nation. She left the reservation when she married my dad."

Ben considered her reply. "So you're First Nation, too?"

Kimi lifted her eyes in annoyance. "Only half."

"That's really cool!"

Kimi stood up suddenly. "No, it's not!" she burst out, startling him. "Why does everybody always say that? I hate being First Nation! It sucks!" She grabbed her backpack and stormed out of the room, leaving Ben gaping.

* * *

Kimi was absent the following two days. Ben found himself deeply worried. He wondered how he had managed to upset her; for the life of him he couldn't figure out what had set her off. He walked home, lost in thought, completely forgetting about Wes and Tyler until it was too late.

Cries of war surrounded him. He ducked with a yelp just as the two boys appeared out of nowhere and pounded him with snow bullets.

Not this time!

He plunged his hands in the snow and shoved it at them as fast as he could. Soon the three of them were flopping around like fish out of water, their arms flailing as they urgently reached for more ammunition to defend themselves. By the time they were finished, Ben lay flat on his back, laughing and hurting at the same time.

"Ah, this is no fun!" Wes said, grinning. "Two against one! Where's that scardycat girlfriend of yours, Ben?"

Ben launched a handful of snow at him but Wes avoided it as he laughed.

"See ya!" Tyler yelled, and the two boys scampered away, pushing at each other playfully.

Ben remained on his back, catching his breath. A shadow hovered above his face and Mesmo came into view.

"Did those boys hurt you?" he asked.

"Nah," Ben replied as he got himself off the ground and brushed snow away from his jacket. "I just wish I could get back at them, is all."

They watched as the two boys walked away. Mesmo bent suddenly and placed his hands in the snow. A flash of blue emanated from them, shooting through the white ground towards a pine tree next to the boys. Ben swore the tree shivered. A mound of snow released from the branches right on to the boys' heads. They yelled in shock as a heap of snow buried them.

Ben's eyes bulged at the sight. He glanced in disbelief at Mesmo, then at the boys, then back at Mesmo.

You've got to be kidding me!

He fell over in a guffaw of laughter.

Wes and Tyler shouted at him angrily, their honour in shambles, as they struggled to get out of the mess. They hurried away, leaning on to each other, while Ben laughed his heart out.

"Did you see that?" he gasped, trying to catch his breath. "That was *awesome*!"

Mesmo stared at him quizzically. "You're doing that thing again," he noted.

Ben wiped his eyes. "What thing?"

"You're laughing and crying at the same time."

That only set Ben off again. "Oh boy, you have a lot to learn! Remind me to teach you about jokes some time." He bent to pick up his backpack, which he had dropped on the field before the attack happened. "Come on, let's get out of here." He peeked over his shoulder to make sure Mesmo was heading off with his back turned, then straightened, holding a huge snowball in his hands. "Timber!" Ben yelled, throwing the big snowball at Mesmo. But it went right through the alien and landed in a useless heap on the other side.

Mesmo stopped in his tracks, then turned slowly, throwing Ben a cheeky look.

"Uh-oh!" Ben moaned, slapping his gloved hand on his forehead.

How could I forget?

Ben turned to make a run for it when what felt like a truckload of snow crashed on top of him from a nearby tree, nailing him to the ground. He spluttered and coughed the snow out of his mouth.

Mesmo bent over him with his hands on his knees, grinning. "Was that a good joke?" he asked.

Ben groaned in surrender. "Not fair."

Mesmo placed a hand on the mound of snow to melt it so that Ben could free himself. Smiling, the alien teased, "You have the wrong skill, my friend."

* * *

"Nothing!" High Inspector Tremblay hit his desk with his fist. A stack of files slid off, crashing in a messy heap on the floor, while an expensive-looking pen did a somersault.

The sturdy middle-aged man with a perm-pressed suit grabbed the one file that was still placed on his desk and pointed it threateningly at the two men standing before him. "For heaven's sake, we are the CSIS, one of the most respected agencies in Canada. And you dare come to me with..." he waved the file in their faces, "...nothing!"

He paced up and down the length of the desk while Hao and Connelly stood before him, weathering the storm.

"What do I care if you picked up a homeless guy off the streets of Chilliwack? What do I care if he ran off with that woman, Laura Archer? It's the little green men I want! Where are they? Not a shred of hair! Not a single fingerprint! My meeting with the Minister of Defense is scheduled next week. What do you expect me to tell her?' The Americans and the Chinese think we're incapable! We're the laughing stock of the international secret services! If you don't deliver pronto, this country will lose control of the biggest case in the history of the planet!"

The muscles on the side of his neck tensed. "You have one week, gentlemen! One week to uncover the little green men! If I go down after that, I'm taking you down with me!"

Hao waited for the blink of an eye before he ventured to speak, "Yes, Sir!" He understood full well that he could be jobless within seven days.

With a visibly superhuman effort to calm himself, the High Inspector barked, "Dismissed!"

Immediately, Hao and Connelly exited the modern office. Once they were in the hallway, Hao said, "We're back at square one. We've got to find that plane!"

"Yes," Connelly agreed. "And while you do that, I'll widen the perimeter for the facial recognition programs."

"Excuse me?" Hao retorted with an offended tone,

stopping in his tracks to face Connelly. "That's searching for a needle in a haystack. Besides, we already have a team accessing public cameras. That plane is our best bet, and I need you on it!"

"Your plane search doesn't require a big workforce. Problem is, your fugitives could be miles away from the plane's landing location by now. Public cameras are our best bet. Trust me, I know what I'm doing."

Hao stepped an inch from Connelly's face and pointed a finger at him. The other did not budge at the menacing gesture. "Listen here, wonder boy. I don't like you. Never have. Never will. But I run the show around here, and when I give you an order, you follow it. I didn't get to where I am by dawdling in front of TV screens all day. If you don't believe me, you can check my track record. Just see how many criminals I've put behind bars. I did my homework and had a look at your record. Guess how many you've caught during your very long small-town police career? None! Zilch! Nada! So when I tell you I need you to work on finding that plane, you get on board, or I'll have you distributing parking tickets in a heartbeat. Do I make myself clear?"

Invisible static filled the narrow space between them. Connelly's mouth twitched as he glared back at Hao with cold, impenetrable eyes.

"Yes, Sir," the bald man replied stiffly, though Hao could almost touch the smouldering anger emanating from his colleague.

CHAPTER 10 *Ice*

"Ben, have you seen Kimi lately?" Ms. Evans asked.

Ben shook his head.

Ms. Evans' shoulders sagged. "I was hoping she would be in today. You know the civics exam is next Friday, right? I'd like her to be ready for it."

Ben offered, "I can go by her house later and give her a copy of my notes."

Ms. Evans smiled. "Well, if it's not too much trouble..." She handed him some photocopies. "She should study these as well."

Ben took the documents and nodded when she thanked him. As he crossed the school field, he remained on the lookout for Wes and Tyler, but the two had clearly learned their lesson because they were nowhere in sight. He walked several blocks, then had to backtrack when he realized he had taken a wrong turn. Finally, he found a door with a veterinary sign on it that he took to be the front of Kimi's house. He pressed the doorbell, which chimed loudly inside.

A distraught voice called, "Kimimela?" It was followed by shuffling sounds and the outline of a woman appeared behind the hazy doorframe. "Kimimela?" the woman's voice came again as she opened the door. She stiffened at the sight of Ben.

Ben stared at the woman in surprise. He barely recognized Kimi's mother: her hair was a mess, a night robe fell loosely over her crumpled pyjamas which were unevenly buttoned up, and there were deep bags under her hazy eyes.

Maggie brushed away at her uncombed hair with the tips of her fingers. "Hi, Ben," she greeted him shakily, her breath smelling foul. "I thought you were Kimimela."

"Hi," Ben said awkwardly.

Maggie attempted to straighten her clothes unsuccessfully. "Kimi's not here. We had a fight this morning. It's not easy for her, you know, taking care of her sick mama. I haven't been very well, you see..." She seemed to remember something. "Oh, were you here about the crow? I released it a month ago. I'm sorry, I should have told you..."

Ben shook his head. "No, no, it's okay. I was just bringing some notes for Kimi. We have an exam next Friday." He pulled out Ms. Evan's photocopies from his backpack and handed them to her.

Maggie's lower lip began to tremble. "You're a good friend, Ben," she said gratefully. "She desperately needs one."

Ben felt sorry for this woman. She had shown a witty spirit on the evening of his birthday, telling colourful tales about the region with great enthusiasm. Not so today, however. He thought of his friend with a pang of sadness, realizing how hard it must be for Kimi to live with a mother in this state. He cleared his throat. "Well, please tell Kimi I said hi, and to let me know if she needs anything."

He took a step back, but Maggie reached out her hand as if to hold him back. "Wait! Please, Ben. Would you mind looking for her? I'm really worried. I haven't seen her since breakfast."

"Sure," he said. He noted her distressed face and added

more firmly, "Yes, of course! Don't worry. I'll find her and tell her to come home." He waved and headed down the street.

Maggie shouted after him, "Check the lake! She likes to go there when she needs to be by herself."

Ben nodded and jogged off with Tike.

The air brushed cold against his skin. The sky was low and grey, reflecting on the fresh, even snow that had fallen that morning. There was no sign of spring, yet. Ben hunched deep into his thick coat, covering his mouth with his scarf, his toque low over his ears. Tike wore a red dog coat, which Kimi had given him for Christmas. They reached the end of an alley and crossed into a large park. It was a bleak, empty landscape, dotted with trees. In the middle stood a small lake bordered by a low hill to the left. In this white world, Ben easily spotted Kimi's black snow coat from afar. There was no one else in sight as she slid elegantly over the ice. He read the sign at the edge of the lake: WARNING. THIN ICE. ICE SKATING PROHIBITED.

Ben looked from the warning sign to the girl who paid no heed to it. Kimi wore her usual black snow trousers, knee-length jacket and military-style boots. But for once, she did not have her beanie hat on. Instead, her dark hair fell freely to her waist, straight and shiny. Ben realized he had never seen it loose before. He found himself mesmerized by the way it changed her face. She was no longer hiding behind her long bangs, which she had pulled back behind her ears. He could see her pixie eyes and nose and noted with a blush that she was very pretty.

"What are you waiting for?" Kimi interrupted his thoughts. She half-walked, half-slid to the middle of the lake, though she didn't get far without ice skates.

Ben glanced at the sign again. He said loudly, "I think you should come off the ice. Your mom sent me to find you. She's worried."

“Ha!” the girl snorted. “Is she, now? Or did she need somebody to pour her a drink because she can't even stand on her own two feet anymore? Yeah, she drinks, did you know that?” She shot him a glance.

“I...” he began, embarassed, but he could tell she wasn’t even listening to him.

“I’m surprised you didn’t know that. Everybody in town knows the vet lady who drinks! Now you know, too. A regular Canmore citizen, you are!”

Ben, who hadn’t expected this outburst, felt anger swelling as she spoke. “Don’t talk like that!”

“I’ll stop if you come on over. I dare you! Or are you scared?” she taunted.

Ben was so upset by her tone that he stepped onto the ice without thinking. Immediately, Tike jumped before him, barring his teeth.

Danger!

Ben stared at his dog in surprise but came back to his senses. He took his foot off the icy surface.

“Oh, poor dear. He’s *soo* scared!” Kimi mocked, laughing snidely.

“Knock it off, Kimi! Get off the ice. It’s dangerous!”

She shrugged and ignored him, skating further away.

“Come on, Kimi. Why are you doing this?”

She whirled around, her face flushed with anger. “Do you know why my dad left us?” she yelled.

Ben lifted his arms helplessly, then shook his head, all the while searching the park in the hopes an adult would come by and talk some sense into the girl.

“He married my mom because she is pure-blooded Dakhona. The lazy bastard thought he’d get tax privileges by marrying a First Nation woman and grow stinking rich. Then, when he realized he'd never get his way, he abandoned us," she retorted. "He left me! My dad left me because I'm First Nation!" She was standing in the middle of the lake, shaking. "He left me because I'm a freak!"

Her words hit home more than Ben cared to admit. "No, you're not! Don't say stupid things like that!"

"Look who's talking!" she yelled at him. "You have the perfect dad, the perfect mom, the perfect family! What would you know about being different?"

A huge lump surged in his throat.

You have no idea!

He almost said it out loud, then gritted his teeth and balled his fists instead. He breathed heavily through his nose several times, then whirled around and stomped off.

"Hey, Ben!" Kimi shouted. "What..."

Her voice turned into a shriek as the ice broke. It made a horrible cracking sound through the lake. By the time Ben turned to face her again, she was already submerged, her hand sticking out like a final farewell.

"KIMI!" he screamed.

He ran back to the edge of the lake, placing a foot on the ice, but it went right through, filling his boot with icy water. He gasped and pulled back. He went up and down the lake, desperately searching for a way to reach his friend, but all he could see were round ripples on the surface where the ice had broken.

Over here!

Tike had scampered to the right of the lake and was carefully testing the ice. The dog lifted his head, his tongue lolling. It was more than instinct that told Ben his dog had found a safe spot to cross. Sure enough, this time the ice felt firm, for it did not crack or wobble under his feet.

Kimi resurfaced with a loud gasp. Her arms flailed in panic, searching in vain for something to hold on to. But the ice crumbled and Ben could picture her big army boots dragging her down.

"Kimi!" Ben yelled urgently. "Hang on! I'm coming!"

Just as he threw his thick jacket off his shoulders, Mesmo appeared on the opposite side of the lake, the part bordered by the small hill. Ben hadn't reached the middle yet when Kimi sank again.

"No!" he shouted, tearing at his scarf. The freezing wind pierced through his sweater, but he took no notice. His panicked breath came up in steam before his eyes as he reached the broken ice and stared into the dark water.

Mesmo had already recognized the situation. He walked straight into the lake, plunging his hands into it. Then he stared at Ben and nodded urgently.

Ben understood.

I have to go in!

Without a second thought for his own safety, Ben took a big gulp of air and dove into the water. He yelled behind his closed mouth, expecting a heart-stopping cold. Darkness submerged him, yet as his skin tingled at the contact with the water, he realized he did not freeze up like he had expected to. He let himself float under the lake, blinking his eyes open, while bubbles lifted around him.

His senses told him that the water was comfortably warm. He could see some feet before him; an eerie blue light filtered to the depth. His heartbeat slowed, and he became confident that he could search for Kimi safely. He swam up, breaking the surface, and gasped for breath. The freezing air entered his lungs and droplets of water froze in his hair, yet his immersed body remained warm.

After taking another deep breath of air and checking that Mesmo was still there, Ben plunged down again. He swam in semi-darkness, white ice hanging ominously above him and rays of soft blue light illuminating the bottom. His lungs were about to burst when he spotted Kimi some way ahead, her boots dragging her down, her arms reaching upwards, her long hair spread like a fan around her head; her eyes were closed as if she were sleeping peacefully.

He had to go up for air again, then immediately swam with all his strength towards her. He reached out for her hand and pulled with all his might. She was heavier than he expected because of her layers of clothing, but he would not give up. He could see the broken ice above him. If only he could pull her up to catch a breath. Her hand slipped and she started to sink again. He shouted in panic behind his closed mouth, then swam to catch her again. This time he grabbed her under the armpits and kicked upwards.

The surface was so close now. His throat burst with pain as he fought not to open his mouth just yet. He reached out his hand and his fingers closed onto the edge of the ice. It was enough to help him heave both of them up. They broke the surface and he opened his mouth to let in a gulp of freezing air, which cut through his throat and lungs. He gasped in pain, swallowing water in the process. Struggling to hang on to the slippery ice, he spluttered and fought to keep Kimi's head up and out.

He blinked the moisture out of his eyes, strove to catch his bearings, and spotted Tike running up and down the side of the broken ice. Ben followed him, pulling himself by holding on to the crumbling side, trying to ignore the contrast in temperature above and below the ice.

Painstakingly, he made it to the shore, to the exact spot

where he had been standing moments ago. In a last, exhausting effort, he dragged himself and Kimi out, their clothes heavy with water.

A heartwrenching cry came from behind him. He turned to find a woman entering the park. His legs gave way in numbness and he tumbled to the ground as Maggie and Mesmo rushed up to them.

"Kimi!" Maggie yelled in anguish. She threw herself on the ground next to her daughter, patting her on the cheek. "She's not breathing! Oh no! She's not breathing!"

Ben rolled over in shock, coming face to face with Kimi. The girl's lips turned blue, her skin was as pale as a ghost, and not a hint of a heartbeat appeared on her skin.

"Kimi! Kimi!" Maggie cried, shaking her by the shoulders. She frantically performed CPR, pressing with the knuckles of her hands on the girl's chest, then applying mouth-to-mouth resuscitation. She did this several times but was so distraught that she lost energy fast. She sobbed in despair. "Kimimela! My butterfly! Come back to me!" Her pleading eyes found Ben's own. "Please, help me!"

Ben hadn't realized that he was sobbing. His chin quivered with cold, his wet clothes covered his body with an icy layer, and he could not feel his hands. Yet all he noticed was the heavy feeling in the pit of his stomach.

This can't be happening!

His eyes fell on Mesmo, begging the alien wordlessly.

Mesmo stared from Ben to Kimi with calm interest. He leaned forward, frowning, then placed his hands two inches above the girl. A faint, bluish light emanated from them, causing Maggie to catch her breath. As the alien's hands floated above Kimi's chest, he said, "I will try to extract the water. But I can't guarantee anything." He gazed at Ben as if sending him a silent message.

"What are you doing? Leave her alone!" Maggie gasped.

"It's ok-kay! T-trust h-him," Ben stuttered through shivering lips.

Slowly, Mesmo's hands moved upwards from Kimi's stomach to her chest, then up to her throat and her mouth. A stream of water appeared at the corner of Kimi's lips like a snake. It flowed to the ground before turning into a small geyser as the warm liquid was drawn from her body.

Maggie grabbed her daughter by the shoulder and shook her. "Kimi! Come back to me! Kimi!"

The girl made a gurgling sound, then suddenly her body heaved to the side as she coughed up more liquid.

Maggie cried in jubilation, while Ben fell back into the snow, an immense sense of relief washing over him. Kimi's eyes fluttered open and she blinked in confusion. Maggie brushed away her hair which was littered with icy droplets.

The girl caught her bearings. "*Iná...*" she began, her face crumpling. "I'm sorry. I didn't mean to..." she sobbed, unable to finish the phrase.

Her mother shushed her as she held her in her arms.

When she could speak again, Kimi whispered with an emotion-filled voice, "*Iná*, are you going to abandon me, too?"

Maggie's eyes widened. She took her daughter's face in her hands, then placed her forehead on the girl's own. With great determination, she answered, "Never!" She looked deep into Kimi's eyes. "I know I am lost, Kimimela, but I will find my way back to you! I promise!" She spoke words in a language Ben could not understand as mother and daughter hugged each other.

"Benjamin!" Mesmo whispered urgently.

Out of the corner of his eye, Ben saw the alien disappear,

while outside the park, two ambulances pulled up, followed closely by a police car. Paramedics swiftly pulled out stretchers from the back, then rushed over to them.

Ben reacted too late. He tried to get up, but his legs wouldn't cooperate. One paramedic covered him with a blanket, then a second one arrived, and they heaved him up with the intent of placing him on the stretcher.

"N-n-o!" Ben protested, realizing at the same time that he was paralyzed with cold. "N-no hosp-pital!" he stuttered as he struggled to roll off the stretcher. He could see the police officers getting out of their car and heading his way.

The first paramedic flashed a small light in his eyes. "What's your name, son?"

"B-Benjamin A-Archer," Ben said automatically, then caught himself. "A-Anderson! I mean B-ben And-derson!" He tried to get off the stretcher again.

The paramedic eyed him worriedly, then took his arm and gave him a swift injection. "You're in shock," he said calmly. "You're suffering from hypothermia, son. Don't worry, you'll be fine. Just try to relax, okay?"

Ben saw Kimi being taken away on the second stretcher. "No b-blood s-sample!" he managed to utter as he grabbed on to the paramedic's coat. But his fingers had lost their strength and his head swam as he felt himself fall into an induced slumber.

A freak! They'll find out I'm a freak!

CHAPTER 11 *The War of the Kins*

Laura Archer's forehead creased with worry over her tired, green eyes as she stared at her sleeping son. Her ash-brown hair was tied in a quick bun, and she bit her lip as she waited for Ben to show signs of waking. She stroked his hair away from his forehead. The boy did not stir but remained in a deep, repairing sleep. She followed the contour of his young face, which had lost its toddler roundness and showed hints of what he would look like as a man. It was only a matter of time before he would be taller than her.

"Laura," someone called softly behind her.

She turned to find Thomas in the doorway. He held the door open to let in a doctor of lanky stature and military-short, grey hair.

Thomas presented him. "This is Dr. Paul Hughes. He is President and CEO of the Canmore General Hospital." Then he added meaningfully, "He is also a faithful Canmore Air client."

Dr. Hughes and Laura shook hands. "That's right," the former said, smiling. "Thomas regularly flies me to conferences and remote locations across the province. I don't know what I'd do without him."

Thomas took over. "Dr. Hughes was kind enough to offer to check up on Ben himself."

Dr. Hughes held Laura's gaze, then said with sincerity, "I came to reassure you that Ben's welfare is our greatest concern, Ms. Anderson. The Canmore General Hospital will do everything to make his stay comfortable. But I must warn you that your son's heroic act may already have spread like wildfire. We will contain this story as best we can. I have instructed my staff personally to turn away any curious reporters. As a minor, Ben has the right to privacy and his name may not be shared without your strict consent."

Laura felt a huge weight lift from her shoulders. "Thank you. We don't want to become tabloid gossip. I really appreciate your discretion."

Dr. Hughes nodded. "You can count on it. Ben only suffers from mild hypothermia, which is quite astounding considering the time he spent in that freezing lake. I could dismiss him now, but encourage you to stay the night so we can monitor him. Physically, he will be back to his old self by tomorrow, though, emotionally, he may be a little shook up." He took out a card from an inside pocket and handed it to Laura. "Here's my card. Call me any time if you notice anything unusual. It will be my pleasure to help out a local hero. You can be proud of him!"

Laura gave him a weak smile as they shook hands again. As soon as the doctor left, Laura glanced at Thomas. "What do you think?" she asked in a low voice.

Thomas pursed his lips. "I think we should wait. We'll know by tomorrow if the media caught wind of this." He paused, before adding tensely, "But if they do, it could mean trouble..."

* * *

Laura dozed off in an uncomfortable armchair by Ben's bed. She half-sat, half-lay with her head resting on her arm, her legs folded against her. She felt a soft whisp of air on her cheeks and blinked, only to find Mesmo kneeling before her, studying her face. She breathed deeply through her nose and stretched her cramped muscles.

"How long have you been here?" she asked, yawning. She checked that Ben was still sleeping.

"A while," he replied, still staring at her. He pointed at Ben. "How is he?"

"The doctor says he'll be fine by morning," Laura said. She noticed his olive-coloured skin. "You look better," she observed.

Mesmo stared at his hands, then said, "I'm eating." He looked at her with his deep honey-brown eyes again, then added with a small smile, "At least, I am trying to."

Laura reached for his face, then followed the contour of his cheek with her hand. She marvelled at how real he looked from so close up. She could see every strand of hair of his brow, the texture of his skin, the detail of his iris. The thought that he was only an illusion when he seemed to be standing before her in flesh and bone was excruciating. She pulled her hand away and held on to the jacket that she had covered herself with to keep warm, never taking her eyes off him. After a silence, she said, "Tell me about your wife."

Mesmo sat on the floor next to her, leaning his arms on his bent knees. "Her name was Sila," he said. "She was beautiful and strong. She was highly regarded in her skill—one of the best. She insisted on keeping her hair short. She said it made it easier for her to shift." He smiled. "She would toy with me and change into amazing beings, but I would always find her in the crowd. It was her expression, you see. No matter who she shifted into, her mouth always made a funny smile, like this..." One corner of his mouth twisted upwards slightly.

Laura frowned as he spoke. "Wait a minute," she interrupted. "You said she could shift. Do you mean shapeshift? Like Bordock?"

Mesmo shook his head. "No, not like Bordock. Bordock was not born with a skill." His eyes darkened. "So he took hers." He wrung his hands together. "She did not survive."

Laura straightened in the chair, a shiver creeping up her spine. "What? Are you saying that Bordock forcefully took Sila's shapeshifting skill? Why would he do such a terrible thing?"

Mesmo sighed. "I will tell you why." He held her gaze the whole time he spoke. "My people are called the Toreq. We have spread into the Universe for billions of years and are accustomed to meeting new species and interacting with them. We respect their growth and search for identity and strive to maintain a balance between helping out and interfering as little as possible. The Toreq have created many alliances and trade fairly, though mostly we are satisfied with our home planet and strive to maintain a healthy balance on it.

"Many generations ago, the Toreq discovered a new species who called themselves the A'hmun. We were astounded by their likeness to us, though they did not possess highly developed skills like ours. Still, we took a liking to them, and them to us. We felt as if we'd found distant cousins and were no longer alone in the darkness. We accepted them into our lives; they settled in our cities, in our homes, and made their way up to the ring of decision makers of our civilization. They, in turn, accepted us in the same way."

He paused. "By the time we realized they were not what they seemed, it was too late. They had infiltrated us to the highest ranks; they had blended into our families. We had been blinded by our joy at finding a kindred species."

"Why?" Laura frowned, fascinated. "What did they do?"

"The A'hmun were jealous of our skills and of our peaceful, balanced lives. They were impatient and wanted to reach the same results without understanding that only respect and long-term dedication could bring them our affluence. Things went from bad to worse and in their haste to get their hands on what we had, they began to exterminate us from within our very ranks. It took a while for us to realize what was happening. We could not comprehend that our brothers could turn against us like that. But too much jealousy had crept into their hearts and they began to scar the land and snatch things with greed. In spite of all our negotiation efforts, we were not able to avoid the Great War of the Kins."

Laura gasped in horror.

"Both our people ended up broken and barely surviving. Yet the Toreq prevailed. In one of the most painful and shameful acts of our history, we extracted the remaining A'hmun from our cities and banished them by force. This happened countless generations ago and we have grown strong again since then. We have not forgotten our past and have grown wiser than before."

He paused long enough to make Laura squirm, then stared away as he continued to speak. "It has come to light recently that some A'hmun managed to remain hidden among us. The majority of my people live in ignorance of this danger, though a small group of us has become aware that dissidents exist. The A'hmun survivors must have found out that I knew of them. That is why they sent a soldier to silence my family and me. And what better way to do that than far away from home?"

"Bordock?" Laura breathed.

Mesmo nodded.

She closed her eyes. How was it possible that she and her

son had got caught up in this mess? She thought of Ben and her skin crawled. Her son had one of these alien skills now.

Mesmo must have noticed her face going pale, because he said, "You see, now, why I do not tell you much? I don't mean to frighten you."

She breathed in shakily, then leaned forward with determination. "There is only one thing I will ask of you."

Mesmo waited expectantly.

"Keep Bordock away from my son!"

CHAPTER 12 *Viral*

Ben was cleared from hospital the next day, though he found out that Kimi had to remain there as she had contracted pneumonia and had to be put on antibiotics. She was reacting well to them, however, and doctors counted on a speedy recovery.

Ben, Laura, Thomas and Mesmo spent the rest of the weekend at home, flipping through TV channels and radio stations to make sure there were no reports of the incident at the lake. Thomas said that he only heard a quick mention of it on a local radio station, but the conversation revolved more around the danger of people ignoring warning signs near frozen lakes or ice skating on their own.

By Monday morning, Laura told Ben that she had spoken to Dr. Hughes, who confirmed that his staff hadn't had any queries from curious reporters and that he had dealt with the police himself. She and Thomas decided it was safe to go about their usual activities. So, Laura headed to Tim Hortons, while Thomas dropped Ben off at school.

Alice, Joelle and Kimberly, the three popular girls of his class, were the only ones still removing their snow gear and rearranging their hair in front of his classroom when he arrived. While he hurriedly took off his toque and gloves, Kimberly turned to him and said shyly, "Hi, Ben."

"Uh, hi," Ben replied, taken aback by the greeting. She had never directed a single word at him before. He realized that all three were looking at him with bambi eyes and smiles that he could not interpret. Ben blushed and concentrated on removing his snow boots.

As he hung up his jacket, an eighth grader slapped him on the back. "Thumbs up, dude," he said as he hurried by.

Ben stared at him, confused, but the boy had already disappeared down the corridor. Was it his imagination, or were several students staring at him while giggling behind their hands? He felt his cheeks go hot and wondered whether there was breakfast cereal stuck to his face. He checked to make sure he hadn't put on his clothes back to front, but everything was in place. He shrugged and decided he was probably part of some practical joke, then picked up his backpack and entered the classroom.

Ms. Evans had already started class, so Ben slipped into his seat and hurriedly copied the instructions on the blackboard. He was late as well when the lunch-bell rang because he lost time separating his and Kimi's notes and assignments. He was still organizing papers when he reached the lunchroom, which was packed with noisy students.

He became aware of the stares by the time he was halfway across the hall. He slowed and saw students chatting behind their hands with their eyes glued on him. Some nudged each other and pointed.

A whole group of his classmates were gathered together, focused on something happening in their midst. When they saw him approach, he heard them whisper, "He's here!"

Some of them began to clap. Then, to his dismay, the cheering spread to the rest of the group, and all the way to the other tables. In no time, the lunchroom burst into clamour: there were whistles, exhilarated yells and hands slapping against the tables.

Goosebumps rose on Ben's arms.

What the heck is going on?

From the center of the group, Wes and Tyler grinned happily.

Ben's face must have been livid because Tyler exclaimed, "Holy moly! Hang on a second! He hasn't seen it yet. Hey, Ben, come check this out!"

With dread in his heart, Ben made his way to the center of the group, where Tyler sat with an iPad in his hands, which he held up for all to see. He punched the screen and a YouTube page appeared. He selected a video and pressed the play button. The person who had filmed the video was not a professional because the image swayed from the sky to the white ground, then back and forth. Wes appeared briefly in the corner of the video, making everyone laugh.

The white background turned out to be a hill covered in snow, and when the camera peeked to the side of it, a frozen lake bordered by trees appeared. The camera stopped at the edge of the hill and focused on the boy and the dog standing before the lake, then on the girl who ice-skated in the middle of it.

"It got twelve thousand views over the weekend, dude!" Tyler announced proudly. "It's gone viral! You're a star!"

As if struck by lightning, Ben froze to the spot. He already knew what he was going to watch. There he was, trying to convince Kimi to get off the lake, then, just as he turned around to walk away, she fell through the ice and disappeared. There were gasps from his companions. Ben ran back and forth over the screen, then around the lake and across the ice to the place where Kimi had fallen. Soon he had removed his jacket and scarf, then plunged into the water. Utter silence fell on the group as they waited for the protagonists to reappear.

By some incredible miracle, Mesmo was nowhere to be seen in the video, as he had been standing on the other side of the hill. Ben's head resurfaced a couple of times, though he was empty-handed, and there were murmurs of worry from his classmates. But when he broke the surface with Kimi in his arms, wild cheers and applause broke out around him.

Crippling fear, anger and despair washed over Ben in multiple waves.

Twelve thousand people watched this video! Jeepers! Twelve thousand!

The adrenaline of the past days boiled over. Overcome with despair, Ben reached over to snatch the iPad from Tyler's hands, but missed. "Make it stop!" he shouted, as the video continued to play.

By the time Ben had dragged Kimi out of the water, Ben's worst fear materialized when Mesmo appeared out of the corner of the screen. The alien turned his face briefly towards the camera, his distinct features appearing under his fur hat.

"Stop it!" Ben cried in panic. He crushed Wes as he reached over him to grab the iPad.

"Hey!" Wes protested from his chair. He shoved at Ben who lost his balance and fell to the ground at the boy's feet, his back pushing the lunch table aside.

Ben sprang up again, his mind bursting with one thought: *Get the iPad!* As if that would stop the video from playing all over the world, from Timbuktu to the CSIS headquarters. This time he got ahold of the device, but Tyler had it in his grasp too tightly.

"What's the matter with you?" Tyler yelled at him angrily.

"I said shut it down!" Ben cried, pulling at the tablet. Both boys fell to the ground in a heap, pulling and shoving at each other. It didn't help when Wes joined the scuffle.

Like ants drawn to a piece of sugar, a chaotic circle of students formed around them, cheering as the fight unfolded.

Ben yelped when he received a punch in the eye. He must have kicked Tyler really hard because the boy groaned in pain. Boys and girls shouted them on excitedly.

A firm hand grabbed Ben by the collar and untangled him from the other two boys. He kicked and punched at the air, even though Joe, the school caretaker, had managed to get a hold of both Wes and Tyler. The circle widened as they were pulled apart.

Tears streamed down Ben's face. "You had no right!" he shouted furiously at Tyler.

* * *

Ben sat in front of the Principal's office with an ice pack over his black eye—something he was thankful for because he could hide his feelings behind it. A sense of utter despair threatened to engulf him, making him want to weep his heart out. But he couldn't.

Opposite him, next to the office door, Wes and Tyler glanced at him glumly. They had been told to sit quietly while Ms. Nguyen talked to their parents.

"Hey! Psst! Ben!" Tyler whispered.

Ben ignored him.

"Come on, man!" Tyler insisted. "We're sorry. We had no idea you'd feel like this. We thought you'd be proud of what you did! You're a hero, dude!"

Ben pressed the ice pack really hard, concentrating on the pain in his eye rather than the pain in his heart. How could Tyler ever begin to imagine what he was going through? His fear of Bordock and Inspector Hao, which he had managed to bottle up since his arrival in Canmore, cut through his body.

What if they saw the video?

The very thought paralyzed him.

Wes pressed a Kleenex against his bloody nose, and Tyler examined the big bump on his leg. Ben heard him note how 'cool' it was. The bruise had turned purple, green and yellowish.

Like my eye.

Wes bent over to whisper something to his friend, to which Tyler replied, "Yeah!"

"Boys!" the assistant at the front desk warned.

The pair stiffened, suddenly taking a quiet interest in the carpet. Several minutes ticked by before Tyler ventured to catch Ben's attention again. "P-s-t! Hey, Ben! When this is over," he gestured to the Principal's office, "Let's do a revenge snowball fight."

Wes joined in excitedly. "Yeah, next Saturday, when Kimi's better. We can meet up at the Millennium Park."

Ben couldn't believe his ears. These boys, who were in deep trouble, were already planning their next stunt. He wished he could have felt that laid back.

Tyler added, "We can sled there, too..." He was cut off when the door to the Principal's office opened and Wes and Tyler's parents emerged. Immediately, the two boys hung their heads in apparent shame.

Ms. Nguyen nodded Ben over, but just before he entered her office, he saw Tyler mouth *Millennium* at him.

As soon as the door closed, Ben fell into his mother's arms

gratefully. He was intent on hiding behind his ice pack for the rest of the day and let her do the talking. But that didn't seem to be on the Principal's mind. The small woman played with her eyeglasses on the desk, staring at him intently. Ben ended up lowering the ice pack, wondering if she needed to see his two eyes before being able to speak.

A look of concern crossed her face when she saw the damage. "Ah, Ben!" she sighed. "What am I going to do with you?" She leaned back in her chair, her eyes boring into him. "I don't know whether to suspend you or give you a gold medal." She paused long enough for Ben to wonder what her verdict would be.

Her face broke into a smile. "Honestly? I think you're the bravest boy I've ever met in my entire career! You put another student's welfare before your own. You risked your life with no second thought as to the danger you were putting yourself in."

She turned her attention to Laura. "Ms. Anderson, your son truly deserves the highest praise. I'm sure there must be some kind of Canmore medal for outstanding deeds to society. This could go much further than you could ever imagine..." She paused for effect, before finishing, "...but only if you want it to."

She focused on Ben again. "Seeing that video and reliving that horrible experience must have been quite a shock for you, Ben. It's essential for you to understand that those boys had absolutely no right to be filming you or posting that video online for all to see, without your consent. That was a fundamental breach of privacy. And I want you to rest assured that the video was taken down at once."

At her words, Ben breathed a little easier. He glanced at his mother, who squeezed his hand.

Ms. Nguyen proceeded very seriously. "Now this unusual event has sent shock-waves through the school and will continue to do so for some time. It is crucial for me to know your mind on this matter so that I can act appropriately. Would you like to share any thoughts, Ben?"

Ben crossed eyes with his mother, then said, "I just want this to go away. I want everything to go back to normal."

Laura added, "We're not looking for the limelight, Ms. Nguyen. We strongly insist on keeping our privacy intact and would appreciate any help you can give us."

The Principal nodded. "Yes, of course. You can count on my full support. In that case, if we are to avoid any interviews, filming, naming, handing out rewards, or such, I suggest you stay at home for the rest of the week, Ben. You are not grounded, but it's best you're not at school until I can calm the situation down. I will hold a staff meeting and instruct the teachers to talk to the students about the dangers of sharing private information on the internet. Goodness knows, we need that kind of debate in this day and age!"

Ben frowned. "But," he objected. "I have a civics exam on Friday."

Ms. Nguyen smiled. "Well, in that case, you can return on Friday if you feel up to it. I'll have Ms. Evans send you her notes and homework by e-mail this week so you can keep up. Does that sound fair?"

Ben nodded. He glanced at his mother, but he could not read her expression.

"The other question I must ask is something you need to weigh very carefully because it can affect the future of certain students." She crossed the fingers of her hands before her and said, "Will you be pressing any charges?"

Ben saw his mother straighten in her chair. "Charges?" she asked.

Ms. Nguyen pursed her lips. "Yes. Charges against Wes and

Tyler for posting video material of Ben and Kimi without their consent. There's no need to answer right away, of course, but I'll need to know if you are going to want the police and lawyers involved."

Laura and Ben glanced at each other in alarm. "No, no!" Laura said quickly. "Of course not! These boys were just fooling around. I'm sure their parents will talk some sense into them!"

Ben nodded vigorously in agreement.

Ms. Nguyen's relief was visible. "I'm glad you see it that way. I'm not defending their reckless actions, but, after all, they did call 911 without delay. At least it shows their hearts are still in the right place."

Ben echoed her words in surprise. "Wes and Tyler called the ambulance?"

Ms. Nguyen nodded. "Yes, Tyler sent Wes for help as soon as they saw Kimi fall through the ice. You can hear it in the video. Kimi was very lucky to be surrounded by so many good-willed people that day."

Ben sat back in his chair, fighting a grin. Those two boys would never cease to amaze him!

CHAPTER 13 *Breakthrough*

They got home by late afternoon. Ben told Laura he wanted to rest, which suited her well because she needed to consult with Thomas about the day's developments.

Thomas arrived one hour later, followed by Mesmo not long after that.

"Sh!" Laura shushed the men when their voices rose at the news. "I don't want to wake Ben," she said.

Thomas pulled out a dining chair and sat heavily, while Laura finished filling Mesmo in. The television flickered with the volume down.

When Laura fell silent, Thomas said, "It's worse than you think. They knew about the ice incident at work."

"What?" Laura exclaimed. "But how?"

"It turns out some guy saw the ambulances at the lake and figured someone had fallen in. He started a thread on a Canmore community page on Facebook. I read it. No one has brought up Ben or Kimi's name yet, but it's only a matter of time."

Laura sagged into a sofa with her hand to her forehead. "Oh my gosh!" she breathed. "All this time we've been checking

TV and radio stations..."

"...when we should have been checking social media." Thomas ended her phrase.

They stared at each other with a heavy silence.

"That's it, then. We have to leave," Laura stated finally.

"I've already looked into it," Thomas said. "But you can't leave. At least not right now. Two storm fronts are heading in from the plains. Once they hit the mountains, they will dump considerable amounts of snow on Canmore. The first one is due in a couple of hours. The second one on Friday night. We're stuck here for the first one, but I'm counting on getting you out before the second one hits, probably around noon on Friday."

Laura's brow creased. "That's a long time..."

Thomas interrupted. "You have no choice. Flying is out of the question right now. Driving would be insane. On the bright side, if we can't get out, no one can get in either. So we shouldn't have any unwanted visitors until then."

Laura sucked in air, then nodded. "All right, Friday it is then."

"NO!"

Laura's head snapped towards the stairs.

Ben grasped the railing, his face flushed with anger. He yelled, "What about me? Is anyone interested to know what I want?" Without waiting for an answer, he stormed up the stairs and slammed his bedroom door.

Laura put a hand to her mouth. The adults fell silent. Mesmo made a gesture as if to follow Ben, but Laura stopped him. "No, it's okay. I'll go," she said, stepping forward.

But Mesmo was no longer looking at her. Instead, he stood frozen in front of the television. He pointed at the screen and gasped, "There!"

Laura was stricken. "What? Is it Ben?" She fully expected to see her son's face on the news. Instead, a reporter spoke in front of high windows behind which multiple large planes were stationed. The caption read: CANADIAN AIRLINE COMPANY IN JEOPARDY.

Thomas turned up the volume.

"...the Alberta oil sands crisis has caught up with Canada's biggest airliner, Victory Air. Stocks have plummeted, and major investors have pulled out of the company. At this point, it would take a miracle to save the airliner," the reporter said.

Another reporter appeared on the screen. He stood in front of a highrise surrounded by a flock of newspeople and cameramen, who ran after a youngish man to the entrance of the building. The man pushed the cameras away with his hand in an attempt to escape the reporters. This time the caption read: VICTORY AIR HEADQUARTERS, TORONTO. The reporter spoke loudly into the microphone as he got shoved around by the crowd. "The spokesperson for the troubled airliner was not available for comments..."

"I don't understand," Thomas broke their concentration. "What are we looking at? That's Toronto, not Canmore."

"I saw him!" Mesmo exclaimed.

"Saw who?" Laura asked, confused.

Mesmo stared at her with wide eyes. "The man who is holding me!"

"Wha...?" She gaped at him in disbelief. "Thomas! Can you rewind that thing?"

"On it!" Thomas' thumb already pressed the rewind button.

"There!" Mesmo said again.

Thomas pushed the play button. They stared at the stocky man with thick black and grey eyebrows and small green eyes behind black-rimmed glasses who appeared on the screen. His stance was relaxed and he smiled smugly as he shook hands with the President of the United States. The woman's voice reported over the images, "...just over a month ago, the CEO of Victory Air signed a billion dollar contract with the American government, leading economists to believe the airliner was in good shape. The CEO will release a statement later today..."

Laura gasped. "I know who that is!"

Thomas' head shot up. "You do?" he asked, bewildered.

"Yes! And so do you. You may not have met him personally, but you will recognize his name."

Thomas frowned.

Laura sucked in air. "That's my father's neighbour, Victor Hayward."

* * *

Laura knocked softly on Ben's door. She did not wait for him to answer but stepped into the bedroom, where she found him lying on his back, staring at the ceiling. When she sat on the edge of the bed, he turned to his side so she couldn't see his face. She rubbed his back, realizing he was crying.

After a long silence, Ben sobbed, "I don't want to leave."

"I know you don't," she said, staring at the floor. "I don't either."

Ben glanced at her with red eyes.

She gave him a sad smile. "This place has grown on us, hasn't it?"

Ben nodded, sniffling.

"Ben," she said more seriously. "We need to look at the bigger picture. We promised Mesmo we would help him. He's already saved us countless times." She leaned on the bed with her hands on either side of him so she could face him better.

"We've had a breakthrough. I think I know where Mesmo is being held."

"Really?" Ben said, his eyes widening.

Laura nodded. "I want to stay here as much as you do, but as long as Bordock and the CSIS are looking for us, we'll never be safe. We have to free Mesmo so he can go home. Only then, will they leave us alone."

Ben's eyes lowered. After a pause, he said purposefully, "How do you know?"

She removed her hands and straightened, taken aback by his statement.

Ben insisted, "Seriously, Mom. How do you know for sure? I've been infected by alien blood. It's inside my body, spreading like a virus, turning me into some kind of freak. Mesmo can beam himself away to safety, but what about me? What about us?" He shook his head as if trying to rid his mind of the idea. "I don't want it. I don't want the skill, Mom. Mesmo can have it back." He rolled to his side again, his arms crossed over his chest.

Laura's shoulders sagged, Mesmo's words echoing in her mind. Bordock had forcefully taken a skill from Mesmo's wife. And she had died. Was Ben stuck with this skill indefinitely?

"Have you talked to Mesmo about this?" she asked, trying to sound in control.

His voice was muffled by a cushion. "Are you kidding? He wants me to have this skill. He's thrilled that I have it! He wants it to grow strong, so I can use it all the time."

Laura frowned. "Use it, for what?"

Ben faced her with angry eyes. "How should I know? Why don't you ask *him*?"

* * *

Laura shut the door to Ben's room and leaned on the wall shakily. She placed her hands over her nose and mouth and closed her eyes tight.

She had gone to see Ben with the intention of reassuring him, but things hadn't gone as planned.

If they ever completed the daunting task of sending Mesmo home, would the police leave them alone? In her heart, she did not believe so.

And what was it about Ben's skill? Intuition told her Mesmo's interest in the skill went way beyond the fact that it had once belonged to his daughter. "I came to assess the planet." That's what he had said. But assess... for what?

Laura realized how little she knew about the alien whose destiny was intrinsically linked to theirs. Her father's letter warning her about Mesmo flashed before her eyes. *"He will crush you if he feels you are standing in his way."*

Her breath halted.

Would he really do that, if it came to it?

* * *

The stocky man's knuckles whitened as he grasped the side of the table, a large golden ring topping his ring finger. His nostrils flared and his small green eyes hardened. He looked like a bull seeing red.

Before him lay a computer screen from which a youngish man rubbed his pale face. Both men sat at desks though the first man had a view of a sprawling desert city while the other cowered in a dim room that resembled a hospital.

The youngish man blinked rapidly and wrung his hands together before him. "I'm sorry, Boss," he said meekly. "We can still contain this."

"We?" Victor Hayward seethed. He looked like he was about to explode. "Who do you think is going to an emergency meeting with the investors? I have the American military breathing down my neck. They are snapping at me like wild dogs." He leaned forward and said menacingly, "Maybe I should feed you to them instead."

The youngish man gulped visibly. Victor Hayward let him suffer for a bit, then said, "How did the media find out? Who told them the oil sands have dried up and we've been stalling to tell the world?"

"I... I don't know, Boss. We're still tracing the news. It obviously came from an investigative reporter..."

"...who slipped through the security you set up," Victor Hayward accused.

The man avoided eye contact. "Tell me what to do, Boss," he said, resigned. "I'll do it."

Victor Hayward leaned back into his tall office chair, letting air escape his nostrils as if he were letting off steam. "Sit tight," he said. "I need to get through this week, restore the investor's confidence, rub the media the right way, put on an angel face." He leaned forward again and jabbed a finger at the screen. "And then," he growled threateningly, "I'm coming home. And we are going to get down to business. Our martian friend's nursing days are over."

CHAPTER 14 *Rejection*

Ben paced his room in frustration. He would honestly have preferred going to school rather than spend long days cooped up at home on his own. His mother had braved the wind and snow to walk to work that morning, while Thomas had had to wait for the roads to be decently cleared before he'd been able to make his way to Canmore Air. There were reports that schools and some businesses would close the next day if the snowstorm worsened. Laura had told Ben that Tim Hortons would remain open, however, due to the high demand for hot coffee, which suited her fine because she needed to work as many hours as possible before their departure.

Seeing as they planned on leaving that Friday at noon, Ben begged his mother to let him take the civic's exam. Laura told him she did not like the idea, but he was adamant and refused to let go until she consented.

Now, alone at Thomas' house, Ben regretted having insisted so hard, because studying proved impossible. Strangely, it wasn't because their lives had been flipped upside-down, again. It was because, in the silence of the house, Tike was talking to him nonstop.

It started with a nudge in his mind, a playful thought, and before he knew it, Ben watched his hands begin to glow while he sat at his desk.

Tike let him know that he was thrilled to have made a connection again. He wagged his tail.

Wanna play?

Ben stiffened. He could feel a heart beating rapidly in excitement. Except it wasn't his heart. He glanced at Tike who rolled onto his back, paws in the air.

"Stop it!" Ben scolded, his own heart pumping a mixture of fear and blue venom. His ears rang with the blood flowing to his brain.

Play?

"No!" Ben yelled. He stuffed his notebooks in his backpack and raced down the stairs.

Tike followed more slowly, his ears and tail drooping.

What's the matter?

"Don't. Talk. To. Me!" Ben snapped, walking out with his boots and jacket unzipped.

A freezing wind slammed into him, sending snow down his throat and neck. He shut the door on Tike and lumbered down the street, welcoming the biting cold.

What am I doing?

He couldn't believe what he had just done. He had shut the door on his best friend. Tears stung his eyes while he nervously tried to cover his bluish-lit hands with his gloves.

Tike was talking to him through the skill. But every time he did so, Ben knew that the skill was getting stronger, taking hold of him in ways he could not begin to comprehend. Every contact with Tike allowed the translation skill to infiltrate his core even more.

I'll never get rid of it!

He took a few steps through the snowstorm.

But this is Tike!

Why was he making such a big deal out of it? Wasn't talking to his own dog kind of awesome? Deep down, he agreed that it was, and part of him wanted to embrace the skill, yet at the same time, every fiber of his body continued to fight against it—because he feared it. What if human bodies weren't compatible with the alien element? What if the skill continued to make him sick until things became irreversible? What if the skill took over his thoughts? Or worse, what if it killed him? He was so involved in his own thoughts that he did not realize his feet were taking him to the Canmore General Hospital.

Kimi!

He felt a wave of comfort at the thought of seeing her. By the time he reached the hospital, the insides of his boots and the bottoms of his trousers were soaked.

When he found Kimi's room, she was resting against several piled-up cushions. Her long hair fell from both sides of her neck down to her arms. Her face was pale, and there were dark circles under her eyes, but her lips were rosy and she smiled.

"Ben!" She greeted him warmly. "What took you so long? I'm bored to death here!" she scolded, then blushed. "Sorry, bad choice of words."

Ben grinned, a fuzzy feeling replacing the cold he felt inside. "How are you?"

Her dark brown eyes twinkled. "They're pumping me with antibiotics. It seems to be working, though they insist I stay here for another couple of days." She rolled her eyes. "I don't know what I'm going to do with myself until then."

"Well, I know exactly what you're going to do," Ben said, dumping his backpack on a small table by the window. He pulled out his notes and handed them to her. "You're going to study for the civics exam."

"Are you kidding me?" she exclaimed, setting off in a fit of coughing.

Ben poured her some water and waited until she could breathe normally again.

"Sorry," she said with a feeble voice. "Happens sometimes."

"Don't talk," Ben ordered. "Just read."

He settled on a chair next to her, rested his chin on his arm with his notes before him on her bed. She eyed him for a few seconds as if trying to find something to scold him with, but in the end, she picked up the papers and began to read as well.

The minutes and hours ticked by as they studied quietly, absorbed by their task. For a brief moment at least, Ben forgot everything else, until a nurse came in and announced it was almost time for Kimi's dinner and medication.

Ben checked his watch, realizing how late it was. "Oops! Gotta go," he announced.

"Will you come back tomorrow?" Kimi asked with hopeful eyes.

"Of course! I look forward to another day of mutual boredom."

Kimi slapped him on the arm with her notes. They giggled, but that only set Kimi coughing again.

"Okay, okay, I'll behave," Ben said, having finished putting on his snow boots and jacket. "I'll see you tomorrow."

"Wait a minute," Kimi interjected, her face becoming serious. "Ben, Ms. Nguyen came and told me about the YouTube video." He stood by the door and saw her studying his face. "Are you all right?"

Ben shrugged, fighting a lump in his throat. "Sure. It's Wes and Tyler who should be worried. They got suspended for the rest of the week."

"Ben," she said again as if reluctant to let him go. "I... I haven't had a chance to thank you, you know, for what you did at the lake." She sucked in air and added, "You saved my life."

Ben stared at his feet, then shrugged again. "I'm just glad you're okay." Their eyes met for a moment.

"Excuse me," a woman said behind Ben. "Visiting hours are over. It's time for dinner."

"Oh, sorry," Ben apologized, stepping back as the nurse pushed in a trolley. The woman busied herself by Kimi's bed, placing a tray before her and arranging her pillows so she could sit up. Kimi pinched her nose and stuck out her tongue at the food tray.

Ben grinned and waved goodbye.

When he stepped into the street, it was already dark, and heavy snow whirled around him. He zipped up his jacket, covered his head with his hood, and stuffed his hands in his pockets.

"Can I join you?" Mesmo said, coming up beside him.

Ben shrugged and kept walking, though he had to admit having the alien beside him was extremely practical because the snow stopped slapping him in the face.

"How's Kimimela?" Mesmo asked.

"Fine," Ben replied briefly as he struggled with his mixed feelings.

Why is it I always feel relieved when Mesmo is around?

"Do you want to talk about it?" Mesmo asked.

"Talk about what?" Ben retorted. He stopped to face the tall man. "You know what I want to talk about? I want to talk about the skill. You see, I don't want it. I want to be normal again. I want to be me. So I've decided I want you to take it back!"

Mesmo frowned. "We did talk about that. I told you it is yours now. It is a valuable gift..."

"It's not a gift!" Ben almost yelled. Pedestrians turned to look at them, so he lowered his voice. "It's not a gift. You can refuse a gift. But this one was imposed on me. I had no choice."

They walked on in silence, then Mesmo said, "I don't know why you struggle with it. All you have to do is learn to control it. I could teach you..."

"Stop!" Ben snapped. "Just... stop." He stepped away from the protective bubble into the swirling snow, leaving Mesmo staring at him.

With a few strides, the alien man caught up with him again. "Why do you fear it so?" he asked.

"Why?" Ben exclaimed, waving his gloved hands at him. "Jeez, do I have to spell it out to you? Maybe its because my hands are glowing? Maybe it's because I'm slowly losing control of my own thoughts? Or maybe because it's turning me into a freak, that's why!"

Mesmo was still frowning. "But why would it turn you into a freak? It is no different than a human skill."

"What are you talking about? Humans don't have skills like you!"

"Of course they do!" Mesmo replied. "I have met people with the skill of music, the skill of dancing, the skill of arts, the skill of invention..."

"The skill of *what*?"

Mesmo searched for the right words. "Take this snow for example. My skill is water: I simply manipulate the snow so it will not fall on us. Humans do not have this skill, so they perfected a different one: the skill of invention. They invented a device to cover themselves so they would not get wet."

Ben gaped. "An umbrella...? You're comparing your skill to... an umbrella?" He scoffed and shook his head.

Mesmo shrugged. "It may seem like nothing to you, but I find human creativity quite original." He fell silent suddenly as if a separate conversation had begun in his head.

They walked on, both lost in their own thoughts.

Even though Mesmo had shone a new light on the problem, Ben was still far from happy.

He's trying to convince me.

* * *

Ben spent the next day studying with Kimi. They tested each other and cleared up any remaining questions they had. Ben had snuck in a couple of doughnuts, which they munched on contentedly while they took a break. Ben lay at the end of the bed, staring at the ceiling.

"You know, I was thinking," Kimi began.

Ben groaned. "Please don't think. My brain is fried enough as it is."

Kimi kicked him with her foot from under the bedsheets.

"Shut up!" she scolded. "I'm serious. I was thinking about the lake."

"Oh," Ben's face darkened.

"No, listen. I was thinking about what I told you, about me not liking being First Nation and all. You were right, I wasn't thinking straight. I didn't mean what I said."

Ben straightened. "That's okay. You were angry. You had every right to be."

Kimi's eyes moved away from him. "No, it's more than that," she said. "You know, I really thought I was done for when I sank to the bottom of the lake. And the only thing I could think of was how stupid I was for hating myself." Her eyes fell on him again, twinkling from some inner fire. "You see, I realized that the problem isn't who I am—the problem is my dad! I can't change what he thinks about my mom or me. But I can change how I think about myself. I don't have to look at myself through my dad's eyes. I have my own eyes to do that."

Her words resounded with certainty. "I am unique: I was born of two cultures. The one doesn't overshadow the other. On the contrary, they complement each other and make each other stronger, through me. Being born with two cultures is a gift, not a burden. I can create a new way of seeing the world and combine the two to solve problems. That's actually pretty awesome!"

She wrung her hands together in excitement as if she couldn't wait to apply her new philosophy. "It's not my problem if my dad couldn't adapt. It's not my job to suffer for it! I don't have to carry his burden. I know that now." She trailed off, consumed by an energy that burned brighter with her every word.

Ben hadn't moved an inch as her vision seeped deep into his core. He knew her words meant something vital to him, only, he wasn't sure if he was ready to accept their meaning. He got off the bed and began gathering his notes and books.

Kimi was still caught up in her revelation. "I'll have to take you back to the lake this summer," she chatted. "It's not that bad, you know? Plenty of kids go swimming there when the days get hotter. And there's an ice cream truck that sells the best bubblegum flavour in the world. You'll see."

Ben had his back to her; he took his time filling up his backpack as he couldn't bear to face her.

I won't be here.

"Cool," he managed to utter.

"Ben?"

"What?" he tried to make his voice sound as normal as possible. He stuck his nose into his backpack as if he were searching for something.

"What's wrong?"

Her question startled him. "Huh?"

"You've been acting weird all week. Like you're trying to be all cheerful for my sake, but you're just pretending. Something's wrong. I can tell."

How can she see right through me?

If he turned to face her, he would fall apart. He would have to tell her everything, and that would be the end of their friendship because she would never trust him again. His eyes welled with tears.

"Kimimela," Maggie's voice filled the room.

"*Inâ*!" Kimi said cheerfully.

Ben watched them hug out of the corner of his eyes. He wiped his tears away swiftly.

"Ben," Maggie said, heading to him with her arms wide.

He had no choice but to turn this time. He was struck by how different Maggie looked. Her hair was neatly tied in a ponytail that went down to her waist. Her smile took years off her face, and the resemblance with Kimi was uncanny.

He fell into her arms gratefully because it allowed him to sob freely. She stroked his head for a long time. Finally, she took his head into both of her hands and placed her forehead on to his. "I thank you, *hokshila*[6]. You saved my butterfly and I am forever in your debt." She lowered her voice and added, "I don't know what it is your father did, but my people tell me he is a great spirit. Even a Wise One from the North has travelled to

[6] *Hokshila*: 'child' in Dakhona

speak with him. But somehow I believe I am indebted to him, too."

They were still standing in this strange embrace when Laura and Thomas arrived.

"Hi," Laura said, casting a worried look in her son's direction. "We were looking everywhere for you, Ben."

Maggie patted Ben on the shoulder and took out a tissue to wipe her eyes. She hugged Laura and Thomas, then went to sit by Kimi's bed. "I am glad you are all here," she said. "I have something to tell you." She took Kimi's hand and continued, "Some years ago, I lost my husband. He abandoned Kimi and me. For a long time, I suffered from this. I blamed myself for it, told myself I could have done more. I turned away from my identity, from my people, and I turned away from my daughter. I became a shadow of myself." She paused, struggling with her words. "I turned away from everything that most mattered to me, and instead, sought refuge in a poison, which I used to drown my grief." She gazed straight at Kimi and said, full of emotion, "I became an alcoholic."

Ben felt a shift in the room at the meaningful confession.

Maggie squeezed her daughter's hand and claimed, "I am Magaskawee. I am of the Dakhona people. You are my daughter, Kimimela, and I will heal now, for you."

Kimi's face crumbled as she fell into her mother's arms. There wasn't a dry eye in the room. When Maggie pulled away from her daughter, she stared at the floor and admitted, "The road will be hard, Kimimela. I will need your help."

Kimi nodded, her face puffy with emotion.

Thomas cleared his throat and went to stand before Maggie. "I would like to help," he said shakily. "That is, if you would let me..."

Maggie frowned as she stood up. "Why?"

Thomas took both of her hands in his and looked deep into her eyes. "I think you know why," he said softly.

"Ben," Laura whispered as she pulled him by the arm. She nudged her head towards the door. "Time to go."

They slipped out of the room. Just before the door closed, Ben saw Kimi glance at him with a huge smile and eyes that sparkled in amazement.

Ben stared at his mother as they walked to the elevator. "Thomas? And Maggie?" he exclaimed, his eyes wide.

Laura only smiled.

Ben jumped in front of her, walking backwards to stay ahead. "Thomas?" he repeated. "And Maggie?"

Laura's smile widened.

Ben's surprise turned into a grin, and he nodded in approval. "Cool!"

CHAPTER 15 *Not Human*

When Kimi entered the classroom on Friday morning, the students broke into loud cheers of welcome. Wes and Tyler, who had been allowed back for the civics exam, hooted the loudest.

Kimi blushed and hid her smile behind her books. Her hair tumbled over her loose turtleneck sweater. The burgundy colour went well with her dark eyes and Ben thought she was easily the prettiest girl in class.

She winked at him as she settled at her desk.

"It's good to have you back, Kimi," Ms. Evans said warmly.

Kimi responded with a raucous cough, but she gave a thumbs up and nodded.

Ms. Evans exclaimed, "Oh dear! All right, good thing it's not an oral exam. Best to leave your voice alone today, I think."

She distributed the exam papers, checked her watch and indicated that they could start.

Ben turned over the papers and scanned through the questions. He glanced at Kimi, and they exchanged a grin; they knew the answers.

This is going to be easy.

Ben pushed the idea that he was flying out of Canmore forever that day to the very back of his mind, and began scribbling. Thirty minutes into the hour, he paused to stretch his back. He checked on his classmates. They hunched over their desks in concentration—even Wes and Tyler, he noted. He rubbed his neck, then leaned over to continue writing, and instead found his hands glowing.

He jumped, heart racing. He glanced around hurriedly to make sure no one had noticed, then froze at the sight outside the window.

On the windowsills, a dozen crows sat with their beady eyes aimed at him. One of them cawed, while the others resembled silent, unmoving gargoyles from a gloomy cathedral.

He tried to ignore the familiar sensation of blood rushing to his ears, but there were too many crows, and their chatter seeped into his mind. The exam answers he had formulated evaporated as if blown away by a cumbersome wind. The birds were trying to tell him something, he knew, but he wasn't willing to hear. A cold sweat broke above his brow as he tried to block off the intrusion into his mind.

I won't listen!

He hung his head a few inches from the papers on his desk so he wouldn't have to acknowledge that contact had been made, but all he saw were blurry words under the tip of his pen. The roaring in his mind became stronger, and part of him knew the message was urgent, that he should listen.

A loud knock startled him back into awareness of the classroom. The Principal entered with a distinctly troubled look on her face. "I'm sorry to interrupt the class, Ms. Evans. I know you're in the middle of an exam, but could I borrow Ben for a minute?" She was clearly unhappy. Her eyes and those of the rest of the class turned to Ben.

Something furry scuttered between Mrs. Nguyen's legs. Tike dashed across the classroom. At seeing him, Ben's mind exploded with an imminent threat.

Run!

Not a doubt remained in Ben's mind. He knew then precisely what Tike was trying to tell him. Panic surged through his body. He jumped to his feet, his chair falling over in his haste. At the same time, Hao and Connelly entered the classroom, shoving Mrs. Nguyen aside.

Ben's eyes searched wildly for an exit, but the only way out was barred by the agents. Like an animal caught in a trap, he staggered back into the wall.

An electric silence fell over the classroom.

Hao took a careful step forward, aware of the twenty-four pairs of eyes glued on him. He forced a smile. "Hello, Benjamin. Would you step outside, please?"

Ben shook his head wordlessly.

Hao raised an eyebrow. His hands twitched by his side. He gestured meaningfully towards the students. "Come now, there's no need to make a scene. Don't make this harder on yourself."

Ben felt his resilience fading like snow in the desert sun, yet he could not make himself cross the only space of freedom that remained between him and the agent. And it wasn't even because of Hao. It was because, from behind Hao, Connelly's cold eyes glued Ben to the ground.

Twisted eyes! There's no way I'm going with him!

Hao's irritation was palpable. He did not need to raise his voice, because his sharp tone was unmistakeably demanding. "Benjamin Archer, you are under arrest. You will step out of this classroom at once!"

The Inspector's words triggered a hidden source of anger within Ben. How dare this man threaten him? How dare he remove him from the safety of his classroom and uproot his life at the snap of his fingers?

"No!" he said, the word born deep within. He wasn't sure what he was doing—he was driven by instinct rather than common sense, but he didn't care. This situation was wrong and he meant to let everyone know it was so.

I'm not going down without a fight!

"No!" he said again, this time with more vigour. "I'm not going with you! I've done nothing wrong and you know it! I'm innocent until proven guilty. It says so in the Universal Declaration of Human Rights. I deserve to be treated like a human being!"

"You are NOT a human being!" Hao's words flew across the room and planted themselves like knives into Ben's heart. He swayed at their power. He fell back as if he had been pierced by a hundred spears.

A deathly silence that would rival the eye of a hurricane filled the room. A pencil rolled slowly off a desk, then clattered loudly to the ground.

Hao blinked and glanced at the multitude of wide eyes that were on him. He sucked in air as he straightened. "Enough," he scowled, gesturing to Connelly. "I don't have time for this. Get him."

The alien who used Connelly's traits as a disguise, strode purposefully towards Ben and Ben cowered at his every step. Then, suddenly, the Shapeshifter stopped and stared down in confusion.

"No, you're not," Tyler announced, planting himself in front of Connelly. Ben's classmate inflated his chest and crossed his arms. "Ben's my friend and I won't let you take him."

"Tyler!" Ben whispered urgently. He could see the muscles in Connelly's neck tighten.

"Me, neither," a voice said, and in an instant, Wes rubbed shoulders with Tyler. Voices flared, chairs scraped on the floor and students flocked to Wes and Tyler's side. Even scared Max joined them.

"Now wait a minute..." Ms. Evans sprung out of her chair, arguing with Hao.

Ben could not escape the Shapeshifter's glare. He could sense the tenseness in the bald man's face as more and more students rushed to stand between them.

"Don't!" Ben said weakly, praying that the alien would not burst like a nuclear warhead, but his warning was lost in the raucous objections.

A gust of freezing wind hit him in the neck. A hand pulled him aside.

"This way!" Kimi urged.

Ben blinked.

Kimi had opened a classroom window and slipped through it. Catching on, Ben picked up Tike and shoved the dog after her. Kimi slid down a ledge and jumped into the packed snow not far below. Ben stuck out his own head and caught his breath: there were hundreds—no, thousands—of crows littering the trees, school rooftop, windowsills and sky all around him.

No sooner had he slipped onto the ledge, than a multitude of wings unfolded around him. A deafening noise of grating caws and clicks filled the air. Ben felt a whoosh of feathers as the birds dove inches from his head, then shot through the open window behind him, triggering shrieks from terrified students caught inside the classroom.

Ben's brain exploded with noise, not so much from the thunderous cawing outside, but from the staggering clamour inside his brain.

Run! Danger! Get out! What are you waiting for? Get away!

Ben pressed his glowing hands over his ears and screamed. His body weight dragged him over the edge and he landed in the snow with a thud. The crows were outside and inside of him. He was a boy lying in the snow, but he was also a thousand birds swirling through the air and diving into the hectic classroom.

"Ben!" Kimi's distressed call came through to him.

He gasped in pain and felt the cold snow beneath his body. It brought him back to his senses long enough to stand and stagger away from the school with Kimi's support. When they were two blocks away, the sudden void in his mind made him retch horribly.

He knew that Kimi was watching his glowing hands with a mixture of fear and wonder. But she grabbed him under the arm and pulled him down the street. The cold seeped through their clothes and their shoes, as they hadn't been able to put on snow gear.

Ben was vaguely aware of his surroundings and of Kimi, who shot him anxious glances as they advanced. He felt utterly exposed to the skill. In his mind's eye, the blue filaments grew arms and attached themselves to millions of neurons in his head, weaving an intricate web through his brain, and he was too weak to fight it.

Tike entered his thoughts, sending him an image of police cars with swirling lights in front of a townhouse. Ben's stomach heaved.

"Wait!" he wheezed as he stopped Kimi from dragging him on. He took a deep breath to settle the nausea and tried to focus on his surroundings. "Not Thomas' place," he said. "Too late. Police are already there."

Kimi gave him a strange look, but said, "Can you make it to my house?"

Ben nodded.

She took him by the arm again, but Ben gasped suddenly. "What?" Her eyes widened as they stopped again.

"My mom!" Ben exclaimed. "She doesn't know! I have to warn her!"

"Come on!" Kimi urged. "I'm taking you home. Then I'll get your mom." She pulled him forward through the snow-packed streets. Light snowflakes floated through the air.

They made it to Kimi's house. She opened the door and shoved him in. "I'll be right back," she said, heading away before he could say anything.

"Kimi, is that you?" Ben heard Maggie say. She appeared in the living room door and frowned. "Ben?" She took him by the shoulders and led him through the door, where he found Thomas sitting on a couch and placing a cup of coffee on a low table.

He took one look at Ben and sprang up. "What is it?" he asked hurriedly, catching Ben in his arms.

Ben choked up into his sweater. "Too late! They're here!"

* * *

"Enjoy your latté," Laura said, as she handed a steaming cup to a customer over the counter. The customer headed to the door of the coffee shop when it swung open and someone collided head-on with him. The latté flew through the air, then landed in a splash on the floor. "Hey!" the customer yelled, but the offender did not offer an excuse and instead searched the place with frantic eyes.

"Kimi?" Laura exclaimed, recognizing the girl's long, black hair.

Kimi rushed around the counter and placed an icy hand on Laura's arm. She wanted to speak but instead broke down in a fit of coughs. "Girl, you're freezing!" Laura scolded worriedly. "Where's your jacket?"

Kimi caught her breath and stared straight at Laura. "Ben said to come quick!" she said sharply.

Laura felt her heart drop. "Where's Ben?" she asked urgently, already removing her Tim Horton's apron.

"My place," Kimi coughed.

"Come on." Laura led Kimi to the back of the coffee shop.

"Some men came to the school looking for him," Kimi said through her coughs.

"Hey, lady," the unfortunate customer called after them over the counter. "I want my latté!"

Laura dropped the apron next to a sink, grabbed her winter jacket and wrapped Kimi in it. "Let's go," she said, heading for the back exit.

"Hold up! Laura!" someone called behind them. A large woman with a similar apron hurried to catch up with them. "Where are you going?" the woman puffed. A pin attached to her apron said MANAGER.

Laura let go of Kimi. "I'm sorry, Rhina, I have to go," she said.

"But... are you coming back?" Rhina asked in dismay.

Laura shook her head. Her chin quivered.

Rhina's shoulders sagged, but she said, "Wait a minute. You can't go without your pay." She dug into her apron and fished out a handful of dollar bills and coins. "Here, take it. Don't worry. I'll figure things out with the others later."

"No... I..." Laura objected, pushing the woman's hand away.

"Take it!" the woman insisted. "It's all I have on me. It's your share of this week's tips. You've earned it."

Laura hesitated, then accepted the money. "Thank you," she said, her eyes falling on the unhappy customer.

Rhina rolled her eyes. "Don't you worry about him, dear. We'll fix him up with a gift card or something."

Laura hugged her. "Goodbye," she said, holding back the tears.

"You take care, now, you hear?" the woman insisted.

Laura nodded, then headed through the exit with Kimi. A gentle snow fell around them as they hurried down the cold streets.

CHAPTER 16 *Dreamcatcher*

Laura found Thomas and Maggie pouring over a large map, which they had spread out on the countertop of the kitchen island.

"Where's Ben?" she asked as she rushed to join them.

"Outside." Thomas pointed to the outer deck which lay off the dining room.

Laura stepped towards it, but Thomas grabbed her firmly by the arm. "There's no time."

Laura set her jaw, then nodded in understanding. "What's the plan? Are we flying?" She stared at the map.

Thomas shook his head. "Too late for that. Canmore Air is swarming with cops."

Laura gaped. "What do we do?"

"Do about what?" Mesmo's voice startled them.

"Mesmo!" Laura felt a wave of relief.

"Who's Mesmo?" Maggie frowned.

Thomas and Laura stared from Mesmo to Maggie.

Thomas took Maggie's hand. "Maggie, this man is not Jack Anderson. His real name is Mesmo. I know this is a lot to ask, but I need you to trust him. I need you to trust me."

Maggie glanced thoughtfully at the tall man in the fur hat. "My people have told me that Angakkuq crossed the country to confer with a great spirit here. I don't know who... or what you are. I don't know what you did to my daughter. But I do know she is alive, thanks to you." Her eyes fell on Thomas. "Tell me what you need."

Thomas' brow relaxed and he nodded in thanks. "It's not Mesmo I'm worried about. We need to find a safe passage out of Canmore for Ben and Laura. Mesmo will follow them in his own manner." He turned his attention to the map. "There aren't many options. We obviously can't send them back west. They need to go east." He followed Highway 1 with the tip of his finger until it reached the city of Calgary. He jabbed at the name on the map. "There!"

"But how?" Laura studied the area around Thomas' finger. "The only way out of Canmore is north, by way of this road that links to the highway. They'll have set up barricades and will be checking every single car driving out of Canmore."

They stared at the map as if waiting for it to give them an alternative.

Suddenly, Maggie said, "The Kananaskis!" She bent over the map and pointed at the main road linking Canmore to the highway. "Look," she said. "Before you reach the highway, you turn left into this small road. It makes a U-turn and will take you south, past Canmore. You follow it all the way down to... here." She indicated a spot that seemed lost in the middle of nowhere. "There is a crossing here that will take you over the Kananaskis Mountain Range."

"That's a huge detour!" Thomas exclaimed.

"It is," Maggie agreed. "But once they reach the other side of the mountain, they can travel north again and rejoin the highway between Canmore and Calgary—here."

Laura contemplated the map. She followed Maggie's instructions in her mind and realized they would basically be making a huge circle around Canmore that would eventually get them back to the highway.

"I don't know." Thomas' voice reflected his uncertainty. "A snowstorm is approaching. I think it's too risky."

"They can make it," Maggie insisted. "If they leave now, they should be over the Kananaskis in a couple of hours, before the worst of the storm hits."

Thomas glanced at Laura. "What do you think? You're the one who has to drive."

Laura straightened, suddenly realizing that she and Ben would be on their own soon. "What about you?" she asked.

Thomas pressed his lips together, his eyes on Maggie. "I think I'm going to stay this time."

Maggie offered him a smile.

Thomas spoke to Laura, his eyes still on Maggie. "I don't think the CSIS will be very interested in me anymore." He fished keys out of his pocket and gave them to Laura. "Here, you can have my car."

"No," Maggie objected. "They'll be looking for it. Take mine. It's a pick-up truck with sturdy wheels. It will get you over the mountains."

"Thank you," Laura whispered, her head swirling at the task ahead.

* * *

Ben stared at nothing in particular. He sat outside on the top steps of a wooden stairway that joined the deck with the yard. He had grabbed one of Kimi's jackets, covered his head with the cape and leaned against the wooden railing.

Mesmo appeared in his field of vision and crouched beside him.

Ben hid his face under the cape unable to face the alien. The boy's words came out with difficulty, his voice empty of emotion. "Hao said I'm not human." His chin began to tremble. "I don't know what I am anymore." He finally turned and glared at the alien. "This is all your fault," he said accusingly, his nostrils flaring.

"Benjamin..." Mesmo began.

"Leave me alone." Ben lowered his face into the cape again. His tone was final. He felt Mesmo pause, then move away. He wanted the alien to stay and comfort him, but the part of him that was angry and unaccepting wouldn't allow it. He heard the deck door slide open and for a moment his mind tricked him into believing the alien had doubled back.

Mesmo can't open doors, he reminded himself.

Black army boots came to stand beside him. "My mom said to try these on," Kimi dangled snow boots at him. "She said you're going over the mountain in our pick-up truck. She's putting together some backpacks with emergency gear. Any Canmore resident knows to never approach the Kananaskis without emergency gear, even if you're in a pick-up truck. The mountains can be unforgiving and must be treated with the greatest respect."

Since he didn't react, she plopped beside him with a sigh, dumping the snow boots before her as if they weighed a ton. They didn't speak for a painfully long time.

Ben heard Kimi's voice waver when she broke the silence. "You knew this was coming, didn't you?" she asked. "Back at the hospital, you already knew you were going to leave..." Her tone wasn't accusing, but it hurt anyway.

He looked at her without answering. He found tears

streaming down her cheeks and his heart tightened. "I don't have a choice." He wrung his hands together. "I have to go."

"But, it's your dad they're after, isn't it? Maybe you could stay, and your dad could go away for awhile..." He heard the false hope in her voice.

Ben shook his head. "He's not my dad."

She knit her brows.

Ben sighed. "My dad died shortly after I was born. I never got to know him." He gestured vaguely inside the house. "His name is Mesmo. And, no, I can't stay. He goes wherever I go. We're stuck together in that way."

She blinked and turned away. After a silence, he heard her say with a touch of unease, "Ben? What did that man mean, when he said you're not... human?"

It hurt to hear her say it just as much as when Hao had said it.

Ben shuffled his feet in the snow, then breathed, "It's true." He listened to his own words, trying to accept them.

She turned to him abruptly, her eyes filled with tears. "No, it's not!" she said vehemently. "Don't be daft! You're my favourite human being in the whole world." She wrapped her arms around him and held him tight.

The sweet gesture cracked his resolve. Overcome with emotion, Ben shut his eyes and squeezed her back.

They were still hugging when Laura stepped onto the deck, her arms full of bulging backpacks. "Ben?" Her voice broke up their embrace.

Kimi stared at Ben with reddened eyes. She leaned over to him and pecked him with cool, soft lips on the corner of his mouth, then ran into the house.

Ben watched her disappear, his heart breaking.

"Ben?" his mother's voice called. "We have to go."

He nodded forlornly, then changed into the snow boots. When he stood up, he began to remove Kimi's knee-length jacket from his shoulders, but Maggie stopped him. "No, keep it. You'll be needing it."

He nodded in thanks, then accepted one of the backpacks that Laura handed to him. They hugged Maggie and Thomas, then got into the pick-up truck, which was parked next to the veterinary building. Laura took the wheel of the four-door pick-up truck while Mesmo sat on the passenger side. Ben slipped into the back. Tike jumped on his lap.

"We'll get the truck back to you somehow," Laura reassured Maggie.

"Just be safe," Maggie replied, squeezing Laura's hand through the window.

The screen door slid open and Kimi came running up to them. Ben rolled down his window as she approached. She reached out and placed something in his hand. It was a flat, circular object, the size of his palm, with a finely woven net inside. Some beads and feathers hung below it.

"What is it?" Ben asked in wonder.

"It's a dreamcatcher," she explained. "I made it with my grandmother on the reservation. It will protect you from bad spirits."

Ben felt a wave of gratitude. "It's beautiful. Thanks!" He stared at the carefully knotted strings that resembled a spider's web. "But, I don't have anything for you!"

She placed her hand on her heart as she stepped away from the truck. "You gave me back my family." She smiled as she joined Maggie and Thomas.

Laura revved up the pick-up, and soon their friends disappeared behind the veterinary clinic. She headed down the main street of Canmore as snow began to fall more insistently.

"Mom!" Ben shouted suddenly, making her hit the brakes with force. Ben and Tike slipped forward into the back of Laura's seat.

"What?" she said in alarm.

Ben rubbed his nose.

"Put on your seat belt!" she scolded.

He did so in a hurry. "Your asthma inhaler!" he said. "Do you have one?"

He saw her eyebrows draw together. She drove slowly for a while as if in deep thought. "No, I don't have one. Truth is, I haven't used one in months." She glanced at Mesmo curiously.

"Like me!" Ben gasped. "I haven't had a panic attack either."

They both stared at Mesmo as if expecting the alien to explain the mysterious disappearance of their symptoms, but Mesmo pointed ahead. "We are nearing the highway ramp," he said.

Ben stretched his neck. In the flurry of snow, he spotted the whirling lights of a dozen police cars in the distance.

"Where's that other exit Maggie was talking about?" Laura's anxiousness was palpable. "Ben, check the map, would you?" She shoved the map to the back and he scrambled to open it wide enough to find their location.

If only we could use Google Maps like every normal person!

The vehicle slowed but inevitably neared the ramp. A line of cars was being monitored one at a time before being released to the highway.

Laura came to a stop. "Ben!" she urged.

"Uh..." Ben scrunched at the map in his haste. "Turn back, Mom! We missed it. Turn back!"

The tires screeched on the snow as she made a full u-turn.

They squinted at the scattered houses and snow-covered trees.

"Got it!" Laura exclaimed, swinging the pick-up to the right into a small street they had previously missed.

Ben glanced through the rear window as they turned the corner, and his heart leapt into his throat. A couple of police cars had detached themselves from the main body of vehicles at the ramp. "They're coming!" he warned.

CHAPTER 17 *Trapped*

Laura grasped the wheel, the knuckles of her hands turning white from the pressure. The windshield wipers worked wildly to keep the snow out of her vision, but even so, it became harder to distinguish anything on the gloomy road bordered by dense forest. There wasn't a soul in sight, so she switched on the headlights and pressed on the pedal to pick up speed. The motor sent a satisfying lurch of power into the tires.

"I thought the storm wasn't due until later," Ben echoed her thoughts. She bit her lip and tried to ignore a nagging feeling in the pit of her stomach. The flashing red-and-white lights pressed her on. There was no turning back now.

The pick-up truck wound its way through the lonesome road bordering the towering Kananaskis Mountain Range. Laura's brow beaded with sweat as she checked the rearview mirror, but she didn't think the police were making any headway on them.

"Watch it, Mom!" Ben warned. "We should be nearing the crossroad going over the mountain."

Laura slowed down reluctantly. They couldn't afford to miss the exit this time. After a couple of minutes, Mesmo's sharp eyes found it. "There it is!" He pointed.

Laura hit the brakes. She switched off the headlights and swerved to the left into an almost invisible crossroad that immediately began to ascend.

"Stop!" Mesmo ordered. "Let me out of the truck."

Laura obeyed without a second of hesitation.

The alien ran to the back of the truck and placed his hands on the tracks that the tires had imprinted into the snow. A wave of blue light flowed from his fingers to the bottom of the road, melting the snow until it looked smooth and even. He hurried back and said, "That should keep them off for a while."

Laura realized he must have turned the snow into a sheet of ice behind them. She revved up the engine again and began the steep climb into the evening sky.

* * *

Hao placed his hand on the dashboard as if that would make the Sheriff's car go faster. He leaned in, trying to make out the pick-up truck in the dark tunnel of trees ahead.

"Don't lose them!" he urged the Sheriff who was at the wheel.

After several minutes of tense silence, the police radio crackled. The Sheriff answered, never taking his eyes off the road.

Hao glanced at him questioningly.

"It's Connelly," the Sheriff said. "He says we need to turn back. He thinks they're heading into the Kananaskis."

"The what?" Hao's face went red.

The Sheriff pointed at the looming peaks alongside the road. "The Kananaskis Mountain Range."

Hao swore as he whirled to check behind them. Two police

cars were still following them, but a couple of others had stopped some way back. "What does he think he's doing? Tell him to get over here! That's an order!"

The Sheriff spoke into the radio, then glanced at Hao. "One of the cars got stuck at the crossroad. They're on a patch of black ice. But Connelly says he can get through. He's convinced the fugitives are on their way up."

"Black ice?" Something triggered in Hao's mind. He remembered the unnatural formation of ice at the Vancouver Police Department.

He squinted ahead. Earlier, he'd been able to follow the pick-up truck in the distance; now there was only darkness and swirling snow.

"All right! Back up, back up!"

The Sheriff did so, but he warned, "The storm is picking up strength. It's going to be hell up there. I may have to pull off the search."

"You're not pulling anything off, Sheriff!" Hao flared. "Or shall I have you reflect on that with the High Inspector?"

The Sheriff straightened his cap and pursed his lips, but made no comment as he drove carefully along the edge of the crossroad to avoid the slippery patch in the middle. An officer tried to manoeuvre his car off the ice patch. A second police car stopped next to it to help.

The Sheriff pointed his Toyota back to the middle of the road, which wound steeply between the fir trees. Hao bent forward, taking in the massive form of the Kananaskis Mountain Range that reached for the sky like jagged knives, attracting black storm clouds to their peaks.

"You've got to be kidding me!" he breathed.

* * *

A heavy silence hung in the pick-up. Laura had switched on the headlights again, but even so, she had a hard time making out the road before her. Large snowflakes hit the windshield. No sooner were they shoved aside by the wipers, than a dozen even bigger flakes replaced them.

"They weren't fooled," Ben said from the back. "They're still after us. I think I saw the headlights."

Laura tensed as she pressed on the speed pedal, excruciatingly aware that she was going too fast. The truck's nose pointed upward as she weaved her way further and further up the mountain. The motor strained on the unfriendly path. After hairraising minutes, the pick-up began to level out again, indicating they were reaching the summit, which was squeezed between even higher black mountain peaks. Breathing a bit easier, she glanced at Mesmo, who was focused on the road ahead. "You don't have to be here, you know?" she told him.

He met her eyes and his voice was firm. "I do."

Laura bit her inner lip, relieved that he wasn't abandoning them.

Just then the pick-up skidded. Laura steered the wheel sharply to the right, but she lost control of the vehicle. It slid for a heart-stopping moment. Then, there was a crunching sound and the truck jolted to a stop.

"What is it?" Ben asked fearfully.

Laura tried to reverse. The tires screeched in protest. "We're stuck!" She opened the car door, inviting a biting cold inside. She stepped out and Mesmo came around to stand by her side. The front tire was buried in deep snow.

"Mom! They're catching up!" Ben rushed up behind them.

Laura could hear the wailing police sirens approaching too fast for comfort. She whirled to face Mesmo. "Get us out of here!

Release the tires!"

"There's no time!" he yelled through the storm. "I sense Bordock nearby. The mountain is our best bet. Follow me!" He turned and stepped headfirst into the darkness away from the road.

"What?" Laura's voice rose in panic. "Are you crazy?"

"Mom, hurry!" Ben followed Mesmo.

"Ben!" Laura yelled as he disappeared into the flurry of snowflakes. "Come back! It's too dangerous! Ben!"

She rushed into the deep snow after him, her breath coming in quick gasps. She hesitated, then backtracked and snatched one of the backpacks from the truck. She wanted to get the other one, but the police cars burst into view behind her. Laura dove after her son just as the first police car slid off the road and collided headlong with the pick-up. The others screeched to a stop just in time.

"Mom!" She heard Ben's muffled shout in the swirling snow before her. Behind her, the lights of the police cars offered the only island of safety on the massive mountain.

"Laura Archer!" A man moved in front of the headlights of one of the police cars. She recognized Inspector Hao's voice. "Don't be foolish. You're heading to your death."

Laura kept on walking away from him, though at a slower pace. Her heart beat as fast as a hare's as she realized he was telling the truth.

"Laura Archer! Think of your son's safety!"

She sobbed and tripped into the snow. "Ben!" she shouted, searching the darkness.

"Over here!" His voice sounded far away.

Laura stood again and walked blindly into the storm.

* * *

"Let's go!" Hao pressed his hand on the gun at his side as he made to follow Laura.

The Sheriff grabbed him by the arm. "That's out of the question. Those fugitives have sealed their fate. But that doesn't mean I'm going to risk my men's lives as well." He shot a glance at Hao. "Or do you want to reflect on that with your High Inspector." The Sheriff didn't wait for Hao to answer and gestured at his other men to get back in their cars. One of them panted up the road towards them. "I can't find him!"

"Find who?" the Sheriff barked.

The officer pointed at Hao. "His colleague. I saw him run to the pick-up when we arrived, but now he's not there anymore."

Hao felt his blood boil all the way to his face. He turned to the darkness and bellowed. "CONNELLY!"

* * *

"Mesmo! Wait up!" Ben shouted as the alien strode effortlessly in the snow. Ben stumbled after him to try and stay in the protective bubble the alien was emitting around him to keep the snowstorm at bay. "Not so fast! I can't see Mom."

They stopped and searched the way they had come. Ben tucked a shivering Tike inside his jacket.

They saw powerful searchlights on top of the police cars sweeping the area, but they did not quite reach far enough to catch the fugitives.

"Where is she? She was right behind us," Ben said worriedly. Then, the light briefly caught Laura's shape as she stumbled on with a large backpack. She was heading away from them.

"Where is she going?" Ben frowned, then his voice stuck in his throat as a dark shape loomed before her in the passing searchlight.

* * *

"Ben? Where are you?" Laura shouted as she raised her arm to protect her eyes from the swirling snowflakes.

"Over here!" Ben said right before her.

She let out a breath of relief and stepped forward, only to stagger headfirst into a bald man.

She opened her mouth to scream, but he clamped a steel hand over her mouth and pulled her down in the snow, just as a beam of light swept over them.

"Hi, *Mommy*," Connelly sneered with Ben's voice. She saw Connelly's eyes switch from green to honey-brown.

She struggled to escape from his grip, but instead, she felt something cold clasp onto her wrist, and before she knew it, they were connected to each other with handcuffs.

They heard Hao shout from the road, "Connelly! Get back here!" Several flashlights pierced the flurry of falling snow as the officers called for the missing agent.

"Let's go!" Connelly growled, picking up Laura's backpack and heaving it onto his shoulder. The Shapeshifter pulled at the cuffs, making Laura lurch after him.

"No, wait!" she yelled, but he held her with an iron grasp, pulling her further away from the road. "Ben!" she gasped. "You can't leave him! He has no protection! He won't survive on his own!" She turned her head and shouted, "Ben!"

"Good idea," Connelly jeered. "Call him. Let's have him join our little party."

Laura's eyes widened and she fell silent instantly.

Catching her look of fear, Connelly chuckled, sending a chill up and down her spine.

* * *

"Mom!" Ben yelled, panic surging through his body when he realized what was happening. He dropped Tike and heaved himself up a snowy ledge to rush to his mother's aid. Instead, his feet slipped beneath him, and he skidded several feet down. Tike bumped into his head as he collided with a tree. He blinked the stars from his eyes and got up immediately, then realized that Mesmo was a little way up with his hands placed in the snow. He had turned the slope into ice.

"What are you doing?" Ben yelled furiously, trying to get up but sliding back every time. "Bordock's got my mom! We have to save her!"

Mesmo reached him with a couple of strides and stared at him intensely. "No! That's exactly what Bordock wants. If you go after him, that will be the end of us."

"But my mom!" Ben shook all over.

"Calm down!" Mesmo urged.

"Calm down?" Ben howled. He threw himself at the alien, only to land headfirst in the snow. "Let me go! Let me help her!" he yelled, punching at the air where Mesmo stood. It was useless, of course. Ben gasped for air and let himself drop to the ground.

"We'll save her," Mesmo said sternly. "But not now. Not like this. We have to get you as far away as possible from the police, find cover, and wait out the storm."

Ben's cheeks were wet with tears. "No!" He felt like a small child who would not listen to reason.

Mesmo crouched beside him. "You must!"

Ben stared at the alien, his mind whirling. His heart couldn't bear to think of his mother spending another minute with Bordock, but his mind knew it was inevitable, for now.

He glared bitterly at Mesmo, then picked up Tike, tucked him back into his jacket, and stepped into the darkness.

CHAPTER 18 *Acceptance*

Even Mesmo's skill was not enough to keep Ben safe from the blizzard. Night had fallen, making it impossible to see far ahead. Mesmo cleared a path before Ben and kept him dry, but even so, the danger that they could be walking beside a precipice without even knowing it became too much of a risk.

Finally, Mesmo stopped before a cluster of rocks and trees. He placed his hands in the snow and swiftly melted a hole into the ground. Ben watched him disappear into the makeshift cave until he reappeared and nodded for the boy to enter. Ben bent through the doorway and found himself in a large, dry igloo below the snow.

"Take off your jacket and snow boots so I can dry them," Mesmo ordered.

Ben did so numbly. He shivered uncontrollably, but not from the cold. He was in shock about what had happened, and he could not shake the image of his mother trudging through the blizzard at Bordock's mercy.

"Here." He heard Mesmo's voice in the dark and saw the alien's hand emit a blue light above the jacket. "You can lie down on it. You should be warm enough."

Ben sat and watched as Mesmo sealed off the doorway, leaving them in silence. He wrapped his arms around his legs and tried to calm his breathing.

"Don't worry," Mesmo's voice said through the dark. "Bordock may be evil, but he is also smart. He won't let anything happen to your mother. There is nothing more we can do but wait for the storm to blow over. He knows we will try to get off the mountain and will follow us."

"I'm not getting off the mountain," Ben interrupted. "Not without Mom."

"You're not thinking straight," Mesmo responded. "As soon as the weather clears, the police will swarm the area. And you may not have noticed yet, but you have no food."

Ben's stomach growled at the word and he squeezed his knees tighter.

"Try and get some rest," Mesmo said quietly. "I'll keep watch."

Ben lay down reluctantly, holding on to Tike's warm body as the dog snuggled up to him.

A thousand images flipped through his mind and he clung to one of Kimi's smiling face. He pulled out the dreamcatcher she had given him and felt the soft web of strings under his fingertips. *Being born with two cultures is a gift, not a burden.* For some reason, her words echoed in his mind. She had lashed out at being half First Nation but then had come to realize her difference was her strength, not her weakness. The idea wouldn't let Ben go. He twisted uncomfortably on the snowy bed Mesmo had made him, knowing, somehow, that those words applied to him, too. Acceptance was inevitable and part of him longed to embrace it, to feel confident and steadfast in his new identity, the way he had witnessed Kimi's transformation.

But the sickness?

He pushed the thought to the back of his mind. There was no time to think about that.

"Mesmo?" Ben's voice pierced the darkness.

"Yes?"

"I want you to teach me about the skill."

There was a long pause, then Mesmo said, "Are you sure?"

Ben sighed in resignation. "Yes." He felt Mesmo approach.

"Why this change of heart?"

Ben stared at the invisible ceiling. "Because it could save Mom," he said.

* * *

Laura woke to clanging sounds. She opened her eyes in a hurry and found the Shapeshifter sitting on a rock opposite her, rummaging through her backpack. He fished out a can of ravioli, a swiss knife, and a plastic spoon. With little effort, he unscrewed the top and began gobbling up the cold contents.

Laura couldn't help staring at the alien, for the bald man named Connelly who had caught her the night before, was no longer there. In his place sat Bordock: a man of muscular build, shorter than Mesmo, though with the same olive-coloured skin and white hair, which spiked out of his head like hedgehog quills.

He must have felt her gaze because he turned her way. She caught her breath and closed her eyes, but he wasn't fooled.

"Wakey, wakey," he said. "Time to get up. We have a long day ahead."

Laura gave up pretending to sleep and struggled to sit, remembering that her hands were cuffed together before her. *How convenient that he's a police officer*, she seethed silently.

She looked out of their rudimentary shelter, which

Bordock had found below some jutting rocks the night before. It had been enough to prevent snow from swirling inside and he had even managed to light a small fire. Still, the night had been long and cold, and by the headache that hammered in the back of her head, Laura guessed she hadn't slept much.

"It's still snowing," she pointed out.

"Yes, but it is also daytime. Which means it's time to go."

"Go where?"

"Down the mountain, of course," Bordock said, munching. Laura tried to ignore her grumbling stomach. Bordock dug into the can of ravioli and said with a full mouth, "We have to get there before they do. We're the welcoming team, see?" He waved an empty spoon at her.

Laura glared at him. "You won't get away with this. Mesmo will crush you."

Bordock burst out laughing. Laura felt fire rise to her cheeks. "Poor little Earthling. Still thinks the friendly alien will save her." Using his tongue, he cleaned out the piece of meat stuck in his teeth, then threw the can at her. It cluttered to the ground. The spoon fell out and ravioli spilled everywhere. Laura picked it up in disgust and stared at the few remaining pasta cushions that plastered the very bottom of the can.

The alien pointed his index finger at her. "Let's get one thing straight. That Toreq scum doesn't care about you. All he cares about is the translation skill. Get this through your little brain. It's not your son he's protecting. It's the skill!"

Laura choked on the ravioli she had managed to extract from the can with her fingers.

Bordock stared at her in amazement. "Don't you realize that yet? Do you really think he's out there looking for you? He doesn't care where you are. He doesn't care whether you're alive or dead. Right now, all he's interested in is escaping these mountains with your son as fast as he can."

Laura's appetite was gone. She dropped the can to the ground. "You're lying," she said with an effort.

Bordock shrugged. He bent to gather their things and shove them into the backpack. "I know the Toreq better than you do. Trust me when I tell you, it's the skill he wants."

"...and you don't?" Laura said in a low voice, launching an accusing glare his way. To her horror, he turned slowly and smirked.

"Yes, all right," he admitted, plopping down on the rock again. "I can't deny the translation skill would be a valuable asset to my collection. But at least I'm honest about it."

Laura shuddered, thinking of Mesmo's wife. "That's where you and Mesmo differ. He would never forcefully take someone's skill from them."

The corner of Bordock's mouth lifted in half a smile. "Ah, I see Mesmo has told you how I became a Shapeshifter."

Laura watched him heave the backpack onto his shoulders. Her heart sank as she realized he knew very well she couldn't survive on her own without it.

"What can I say?" he said as he fished out a tiny key from his pocket. "War comes fraught with sacrifices."

"What war?" she chided. "The War of the Kins happened millennia ago. And you lost. He told me so."

A funny smile crept into Bordock's face, one she did not like at all.

"Strange..." he said thoughtfully, releasing one of her hands, then attaching the empty cuff to his own wrist. "...strange that he should open up to you, yet tell you only half the story..." he trailed off.

"What story?"

The weird smile crept on to his face again. He shook his

head. "No," he said as if speaking to himself. "No. It would be a lot more fun to watch him tell you."

He turned and pulled her away from their rocky shelter.

"Tell me what?" she insisted.

"Enough!" he snapped, making her cringe. She did not like the way his eyes had hardened. "If you want to see your son again before Mesmo takes him away, you'll want to get down this mountain as soon as possible."

Laura struggled behind him with the faintest glimmer of hope blossoming in her mind. From Bordock's last phrase, she gathered that he was not aware of Mesmo's current condition. Mesmo was reduced to a mere apparition. He could not physically force Ben to go anywhere.

* * *

Ben woke to a ray of light that shone in his left eye. He blinked and gathered his bearings, then remembered where he was.

Faint daylight seeped through cracks in the makeshift igloo. Tike scratched at its snowy surface, making some of it crumble. The terrier trotted back to the boy to check that Ben was satisfied with him.

Ben stared at his dog as if seeing him for the first time.

Can you hear me?

The blood rushed to his ears as soon as he directed the question at Tike with his mind. The dog wagged his tail vigorously.

Of course, I can! What took you so long?

Ben shrank back into the snowy wall. He willed himself not to think anything for a moment, but the connection was crystal-clear in his mind. The part of him that was Tike, was overly thrilled and happy, while the part of his brain that was still his own was more cautious. An image of blue filaments flashed through his mind, but he pushed it away before he could panic. There was no time to think about that. He had to master the skill if he was going to help his mother—even if it meant losing himself to it.

What's wrong? Are you still angry at me?

Tike's words were unmistakable as, for the first time, Ben opened up to them entirely. It also meant feeling all of his dog's feelings, and he realized just how much he had hurt his companion in the past weeks by ignoring him.

Oh, Tike!

He picked up the terrier and hugged him.

I'm so sorry I was mean to you. I'm an idiot!

Tike licked his face.

No, you're not. I love you.

Ben was taken aback by such innocent sincerity. He hugged his dog harder.

I love you, too!

They stayed close like that for a long moment, Ben stroking Tike's back and Tike kissing him in the neck with his snout.

Light poured into the igloo as the snow melted and Mesmo appeared in the open doorway.

"Benjamin?" he called. "Time to go. It's a long way down. I'm hoping to reach the road by tomorrow morning."

"After we've saved Mom."

"Right."

"Before that you have to teach me to use the skill."

Mesmo didn't answer right away. "First, let's get this day over. I need you to save your strength."

"I'm fine," Ben reassured him, before noticing the

emptiness in his stomach.

Mesmo must have noticed his face change, because he said, "Time to go."

Ben stepped out of the igloo and caught his breath. Though it was still snowing, the clouds were high and grey in the sky, allowing him a glimpse of the vast landscape ahead of him. The steep Kananaskis Mountains sloped dangerously before leveling out into the plains that crossed half of Canada. Somewhere, down below, a road followed the mountain and rejoined the highway. Ben suddenly understood Mesmo's urgency. If another storm hit, he could be stuck here for days without food. Ignoring his hunger, he stepped after Mesmo as they began their descent.

CHAPTER 19 *Grizzly*

Ben fell headlong in the snow.

"Benjamin?" Mesmo called, hurrying to his side.

Ben turned his head but was too weak to flip onto his back.

"Get up! You have to keep going!" Mesmo urged.

"Can't," Ben muttered. He had walked for seven hours straight and he was exhausted.

Mesmo melted some snow by his mouth. "Drink!" he ordered.

Ben obeyed, feeling the fresh water flow down to his empty stomach. The descent had been brutal, especially when Mesmo had had to cut the connection with the spirit portal to return to his physical body, leaving Ben on his own for several hours. Ben's progress had been excruciatingly slow during that time because Mesmo had not been there to melt the snow in his path.

Fortunately, sometime after two o'clock, the alien had returned, allowing Ben to make good progress.

But now, Ben was done. He needed rest. And he needed food.

"You can't stay out here in the open," Mesmo said with his back to the boy. "Come on. You need to make it to the edge of the forest at least."

Ben raised his head slightly.

What forest?

He spotted it way below.

I can't.

Yes, you can. Get up!

Tike was by his side. Ben stared at his dog, whose exhaustion was more palpable even than his own. Ben felt a pang of guilt and picked himself up. Then he grabbed Tike and covered him under his jacket. His dog sent him a wave of gratitude, giving him the energy he needed to clamber down to the forest.

Ben, Mesmo and Tike made it to the border of trees by early evening. The boy collapsed in the igloo that Mesmo melted out for him and fell into a troubled sleep. His dreams bordered on hallucinations. He shivered from cold in spite of the protective snow-womb he lay in, the low temperatures having anchored themselves to his clothes. Sometimes he was talking to Tike, other times he was calling Mesmo's name, but he couldn't tell if the alien was there or not. He dug his mouth into a juicy steak, only to realize it was made of thin air, and he woke to his stomach grumbling painfully.

By morning, he couldn't shake off the fuzziness in his brain and his eyes blacked out for a second as he tried to sit up. His legs felt like numb stumps. He rubbed his face with his hands to try and get rid of his exhaustion, then broke out of his snowy shelter.

The sun shone, warming his cheeks. He lay in the snow, half-in and half-out of the igloo, unable to move. Finally, he attempted to stand shakily, his legs feeling like stubborn logs. He scanned the barren landscape with his eyes. There was no sign of Mesmo.

Having nothing better to do, Ben followed Tike as the dog wandered off into the trees. It wasn't long before they reached the edge of a lake. Ben knelt at its edge and broke a hole in the ice. Tike lapped at the water thirstily while Ben struck at the ice to make a second hole. He plunged his cracked lips into the icy liquid, ignoring its stinging cold. Satisfied at having filled his stomach with something, the boy wiped his mouth with the back of his hand.

Suddenly, Tike tensed. The dog crouched to the ground, ears laid back, teeth bared.

Ben froze with his arm half-way up to his mouth. A low growl reached his ears, chilling his blood. Filled with a sense of foreboding, he turned to face the source of the menacing sound.

The towering grizzly bear's mouth bristled with saliva. Its nostrils huffed. It shook its robust body, making its shaggy coat sway to-and-fro. The beast sniffed at the air, then rose on its hind legs and let out a furious roar, displaying its sharp teeth.

Ben scampered back in terror. His brain exploded with stars, the blood rushed to his ears and instantly, he was pulled into the grizzly's mind. He saw himself through the eyes of the bear with a powerful sense of irritation at the sight of this insignificant, trembling creature before him.

You trespass!

The words boomed in Ben's mind. The beast shook its mane to show off its power and might and the small creature shrank into a ball of fear before it. This only made the grizzly angrier. It wanted to swipe at the thing with one mighty paw.

A tiny part of Ben's mind was still his.

If I want to survive, I must give in to the skill.

It was imperative. It was urgent. It had to be now.

For Mom.

He let go willingly. He resigned to the translation skill and instantly slipped into the bear's thoughts, the words he needed forming in his mind's eye.

Yes! I trespass! This is your domain, mighty one. Forgive me.

The bear fell back down to its front paws in bewilderment. It sniffed at the air, trying to decide whether the insignificant creature was a menace.

Ben crouched on the ground, making himself as small as possible. He pushed aside his feelings of fear and made the bear aware that he was completely harmless. He bent his head, avoiding eye contact, and reached out a glowing hand in submission.

The grizzly blew angrily through its nostrils, but its curiosity was piqued. It spoke with a deep, authoritative voice.

You kill my family with thunder. You steal my food. I do not like your kind.

Ben knew it was referring to hunters. He also knew it was no use lying. His mind was open to the bear, just as much as the bear's was to him.

Yes, my species can be unkind. But I am just a cub. I have no thunder. I do not like thunder.

He remained silent, allowing the beast to scan his mind, ignoring a surge of nausea.

You are strange, different. Not like the others.

Ben bit his lip.

That is because I speak your language. I can listen and obey your will.

The bear relaxed slightly and took a step back.

Ben dared lift his head to peek at the animal. It observed him curiously, deciding Ben wouldn't make a worthy meal after all. Instead, its threatening mood fell away and it was replaced by compassion.

You are hungry.

The bear could read his every feeling.

No cub in my domain goes hungry!

The grizzly lurched forward, making Ben jump. But it headed straight for the lake. Ben watched, awestruck, as the majestic creature waded into the water, scanning the depths for fish.

Not long after, Ben plodded through the snow, away from the lake, through the forest, and out into the sun. A sleepy corner of his brain knew that he was still submerged with the bear, at the animal's complete mercy. He spotted a movement a little way off. The intrusion of another being in the bear's territory angered him and he advanced with determination.

The being had flimsy arms and legs, and fur on its small head. The being turned to face Ben the Bear and looked straight at him. "Benjamin? What's wrong?" it said, frowning.

Why do you call me Benjamin? Why do you not fear me?

Confusion entered Ben's thoughts.

Am I not a bear? What am I?

A part of his mind detached itself and became that of a boy. Ben's awareness slowly replaced the bear's thoughts as it focused on the being.

I know you.

"Ben!" Mesmo urged. "Snap out of it!"

Ben's mind uncurled entirely from that of the grizzly, which had remained by the lake, and through a hazy fog in his mind, he remembered who he was. He looked down, expecting to see huge paws, but instead found that he had hands, and that he was carrying a large trout. He let the fish slip to the ground.

I'm not a grizzly. I'm a human boy.

He stared at Mesmo in utter confusion. "Grizzly," he muttered. Then everything swam before his eyes, and he fell into darkness.

* * *

When he woke, Ben found himself lying on his back in the snow. He turned his head, but when he did, his stomach heaved, and he retched. Nothing came out of his mouth as he had not eaten in two days. He found Mesmo staring at him intently. He remained on his side, panting, holding Mesmo's eyes as if they were anchors. His mind was free from the bear's thoughts. He was just Ben again. But he was also paralyzed with fear. He had used the skill and it had knocked him out, making him weak and nauseous. It took a while before he found enough strength to speak. "Am I going to die?"

Mesmo studied him with deeply knitted brows. He approached Ben and knelt beside him. "No, Benjamin Archer, you are not going to die."

Ben rolled to his side, ignoring the dizziness in his head. "Then why is the skill making me so sick?"

Mesmo's gaze bore into him. The alien's shoulders sagged as if a great burden had been placed on them, and Ben thought he saw the shadow of a deep sadness pass before his eyes. "It is not you who is sick," Mesmo said. "It is the animals."

Ben stared at the alien in stunned silence. The words repeated in his mind.

It's not me. It's the animals!

He was dumbfounded at their meaning. "But how?" he breathed.

Mesmo wrung his hands together. "I have thought about it, ever since you mentioned the symptoms the first time. I thought perhaps your body was adapting to the skill, but soon it became clear that something else was going on—something that, as far as I know, has never been recorded by previous Observers of my kind. There is only one explanation: when you use the skill, you experience the animal's illness. That is my conclusion." He held Ben's gaze and asked, "Do you agree?"

Ben caught his breath. As soon as Mesmo had uttered the question, everything became evident in his head, as if a veil had lifted. And he knew, deep in his heart, that Mesmo was right. "Yes," he said in agreement. He pushed himself into a sitting position, his eyes never leaving Mesmo's gaze, and said again, "Yes!"

His nausea was replaced by horror at the seriousness of the discovery. "But Mesmo," he gasped. "It's all of them! All the animals: the seals, the bear, the ants..." He broke off, unable to continue. The implication was staggering.

Mesmo nodded and Ben knew instinctively that the alien had reached this conclusion some time ago.

"But it doesn't make sense," Ben reflected. "They don't act sick."

"I don't think they are aware they are sick. I think it is more like a hidden cancer that has not yet declared itself," Mesmo said. "When you connect with the creatures, you are not only communicating with them, you are also entering their whole being. You become one with them. Your body and your mind synchronize with their bodies and their minds. My daughter did that, too, when she was a small child and did not understand her skill. Where I come from, it is against the law to take over a creature's mind and body without their consent. The translation skill is used for communication only, and only if the creature is willing to communicate. The trick is to refrain from using the skill's full power unless the creature agrees to it.

"Because you are new to this skill, you have not yet learned to separate yourself from the creature. You become one with them. You forget yourself. The problem is, when your body synchronizes with theirs, it picks up any illness they may have, and its symptoms translate into your body. Hence your physical reactions.

"You are strong. You are healthy. But if you don't learn to disconnect yourself from the creatures you communicate with, your body may not recognize the difference between you and them anymore, and it will keep the symptoms. And, yes, then you truly will be sick."

Ben listened to Mesmo speak and knew that everything he said was true. It was as if some part of him had always known things were this way, but he had not known how to distinguish the animals' feelings from his own. He had connected with his whole being with many creatures already, and he shuddered when he remembered how sick he had felt after synchronizing with them. He was afraid to hear the answer but needed to ask the question. "Mesmo, why are the animals sick?"

Mesmo considered him for a moment, then replied, "I think you already know."

Ben did. "Are we—humans—making them sick?"

Mesmo did not need to answer.

"But how's that possible?" Ben blurted. "We're miles away from any city. There's no pollution here. How could that bear be sick?"

Mesmo replied, "Humans are not only poisoning the cities. Pollution is seeping into the air and the water, which carries it to all corners of the globe. No mountain or ocean has been spared. I have felt it in the water, everywhere I have travelled. This poison has been absorbed by all the living creatures on this planet. It is lying in wait in their bones, in their blood. If nothing is done soon, this terminal illness will declare itself and a massive extinction will be unchained among the animal kingdom. I fear none will be spared, perhaps not even humans."

Ben gaped. The enormity of these revelations was almost too much too bear. He thought of the gentle giant, the humpback whale, who had taken him into the deep ocean for a brief instant. And the seals, who had wanted to play with him under the surface of the water. Poisoned by his own species.

I can't let that happen!

From that very moment, something was born inside of Ben, like a calling or a lifelong purpose, and he knew things would never be the same again. A sudden realization came to him. "Is that why you came to Earth? To save the animals from dying out?"

A strange look crossed Mesmo's face—one that he could not read. The alien stood and said, "You need to eat." He placed his hands in the snow and melted it, so it covered the trout that the grizzly had offered Ben.

Ben stood as well, joining Mesmo hastily. "I want to help! I understand everything now. I want to master the skill and help you save the animals."

Mesmo did not seem to share his enthusiasm. He smiled, but his eyes remained sad. "You can't do that on an empty stomach," he said. "I know you said you want to become a vegetarian, but right now I think you need to break your vow."

Ben watched as bubbles and steam appeared on the surface of the water, rising from under the trout. A delicious smell seeped from the fumes. "You're boiling the fish?" he asked in wonder.

Mesmo smiled. "I can't light a fire, so this will have to do."

Ben's mouth watered.

CHAPTER 20 *Convergence*

Laura stumbled after Bordock in a daze. She wanted to lie down and drift into a deep sleep, but the idea that Ben might be alone on the mountain kept her going. She prayed that Mesmo had not abandoned him, though she knew that, considering Mesmo's condition, it would be impossible for him to remain at Ben's side at all times. He would have to return to his physical body at some point.

Her mouth dried at the thought that Mesmo could betray them somehow; that he was in fact the enemy. She could not, would not, believe it. Bordock was the one who had killed Mesmo's wife and daughter, shot down Mesmo's spacecraft and threatened Ben. She hated his ability to plant doubt in her mind and she pictured him as a deceitful chameleon that changed colours according to what suited him best.

Bordock pulled at her numb arm to keep going. She faintly registered that they were marching along a dense forest of fir trees.

Then a sound reached her ears. She forced herself to pay attention, as her fuzzy mind could not determine what it was.

Bordock stopped and they both listened as the rumbling

drew nearer and nearer at incredible speed.

Suddenly, Laura identified the source of the noise. "Helicopter!" she shouted.

Bordock pulled her away from the clearing and into the forest. He pushed her between some thick roots and held her down until the helicopter had zoomed over their heads.

Laura regained complete consciousness in an instant. Her heart drummed in her chest. She risked a peek into the clearing and spotted a couple of helicopters the size of flies high up on the mountain. The sky had turned blue, with scattered white clouds. Before long the area would be crawling with search teams.

Bordock grabbed her wrist and dragged her deeper into the forest until they reached the edge of a small lake, hidden under the branches of the trees. They stopped again, breathing hard, listening to the muffled silence.

This time it was not a sound that caught their attention. It was a smell. The smell of cooking fish: unexpected and penetrating.

"Smells like breakfast," Bordock smirked.

Laura's eyes widened. They were both thinking the same thing.

"Ben!" she gasped in horror.

Instantly, Bordock had a key in his hand. He unlocked the cuff on his arm and dragged her to a young birch tree.

"No, wait!" she yelled, fighting him. He was too strong and in no time had passed her arms around the tree trunk and closed the handcuff around her other wrist. Then he was off, following the direction of the smell.

"No!" she shouted, struggling to free herself. "Ben! Ben!"

* * *

Ben had gobbled up half the trout when the helicopter came. He plunged into the igloo with Mesmo just before it roared over their heads. He listened to the main rotor blade cutting through the air until long after it was gone.

Carefully, he and Mesmo extracted themselves from the snowy shelter and checked their surroundings.

"Up there," Mesmo said, pointing to the Kananaskis peaks. Helicopters circled an area high up the mountain which Ben judged was where they had left the pick-up truck. "Time to go," Mesmo urged.

"What about Mom?" Ben asked in alarm. Now that his hunger was stilled, his brain was sharp as a tack.

"Don't worry, we'll find her," Mesmo answered.

Really?

Ben put on his snow jacket slowly, struggling with doubt.

A crow hopped over and stole a bit of fish, which did not please Tike. The dog made as if to attack it, and it flew back a few feet, cawing indignantly. Tike went back to gnawing at the fish bones, eyeing the bird suspiciously.

"Hey, I know you!" Ben said, startled.

You're the crow with a broken wing.

Inevitably, Ben's blood swirled in his ears and already he felt himself drawn to the bird.

"Not now, Ben," Mesmo warned.

"Yes, now!" Ben spoke sharply. "This might be the only chance I get to find my mom." He glared at the alien, challenging him to object.

Mesmo scanned the sky rigidly. "All right," he said. "But be quick. And ask for permission first, and don't lose yourself in the creature. Remember who you are."

Ben nodded. "Move away, Tike," he said. "Let our friend

have some."

In his mind, he heard the dog growl as he moved away with the fish's tail in his jaw. The crow approached them again, then helped itself to another small piece of trout skin.

Ben hunched down next to it.

Hello, I am Benjamin Archer. Do you remember me?

The crow eyed him with beady eyes.

Greetings, Benjamin Archer. I am Corbalyn. Yes, I remember you.

Ben breathed in sharply. He had just approached the skill in a new way. He checked Corbalyn's wing, reminding himself that the crow was a she.

How is your wing?

It has healed well. You saved me. You may ask any favour of me.

I'm glad you are better. And I do have a favour to ask. I seek my mother. She is in danger.

I know where she is. I will take you. You may come.

Immediately, Ben felt drawn into the crow, and for a second he forgot who he was. But then he remembered Mesmo's words and gently rested his mind's eye on the crow's back.

I am still Ben.

He managed to keep control of his thoughts, instead of being swallowed up body and mind into the bird.

Corbalyn took off and soared above the trees, leaving a tiny Mesmo, Ben and Tike behind. The Ben whose spirit was flying with the crow watched as the physical Ben crumbled to the ground below him. He was not worried. A sense of exhilaration made his mind soar with the bird. The earth fell away beneath him revealing an immense landscape covered in a blanket of pristine snow. The mountains towered to his left; to his right, plains stretched as far as his mind's eyes could see. A faraway lake glimmered in the sun; the air was gentle and fresh on the bird's wings. Ben's soul experienced a moment of utter happiness, and for the very first time, he understood that the skill was indeed a gift. He told the crow, *Thank you!*

The bird swooped to the right, passing a large patch of snow that rolled down to a shimmering river at the bottom of the mountain. Several dots moved on it, and with a start, Ben realized that it was not a river, but a road.

We're almost there!

He smiled inwardly at the thought that escape was near.

Now to find my mother.

She is here.

Corbalyn glided down to a forest not far from Ben's shelter. The small lake where the grizzly had caught the trout came into view, and Ben's adrenaline increased when he caught a movement in the trees. He spotted his mother and panic careened through his mind. Corbalyn landed on a branch in alarm.

Below them, Laura fought to free herself from a tree trunk, shouting in panic, "Ben! Ben!"

* * *

"Are you sure this is a good idea?" Hao asked.

He struggled to place one foot in front of the other as, each time, he sank knee deep in the snow. Below him, the lights of half a dozen police cars whirled, stationed at the edge of the road, at the bottom of the Kananaskis. Hao believed they were miles away from where they should be.

"We've got the mountaintop covered," the Sheriff said as if reading his thoughts. "If they survived the storm, they will be heading this way. We'll comb the area from the road upwards, and the helicopters will do the same from the top down."

A dozen officers followed Hao and the Sheriff as they headed through the forest.

This is going to be a long day, Hao thought. He clenched his teeth as he trudged on. He still couldn't believe that Connelly had been foolish enough to follow the fugitives into a raging snowstorm. High Inspector Tremblay had been furious—as if Connelly's stupidity had been Hao's fault.

Hao mulled over the unfair situation—focusing on his anger rather than on the rugged terrain—when an officer yelled a warning. He tensed, eyes alert, scanning the trees for signs of danger. Then he saw it, a movement in the trees, a giant shadow lumbering at an uncomfortably close distance.

"Grizzly!" the Sheriff cautioned.

With a swift motion, Hao pulled the gun from his side and aimed.

"Whoa!" the Sheriff yelled. "What do you think you're doing?" He yanked Hao's arm down so the gun was pointing at the ground.

"For goodness sake!" Hao snapped. "You just said: that's a grizzly!"

The Sheriff shook his head as if Hao was a small child. "You aren't from around here. The dangers aren't where you think they are. First, if you shoot, there is a high chance you will injure the bear. Trust me, you do not want to irritate a grizzly. Second, we just had a snowstorm in early spring, which is melting as we speak. A shot like that could trigger an avalanche and that would be ten times worse than a charging bear." He let go of Hao's arm. "Believe me, it's best to leave it alone."

Hao watched as the brown animal disappeared into the forest. "So, how, exactly, are we supposed to defend ourselves?

Do you really think those fugitives are going to run into our arms willingly?"

The Sheriff sighed and shrugged. "Guns are for last resort only." He signalled to his men to move forward.

Hao put away his sidearm but kept his hand close to it. The memory of an attack by another massive animal—the humpback whale—was still fresh in his mind. The Sheriff had no idea what they were up against, and Hao wasn't going to let himself be fooled twice.

CHAPTER 21 *Confrontation*

Ben's mind did a double flip at his mother's cries, his thoughts getting entwined with that of the crow.

Stop it!

Corbalyn struggled.

Ben couldn't make sense of who he was anymore. He wanted to speak. He tried to use his voice to reassure Laura, but all that came out were exasperated caws.

Corbalyn took off.

No, wait!

Ben was powerless under the crow's will as it flew back to the snowy shelter. As it prepared to dive, Ben's inner eye caught Bordock hiding behind a tall fir tree, his hands glowing with intense power, ready to strike.

Dread shot through Ben's mind like lightning, making Corbalyn lurch. Unable to control her movements, the crow fell in a messy heap to the ground. With superhuman effort, Ben tore himself from the bird's mind. Full consciousness returned to his body at once. He swallowed cold air through his mouth with a loud gasp as his eyes shot open. "BORDOCK!" he shouted.

Too late.

Bordock thrust the mysterious power from his hands and it swept at them like a whip, hitting Mesmo first but avoiding Ben whose body still sprawled on the ground.

Mesmo vanished. The trunk from the fully mature fir tree next to Bordock detached itself from its base with a loud crunch. It teetered, then plummeted towards Ben who watched in dismay. He yelled, raising his arms to protect his head.

There was an immense thud as the trunk hit the ground. The branches plastered the snow, releasing a sprinkle of pine needles in the air as they swayed. Static dissipated slowly, a remnant from the alien impact. Then everything went silent.

Ben peeked carefully from behind his arm and found a thick branch a foot from his face. Its twigs had scraped his cheeks and a strong smell of earth filled his nostrils. But he was unharmed.

He daren't move, his heart beating like a frightened hare in his chest, while he took in the protective cocoon of branches that could have killed him had he been lying a little to the right. A light sense of claustrophobia enveloped him under the stuffy branches.

I need to get out.

The regular, crunching sound of footsteps in the snow froze him to the spot.

Bordock!

He peeked through the branches and saw the shapeshifter moving slowly along the tree.

Ben scrambled backwards, using his elbows and feet to push himself further away, but Bordock must have heard him. He stopped and straightened.

"Well, well," Ben heard him say. "A spirit portal. How convenient. As soon as our Toreq friend senses danger, he zaps away to safety."

Ben watched Bordock bend and search under the branches. The boy remained still as stone, hardly daring to breathe.

"I find that very disappointing," Bordock continued. "Don't you?" He stepped slowly along the fringe of the tree, causing Ben to scamper under its trunk for refuge. It only hid him partially, meaning he was nearing the treetop. He shut his eyes tight and prayed that the alien would walk by him.

"You and I are more alike than you know," Bordock said, his voice too close for comfort. "Think about it. Both of us were born without a Toreq skill." His footsteps paused. "And someone had to die for us to inherit one."

Ben placed his hands firmly on his mouth. Images of a fading Kaia with her long, white hair flashed before his eyes and he wanted to scream. Yes, she had died after she had given her skill to him, but he had not taken it from her forcefully. Unlike Bordock.

We are not alike!

"Huh," Bordock said with interest, his voice moving away. "There's your dog. I hope it's not hurt."

Ben's eyes shot open.

Tike!

His hands began to glow and blood rushed to his ears. He listened, but there was only silence.

Tike?

He called his dog with his mind, anxiously trying to make contact. There was no answer.

Ben's heart leapt. He turned to lie on his stomach and frantically pulled himself through the snow with his arms. Tike suddenly rustled the branches not far from him.

I'm right here. I'm stuck.

Ben found the terrier trapped in a natural cage made of

twigs laden with pine needles.

"Hold on..." Ben whispered, reaching out to release his dog. Something grabbed him forcefully by the collar of his jacket. "Aargh!" he yelled, struggling as Bordock's strong grip dragged him from under the tree and into the open.

He lay helpless on his back, unable to reach Bordock who held him from behind. His arms flailed, searching for something to grab on to as Bordock continued to drag him away from the tree. His hands only found snow. Frantic, he raised his arms and let himself slide out of his jacket. Bordock whirled.

Ben sprang to his feet; Bordock was too close for him to be able to make a run for it. He staggered backwards, Bordock shadowing his every step.

"We are *not* alike!" Ben burst out.

A sliver of a smile appeared on Bordock's face. "Ah, but we are. If only you would stop running and let me explain. We could get your mother. We could sit down, the three of us, and talk. She is not far. I took good care of her. You can trust me." He reached out his hand.

Ben's heart leapt in anger. "You're lying! I saw her—in there." He pointed to the forest behind them, vaguely surprised that his hands were still blue from connecting with Tike. "I'll never trust you!" he said, taking another step back. His foot caught in something. He tripped and fell heavily on his backside.

In a flash, Bordock was on top of him, choking him with his hands. "Clever boy," he said with a low voice.

Ben squirmed. The more he struggled, the more Bordock pressed on his neck, until he saw stars. He grabbed Bordock's arms weakly, his hands gleaming from the skill.

Bordock nodded satisfyingly. "Good. The skill is strong. It has lost nothing of its essence." His face was strangely calm and his eyes were emotionless black pearls. "No need to resist," he said quietly. "It won't hurt."

He waved a hand over Ben's face and Ben felt his eyes roll back in his head. In his mind's eye, he watched the blue filaments seep away from every blood cell.

And it hurt. It hurt as if a million healthy teeth were being extracted at the same time.

Whales, ants, crows, bears—Tike—all flashed before his eyes and it was as if his closest friends were being torn away from him.

Not the skill!

For the first and briefest moment, Ben knew he never wanted to part with the skill. It was his, and his alone, and Kaia had seen it in him that he was worthy to wield it.

Determination broke through the pain and Ben focused all the strength he had left towards the skill. He sensed his hands glowing ever stronger and the blood in his ears rushed like waterfalls. Yet that action only made it easier for Bordock to absorb the skill like a magnet.

There was a scuffle, and Ben heard a short yell. The connection broke for a fraction of a second. It was all Ben needed. His thoughts exploded outwards. His mind's eye caught Tike biting Bordock's arm and Bordock casting the dog away. He sent his thought whizzing on through the forest and collided with the mind of the grizzly.

HELP!

Ben's eyes fluttered open. He lay flat on the ground. Bordock sat not far from him, looking as though he had been hit by a truck. His eyes reflected surprise mixed with a touch of fear. There was also anger. And it was directed at Ben.

Ben wanted to get up, but his limbs were useless. He knew he couldn't handle another attack. Bordock knew it too.

The shapeshifter stood slowly and approached him. Ben

shivered uncontrollably, his energy utterly depleted.

The alien kneeled next to him, his eyes once more becoming emotionless pebbles.

Ben knew he was done for.

Then suddenly Bordock's eyes moved away from Ben's and his mouth twisted in horror.

A gigantic shadow covered the sky above Ben, and just like that, Bordock was gone. There was a deafening roar and a yell.

Ben forced himself on his stomach and watched, dumbfounded. The grizzly bear had Bordock in its paws, but with a mighty bang from the alien's hands, the two bounced away from each other. The grizzly collapsed on its side, Bordock crouching not far from it.

No!

Ben's skill searched the bear's mind frantically as he dragged himself up. Abruptly, Mesmo appeared out of nowhere. He placed his hands in the snow and a wall of ice surged before them, separating them from the shapeshifter.

Ben staggered to the grizzly's side.

Are you hurt?

He scanned the bear as it huffed heavily through its nostrils.

I am fine. Run, little cub. The men with thunder are here.

An image of whirling police car lights flashed through Ben's mind. He caught his breath, consumed by a sense of urgency. He made sure the bear was only dazed and would recover, then sent him his thanks.

He turned to Mesmo, who was staring at the icy wall he had created. The alien's face was very pale and grey. Whatever Bordock's attack had done to him, it had left a mark.

The shapeshifter stalked them from behind the ice. Something abnormal was happening to the outline of his body.

It expanded, surrounded by a halo of blue light. It twisted and deformed, inflating like a balloon.

Ben's mouth dropped as he realized the alien's intentions.

He's turning into a grizzly!

Ben and Mesmo watched, stunned, as the shape of a grizzly bear, identical to Ben's friend, reflected through the ice. It contemplated them, then took off suddenly.

Ben's pulse raced. "My mom! He's going after my mom!"

Ben picked up Tike who had wobbled shakily to his side. They rushed into the trees after the shapeshifter.

By the time they came to the edge of the lake, the fake grizzly had almost reached the other side. Mesmo plunged his hands in the half-frozen water and sharp, crystalline stalagmites shot up from its surface, forming a new wall that crackled with immense, sharp edges, cutting off the grizzly's path to Laura.

Ben didn't wait to see what Bordock would do next. He raced along the far edge of the lake, taking the long way around the sharp-toothed wall. Every time a wave of power emanated from either alien as they battled, he staggered, then forced himself onward.

He reached his mother as she crouched by the tree, trying to protect herself from flying ice-debris.

"Ben!" she gasped as he dropped Tike next to him and threw his arms around her.

Ben saw the handcuffs and understood why she couldn't get away. He pulled at them, knowing it was useless. He glanced around for Mesmo and spotted the alien on the other side of the lake, catching his eye with a meaningful look. Again, the alien hovered his hand above the surface of the lake.

"Watch out!" Ben yelled, covering his mother's head with his arms.

A silent explosion hurtled him backwards. He hit his head

on a tree trunk and saw stars. Blinking several times, he saw that the lake no longer existed. It had transformed into a thick fog filled with glittering droplets of water suspended in mid-air.

Already Mesmo was at Laura's side. He surrounded the handcuffs with snow and froze it to such a degree that the metal cracked.

"Ouch!" Laura yelled when the sub-zero metal scraped her arm.

"Sorry," Mesmo said, but Laura was already up, kneading her wrist. She rushed over to Ben.

"Are you okay?"

Ben nodded, rubbing the back of his head.

They helped each other up and followed Mesmo hastily as he parted a way for them through the thick mist.

* * *

The officers heard the strange sounds coming from the forest: low but powerful rumblings. Pine needles shook off the trees. Waves of cold air, not like natural gusts of wind, slapped their faces. They crouched down, glancing at each other with wide eyes.

"What's going on?" one of them asked.

Hao saw tiny, blue sparkles of ice floating by. "It's them!" He straightened and spotted a clearing some way ahead. "Let's go!" he urged.

The Sheriff spoke into his walkie-talkie, directing the helicopters towards the source of the noise.

CHAPTER 22 *The Wrath of the Kananaskis*

Suddenly, they were out in the open.

Laura and Ben stopped at the edge of the forest, hesitating to step onto the fold of the mountain.

Ben gasped. He recognized the clearing; he had flown over it with the crow's help. "The road's over there!" He pointed to the other side of the snow-packed open area. Spotting a corner of the road from where they stood, he took Laura's hand and urged her on. She didn't budge as she scanned the area, her face tightening.

"Maybe we should follow the trees..." she began, staring down the slope.

At the bottom of the mountain, Ben saw a lone man venture onto the open snow. Even from so far away, Ben recognized Inspector Hao. Along the side of the forest, other men slowly made their way toward him and his mom.

A sound like firecrackers sent them flying for cover. Ben whirled to find Bordock the Grizzly emerging from the shadows of the forest, the animal's body fluctuating from an intense heat that surrounded it, its eyes gleaming a cold blue. The trees scorched black at its passage. Large branches snapped like twigs in a hurricane and fell to the ground around it. Ben felt goosebumps rise at the tension emanating from the shapeshifter. Bordock was livid.

"Go!" Mesmo yelled.

Ben and Laura sprang in the opposite direction.

Bordock the Grizzly glowed steadily from a blue halo of power, which he concentrated before him and thrust at them with a movement of its large head. It was all Mesmo could do to stop the formidable attack. He barely had time to erect a vast wall of ice before it curved under the force of the blow and bent towards Ben and Laura like a massive, frozen hand rushing to engulf them.

The crackling blue static slipped off the arched crest like lightning and projected skyward, catching a passing helicopter, which was hurled aside as if a giant finger had flicked it away. The pilot managed to straighten the craft just in time before flying headlong into the mountain.

Mesmo lifted his fist from the ground at the base of the gigantic hand made of ice. Behind it, Bordock the Grizzly moved up and down like a trapped beast searching for an exit, its form visible as if through cracked glass.

Mesmo urged Ben and Laura away. They had been rooted to the spot, mesmerized by the alien confrontation. Needing no further encouragements, Ben struggled forward after his mother, their progress hampered by the deep snow.

He was almost halfway across the mountain artery when something pulled at his mind and blood rushed to his ears. He cringed in terror as a name left his lips.

"Tike!"

Ben merged with his dog in an instant. He watched through Tike's eyes as it sniffed at the icy wave Mesmo had created, searching for a way out.

Finding none, the terrier turned to face Bordock the Grizzly. The shapeshifter spotted him and roared with mad fury. The electrifying fear that grasped Tike was so strong it ejected Ben from his dog's mind. The boy tumbled to the ground and watched helplessly as the beast lurched after his dog. The two animals scrambled down the mountain.

"Tike! No! Over here!" Ben shouted in a frenzy. He dove down the mountain after his dog, who scurried straight towards Hao.

* * *

Hao's blood went cold when the furious grizzly emerged from the trees. The beast headed into the clearing and bolted headlong in his direction. He briefly registered the boy and his mother, then a man unexpectedly rushing after it. *What's wrong with them?* "Grizzly!" he yelled in warning to the Sheriff. He seized his gun, aimed at the animal, and expertly pulled the trigger. There was a deafening bang, followed by a whimper.

The boy's cry was heartwrenching. "NOOO!"

The grizzly scampered away, unhurt, but remained in close proximity by the trees.

Hao watched, confused, as the boy continued to run towards him. *I thought I missed?* He saw the boy throw himself behind a mound of snow.

The grizzly shook its mane, undeterred, then slowly approached the fugitives.

Hao raised his gun again but just then the mountain heaved. A huge slice of snow detached itself in front of him with an unmistakable rumbling. He watched in numb horror as the slice of snow became a wave. The wave became a wall that reached for the sky and, as it advanced, swallowed the grizzly and the three fugitives.

The Sheriff's scream chilled Hao's bones. "Avalanche! Fall back!"

Hao had a moment to think. *This was not how I expected to die,* before the avalanche caught up with him and plunged him into darkness.

* * *

Ben longed for silence. He didn't care about the overpowering noise that surrounded him, the threatening roar that resembled a furious gust of wind, the trembling ground beneath him, or the strange blue light that covered him. He didn't care about the alien who yelled under the effort to keep them safe from the raging avalanche, his hands spread out before him in an attempt to shove the descending snow above and around them. Ben didn't care that, when a muffled silence finally settled, the alien had almost become transparent as he staggered to the ground. Somewhere far away, his mother was calling his name. He didn't care about that either.

All Ben cared about was the heartbeat. Tike's heartbeat: very slow, very weak. Just like his. The excruciating pain that had blasted through his chest was almost too much to bear. It throbbed with each pulse, sending a flood of agony through his body. Or was it Tike's? He couldn't tell. They were one and the same. But as long as they held each other's gaze, maybe there was a chance, a glimmer of hope.

Tike blinked. A tiny light gleamed in the dog's eyes and Ben held on to it with all his might.

"Ben!" Mesmo's voice barely reached him. "Break the connection!" The alien's shouts were a mere irritating buzz in Ben's ear.

Don't listen to him. I'm staying with you.

It hurts!

It's okay. Give me your pain. I'll help you carry it.

Searing pain gushed through Ben's body and he groaned.

"Ben! Break the connection or you'll die!" The words were vital, pressing, yet unimportant.

"Ben! Wake up! Ben!" His mother called frantically.

Why don't they leave us alone?

Ben held his dog's gaze. It was the only thing that mattered in the world.

Laura's voice called from far away. "Tike!" Tike's eyes moved away from Ben's and the boy struggled inwardly, not wanting to break the only bridge remaining between them.

"Tike," Laura sobbed. "You beautiful, beautiful dog. Please don't take Ben away from me! You have to let him go."

Ben didn't catch the meaning of the words, but he did not like the sound of them. Tike licked Laura's hand once, then his eyes fell on Ben again.

It's okay. I feel better already. I'm going to sleep a bit now. I love you.

I love you, too.

Ben felt reassured. His dog was going to sleep for a while. Maybe he would, too. Ben sent him a blanket of comforting thoughts, wishing his dog a good rest. They did not get through. The bridge between them faded. The light in Tike's eyes faded. Something was wrong.

No, wait!

The dog's body sagged and Ben felt a rush of consciousness return to his mind. Cold under his body, a hard roof of ice above his head, the touch of his mother's hand on his shoulder.

He swallowed a tremendous volume of air, which

triggered his body functions. He heaved and wailed, "NO! TIKE!"

CHAPTER 23 *Doubt*

Hao blinked his eyes open. His brain was scattered and he felt completely disoriented. He tried to move, but for some reason his body would not respond. His eyes focused and he saw white. Everything was white. He wiggled his gloves; the stuff that surrounded his fingers seeped cold through the material.

And suddenly he remembered. His body jolted at the realization. He had been caught in an avalanche. And he was trapped in it, alive. He gasped in panic as his mind scrambled to grasp reality. Never in his life had he been more afraid.

He almost lost consciousness again, but then his years of harsh training in the police kicked in. He shut his eyes, willed his breathing to slow, and focused on forming coherent thoughts. It took him a while to quiet the horrendous thoughts of being buried under miles of snow, alone. He blocked the image out of his mind and concentrated on facts.

For one, he wasn't alone. He was confident that the Sheriff and his men had survived the avalanche, for they had been near the trees and would have had time to run for cover. One of them, at least, would rush for help.

Then, there were the helicopters. They would have seen the event from up high. Hao reassured himself with as much confidence as he could muster that help was on the way. A couple of hours at the most—that was the amount of time he would need to wait before rescue teams were set into action. He could handle a couple of hours.

Now to figure out how to catch their attention. Hao's heart skipped a beat as he realized the extent of the area they would have to search. He struggled for several minutes to restrain his reoccurring panic.

He licked his dry lips, still breathing hard, but in a more controlled way. He checked his body, moving one muscle at a time, testing for injuries. Everything seemed in one piece until he reached his left leg. A searing pain sent him yelling in shock. Black spots floated before his eyes and he puffed air like a locomotive.

"Broken leg, check."

He tried to move his hands and arms. The right one was trapped, but the left one had a bit more space. He loosened some snow with his fingers, feeling which way it fell.

At least I'm not upside down, he thought scornfully.

He moved his head to his left and caught his breath. He could see the blue sky through a small crack in the snow just above him.

"Help! Help!" he shouted before realizing it was useless. He wasn't too far from the surface. If only he could free his arm.

Painstakingly, Hao began to scratch away at the snow.

* * *

Laura cradled Ben in her arms. She had covered Tike's ruined body under her sweater. Mesmo sat with his legs bent upright, his arms resting on his knees, his head hanging in total exhaustion. Laura noticed his grey skin anxiously. Eventually, he lifted his head and said determinedly, "You can't stay here. You need to get away and find a safe place to hide. I won't be able to follow. You'll be on your own."

Laura held his gaze and fished a notebook page out of her back pocket. She scanned the five names on the small document that her father had left her.

"Bob M.?" Mesmo asked, pointing at the last name on the list.

Laura sighed, then folded the notebook page again. "Yes: Bob M.," she confirmed with a final tone in her voice, indicating she wasn't inviting any more questions. She stuffed the paper in her back pocket. "Ben needs a place to heal. We'll be heading to Toronto. Bob will help us." She lowered her gaze, burning to ask how bad his wounds were. But Bordock had shaken her faith in him. *Mesmo just risked his life to save ours,* she reminded herself guiltily.

"What is it?" Mesmo asked.

She bit her lip.

"It's Bordock, isn't it?" Mesmo pressed. "What did he tell you?"

She shot him an accusing glance. "Not enough." She could tell he was struggling to remain present and her heart ached to reassure him.

Mesmo considered her, then said quietly, "I never asked anything of you, Laura Archer. You were the one who offered to help me."

When she didn't answer, he said, "Look at me."

She did.

His honey-brown eyes did not reflect any resentment or accusation. He held her gaze and said, "I know you don't trust me. And you probably shouldn't. But there is one thing you can be certain of. I would never harm Ben." He paused to make sure she was listening. "You need to realize, I could have taken Ben's skill away from him any time, killing him in the process. But I didn't. And I won't."

Laura swallowed and lowered her eyes in shame.

"Laura," he said, forcing her to look at him again. "You don't owe me anything. You are free to go."

She opened her mouth, but couldn't find anything to say. He stood and backed away into the wall of their icy cocoon. He placed his hands on its surface and began melting away the snow, thus creating a tunnel coated in bluish light.

If her heart had been heavy before, now it weighed like a brick. "Ben?" she said, shaking his elbow.

Ben winced and placed a hand to his chest.

Laura's face tightened with worry. She lay him down and lifted his sweater and shirt. Her hand flew to her mouth. On Ben's chest, near his heart, was a large, black-and-blue smudge that corresponded with the area where Tike had been hit. A sob escaped as she realized how close she had been to losing her son.

Mesmo came back, hunched over and pale. His image faded, she could see the tunnel right through him.

"Ben, we have to go." She nudged him gently, but he remained limp in her arms. He opened his eyes and saw Tike. His face crumpled.

Laura and Mesmo exchanged a glance.

She didn't think he still had it in him, but the alien placed his hands around Tike's body. Water flowed around the terrier until it formed a block. Mesmo froze the water in such a way that it became smooth and transparent, like resistant glass.

The three of them remained there for a long, silent moment, watching Tike who seemed to be sleeping peacefully in his icy coffin.

* * *

Hao squeezed his hand open and closed to restore some circulation to it. His gloved fingers cramped, but he was making headway. This was no time to give up. He sweated profusely and panted under the effort until he was finally able to bend his arm up to his shoulder. Next feat would be to reach his arm through the hole above his head. He decided to take a short break to calm his thoughts and rest his arm. He just wanted to close his eyes for a minute...

Cold drops splattered on his cheek. Hao woke with a start, panic surging through his body. Had he really fallen asleep? He swore angrily. His body ached from being forced into the same position for...how many hours?

How long was I asleep? Dread overwhelmed him.

A shadow passed overhead. He twisted his head to peek through the hole, fully expecting to see a cloud or, worse, setting dusk.

Instead, he saw a man standing right above him. Hao could see the underside of his chin and his nose. The man glanced in the distance.

"Hey!" Hao shouted. "Heeey!"

He yelled and yelled for help, but the man just stood there, impassive.

He can't hear me! Hao realized in horror. Despair gripped him.

"Help!" he said weakly, his eyes filling with tears.

The man glanced down, his bald head reflecting the late sun.

Hao blinked in a hurry. "Connelly!" he shouted frantically.

"I'm down here! Help!"

Connelly seemed to be looking straight down at him, yet his face was expressionless.

Why can't he see me? Hao thought in alarm.

Something was wrong with the bald man's eyes, but he couldn't put his finger on it.

I'm delirious, Hao thought.

Connelly straightened and moved away, disappearing from his view in a second.

"No! Connelly! Come back!" Hao shouted in a strangled voice. He sobbed, unabashed, giving in to exhaustion and fear. When he finally calmed down, snippets of thoughts and images haunted his mind. Grizzlies that charged him, innocent-looking boys that transformed into alien monsters, dark spaceships hiding imminent threats...

He had not been ready for this assignment. It was beyond his human comprehension. "I just want to make sure you stop in time." His sister Lizzie's words scolded him from the border of his sanity. If only he had listened to her!

Connelly's face floated on his eyelids, strangely twisted as he stared at Hao without seeing him.

But he DID see me.

The thought jolted him awake. Hao's body shook with cold and shock, but a spark lit deep within him.

"He D-DID see m-me!" he stuttered, his eyes widening in disbelief, consciousness returning with force.

That one thought, whether originating from a hallucination or reality, sent a rush of power through his body, willing him to live. His ears caught the sound of a passing helicopter.

Using this new source of energy, Hao began to scratch frantically at the snow again. He could not feel his fingers but went on anyway, and before long, he shoved his arm through the opening above his head, sticking his hand out to the surface, like a signalling flag.

* * *

On the verge of being overcome with emotion, Laura heaved Ben to his feet, placed his arm around her neck and encouraged him to walk away. He was too numb to resist and let himself be guided through the tunnel.

Mesmo closed up the tomb and, once they were out, made the snow collapse into the tunnel behind them.

The sun shone warmly on their skin from a beautiful, crisp sky. The significant flow of the avalanche was visible, and there wasn't a soul in sight, though a helicopter hovered some way up the mountain.

Laura spotted the road they had been trying to reach for two days.

Has it only been two days? she thought in wonder.

Before long, she and Ben took a place in the back of a camper of a friendly couple of skiers who were headed to the city of Calgary. Ambulances and police cars sped by them in the opposite direction, rushing to the scene of the avalanche.

As they drove off, Laura stared out the back window and saw Mesmo standing on a ledge, his form barely visible. She knew instinctively that he had gone too far. A lump formed in her throat and she realized that, friend or foe, she would end up helping him.

* * *

Victor Hayward leaned back in his chair and peeked under the business table. He didn't care whether the investors who surrounded him thought he had fallen asleep. He had stopped counting the hours since he had begun negotiating with the twenty-or-so businessmen, split evenly to his left and to his right. One of them spoke angrily, jabbing a finger at the perfectly polished oak table.

Hayward had long given up listening to the man's accusations, especially when his emergency phone buzzed, indicating something was up with the alien.

He held the phone under the table and watched the video clip his contact had sent him. The grainy black and white image that filmed the alien non-stop had captured an unmistakable scene: the alien was having seizures. The video stopped when men clad in doctor's coats and masks rushed to the alien's side.

Hayward typed hastily: WHEN?

His contact replied: 15 MIN AGO.

Hayward waited impatiently for more. When nothing came, he texted: REPORT!

His contact wrote: ALIVE. BUT BAD SHAPE.

Hayward sighed in frustration, then texted: ON MY WAY.

He put away the phone and realized that the bothersome investor stared at him condescendingly while he continued to enumerate his grievances.

Hayward placed both his hands flat on the table, feeling the cool, soft surface on his skin. He let the investor blab away for some time, then said sharply, "Enough."

The investor barely paused in his lecture, addressing the other men at the table who were all ears.

Hayward smacked both hands loudly on the table. "ENOUGH!" he shouted.

The investor plopped on the chair, his face turning pale as

white bedsheets.

Hayward stood slowly, his imposing presence making up for his short stature.

"Enough of your whining," he seethed. "Whining never made anyone rich. Whining isn't what's going to put money back in your bank accounts." He displayed the back of his stubby hands, fingers spread out before his face. "These two hands built an empire through hard work and sweat. You wouldn't know what that means because you're just a bunch of scavengers, scrambling over each other to catch the falling crumbs. But I say, enough! I have an empire to rebuild, and I have two hands to do it with. You have delayed me far too long. I am needed at headquarters. This meeting is over."

"But the oil..." someone ventured meekly.

"Forget the oil." Hayward cut in. "Oil is a thing of the past. It is time to introduce new, boundless energy to the aviation business. Heed my words. Victory Air will be the first company in the world to introduce cutting-edge technology never heard of before."

He glared at them, all twenty investors in turn, then straightened the jacket of his business suit and headed out with a confident stride.

He paused by the door and said, "Don't forget who you're dealing with. I am Victor Hayward. Remain loyal to me and gold will roll off the table into your laps. Or else, scatter back to the filthy gutter from whence you came."

He waited until an assistant hurriedly opened the meeting room doors for him, then headed down the hall with a determined stride.

He had delayed too long. He needed answers, and he needed them now!

EPILOGUE

The crow rested on a rooftop, watching as a grey bus pulled out of a large station topped with the letters GREYHOUND STATION CALGARY. It kept its beady eyes on the boy seated with his forehead pressed against the windowpane. Their eyes met briefly before the bus turned into a bustling street.

The crow took flight, escaping the fumes coming from noisy cars and the shiny skyscrapers. It followed the sun as it descended in the sky, caressing the tips of the Canadian Rockies. Their snowy caps put on gowns of orange and red while stars began to appear in the dusk.

The crow beat its wings rhythmically, purposefully, until she found the Kananaskis Mountain Range and, further up, the town of Canmore. She swooped down just as streetlights flickered on and landed on a leafless apple tree of a yard she knew well.

Warm light splashed onto the ground from inside the house, rich smells seeped from the kitchen, and a man's contagious laughter escaped from the dining room.

Corbalyn cawed and ruffled her feathers.

The girl with the long, black hair lifted her head. She was sitting at the top of the deck stairs and when she saw the crow, she got up and approached the tree slowly.

Corbalyn began to clean her wings.

"Hello, you," the girl said. "Feeling better?"

The crow took no notice and continued her task. Then she pulled at her tail, releasing a feather—her longest and most beautiful one. Holding the feather in her beak, Corbalyn observed the girl for a moment, then let go.

The feather floated to the ground, and the girl picked it up. She held it up to admire it. Finally, she looked at the crow with a gleam in her eyes. "A gift," she whispered. "Thank you."

Corbalyn ruffled her feathers once more, then took off into the night.

The girl remained immobile, holding the feather in the palm of her gloved hands.

"Kimi? Dinner's ready!" a woman's voice called from inside the house.

The girl didn't move, but when she finally did, she had a smile on her face.

BEN ARCHER

and

THE MOON PARADOX

The alien's choice.

Rae Knightly

CHAPTER 1 *Bob M.*

When Ben and Laura stepped through the elevator door into the penthouse, they found Bob M. waiting.

Not that Ben took much notice: at that point, he felt emotionally and physically drained. He slouched behind his mother, studying the marble floor, anxiously waiting for her to get over the tedious but obligatory introductions, and then, maybe, they would finally let him get some rest.

Hang on for a bit longer.

A movement out of the corner of his eye startled him.

Tike?

But it had only been a flickering shadow cast by candlelight on the countertop of an open kitchen.

Ben swallowed.

He had already caught himself thinking that his dog was scampering at his feet several times in the past days, sending flashes of raw pain through his body. But that wasn't possible, of course.

Tike's dead.

"Laurie, baby!" The man who greeted them as they entered the tenth-floor penthouse, reached out his arms and pecked Laura's left and right cheeks. He stood back and held her by the shoulders so he could take a better look at her. "It's been so long!"

Ben heard the strain in his mother's voice. "Hello, Bob."

He glanced over her shoulder, remembering that Bob was the last name on the list his grandfather had left them, which meant it was someone they could trust.

The man with short, brown hair and neatly trimmed beard stuck his hands in his pockets casually. "Long trip?" he asked, drawing his eyebrows together.

Laura nodded. "Yes, we've been travelling for three days non-stop and just walked from the Greyhound Station."

Bob sighed. "You should have told me. I would have picked you up."

Laura shrugged. "It's okay. I didn't want to bother you..." She glanced around the apartment. "...and I wouldn't have come if I'd known you were having a party."

Ben realized there were wine glasses on the kitchen countertop and chatting voices coming from a balcony.

To their surprise, Bob burst out laughing. "This? A party? Oh, come on, baby. Have you forgotten already? This is Toronto. It's Friday night. This is just a little get-together." He cleared his throat as if he hadn't meant to laugh so hard. "Don't worry about it. These are just some friends. I'll introduce you to them later. But I guess you want to freshen up first."

Ben stared at his own frumpled clothes and muddy snow boots, suddenly aware of his appearance. After all, Bob wore an elegant, black suit and white shirt, unbuttoned at the neck. He fit perfectly in the minimalist apartment with uninterrupted windows overlooking the Toronto skyline.

"And, who's this?"

Laura had been standing before Ben this whole time, for

which he was grateful, but now she moved aside purposefully and placed a hand on his shoulder. "Bob, this is Benjamin. Benjamin, this is Bob."

Ben glanced at his mother. "Bob M.?" he whispered. He hadn't really cared to ask where they were going until then.

She nodded.

"Is he a wit..." He was going to say "witness of *The Cosmic Fall*," but she widened her eyes in warning and cut him off, "This is Bob *Manfield*."

Ben turned his attention from his mother to the man, confused. "Manfield? Isn't that Dad's last name?" His mind whirled.

Bob tilted his head, his brown eyes boring into Ben's. He held out his hand, which Ben accepted. "Hey there, squirt," he said. He glanced briefly at Laura, then added, "I'm your Uncle Bob."

Ben searched his mother's eyes, but she looked away.

Bob shook Ben's hand firmly, and for an instant, the boy forgot about their troubles.

I have an uncle!

"It's good to see you again, Benjamin. It's been too long," Bob said, putting extra stress on the last words. He couldn't take his eyes off Ben and looked as though he were hoping for recognition from the boy.

Laura shifted and placed a hand on Ben's shoulder again. "Actually, everyone just calls him Ben. And we're pretty tired, Bob. Do you think we could talk later?"

"Of course," Bob clapped his hands together, smiling. "Follow me." He led the way into a stylish living room with black sofas and a glass coffee table.

Ben spotted several elegantly dressed people on the balcony which was decorated with white, Christmas-styled lights and candles, while upbeat jazz music played at a decent volume—enough to lighten conversation without drowning it.

A young woman wearing a tight, one-piece dress entered the apartment with a glass of wine in her hand. With the other, she removed her high-heeled sandals and thrust them aside, then smiled when she spotted them. "Hey, Bobby! There you are!" she called, pattering lightly over to them. "Who are your friends?"

"Hi, Pearl," Bob said. "This is Laura Archer. And this is her son, Ben. He's my nephew."

Pearl squealed. "Your nephew? You never told me you had a nephew. Look at him! He's your spitting image. But much more handsome." She squeezed Ben's cheek.

Ben prayed the dimly lit apartment hid his crimson face.

"This is Pearl," Bob said, seeming a bit jumpy. "She works for me."

Pearl waved a manicured hand at him. "Yeah, right. I clean up after you, honey." She rolled her eyes at Laura. "He has such a scattered brain, this one. You'd think he'd be capable of organizing a simple social event, but guess who did all *this*." She waved a hand at the decorated balcony.

Bob wrapped his arm around her shoulders. "Yes, all right. I couldn't do it without you, baby. You know that."

She smiled approvingly, then waved her wine glass at Laura, "So, is it just you two, then?"

"...and Mesmo," Ben blurted.

Laura tensed sharply beside him.

Bob frowned. "Mesmo? What's a Mesmo?" Then his eyes widened. "Hold on a minute! No cats in my house. I hate cats. I'm allergic."

Picturing Mesmo as a cat, Ben snorted before he could stop himself.

Laura coughed into her hand. "Hum. Mesmo is a friend. And no, he won't be staying. It's just the two of us."

"I see," Bob said, raising an eyebrow. Then, addressing Pearl, he explained, "Laura and Ben arrived from the West Coast earlier. They'll be staying with me for a while."

Pearl's face brightened. "How lovely! I'll finally have a decent girlfriend to talk to." She winked at Laura, then turned to Ben. "And you? Have you ever been to Toronto before?"

"Erm... n-no."

"Really?" she exclaimed. "You'll love it here! There's so much to do. Have you seen the CN Tower?" She took his hand and skipped lightly to the window with him in tow. "Look! You can see it from here."

Ben swallowed and glanced back at his mother who directed a small smile at him.

* * *

Laura woke with a start. She stared at the darkness, trying to remember where she was. She had only meant to lie down for a couple of minutes, but instead, had fallen fast asleep, fully dressed, in the bedroom Bob had provided for her and Ben.

A light tapping on the door made her jump. She realized it was the sound that must have woken her. She rolled over and found Ben sleeping beside her, also fully dressed. He hadn't even taken off his boots.

She stood and quietly opened the door a crack.

"Hi," Pearl whispered. "I didn't want to wake Ben."

Laura nodded, blinking the sleep from her eyes.

"Um, I didn't want to wake you, either, but we ordered sushi and Bobby said you might be hungry. Do you want to join us?"

Laura turned to check that Ben was still sleeping, trying to figure out what to do.

"I made Ben a sandwich, earlier," the young woman said as if reading Laura's mind.

"Thanks," she replied gratefully, not used to having someone take care of things for her. She felt tired, but she was starving, too. Should she step out in her muddy clothes? The idea of mingling with a crowd of well-dressed, casual people was daunting.

"Um," Pearl interrupted her thoughts. "Bobby said you didn't bring any luggage. I thought maybe you'd be more comfortable in this." She held up a black dress.

Now, where did she get that from? Laura wondered.

"Bobby entertains every weekend. I always keep a spare dress around," Pearl said, seeming to read her every thought.

Laura accepted it, studying the young woman curiously. "Are you and Bob..." she began.

"...together?" Pearl finished. She rolled her eyes. "Oh, goodness, no! We'd get into each other's hair all the time. He's so unpredictable. It drives me crazy."

She's trying too hard, Laura realized.

Pearl locked eyes with her. "What about you? I guess you and Bobby have quite a history?"

Laura dropped her eyes. "Yes. But that was a long time ago..." She let the phrase hang. Then she smiled at Pearl. "Thanks for the dress. We won't be staying long—a couple of days at the most. I'll make sure to return it to you before we leave."

Did a wave of relief pass briefly before the woman's eyes?

Pearl grinned. "Well, go on then. Try it on. We'll be waiting for you." She waved as she turned to leave.

Laura closed the door and let out a long, shaky breath. Her

heart pounded in her chest. Had this been a bad idea? Something in the back of her mind told her it was, but she had no choice. Ben worried her more than she cared to admit. The events that had taken place on the Kananaskis Mountains were excruciatingly fresh in her mind. She needed a place where she could watch over him and make sure he hadn't come out with permanent injuries—physical or mental.

"That goes for me, too," she thought sarcastically, heading for the attached bathroom.

The hot water from the shower triggered a flow of emotions, and she found herself sobbing as she let go of the stress of the past days. She cried for Ben, she cried for Tike, and she cried for Mesmo, who hadn't given a sign of life since their escape from the mountain. She wished she could go back in time and do things differently.

By the time she stepped out of the bedroom wearing the cocktail dress, she had resolved that, from now on, she would do whatever necessary to let things end well.

"Ooh, look at you!" Pearl quipped when Laura stepped onto the balcony. She took Laura's hands and extended her arms so she could see the dress better. "It suits you perfectly." She placed her arm through Laura's own and directed her into the crowd. "Come on, I'll present you."

CHAPTER 2 *An Honest Conversation*

Laura sagged into the living room couch as soon as the last guests entered the elevator. She had put on a false smile and made polite conversation well into the night, thankful that her years working as a server in bars and restaurants had taught her the appropriate social manners to survive through the evening.

"Bye, honey," Pearl said as she kissed Bob on the cheek. The young woman waved at Laura, who returned the gesture. Then the elevator swallowed her up, and Laura was left alone with Bob Manfield.

He removed his dark jacket, threw it to a chair, then settled into the couch opposite her with a plastic water bottle in his hand. He crossed his ankle over his knee and rested his arm on the back of the couch in a relaxed stance. "So," he said after drinking a sip of water. "Here we are."

Laura noticed an unruly mesh of hair sticking out from the back of the man's head, and felt a pang of recognition. She cleared her throat and gestured to the apartment. "Is this yours?" she asked, her mind still in a polite-conversation mode.

Bob nodded with a gleam in his eye. "Yup. It's all mine. I bought it a year ago. I still have unpacked boxes in storage, though. It's been too busy, what with my business expanding and everything..."

Laura wasn't really listening. Facing Bob in flesh and bone after so many years destabilized her. Sure, his brown beard and nice outfit were new, but for the rest, he hadn't changed a bit, which didn't help the pile of unresolved emotions she felt for him.

She realized he had stopped talking and was staring at her, so she said hastily, "You've done well for yourself. I'm happy for you."

"Are you, really?" he replied with a touch of scorn.

I don't need this right now, Laura thought. Out loud, she said, "Yes, I am. Really."

She rested her elbows on her knees and rubbed her arms. "I'm sorry I called you out of the blue like that. I didn't mean to crash in on you, but things didn't work out the way I had planned."

Bob placed the bottle of water on the table and shrugged. "It's okay," he said. "I already knew you were coming."

Laura stiffened. "You did?" Her voice rose in alarm.

He waved a hand at her. "Calm down, baby. There's nothing to worry about." He locked eyes with her. "Your dad warned me you'd come."

"My dad?"

Bob grinned. "Yeah, I know, right? I'm sure I pulled the same face as you right now." He leaned back on the couch and crossed his knees again.

"He came here about six months ago. He was waiting for me in the lobby." Bob chuckled. "I thought he'd come to give me a good beating, I'll tell you! But no, it turns out your old man wanted to have a chat, face-to-face. I invited him up, and he sat right where you are now. He told me, basically, that you and

Ben were going to need help and that I wasn't to ask any questions but that I was to give you any assistance you needed. And boy, did he make it clear that I was to accept." Bob laughed out loud.

Laura burst into tears. She pressed her hands to her face hurriedly. This was the last person she wanted to show weakness to, but the mention of her dad hit her hard. It was as if Bob had pointed out that her dad was sitting right next to her and she hadn't even noticed.

Bob fell silent for a second, then said, "Hey, baby! What's the matter? I didn't mean to..." he broke off, his voice thick.

When she finally felt calm enough to peek through her fingers, he was holding a box of Kleenex in front of her. She plucked a couple of tissues and blew her nose. "I'm not your baby," she said gruffly, trying to recover some dignity.

Bob plopped on the couch with his arms resting on his knees, the box of Kleenex hanging loosely in his hands. "Right. Sure, bab... er..." He sighed and shook his head, then said, "How is the old man, anyway?"

Laura pressed the tissues to her face and hiccupped. "He passed away, not long ago," she managed. "Heart attack."

Bob gasped. "Oh, baby, I'm sorry," he exclaimed. He seemed genuinely crestfallen. "I don't believe it! The old oak, gone? Jeez! No wonder you're so upset." He pushed the box of tissues over the table to her side.

They both stared at it for a long moment.

"Do you want to talk about it?" he asked gently.

Laura shook her head. "No." She spoke in a final tone, then straightened. "We won't be staying long, Bob. We just needed a place to land on our feet, then we'll be off again."

"Now wait a minute. I agreed to take you in. And on your own terms at that. But now that you're here—and that *Ben* is here—you can't go disappearing on me. We have an opportunity here..."

"Stop it, Bob!" Laura snapped. "You promised over the phone you wouldn't go there."

"No, you listen here, little lady." He pointed his index finger at her. "Come now, *Uncle* Bob? Are you *serious*?" He snorted. "Ben looks like a smart kid. How long before he realizes Robert and Bob are not brothers, but one and the same? Jeez', baby, everybody knows Bob is a diminutive for Robert." He slapped his leg. "*Uncle* Bob! How did you come up with such a stupid thing?"

Laura glanced in the direction of the room where Ben was sleeping. "Sh! Okay, okay," she whispered through gritted teeth. "It was a dumb idea. I was desperate. But Ben can't handle the truth right now, Bob. Please, trust me! You promised you'd go along with it."

Bob stared at her in obvious irritation, then said with determination, "I want Ben to know I'm his dad."

Laura bit her lip hard. Her mind scrambled for a reply, but she felt so drained. She couldn't handle another drama.

Bob glared at her, and when she didn't answer, he said, "What? Am I not worthy? Is that what you're thinking?"

Please, not now!

Bob fidgeted in apparent anger. "Come on, say it, then! It's not that hard!"

Laura's exhaustion turned to anger. Didn't he understand that this wasn't the right time, nor the right place? Emotions bubbled inside and threatened to explode.

He leaned forward and stared at her with hard eyes. "Say it!"

"You promised you'd watch over Ben!" she burst out. "You said you'd only be gone for five minutes, but you were out for five hours, drinking with your buddies. What kind of a dad gets into a car without a driver's license, crashes into another car, then runs off in a panic?"

Bob didn't move an inch. He waited to make sure she was done, then said in a low voice, "Now that wasn't so hard, was it?"

They glared at each other.

A candle died out, leaving a smell of burnt wax.

"Look," Bob said. "I can tell you haven't read a single letter I sent you these past eleven years..."

"Thirteen," she corrected.

Bob raised his eyes. "All right, twelve, thirteen, whatever. The point is, if you'd read any of them, you'd know how often I repeated those very phrases to myself, day in, day out, night after night, going over what I'd done, wishing I'd reacted differently, hating myself every single minute for my stupid reaction.

"But you turned a deaf ear on me. You visited me only once in my five-year jail term, and it was to tell me you gave Ben your dad's surname instead of mine, that you told Ben I'd died in the crash and never to contact you again." His pale face trembled with rage. "And I felt so bad I fell for it and agreed."

He intertwined his fingers, their knuckles going white. "And then, it came to me one day. I was wasting my life away—waiting, hoping, praying—for you to forgive me. But I realized, the only one who could forgive me was *me*. If I were ever to move forward, I would need to make my own peace, stop looking back and live my life. I figured no one was badly hurt in the crash. I paid my dues. So I forgave myself, respected your wish and moved on."

He waved his arms at the apartment. "You could have been part of it, you know? But you chose not to. And I wonder, sometimes, when are *you* going to get over it, Laura?"

His eyes dug into hers, forcing her to look down.

In her haste to find a safe place to hide, Laura had conveniently discarded the thought that this conversation would take place. How wrong she'd been! Had she really thought Bob would let them stay with him without attempting to resolve their decades-old fight?

If it hadn't been for Ryan Archer's contact list, Laura realized she would never have ended up here. *Dad, why did you leave me Bob's number?*

But it was too late now. The day she had always dreaded loomed before her.

Ben is going to hate me.

Bob's stance softened a little. "If you think I no longer care about what I did, you're sorely mistaken. I still think about that crash every day. I was irresponsible and young, I know that. But I'm a grown man now, I've learned from my mistakes. I would never turn my back on you or Ben like that again. You've got to believe me."

Laura studied his face and saw honesty reflected in it. She had shut him away from her life the minute she had learned he had been responsible for the crash, disgusted by his narrow-minded escape after his botched hit-and-run.

We were so young!

They had met in high school. They had been carefree. And then Ben had come along...

She stood and brushed at the folds in her dress. "I don't know if I can ever forgive you, Bob, but that's my problem, not Ben's. It would be selfish of me to continue keeping him from his dad." She took a deep breath. "So, I agree. We'll tell him, together. But please, Bob, give me a week, two at the most. There's something I need to take care of, first."

I have to save Mesmo.

* * *

Ben woke, feeling rested for the first time in a long while. He had had a deep, dreamless slumber, no Tike or Bordock to torment him. He stretched, then realized his mother lay fast asleep next to him. He got out of bed as silently as possible, then took a long, refreshing shower. After days spent on the freezing Kananaskis Mountains and travelling day and night across the country, the hot water felt glorious.

Having to wear his same clothes satisfied him much less, however, but, with no other option, he stepped into Bob's living room with his torn jeans and dirty hooded sweater.

He blinked at the bright light coming in from the windows and ruffled his wet hair, before realizing Bob was sitting on a stool at the edge of the kitchen counter, working on his computer while sipping on a cup of coffee.

"'Morning, squirt," Bob said, turning to face him. "Did you sleep well?"

Ben noticed his uncle's hair was as disheveled as his own, which was a bit of a relief. He smiled and replied, "Hi, Uncle Bob. Yes, thanks."

"I think your mom's going to be knocked out for a good while yet. She went to bed pretty late. We had a lot of catching up to do."

Ben felt a pang of envy at having been left out of the conversation. He would have liked to learn everything he could about his newly-discovered uncle.

"You must be hungry," Bob said, getting off the high stool and opening the fridge. "Ah, you'll have to forgive my manners. This is a typical bachelor's fridge. Not even an old piece of cheese in sight." He straightened and pursed his lips. "How about we get a decent plate of eggs and bacon? I know just the right place!"

Ben wanted to hug the man. "Yes, thanks."

"Okey-dokey. Get cleaned up, and we'll head right out."

Ben's face drooped.

Do I look that messy?

Bob put his hands to his hips. "You don't have anything else to wear, do you?" he said with half a frown.

Ben blushed and shook his head.

"All righty! Looks like we'll be doing some shopping as well, then!" He clapped his hands together.

Ben's nose curled automatically, making Bob laugh. "Oh, come on!" he said, wrapping an arm around Ben's shoulders and directing him towards the private penthouse elevator. "It will be fun! Just you and me. Men only."

Ben grinned. "Thanks, Uncle Bob. I'd like that."

CHAPTER 3 *Beetrix*

Over a hearty breakfast, Bob chatted about life in Toronto. He told Ben how he successfully launched and ran three nightclubs and that he was a big fan of professional ice hockey. He promised he'd take Ben to a game.

But Ben wanted to know about his dad.

Bob shrugged. "Sorry, squirt. I can't say much. I left home pretty young and backpacked around the world for several years. Then, I figured I needed to settle down someplace—do something with my life—and Toronto seemed as good a place as any."

His eyes became distant. "Your dad and I weren't that close. I'm sorry to say he was a pretty irresponsible guy and probably would have continued down that road if things hadn't ended the way they did."

He leaned his arms on the table and bent forward to be eye-level with Ben, who was sipping on his milkshake. "Now, I will tell you this: he and I, we had the magic touch when it came to hockey passes. You should have seen him on the ice! He was the best! A natural skater with loads of potential."

Ben's eyes widened as he imagined his dad sliding on an

ice-skating rink, dressed in hockey sportswear. "Really?"

Bob pulled back and grinned. "Yes, really!" He knocked with his knuckles on the table as if to indicate that their conversation had ended and searched for a waitress to pay the bill.

Ben continued to daydream as they left the restaurant and crossed the street to a triangular-shaped park.

"What about you?" Bob interrupted his thoughts.

"Huh?"

"Yeah, what about you, squirt? You haven't told me anything. What types of things do you like?"

Ben swallowed. "Um, I like dogs, I guess."

"Dogs?" Bob said with a touch of amusement. "Ah, well. These are the types of dogs that I like." He stopped walking, and Ben bumped into him.

They were standing in front of an impressive, two-tiered fountain. Spouts ejected water from the base up, the majority of these originating from a dozen statues placed around the fountain.

In a different life and a different time, Ben would have found these statues amusing, but not so at this very moment, because the figures happened to represent dogs of all kinds. Some were placed outside the fountain, others, inside, and out of their snouts, water arched in clean lines into the basins above.

"We're in Berczy Park," Bob explained. "And this is—you'll never guess—Dog Fountain." He chuckled. "I thought you might like it."

Ben knew he was waiting for some kind of sign of approval, as any typical boy would have, but he couldn't do it. He offered Bob a forced smile. "Cool," he said, struggling to contain his loss. "Can we go, now?" He needed to get away or he was going to break apart.

Bob pouted his lower lip and shrugged. "Sure."

They walked towards busier streets and glanced absentmindedly at store windows.

"So," Bob said with his hands in his pockets. "Who's this Mesmo guy, anyway? Your mom's boyfriend?"

Ben poofed, then bit his lower lip to get a hold of himself. "No." He giggled, then thought the better of it. "He's a good friend, though. We're supposed to meet him here."

He shut his mouth, wondering if he was saying too much, then suddenly remembered Kimi's surprised face when she had found out that her mother, Maggie, and their host, Thomas, had revealed that they had feelings for each other. Was he missing something similar between Mom and Mesmo?

Adults can be weird in that way.

His thoughts were interrupted when Bob led him into a clothing store and began fishing out jeans, shorts and sweaters. Before long, Bob shooed him into the dressing rooms, his arms laden with clothes. It took Ben a while to sift through the mound.

"Are you okay in there?" Bob called after a long while.

"Humph, I think this shirt is too small." Ben pulled open the curtain to show him.

Bob checked the price tag for the size, then clicked his fingers. "Off with it. I'll get you a bigger size."

Ben pulled the shirt over his head, then winced. He stared at his chest and found the black mark near his heart—a painful reminder of where Tike had been hit. He removed the shirt with more care and handed it to Bob, but found the man staring at him with deep worry lines on his forehead.

He saw the wound!

"Um... skiing accident in Alberta," Ben muttered.

"Ah," Bob said as he accepted the shirt. "That looks bad.

Maybe we should have it checked..."

"Oh no, that's fine." Ben jumped in a little too quickly. "I'm much better already." He closed the curtain in a hurry and shut his eyes to prevent tears.

From then on, the mood between them changed, and even though Bob bought him a cupboard-full of clothing and sneakers, Ben couldn't quite get that frown off his uncle's face for the rest of the morning.

"Do you want to get some ice cream at the lake?" Uncle Bob asked after they were done shopping. It was almost noon.

Ben wanted to go home, but at the same time he didn't want to darken his uncle's mood further, so he accepted.

They ended up at the edge of a lush park called Tommy Thompson Park, which formed a curious web-like net of paths straight into Lake Ontario. The Canadian/US border ran through the middle of it. Ben squinted, hoping to spot the other side of the vast body of water, but the US shore was too far away.

He sat and rested his back against the trunk of a tree while Bob went to get their ice creams from a local vendor. He stroked the grass with the palm of his hands and enjoyed the occasional ray of the sun on his face.

I wonder if Kimi is eating ice cream, too?

"There's an ice cream truck that sells the best bubblegum flavour in the world. You'll see." Her voice echoed in his head, and he wished he could have stayed in Canmore long enough to taste it.

If you crush me, I'll sting you!

Ben gasped. He looked down and found his hands glowing. Blood rushed to his ears as his alien skill kicked in. He glanced around to make sure no one had noticed, then stuffed his hands hurriedly in the pockets of his new, hooded sweatshirt.

A gentle humming reached his ears, and when he searched

through the grass with his eyes, he found a rather large bee lumbering around the green stems, close to where his hand had been.

Oops! Sorry!

It seemed proper to apologize. Remembering what Mesmo had taught him, Ben presented himself.

I am Benjamin Archer. May I speak with you?

There was no immediate answer, but rather, a wave of desolation brushed at his mind. Ben quickly set up a mental barrier between his and the bee's feelings.

Hello, Benjamin Archer. I am Beetrix. Yes, we may talk.

Ben smiled briefly at the bee's name, but at the same time knew instinctively that something was wrong.

What's the matter?

The insect brushed at its antennas.

I can't find my hive. My children won't make it without me.

Ben frowned.

Why?

Beetrix buzzed her wings.

Because I am their queen.

Ben's mouth dropped.

No wonder she seems bigger than an ordinary bee.

The thought escaped before he could hold it back, but she heard him anyway. She did not seem to mind, however.

I am larger than the others because I am the mother of a thousand children. They are lost without me—if we are not lost already...

What do you mean?

An illness has spread in our midst. I cannot identify it. I had hoped that, by moving my hive, we would find a healthier home. But that is when we got sepa... aah!"

A gigantic foot stepped on Beetrix, rendering everything dark in Ben's mind.

Bob stood right beside him, plastering the grass with his shoe.

"Get off!" Ben cried, jumping to his feet and shoving his uncle aside.

An ice cream cone slipped out of Bob's hand, its contents splattering to the ground. "Whoa!" he yelled. "Take it easy, squirt!" He gestured toward the grass. "Those things sting!"

"No!" Ben said vehemently. "Not this one." He crouched and searched the grass with his mind.

Beetrix?

A tiny movement indicated she was still alive.

Ben let out a breath of relief.

Beetrix buzzed angrily a couple of times and climbed to the top of a grass stem.

Are you hurt?

She tested her wings.

I am fine. But tell that giant troll to watch where he puts his paws!

Ben fought a smile.

Come with me. I'll help you find your hive.

Beetrix considered the offer for a second, then clambered onto Ben's sleeve and nestled in the boy's hoody.

When Ben stood again, Bob was staring at him with his nose curled and one eyebrow raised. "Are you serious?" he said, licking at his ice cream.

Ben grinned. "Yep." He checked that his hands weren't glowing too much, then picked up the shopping bags with his new clothes inside.

"I'm allergic," Bob warned as they headed out of the park.

"It's okay. I'll tell her not to sting you."

Bob paused a fraction of a second, before biting into the sweet dessert. “You’re a weird kid,” he said.

“I know.”

“And I’m not getting you another ice cream,” he added, a drop of white vanilla landing on his beard as he bit into the cone. “This is mine.”

Ben laughed. “That’s okay. Sugar is bad for kids my age anyway.”

They walked, side by side, the dark mood between them having lifted somewhat.

“Uncle Bob?”

“Hm?”

“You know bees like ice cream, don’t you?”

CHAPTER 4 *Suspicion*

"Hi, Mom!"

Laura heard Ben greet her as she stepped out of the bedroom. But he didn't stop to talk to her. He dropped shopping bags on the floor and headed straight for the balcony.

She pulled on a sweater and followed him. "Hi, honey. Where have you been?" She wanted to give him a hug, but he said, "Careful!" She pulled back and watched him remove a bee from his hoody with extreme care. His hands glowed a soft, blue colour. He placed the bee on a decorative shrub, then spoke to it, "I'll get you something more comfortable in a bit."

Only then did he turn his attention to Laura. "Her name's Beetrix. She lost her hive. I'm going to help her find it."

Laura smiled and ruffled his hair.

"Oh! And Uncle Bob took me shopping. He bought me tons of clothes and these sneakers." He pointed at the clean, new shoes on his feet.

"Really?" Laura said thoughtfully. "That's nice of him."

Ben nodded, checking up on his new insect friend. "Yeah. He took me for breakfast and everything!"

Laura stopped stroking his hair and stared at him, but he

seemed to be in a genuinely good mood.

She let out an inward sigh of relief.

Bob didn't tell him.

"Ben," she said. "Have you heard from Mesmo?"

Her son's face darkened as he shook his head. "I tried contacting him this morning," he said, tapping his wristwatch.

Laura admired the tiny stone in the centre of the watch. It sparkled too much for it to be a diamond, reminding her that it was in fact an alien device used by Mesmo to spirit travel.

Only, Mesmo was not connecting with them.

Laura's heart thumped loudly, but she didn't want Ben to notice her worry. He had enough on his mind. Her thoughts had been on the alien ever since she had seen him last, standing on a snowy ledge, his spirit almost transparent from the effort of having saved them repeatedly on the Kananaskis Mountains. That had been four days ago.

Way too long.

"Keep trying, okay?" she said.

Ben nodded. They both automatically glanced inside the apartment, where Bob was busying himself unpacking Ben's clothes.

"I'm going to stay here for a bit," Ben said, indicating his glowing hands.

"And I'm going to look for a job," Laura said. "Will you be okay on your own?"

He nodded, and they gave each other a quick hug.

Laura stepped back into the living room to find Bob staring at her, as he drank from a bottle of water. He had an unreadable look on his face.

She forced a smile. "Ben said you took him shopping?" She went through the clothing that lay on the edge of the couch. "Thank you," she added, not sure yet if she approved. Hadn't she always been Ben's provider?

He nodded briefly.

Laura tried to fill the silence between them. "I'll pay you back as soon as I can. I'm on my way to look for a job. Do you mind if Ben stays here in the meantime?"

He took her gently by the wrist, still with that serious look on his face. "Come," he said. "We need to talk." He led her to the kitchen counter and invited her to sit on the high stools.

What now?

"Look, baby," he began. "Why do you need to look for a job? I told you already, I run three successful nightclubs. I'm opening a fourth location in three months. I'm always looking for people..."

She lifted her hand firmly. "I'm not working night shifts again, Bob."

He cocked his head. "Who said anything about night shifts? Hear me out, for once! My accountant is going on maternity leave next month. I need someone I can trust to replace her. She could teach you. It's a nine-to-five job, five days a week. The wage is above average. I treat my staff well, believe it or not."

Laura listened to him with a slight frown. He was speaking with a stern voice that was new to her.

Must be his business voice.

She found herself liking this grown-up side to him. She couldn't help seeing Ben's face in his, only it was the adult version of the one she'd fallen for so many years ago.

"And there's another thing," he continued, pulling her back into the conversation. "I may not know much about kids, I'll give you that, but I know this boy should be in school right now. There's a private school not far from here. Very well rated. I know the Principal. I could get him registered in a heartbeat." He kept talking, but unexpected feelings washed over her again.

I fend for Ben!

She struggled to push back the emotion.

In less than five minutes, Bob had solved two of her biggest issues: money and keeping Ben occupied. She didn't like it, something in the back of her mind resisted for no sound reason.

Don't be so selfish! It's only until I find Mesmo.

She waited patiently for Bob to finish talking, then said, "All right, I accept. Thank you, Bob."

He gaped, his hand still raised before him as if he was preparing for another round of convincing. "Oh," he said, leaning back. "It's that bad, then?"

She frowned. "What do you mean?"

He sighed and stroked his beard. "The Laura I knew wouldn't have accepted that easily."

She lowered her head. "I guess we all have to grow up sometime." She cleared her throat and stood. "I still need to get some clothes. Don't worry, I'll pay for them myself," she added quickly.

He grabbed her wrist again and bore his eyes into hers. "I don't know what's going on with you two, but I'm not blind." He glanced at her wrist, which still had the mark of Bordock's handcuff on it. "I won't accept anyone hurting you or Ben. Your dad said not to ask questions, but I hope you'll smarten up and spill the beans." He let her go and sat back. "When you feel up to it, that is."

His eyes were glued to her, making it extremely hard for her to maintain her composure. She took a few steps back and nodded unsteadily. "Yes. When I'm ready." She turned before he could say anything else and entered the elevator, letting out a shaky breath as she did so.

* * *

Inspector James Hao stared fixedly at an invisible point on the opposite side of the room. The concrete wall of the Dugout infirmary was dull, to say the least, but after its hasty construction, painting the walls a clean or cheerful colour hadn't exactly been on anyone's mind.

He pouted in concentration, oblivious to his surroundings or the throbbing pain of his broken leg, which lay tightly wrapped in a cast before him on the hospital bed.

Doctors and nurses slid by his open door, going about their business, which suited him fine because right now he was burning with anger. He had placed a lid on his feelings, concentrating solely on getting better so he could get back to work as soon as possible.

A shadow stopped before the crackled glass of the window that separated his room from the corridor. Then a man stepped into the doorframe and leaned against it nonchalantly.

"Hi, partner," Connelly said with his hands in his pockets. "I thought I'd check up on you."

Hao set his jaw, the lid on his inner cauldron sliding off to reveal burning coals.

Connelly entered, checking the room with vague interest. He stopped by Hao's bed and tapped the cast lightly with his fingers. "That looks painful," he said. "Did they tell you how long you'll be in here for?"

Hao signalled for Connelly to approach, which he did. Then, with lightning speed, Hao grabbed him by the collar and pulled him close, so their faces were inches apart. "You saw me!" he growled. "You saw me, buried in the snow under your feet. And *you left me there*!" Every word was laden with fury and disbelief.

Connelly struggled to release himself from Hao's grip. He pushed against Hao's shoulders, but Hao wasn't going to let him go so easily. Connelly's hands slid closer to his throat.

"Hey! What's going on here?" A woman's voice shrieked down the corridor, "I need assistance!"

There were thudding feet, then several hands tried to unlock the two fighting men from each other. Arms appeared around Connelly's chest, and a doctor yanked him away.

"You saw me!" Hao screamed, his face livid.

Connelly staggered back, then caught himself. In a defiant gesture, he straightened his tie, shot a deathly look at Hao, then stepped out of the room.

"I'm on to you!" Hao yelled after him.

CHAPTER 5 *Headquarters*

The sun reflected so brightly on the skyscraper that Laura had to look away. She stood at the corner of a busy crossing, lost in a crowd of hasty pedestrians who brushed passed her, handbags swaying, work shoes clicking hurriedly on the walkway.

The Victory Air headquarters filled the shiny, window-clad building, with a long set of stairs leading to a modern reception. Some employees sat on the steps, enjoying a ray of sunlight while on their lunch break, or scanning their phones while they chatted with a colleague.

Laura unzipped the raincoat she had bought and straightened her new, olive-green sweater. It had felt good to get rid of the clothing damaged by the frigid weather on the Kananaskis Mountains.

She plunged into a coffee shop opposite the building and lined up for a coffee and sandwich.

"Busy, isn't it?" she said pleasantly to the young man on the other side of the counter who was preparing the items.

"Actually, this isn't too bad," the man said, working the coffee machine. "You should've seen the line-up an hour ago!"

Laura smiled at him. "Is that when all the Victory Air

employees have lunch, then?"

The man laughed. "Yeah, I guess so."

"I saw the news yesterday. I thought they were on strike?"

"Yesterday, yes. Tomorrow, who knows? Everybody's expecting the company to announce bankruptcy."

"That's awful," Laura sympathized.

The man shrugged as he passed her her sandwich and punched in the cash amount of the food. "Nah, I wouldn't worry about it. You should see the CEO. He walks up those stairs with his chest puffed, like he owns the world. I bet he's got it all figured out."

Laura stopped counting the coins she had pulled out. "You mean Victor Hayward?" She slid the money towards him slowly.

The man nodded. "He's like a well-oiled clock. You'll see his limo drop him off at 8.45am and pick him up at 6pm sharp, every day. With everything going on, you'd think he'd take a back entrance. But not Victor Hayward. He barges through the crowds of protesters and media as if he didn't have a care in the world."

Laura stepped aside while he spoke as impatient customers made it clear she was taking up too much time. She thanked the man behind the counter and squeezed into a chair facing the window, beside two men working on their laptops.

She stared at the infamous building. Would she find answers here? Would Victory Air or its boss lead her to Mesmo?

She settled in her chair, and waited.

* * *

Hao munched on his lip, then realized he was staring at the wall with a deep frown again. It wouldn't do to lie around for days doing nothing. It was time for some action.

He picked up the phone on his bed stand and pressed an extension.

"Yes, sir?" his assistant said on the other end.

"Bring me my laptop. I want access to *The Cosmic Fall* files. Make sure I still have clearance. Also, bring me the boxes in my office. And be quick about it!"

"Yes, sir," the assistant said, but Hao heard the hesitation in his voice. "Hum, but will the High Inspector agr...?"

"Just bring me the damn things and let me deal with the High Inspector."

In his mind's eye, Hao imagined the assistant jump to a salute. "Yes, Sir!"

* * *

Laura fidgeted on her seat. She had been at the coffee shop for almost five hours, and her back hurt. She'd had to spend her last coins on a lemonade when she noticed the baristas at the counter glancing her way.

It was close to five minutes before six when a sleek, black limousine pulled up in front of Victory Air.

Laura pushed back the stool, making it screech on the floor, but she took no notice and was out in a jiffy. She had to wait at the pedestrian crossing until the light turned green, because heavy evening traffic blocked the way, and by the time she made it across the street, the man she had been waiting for was already exiting the building.

She jogged diagonally up the imposing stairs, bumping heavily into one of Victor Hayward's bodyguards. Her handbag flew to the ground.

"Hey, lady! Watch it!" the bodyguard warned, shielding Victor Hayward with his muscled body. He did not need to speak loudly as his stiff posture was indicative enough that he wasn't up for any nonsense.

"I'm so sorry!" Laura apologized. "I wasn't paying attention."

The bodyguard regarded her sternly, then picked up her handbag, giving her a good view of the short man with mixed black-and-grey hair and black-rimmed glasses who was about to enter the limo.

"Mr. Hayward!" she called.

The bodyguard jumped to attention, holding out his hand defensively. "That's enough! Stand back please."

Laura tried to glance behind his hulky body. "Mr. Hayward! It's Laura Archer," she shouted. "From Chilliwack."

Victor Hayward froze with his head already inside the car. Then he straightened and turned to see who had spoken.

Laura waved and smiled at him, trying to look as innocent and harmless as possible.

The man's suspicious eyes softened. He gestured at his bodyguard to let her pass.

"Mr. Hayward!" she said breathlessly. "Do you recognize me? I'm Ryan Archer's daughter, Laura. You know? Your neighbour in Chilliwack?" She stood before him and held out her hand. "Imagine bumping into you here!"

The CEO of Victory Air shook her hand, then recognition filled his eyes. He broke into a genuine enough smile and said, "Laura? My, my! Yes, I remember you, though if my memory serves me well, the last time we spoke you were about this high..." he lifted his hand parallel to the ground to indicate her height, "...and you were trespassing on my property, if I recall."

Laura let out a giggle, her blush coming out naturally. "Oh, gosh! Please don't remind me. Dad was so angry with me!"

"You can say that again," Hayward said, his grin widening

to show a set of small, extra-white teeth. "Ryan came over and apologized profusely. So how is my old neighbour?"

Laura's face fell instantly. "My dad passed away some months ago, Mr. Hayward. He suffered a major heart attack."

Hayward's grin faded. "Ah, dear girl. I'm sorry to hear that." He glanced around hastily. "Look, I can't talk now. But I want to see you in my office next Monday, 9am sharp. Ask for my Executive Assistant, Charlene. She'll be informed." He slipped into his car and pointed his index finger at her. "Don't be late!"

His chauffeur closed the door on him and hurried to the driver's side.

Laura blew her hair out of her eyes and watched the limo disappear into traffic.

* * *

"Where were you?" Ben asked, standing hastily from the sofa and dropping the X-box control on the coffee table. He'd been out for hours, unsuccessfully looking for Beetrix's hive, and had been disappointed not to find his mother on his return.

Laura removed her raincoat and checked the apartment. "Are we alone?"

Ben nodded. "Uncle Bob's at work. What happened?"

She placed her hand on his shoulder and led him back to the couch. They sat down and faced each other.

"I saw Victor Hayward," she said, a little out of breath. "I'm meeting him on Monday morning."

"*What*? Are you crazy? How did you do that?"

"He was my neighbour growing up, remember? I know him personally, though not very well, of course. He was away most of the time, but he'd drop by to catch up on local news with Grampa."

Ben shivered. "Do you think he witnessed *The Cosmic Fall*?"

Laura pursed her lips, then nodded. "Yes. I'd bet my bottom dollar on it."

Ben's hands flew to his face. "So now what, Mom? You can't just walk up to him and say, 'hand over the alien.'"

"I know, I know. We have to come up with something."

They both fell silent, deep in thought.

Suddenly Ben's face lit up. "I have an idea."

CHAPTER 6 *A Dangerous Device*

Laura's footsteps echoed on the perfectly polished marble floor. The imposing symbol of Victory Air hung above the impeccable reception where receptionists wearing bandanas with the red-and-grey colours of the company spoke into extra-thin headsets.

One of them glanced up and said, "Good morning, may I help you?"

Laura tried to make herself look important. "Yes, I'm here to see Mr. Victor Hayward."

A brief shadow of disbelief passed before the receptionist's eyes, so Laura added quickly, "My name is Laura Archer. Please refer to his Executive Assistant, Charlene."

The receptionist's fingers were already typing away and before long, Laura was given a printed badge that allowed her to override the elevator security to reach the CEO office on the top floor.

Laura's legs felt like jelly as she scanned the badge and pressed the highest number on the button panel, a staggering flood of doubt almost making her turn back.

This isn't going to work!

She had argued extensively with Ben, telling him that his

idea was way too risky. They could lose contact with Mesmo forever. Not only that, Ben was basing his idea purely on a hypothesis, one they had never tested.

The problem was, they hadn't been able to come up with any other plan. Most of their ideas involved tedious research and time-consuming spying on Victor Hayward. And time was not on their side. Laura was constantly reminded of Mesmo's words: if he did not reach Saturn's moon, Enceladus, within a week, he would never be able to return to his home planet.

She wished they had been able to make contact with the alien to confirm their theory and give him a heads up. But after multiple attempts, Mesmo still had not answered Ben's calls, meaning he was not in good shape.

Or maybe worse.

Laura shuddered.

Hang in there, Mesmo.

She set her jaw, straightened her shirt neck and pulled back a strand of ash blonde hair behind her ear as she watched the floor numbers flash by.

The elevator door pinged and slid open, revealing a posh reception decorated in tones of soft grey and splashes of red.

A woman with shallow cheeks, glasses and a tight bun stood as soon as Laura entered the spacious area from which she caught stunning views of the city.

"Ms. Archer, I presume?" the woman said in a business-like tone, which she had clearly practiced over many years.

"Yes."

"I'm Charlene. Please, follow me." The woman reminded her of a stern middle-grade school teacher.

Laura pinched her lips. In a matter of seconds, she was led into a large office with an impressive oak desk and two leather sofas with an oak coffee table in the middle. Victor Hayward sat in one of these chairs with his legs crossed as he studied documents over his black-rimmed glasses.

He dropped the documents as she approached and stood to shake Laura's hand. Laura felt his thick, golden ring under her fingers. "Laura," he stated. "Welcome. Can I get you something to drink? Coffee? Tea?"

"Oh, um, a glass of water, please."

Hayward nodded to Charlene, who left instantly, while he invited Laura to sit.

"Thank you for being so timely," he began. "I can't stand people who are late. It's a habit I caught from my line of work. No one likes a delayed flight, you will agree." He sat opposite her and Laura thanked the stars she had categorically refused to let Ben accompany her.

"It's the least I could do, Mr. Hayward," Laura replied. "I'm surprised you were able to make time for me at all. I appreciate it."

"Nothing's too much for my dearly departed neighbour. I miss him sorely."

Laura glanced at the businessman, trying to determine whether he was being genuine, but Hayward showed nothing of his feelings. She shuddered at the thought that he could be holding Mesmo against his will.

"So, tell me, what brings you to the city?"

Laura accepted a glass of water from Charlene and said, "I needed a change of setting. You know, to get away from the memories..."

"Yes, of course. Both of your parents passed away, if I remember correctly. There isn't much holding you back on the West Coast, is there?"

Laura shook her head, going along with the small talk, wondering what she should say next.

"And... what is your line of work, exactly?"

Laura's throat went dry, so she took a sip of water. "Oh, uh, I wasn't much good in school. I didn't get a degree or anything like that. I've been working odd jobs here and there."

And taking care of Ben.

"I see. Well, if there's anything I can do in that department, don't hesitate. Charlene can set you up with Human Resources and look at your options..."

"Oh, no, no. There's no need. I've already found a job. But, thank you."

Hayward rubbed at his chin, then narrowed his small, green eyes. "Don't let the media get to you, Laura. They are pure sensationalists, shouting to all who will hear that Victory Air is taking a dive. But they have no idea what I have in store for them. My company is at the dawn of its existence, not at its end."

He stood and paced before the windows overlooking Toronto and Laura could hear the pride in his voice. "The media is not far from the truth, Laura. Oil is a thing of the past. It's time to fuel our cars and planes with brand new, cutting-edge technology."

His hand curled into a fist, as if he were holding a miniature Earth within it. "Victory Air holds that technology, the power to generate unlimited, low-cost energy for all!"

Laura felt the blood drain from her face.

So that's what he's after!

She understood everything now, Victor Hayward needed the alien to reveal the source of energy that fueled his spaceship. Hayward would use it for his own airplane company. Investors, governments, the military... all would flock to him to get their hands on such a source of power.

She almost dropped her glass of water as she placed it on the edge of the table. She was no longer able to concentrate on the magnate's self-centered speech, but nodded in what she considered were appropriate places.

Hayward sat heavily in the sofa, the leather squeaking under his weight. "But enough of that. This is our little secret, between you and me, and is a work in progress." He tapped the tips of his fingers together and bore his eyes into hers.

She braced herself as she sensed more was coming, then picked up the glass again to keep her nervous hands busy.

"Tell me about *The Cosmic Fall*," he said.

Laura lurched, spilling some water. "The... the what?"

He leaned back as if he were suddenly tired. *"The Cosmic Fall.* You've heard of it, of course. Did you know it occurred on my land?"

"It... it did?"

"Yes. Picture this: some interstellar rocks lurch towards the Earth and, bingo! they fall right into my lap, so to speak. You'd think anything that landed on your property belonged to you, but no, the government stepped in and took it all away from me. I was wondering, did that happen to your father, too?"

What's he getting at?

"Er... no, of course not..." she stammered.

He nodded, raising his eyes to the ceiling as if in deep thought. "I didn't think so. However, considering your precarious financial situation, I am sure you will be happy to hear that I am interested in purchasing your father's house and land, since you clearly have no further use for it. How would you like to step out of my office with a two million dollar check in your pocket?"

Laura's jaw dropped.

She made a superhuman effort to close her mouth and swallow a large lump in her throat. "Th-that's unexpected. I... um... would need to think about it."

He waved his hand at her. “Of course! Of course! It’s a lot to take in. But my offer is on the table. You should take it while the deal is hot because I can’t promise it will still be there tomorrow.”

“Thank you.” Laura forced the words out. She was on the verge of a nervous breakdown.

I need to finish this!

She stood hastily, as did he.

“Here’s my card,” he said. “Call me anytime. I’ll even add in an extra two hundred grand, as a last show of goodwill to my dear neighbour.”

She took the card hastily. “Thank you, Mr. Hayward. You’re very kind. I will consider your offer.” She needed to change the subject at once, or she would crumble.

It’s now or never!

She opened her handbag and said, “Talking about goodwill, I have something for you, as well.”

She pulled out a square box, neatly wrapped in grey paper with a red ribbon around it. “It’s not as generous as your offer, of course, but I wanted you to have this.”

Hayward glanced at her in surprise, then proceeded to remove the wrapping. A velvet box appeared, resembling one that would contain a wedding ring. Only, this one was bigger.

“What’s this?” Hayward said, opening the lid.

“It was my father’s,” Laura explained. “I have no use for it. It’s a men’s model. I think Dad would have felt very honoured to have Victor Hayward wear it.”

The businessman pulled out a silver watch and studied it closely.

“You see?” Laura said, pointing to its centre. “It even has a diamond in it. Go on. I want to see it on your wrist.”

* * *

Inspector Hao burst into High Inspector George Tremblay's office, located at level -1 of the Dugout, ignoring the assistant who tried to stop him.

"Why does Victor Hayward have access to the spaceship?" he blurted.

Documents slid out of his hands as he tried to keep a hold on his crutches. He swore, then bent with his cast leg teetering dangerously in the air, until he managed to recover the papers.

When he straightened again, the High Inspector—who cast a distasteful look his way—said into his phone, "I'll call you back." He hung up, then waved the assistant away.

Hao hopped inside the office and landed in the chair opposite his boss.

"James," the High Inspector greeted, his voice absent of emotion. "I see you're up and about."

Hao dropped the documents on the desk and stabbed his finger at them. "Why does a civilian witness to *The Cosmic Fall* have access to the spaceship?" he repeated, ignoring the greeting.

The High Inspector remained impassive. "Agent Connelly is a civilian witness, as well," he noted. "And he has access to the spaceship."

"Yes. But this is different. Why wasn't I notified? Why did I have to go through the registry to find out?"

"Victor Hayward isn't just anybody. After making his witness deposition, he offered us his own flight engineers—some of the best in the country. His navigational expertise can help us pierce the mysteries of the extraterrestrial spacecraft. Not to mention that he is one of our highest esteemed patriots who—by the way—deserves your utmost respect."

Hao pressed his hands to his eyes. "I don't believe this. You gave him clearance? Just because he knows some engineers? Do you realize he signed a billion dollar contract with the United States military last month? Don't you find that a little suspicious?" His voice trailed off suddenly and his mouth fell open. "But you already knew this..."

The High Inspector humphed, clearly not in the mood for this conversation. "Canada and the United States have common goals. We have the technology; they have the manpower. It's only natural we work together."

Hao sat back and clenched his teeth. "What about the fugitives, then?"

"The ones whose bodies we never recovered from the avalanche?" the High Inspector jabbed. "What about them?"

Hao ignored the criticism and searched through the papers, then pointed at a list. "Ryan Archer, Wayne McGuillen, Susan Pickering, Thomas Nombeko... do you see any pattern here?"

The High Inspector shrugged. "No. But I'm sure you're going to tell me."

"Over the past months, our fugitives have had contacts with all *The Cosmic Fall* witnesses on this list—save one. They even sought refuge with some of them."

"So?"

Hao tried to remain patient. "So, our intel has told us the fugitives are alive and heading east." His finger slid down to the last name on the list. "And who is the last witness we know is located in the east?"

The High Inspector bent forward to look at the name. "Victor Hayward," he read.

CHAPTER 7 *Safe Haven*

The ball hit Ben square in the cheek.

"Pay attention, squirt!" Bob yelled from a distance. "Are you okay?"

Ben rubbed the side of his head. "Yeah." He picked up the soccer ball, checking his surroundings for the hundredth time, then spotted his mother. She was walking at a fast pace on the footpath that crossed Tommy Thompson Park.

Ben dropped the ball and ran over to meet her. "Did it work?"

She nodded, heading towards a tree where Ben and Bob had left their sweaters. She dropped to the ground and let out a long, shaky breath.

"Way to go, Mom!" Ben said, full of wonder. "Is he wearing..."

"Sh!" she warned, glancing over his shoulder.

Ben turned and found Bob jogging up to them.

"Hi, baby. How was your meeting?" Bob said, out of breath.

"Exhausting," she answered, studying their green surroundings. "This is nice. I could take a nap, right here." She grabbed the sweaters, rolled them up and placed them behind her neck, then closed her eyes.

"Come on," Bob gestured to Ben. "Let's give her a breather. Three-to-one. I'm winning, squirt. Better get at it!"

He bent to pick up the ball, but Ben called after him. "Thanks, Uncle Bob, but I don't feel like playing anymore. I think I'll go for a walk."

Ben caught a brief look of disappointment on his uncle's face, but the man shrugged and showed off his soccer skills by repeatedly kicking the ball on his knee and heel.

A small buzz near Ben's ear made him raise his hand to it.

Hey! You're tickling me.

Beetrix hovered in front of his face.

You're going the wrong way, Benjamin Archer. We've searched this area already.

I know, I know. Bear with me for a minute. There's something I need to do first.

Ben pushed through some shrubs until he was satisfied that no one could see him. Then he sat, Beetrix settling on a leaf nearby, observing him.

When Mesmo had indicated the glittering diamond in the centre of his grandfather's watch, and had told him it allowed the alien to travel in spirit to Ben's location, it had never crossed Ben's mind that *he* might be the one who would, one day, need to use the device.

But could he? He had never attempted it, nor had he asked Mesmo if it was remotely possible for a human to disconnect his spirit from his physical body.

"I guess you are more than a normal Earth human now..." Mesmo had said, many months ago. Ben felt a pang of loss at the memory. He missed Mesmo more than he cared to admit.

Beetrix buzzed next to him, pulling him away from thoughts that threatened to drown him if he lingered on them for too long.

He moved restlessly, trying to find peace in body and mind. Would Mesmo realize that Victor Hayward was wearing the watch? Would Ben be able to connect to it?

The idea was completely crazy. If the plan didn't work, they risked losing contact with Mesmo for good.

Why didn't you send me?

Ben glanced at Beetrix sternly.

Don't be silly. It would have been way too dangerous. Besides, we have to find your hive.

Ben was going to close his eyes again, but he changed his mind and shot an annoyed look at the insect again.

And stay out of my thoughts!

* * *

"So, you like it here?" Bob asked as Laura opened her eyes. He was sitting close to her, smiling.

Oh boy, he still has those deep, brown eyes. Not like Mesmo's, but...

Laura rolled to a sitting position. She removed soil from her hands by wiping them together, then looked up at the trees with their fresh, spring leaves. "I could get used to living here, I guess..."

"Then do it," Bob said.

"What?"

"Live here. Permanently. With me." Seeing the look on her face, Bob raised his eyes to the sky. "Okay, okay. Not *with* me, then. But close, so I can spend more time with Ben."

She squinted her eyes. "I hope you're not considering joint custody." It was meant as a joke, but she suddenly regretted saying the words.

Bob shrugged. "No. Yes. Maybe. Why not?" He glanced at her.

He is *thinking about it!* she realized in shock.

He crossed his hands behind his head and lay down. "Oh, I don't know. It's just that, he and I, we're bonding, you know? He's a great kid—apart from his insect craze. But that will wear off. Those things always do."

"I don't think..." Laura began.

"Just look around you, Laura. There's everything he needs here: good schools, good jobs. He'll make tons of friends. He can come work for me later. Jeez, for all I know, he could take over one day..."

"Bob, Bob!" Laura snapped. "You're daydreaming. Bounce back to reality already!"

Bob straightened. "What? Does that sound so off the beaten track? Do you still think so low of me then? I could be a great dad, you know?"

"It's not that easy," Laura seethed.

"Of course, it's not that easy. But give me a chance to learn, Laura. Can you give me that, at least?"

Laura looked away. She felt like Ben was slipping away from her. After fighting so hard to stick together, she was finding this to be the toughest challenge she had yet faced.

Joint custody: one week with me, one week with Bob.

That's what life would look like.

I can't do it!

Her mind tripped over itself, searching for a way out.

I can't keep Ben away from his dad, either.

She was so lost in an inner debate that she didn't realize Ben had walked up to them until his shadow fell over her.

"Can we go home, now?" he said, his face looking crestfallen.

* * *

They sat on the bed opposite each other, their legs crossed, speaking in low voices so Bob wouldn't hear them.

"This isn't working, Mom," Ben said, discouraged. "Mesmo isn't connecting with me."

Laura took his hands in her own. "Be patient. Mesmo may not have realized that Victor has the watch yet."

"What if he does, but we aren't able to make contact?"

"We talked about this. We decided it was worth a try. If it doesn't work, we'll think of something else. Let's give it a rest for now. It's late. You can try again tomorrow morning."

Ben sighed in exasperation, then lay down on the bed.

"Come on," Laura said. "Let's get some sleep."

She switched off the light and Ben stared at the dark with his eyes wide open.

"Mom?" he said softly, fighting a sudden lump in his throat.

"What?"

Around this time of night, Tike would be lying beside him—he could almost physically feel the dog's warm body. But he reached out his hand and touched only emptiness. Feeling crushed, he said, "I wish Tike were still alive. I wish that police officer hadn't shot him. I wish..."

"Shush," Laura said in a hushed voice. He heard her turn to face him. "You know, I've been meaning to tell you, I don't think that police officer meant to kill Tike. He was aiming at the grizzly. I don't think he even realized Tike was there."

"But it's not fair, Tike never hurt anybody..." Ben sobbed.

"I know, honey," she replied. "But sometimes I wonder where we'd be, if it hadn't been for that avalanche triggered by the shot..." She fell silent, then said after a while, "Ben?"

"What?" he sniffed.

"Remember when I promised you I'd find a place where we could belong?"

"Uh-huh."

"Well," she said. "What if that place was here?"

Ben raised his head from the cushion. "With Uncle Bob?"

Laura didn't answer right away, but when she did, her voice was muffled. "Maybe not *with* Uncle Bob. But nearby. He can help us settle in. Would you like that?"

Ben thought about it. He liked Uncle Bob. They had their differences, but it was like having a piece of his dad. "Maybe," he answered slowly.

"Let's sleep on it," Laura said. "You can check out your new school, and I'll give my new job a try. We can talk about it again in a week."

"After we've saved Mesmo," Ben added.

"Yes," Laura agreed. "After we've saved Mesmo."

They fell silent. Ben stared at the darkness, lost in thought.

* * *

Victor Hayward paced the floor with his head down and his hands on his hips, while a young assistant whispered the latest updates to him.

"Placing humans in an induced coma gives their body a chance to heal. But that's not the case with the alien. Every time we wake him up, he gets worse. We're running out of options."

Hayward removed his glasses and rubbed his face. "*I'm* running out of options." He paced a moment longer, then put his glasses back on. "I'm going to deal with him, once and for all."

"Boss!" the man warned, but Hayward picked up a grey object from an examination table and then scanned his badge to unlock a metal door.

When he entered the bare room, the first thing he noticed was the alien's white hair. Even observing the being from this distance in the dim light, Hayward had to admit it had a deathly look. The businessman approached the hospital bed. He held the metallic object inches away from the subject. The object began to levitate.

The alien who lay on the hospital bed with feeding tubes sticking out of its arms opened its eyes a crack.

Hayward met the being's gaze. "I know you can hear me. So, I want you to listen closely, friend. I'm a wealthy and powerful man. I own thousands of airplanes that have crossed the world countless times.

"But the fuel we use for these airplanes is running out. If I don't find alternative energy soon, my company will go out of business. I will be forced to fire thousands of people who depend on me to feed their families..."

He gestured towards the floating object. "This piece was extracted out of your spaceship, and it reacts to you. Therefore, I believe you hold the solution to my problem."

Hayward snagged the object from the air and slipped it into his pocket. "I will ask you one final time. Tell me about the energy that fuels your craft, show me how it works, and I guarantee your freedom. I can get you on a plane by morning, to any destination you may desire."

He stopped at the end of the bed. "I can make you a special deal, friend. This one time only." He stared at the floor, choosing the words carefully. "What if I saw to it that you could get home? You see, I have no interest in you—I'm only interested in your technology. So, help me duplicate your flying saucer, show me how it works, and I will provide you with access to your own spacecraft. Because, you see," he straightened his glasses. "I know where it is, and I can lead you to it."

The extraterrestrial hadn't moved an inch, but Hayward knew it was listening because it followed him with its eyes. The subject opened its mouth, and a sound left its lips as if it wanted to speak.

"What?" Hayward said, lifting his hand to his ear and approaching the alien's head. "Speak up!"

The being tried again, but only a croaking sound left its throat.

Hayward's adrenalin rose slightly. It was the first time he was getting a reaction. Maybe he was finally getting a breakthrough. He checked that the subject's arms and legs were firmly attached to the bedframe, then leaned forward expectantly.

Something caught at his wrist. Yelping, Hayward jerked back. But the alien had wrapped its fingers tightly around Hayward's wrist and was staring at him with intense eyes. Hayward struggled, watching in horror as the subject lifted its head, its voice coming out in rasps.

"I will not speak a good word for you," it said. The faintest trace of a smile appeared on its face, then it sank back weakly.

Hayward roared, just as his men erupted into the room. But the alien had already let him go.

The businessman rubbed at his wrist, his teeth bared. "You've sealed your fate, friend," he snarled.

As he stormed out of the room, his edgy assistant followed closely. "What did he say?"

"Baloney!"

* * *

It happened all at once. One second, Ben was fast asleep; the next, he felt a jolt and tumbled into the void. He wanted to scream, but the high velocity pushed his voice to the back of his throat. He tried to grasp on to something, but could not find his hands.

Then, as suddenly as it had begun, the sensation vanished, and he was himself again. Or at least, he thought he was.

His senses on high alert, he reached for the bed light but found only air around him. His eyes focused slowly. Soft light washed over him, then forms began to take shape.

Where am I?

A corridor, illuminated by dull night lights, stretched out before him. Several doors took shape to his left and right, while the corridor continued behind him. The door in front of him stood open.

He tried to remember where he had been last, but his thoughts were jumbled. He checked himself and found that he was in one piece, wearing pyjamas.

I must be dreaming.

Deciding to go along with this mind trick, he stepped through the door and found himself in a room filled with strange apparatus. Computer screens flashed strings of information, science jars contained mysterious liquids, baffling instruments lay strewn across a table. Ben concluded he was in some kind of laboratory.

To his right, he discovered a large window. He glanced through the smoked glass and found a dim, empty room that only contained a hospital bed. A man with white hair lay on it.

Ben gasped. "Mesmo!"

CHAPTER 8 *Contact*

Ben stepped back from the window giddily. He stared at his hands, which seemed solid, but when he tried to make them touch, they passed right through each other. His mouth fell open in exhilaration mixed with fear.

I did it!

His spirit had disconnected from his body and had travelled to Mesmo's location, at the alien's call.

Mesmo has the spirit portal!

He turned to the window again.

I have to tell him I'm here.

Loud voices filled the corridor.

Tensing in dismay, the boy searched for a hiding spot, then dove frantically behind a filing cabinet in the nick of time, just before two men entered the room. Ben heard them close the door, then settle in front of their computers on the opposite side of a lab table.

Making sure they were concentrated on their work, Ben crawled behind the lab table to the door, then reached for the doorknob. His fingers slipped through it.

Drat!

He checked on the men hurriedly, and instead found a security camera in a top corner of the room, aimed in his direction. A green light flickered on it. Beside him, several screens projected images from other security cameras. Mesmo was visible on one of these screens, a wobbly, static image of Ben on another.

He retreated with his back to the lab table and shut his eyes tight.

Think!

To begin with, he couldn't save Mesmo. Not in his spirit state. What he needed to do was find out Mesmo's location. He checked his surroundings for any clues but found none.

I'm going to have to inspect the whole facility.

Ben closed his eyes again, trying to accept that the laws of physics had changed now that he was intangible. He opened his eyes to study the door, and, instead, found himself in the same room as Mesmo.

* * *

Victor Hayward considered his options while he brushed his teeth. As he pushed out the toothpaste, he considered the pros and cons of delivering the subject to the American military. Or, he could start a bidding war between major world powers. It would pay off a good deal of his debts. If only he had been able to make the alien talk, things would have been so much easier, but that alternative was fading fast.

The important thing was to keep the Canadians out of it. They had, after all, stolen the spaceships off his land, claiming it was "federal property."

"Federal property," he snorted with a mouth full of bubbles.

"What, sweetheart?" his wife called from the bedroom.

He spat into the sink. "Nothing, dear. I'm talking to myself."

He got back to brushing his teeth, mulling over the idea, but he didn't like it. The extraterrestrial was *his*. He had caught the alien. Not the CSIS, not MI6, not the KGB. Not any of those secret services, but *he*, Victor Hayward—because *he* was the one who had discovered the alien lying among the debris of the crash.

Hayward quickly dismissed the uncomfortable memory of his first contact with the being. He had approached it, thinking it dead. But when the alien had moved its head, Hayward had shrieked and run for his life. Not one of his finest moments, he had to admit.

Fortunately, the alien's facial traits had been burned into his mind—enough for him to send out a quiet face recognition search among his Victory Air crew across the globe, with a positive outcome.

For goodness sake! This creature had been travelling the world doing God-knows-what since its arrival. If not for Hayward, it would most likely still be going about its business with complete impunity.

He filled his cheeks with water and pressed on his phone to pull up the security screens of his underground laboratory, his toothbrush still in his hand.

That's when he saw the boy.

He gagged on the water in his mouth.

"Are you okay, sweetheart?" his wife called while he coughed raucously into the sink.

He rushed into the bedroom—toothpaste stuck to the side of his mouth—and jumped into a pair of trousers and shirt.

"Sweetheart?"

He left his startled wife, grabbed his phone and jacket and practically flew down the stairs of his mansion. He swung open the front door, struggled to put on his coat, then dialled a number on the phone while sprinting towards his limousine.

When he knocked loudly on the windowpane, his chauffeur—who was fast asleep in the driver's seat—jumped so hard Hayward thought he was going to have a heart attack. The man scrambled to catch the hat that slipped off his head, then clumsily extracted himself from the vehicle.

Hayward's cellphone was stuck to his ear, ringing on the other end. He heard a click as his assistant picked up.

"A boy! There's a boy in the room with the alien!" Hayward screamed into the receiver.

He grabbed the chauffeur's car keys and pushed him aside. "Move over!" he yelled, plunging into the car, then turned on the ignition and screeched away into the night.

* * *

Forgetting his own safety, Ben rushed to the hospital bed and found the alien extended on it. Mesmo's cheekbones protruded through his grey skin. Gone was his friend's rock solid frame.

Ben held back a cry.

What if he's... dying?

The alien turned his sunken eyes to him and managed a small smile. "Benjamin," he whispered, opening his hand. The watch with the spirit portal rested in his palm.

"It worked!" Ben gasped, though he had to muster up the courage to speak.

Has Mesmo been in this state all this time?

Could Mesmo make his spirit appear healthy and strong,

while in fact, his physical body ailed? Ben didn't dare think of the answer.

"I'm here now," he said encouragingly. "Don't worry, I'll get you out. I just need to figure out where we are."

A phone rang outside the room. Ben heard the man's voice who answered it turn to alarm. There was a thump and the sound of running feet.

"Go!" Mesmo urged. "You are a spirit. You can go anywhere, as long as you stay in the vicinity of the portal."

Ben nodded, his eyes wide. "Hang in there, Mesmo," he begged.

He turned, closed his eyes and headed straight for the wall. When he opened them again, he was standing in the corridor once more, the two men staring at him from the lab door, mouths agape.

"Get him!" one of them yelled.

Ben turned and sprinted down the corridor, the men's heavy shoes thudding behind him. He headed for a door with a red EXIT sign on top of it, raised his arm and plunged, expecting to crash straight into it. Instead, he landed on the other side, unharmed.

Sooo cool! ...I think?

He hiccupped in nervous excitement. He could have sworn his spirit body was covered in goosebumps at the idea that he was passing through physical objects. But there was no time to analyze the idea.

The men pushed against the emergency exit door behind him.

Ben clambered up several flights of stairs—his pursuers huffing loudly behind him—until he found a sign that said 1ST FLOOR.

Charging head-first through the door like a bull, Ben

suddenly found himself in an enormous reception area. The massive, red symbol of Victory Air ornamented the back wall. A night guard stood behind a reception desk, talking to a group of police officers who wore jackets with the letters CSIS on the back. In their midst, stood Bordock.

Ben froze.

The two men burst through the emergency exit behind him.

All groups faced each other, their eyes wide.

Ben didn't wait for them to come to their senses. He dashed over the marble floor—the hall erupting with warning shouts around him—and slipped through the main doors to the outside world. Taking refuge behind a column at the foot of an extended flight of stairs, he shut his eyes tight.

Take me back, Mesmo! Take me back!

Panic engulfed him as threatening voices neared his futile hiding spot.

There was a whoosh of air, and the ground beneath him fell. His spirit connected to his body with a bang. He yelled as if someone had just hit him with a hammer.

"Ben?" Laura's shrill voice called him in the dark.

The bed light came on, and Ben found himself sitting upright, gasping for breath.

"Ben! What is it?" Laura cried.

He cast a distressed look her way and burst, "We have to get Mesmo out, *NOW*!"

CHAPTER 9 *Deliverance*

Laura ran into the middle of the road to hail a passing taxi cab. The driver barely had time to hit the brakes, the bumper ending so close to her that its headlights illuminated dust rising in front of her jacket.

She gestured for Ben to get into the car, and soon they were racing down Toronto streets towards the Victory Air headquarters.

It didn't take long for them to get there, and as they neared the building, the red and blue lights of half a dozen police cars became visible from afar.

"Stop here!" Laura ordered the taxi driver. She threw several dollar bills at him and clambered out after Ben. They both hurried closer to the scene of the tumult.

"What should we do?" Ben asked worriedly.

"We'll have to find another way in," she said. "Maybe through that service street there."

"No, wait!" Ben held her back. "I have a better idea."

* * *

Victor Hayward's phone continued to ring. He had no intention of answering, his eyes were glued to the road before him as he sped into town way over the speed limit. But the phone rang again, and when he glanced at it, he realized it was his assistant. He picked it up at the risk of ending in a ditch.

"What?"

"Boss, the police are here."

"The what?" he bellowed.

His assistant's voice wavered. "Yes, Boss. The CSIS is here with a warrant to search the building. They say they are searching for proof that we knew our oil extraction fields were depleted."

Hayward snorted into the phone. "Yeah, right! Bunch of liars. They know we have the 'package.' Resort to Plan B. I want the 'package' removed at once. You have two minutes. Do you understand?"

His assistant sounded distant and nervous. "Yes, Boss. Removing 'the package' at once."

* * *

Ben decided he wasn't enjoying this spirit travelling much. He'd much rather soar on a bird's wings or dive into the deep on the back of a whale, but right now he had no choice.

He wasn't sure where he would end up, or even if Mesmo was up to the task of connecting with him, but as soon as he focused on the alien, his spirit jolted out of his body and materialized in an underground parking.

Hearing voices, Ben hid behind a car and watched as Mesmo was rolled on the hospital bed into a waiting ambulance. They caught sight of each other for an instant before the ambulance doors were shut on him.

Pursing his lips, Ben noticed the ramp that the vehicle would use to escape—and he instantly knew what he needed to do.

* * *

The limo screeched to a stop. Victor Hayward exited the vehicle and ran up meticulous stairs to the entrance of his headquarters. He pulled the doors wide open, making sure his voice boomed into the reception. "What's going on here?"

His short legs took him to the dozen-or-so police officers who were assembled under the red symbol of his company.

A man detached himself from the group. He was not wearing the CSIS vest like the others, but a neat, light-grey suit that Hayward would have approved of in other circumstances. A sense of authority hung around the agent. The lights reflected on his shaved head but not in his emotionless green eyes. Either way, Hayward knew instinctively that he had to tread with care—he recognized a person with his level of intellect when he saw one.

"Mr. Hayward?" the bald man said, showing him a piece of identification. "I'm Agent Theodore Connelly, with the National Aerial Division of the Canadian Security Intelligence Service. We have a search warrant for the premises."

"Naturally," Hayward growled icily, noting that Mister Bigshot here wasn't even hiding which department he was working for. *He can wipe his nose on his search warrant for all I care—as long as he doesn't find the alien...*

"Mr. Hayward, I need to talk to you privately," the agent said.

Whatever keeps them busy, Hayward thought. Out loud,

he said, "Follow me."

Agent Connelly gestured for his men to spread out and Hayward noted with satisfaction that they were heading to the elevators, which—he knew—did not go down to his secret, underground laboratory. A makeshift laboratory, for sure, but one he had had the visionary presence of mind to build after witnessing The Cosmic Fall. Only one separate elevator connected to it from the reception—and he had the key.

Both men entered the room that the receptionists used to work in when they weren't out front.

Hayward leaned against a desk and crossed his arms. "Well? Let's have it. What's this all about?"

Connelly closed the office door, and when he faced Hayward, he wasn't smiling. The agent's eyes bored into him. "Mr. Hayward," Connelly said in a low, threatening voice. "You have exactly two minutes to deliver the alien to me."

Hayward's arms dropped, as did his mouth. "Wha...?" But his voice caught in his throat because something entirely abnormal was happening to Connelly's face.

* * *

Ben raced up the ramp of the underground parking area. Far below him, the ambulance roared to life. He ignored the closed garage door and dashed through it, finding himself in a dark service street close to where Laura and his physical self were located.

It took him a few seconds to find what he was looking for.

"Please let this work, please, please, please," he begged, as tires squealed up the ramp of the garage door behind him.

Ben hid beside it and waited.

* * *

Connelly called for reinforcements as he headed for a separate elevator located not far from the receptionist's office. It was locked with a security system.

Unfazed, Connelly pulled out the security card Hayward had given him willingly only moments ago as he begged for his life. Connelly scanned it and the elevator door opened, allowing him to head down to the level indicated by Hayward.

The shapeshifter glanced left and right at the corridor that appeared before him. He headed to the right, finding an open door at the end which led to a laboratory.

His sharp ears caught the sound of distant, screeching tires. He tensed, then doubled back and searched for the source of the noise.

* * *

The garage door lifted slowly, the driver of the ambulance pressing on the gas pedal impatiently, making the motor roar.

The door had barely raised when the vehicle lurched forward into the service street, which was closed at one end. It turned left with the intention of joining city traffic.

Only, a young boy stood right in its path.

The driver swerved so hard that the ambulance swayed and collided into a fire hydrant located at the exit. The jet of water that was released upon impact was so powerful that it enveloped the ambulance under a swirling waterfall.

Ben watched expectantly.

It didn't take long. The flow slowed and hardened, turning to ice in answer to Mesmo's skill. It crackled and gleamed under the street lights, its churning form caught in time.

Ben heard shouts coming from inside the ambulance. The driver struggled with the door, which resisted under the weight of the ice. It finally gave way with a loud crunch, allowing him to make his escape.

But Ben had stopped watching. He closed his eyes and returned to his physical body with a jolt.

"Ben!" Laura called from far away. He groaned at the force with which his spirit reconnected to his body.

"Get up! Hurry!" Laura half lifted, half dragged him to a standing position.

He became aware of a grating sound. He focused his eyes and ears and found the back doors of the ambulance opening with difficulty, scraping at the ice that surrounded it. Four men, who shouted frantically to each other, spilled out and scampered away, while water continued to flow from the fire hydrant, flooding the street.

Ben and Laura approached the opening at the back of the ambulance. Just then, the shadow of a man appeared, making them gasp. The man stepped into the light. His white hair was disheveled, the tone of his skin light-grey.

"Mesmo!" Ben cried with relief.

The alien slumped against the side of the ambulance.

Ben and Laura reached out to him. He made to step down, but his legs gave way, and he toppled forward out of the van. Ben and Laura almost collapsed as he fell into their arms, but they managed to hold on just long enough for him to regain his balance. Laura swung one of his arms over her shoulders, Ben hurriedly trying to do the same, but the alien's height meant he wasn't much help. Still, shifting his weight between them, Mesmo managed to hunker forward, groaning painfully.

The three of them hugged the shadows and made their

escape.

* * *

Connelly sprinted up the garage ramp, anxious to discover the origin of the racket outside. He found the ambulance wrapped up in a small iceberg at the end of the service alley, with water flooding the main street.

The shapeshifter rushed to the vehicle's back doors and peered inside. It was empty. He balled his fists and hit the floor of the vehicle so hard it left a dent. His body shook with fury. His eyes switched colour as he struggled to keep Connelly's appearance under the weight of his anger.

Running footsteps approached behind him, and it took all of his willpower to contain himself. If he turned around now, he would explode.

"What's going on? Is anyone hurt?" a man asked, bumping into him as he tried to glimpse over Connelly's shoulder into the ambulance.

The shapeshifter shut his eyes tight.

Some more men arrived. "Agent Connelly? What are your orders?"

Connelly inhaled deeply through his nostrils. He opened his green eyes slowly and was about to respond when he noticed an object at the base of the hospital bed which lay overturned on the floor of the ambulance. He reached for the object and his hand closed on a silver watch.

At first, Connelly couldn't believe his luck, but the way the tiny diamond shone in its centre was unmistakable.

"Agent Connelly?"

Police sirens whirled to a stop behind him, and more people gathered around the ambulance.

Connelly clasped the watch tightly and smirked.

CHAPTER 10 *Arrest*

Ben and Laura shoved Mesmo into a doorway just in time to avoid the headlights of a passing police car. Ben peeked out of their hiding place to make sure it didn't turn back, then let out his breath as the swirling lights faded away.

"Let's go!" he urged, glancing at his mother and the alien. His mouth fell open.

Wait a minute! Are they kissing?

Had he just caught Mesmo and Laura in an embrace? He couldn't be sure, because his mother pulled back with an incredulous look on her face.

"Hey! Time to go!" Ben tugged at his mother's arm.

She blinked at him, then placed Mesmo's arm around her shoulder again. "Come on. Bob's condo is just a block away."

They stepped onto the sidewalk, but Mesmo dropped to his knees, almost dragging her down with him. "No!" he gasped. "Outside. Water."

Ben exchanged a worried look with his mother. His mind whirled. "Let's take him to the park! It's not far."

Laura nodded. "Good idea. You can make it, Mesmo."

Ben couldn't avoid staring at the alien's face. It was drawn, his skin almost as grey as Kaia's had been...

...when she died.

He took Mesmo by the arm and stared at the man with intense determination.

You can't die.

As if reading Ben's mind, Mesmo set his jaw and forced himself up.

The dark outline of trees came into view some painstaking minutes later. It took all of Laura and Ben's strength to haul the tall man through the wooded park. They grunted under his weight and had to pause every now and then so Mesmo could lift his head and take in a deep mouthful of fresh air.

The sound of tiny, lapping waves reached Ben's ears. Mesmo must have heard it, too, because his pace quickened. They broke through some bushes and found themselves at the edge of a short beach that led to Lake Ontario.

Mesmo let go of them. He stumbled forward, walking straight into the water without slowing down.

Laura reached out her hand as if wanting to hold him back, but remained by Ben's side. They watched the alien wade up to his knees into the lake. He paused, then let himself drop face first into the water like a rigid plank. The dark liquid submerged him until only rings on the surface indicated where he had stood.

Ben shadowed his mother's footsteps as they hurried to the edge, searching the darkness for his presence. They waited, the seconds ticking by in slow motion.

"There!" Laura whispered suddenly, pointing to her right.

A barely visible glow moved under the water but became stronger as it glided to a standstill some distance before them. Then it approached the surface, and Mesmo's head broke through the water. He looked in their direction, a bluish halo emanating from his body.

Ben watched, astonished.

Woman and boy stood by the edge, slightly out of breath, wondering what would happen next.

Then, to Ben's utter surprise, Mesmo threw his head back and laughed. It was a strong, heartfelt sound that caught him completely off guard. It resonated through the night, open and sincere.

I've never heard Mesmo laugh before.

Ben cast his mother a quizzical look.

Laura frowned at him with the same wonder reflected in her eyes, while a smile crept on to her face.

Ben couldn't contain a grin, his nervousness overcome by a sudden sense of pride at what they had accomplished.

We did it!

The thought made his whole body tingle. After all their hardships and turmoil, they had done it! They had freed Mesmo. He chuckled at the realization, though Mesmo's elation fueled the rising feeling inside of him.

Beside him, Laura's timid giggle turned into real laughter, and before long, she cracked up completely.

Ben followed her lead, whooping loudly into the night, letting go of months of bottled up emotions, thrilled at the idea that they had outsmarted both Victor Hayward *and* Bordock, not to mention an overwhelming relief at being together for real at last.

He let it all go and found himself splashing, fully dressed, into the lake to join Mesmo. The water enveloped him in a warm blanket, glowing a soft blue in response to the alien's skill. Ben threw himself into Mesmo's arms, his tears of laughter turning into emotional ones.

Mesmo became silent, then wrapped his own arms around

the boy.

They remained like that for a while, Ben feeling slightly bewildered at hugging the alien in flesh and bone for the first time.

* * *

"You should eat something," the nurse said. She placed a food tray next to Hao's bed.

"Yes, yes," Hao replied impatiently, as he typed away at the computer on his lap.

The nurse remained by his side, but the Inspector was so absorbed by his work that it took him a while to acknowledge her.

Finally, he looked up, then at the tray. "Yes, yes, I'll eat," he insisted, grabbing a piece of toast and stuffing it in his mouth.

The nurse pressed her lips into a fine line, then exited the hospital room.

Hao got back to his screen, his cheeks full, then reached out for a folder on the side of his bed.

The room lay littered with boxes, files and documents from *The Cosmic Fall*. If the High Inspector got wind of this, Hao would be in deep trouble. But at this point, he didn't care. After all, he had set the High Inspector on Victor Hayward's track and was waiting for news of the raid on the businessman's headquarters.

As he picked up the folder, his eyes fell on the TV which was constantly streaming news.

VICTORY AIR—CEO ARRESTED, the red banner at the bottom of the screen read.

Hao left the piece of toast dangling from the side of his mouth and reached hurriedly for the control to turn up the volume.

"...in what investigators claim to be the biggest fraud in the country's history. The founder of Victory Air and owner of the billion-dollar industry responsible for extracting oil for the airliner is accused of having lied about the years of resources still available in Alberta. It is thought the tar sand oil was depleted over four years ago, and that, instead, Mr. Hayward redirected substantial Federal funding—destined to modernize the industry—to the United States, where he obtained the fuel for his airliner, thus avoiding bankruptcy..." the reporter explained.

Hao munched slowly as he watched cameras flashing at the businessman who was being led down the stairs of his Toronto building. The man's face was ashen. His eyes were glazed and unresponsive to the shouting reporters around him.

A police officer wearing a CSIS vest helped Victor Hayward into the back of a police car.

The phone next to Hao's bed rang. He reached out for it, groaning as he twisted his broken leg.

His assistant's voice said, "You were right. The extraterrestrial was here. We have footage from security cameras..."

"What do you mean *was*?" Hao barked.

"We think the fugitives helped the alien escape just before we arrived. We're combing the city for them as we speak."

Hao's knuckles went white as he grasped at the bedsheets. But he said in a calm tone, "Send me the footage as soon as you can."

"Yes, Sir."

Hao hung up. He stared at the TV without really seeing it. He should have been there. The High Inspector had put Connelly in charge of the raid, but his partner had not been up to the task.

Hao carefully slid his cast leg to the edge of the bed, so he was in a sitting position. There were so many unanswered questions. What was the relationship between the fugitives and Victor Hayward? What was the alien doing there? And then there was the question of the boy, Benjamin Archer.

Hao stared at two contradicting documents laid out on the bed. One contained the blood results from the boy, proving the child was not human. The other was a birth certificate recently uncovered at a hospital on the West Coast. In it, the hospital declared the birth of a healthy, *normal* boy. There had been no mention of a father.

How could the hospital not have noticed anything unusual? How could an alien child have been hiding in plain sight among humans for so long? And if an alien child could be born in a hospital undetected, how many more were out there?

There were too many inconsistencies in this whole investigation, and Hao did not like inconsistencies. He wanted clear, logical answers.

His eyes fell on the box labelled WITNESSES. He had put a team of researchers on to each witness, they had dug up every last detail on these peoples' lives, but only Victor Hayward had given any result.

A name stuck out of one of the folders in the box: THEODORE EDMOND CONNELLY: the only one who had not undergone the same rigorous investigation as the other witnesses. Seeing as Connelly was a police officer, all had automatically assumed that his testimony was reliable.

But what if it wasn't?

Hao set his jaw and pulled out Connelly's file.

* * *

Laura caressed Ben's hair. The boy had fallen asleep with his head on her lap. Laura sat, cross-legged, on the little beach that bordered Lake Ontario, watching Mesmo as he floated in the water, staring up at the night sky.

Laura glanced up as well and let her eyes adjust until stars became visible. She would have liked to stay like this for hours. Everything was peaceful; an almost imperceptible breeze moved the leaves of the trees above her, the water lapped quietly at the shore, and a comfortable warmth enveloped her.

But the crack of dawn neared with every passing minute, and she knew the city would wake up soon. She shook Ben's shoulder gently. "Wake up, honey. We should go."

He moaned and rolled off her lap into a sitting position, then rubbed his eyes.

They both stood and approached the edge of the lake, while Mesmo straightened, still submerged in the water.

"We have to go, Mesmo," Laura said. "The park's going to be full of joggers and people walking their dogs in an hour."

"You go," the alien agreed. "I'll stay here. I need time to recover and this is the perfect place for me." He let himself sink into the water to show them that he could hide easily.

When he emerged again, Laura asked worriedly, "Are you sure?"

Mesmo nodded. "I'm sure. It's you two who have to be careful. You're the ones who are out in the open."

"We'll be fine," Laura said. "We're safe with Bob."

They agreed to meet that afternoon.

"I'm going to dye your hair," Laura said. "You won't make it very far looking like that." She pointed at his white, wavy hair.

Laura and Ben said their goodbyes, then slipped through the park.

Laura plodded behind Ben in semi-darkness, fighting off the morning chill that seeped into her clothes.

Suddenly Ben stopped. Laura bumped into him.

"Shh!" he said, raising his hand in warning.

"What is it?" she asked hurriedly.

They stood still, listening to the rustling leaves and far away sound of cars.

"I don't hear anyth..." she began, but Ben raised his hand higher.

He stepped slowly towards a compact group of shrubs, Laura following closely behind with her heart thumping. Behind the bushes, she found a small, arched bridge made of bricks. A stream trickled under it. Ben headed for it.

She was about to ask what on Earth he was doing when she noticed the sound. It was faint at first, but the closer she got to the bridge, the louder it became.

It was a humming sound, one that she recognized immediately. A buzz whisked by her ear, then several others, and soon she found herself surrounded by a cloud of insects.

"Bees!" she exclaimed.

Ben grinned. "Beetrix' hive," he confirmed.

* * *

"Hello? Is this Tamara Connelly?" Hao spoke into the phone. Connelly's file lay open before him, and he stared at the picture that was clipped to the side. It showed a youthful woman with curly hair and a dark-skinned face. Her smile revealed neat, white teeth. Even from this single picture, Hao got a sense of a fundamentally confident and happy person.

He hadn't seen the picture since his meeting with Connelly and the High Inspector months ago, when they had first been assigned to *The Cosmic Fall* case.

The woman who answered the phone did not reflect any trace of confidence or happiness in her voice, and Hao could hear a baby crying in the background. "Connelly?" the woman said scornfully. "I don't go by that name anymore. Who's this, anyway?"

Hao cleared his throat. "I'm sorry to bother you, Miss. My name is Inspector James Hao. I'm with the CSIS."

The baby's cries became louder but then died down, and Hao could hear it cooing near the receiver.

"What do you want?" Tamara asked curtly.

"I'm calling about your husband, Theodore Edmond Connelly."

To his surprise, Tamara cackled darkly. *"Theodore?* He lets you call him that?"

Hao knit his brow. "Excuse me?"

Tamara sighed. "Anyone close to Ted knows not to call him Theodore. He'd punch you in the nose if you dared utter that name. He hates it! Says it makes him sound like an old uncle or something." Her voice faltered.

"Mr. Hao, have you heard from my husband? I've called your office hundreds of times. They won't patch me through. He hasn't spoken to me since that crazy meteor business. He's literally disappeared off the face of the Earth! And I can't live like this anymore, Mr. Hao."

The baby began crying again. "Hold on," she said.

Hao heard her shushing the baby, then her voice came through again. "What was it you were calling about again?"

Hao searched for the right words. "Oh, er, I was calling to let you know that your husband is doing a great service to his country..."

"Are you serious?" Tamara blew up. The baby cried in the

background again. "I had a baby girl two months ago, Mr. Hao. Are you listening to me? Ted became a father for the second time, and he hasn't come home once to meet her!"

Hao heard her burst into tears. It took her several minutes to calm down.

She sniffed and said with a broken voice, "It's just not like him. We were happy, before. But I've had enough! You can tell him I want those divorce papers signed. I'm tired of waiting. Goodbye, Mr. Hao."

He thought she would hang up, but instead, she added. "And tell him... tell him, if he won't talk to me, to at least call his son Kyle for his fifth birthday. It's the day after tomorrow, April third." Her voice broke again. "That's the least he could do."

Silence fell between them, Hao at a loss for words. Then he heard a click, and the line went dead.

CHAPTER 11 *Light Years*

"Well, hi there, lazy heads," Bob said.

Laura entered the living room, following Ben who rubbed his hair and yawned. Bright sunlight seeped into the apartment.

Bob was sitting on the sofa with one foot resting on the coffee table, his hand on the TV control. "I thought you'd never get up. It's two in the afternoon! Were you partying all night or what? I heard you come in at dawn."

Ben glanced at Laura.

"We met up with an old friend," Laura said quickly. "We had a lot of catching up to do."

"I see. The friend with a cat name, huh?"

Laura opened her mouth to answer, but Bob had already lost interest and was pointing the control at the TV. "Hey, didn't your dad know this guy, Victor Hayward?"

Laura tensed and stared at the screen. They watched as the pale businessman was led away by police in front of the Victory Air building.

He looks like he's seen a ghost!

Even Laura could tell there was something going on with the man. But there was no time to analyze the thought because

Victor Hayward's image was replaced by one of Mesmo.

POLICE SEARCHING FOR CRIMINAL IN CENTRAL TORONTO, the caption read.

The image was a grainy one. Mesmo's high cheekbones, square chin and straight nose, along with his white hair, was unmistakable.

Laura slipped in front of the TV. "Victor Hayward?" she said. "Yes, I think that was my parent's neighbour back home. I don't remember, really." Anxious to change the subject, she asked, "So, what are your plans for today?"

Bob sighed, switched off the television and said, "I know it's Saturday, but I've got to head into work for a couple of hours. Want to meet up at the park later?"

Laura straightened some cushions nonchalantly, while Bob picked up his jacket that hung from a kitchen stool. "Uh, I think Ben and I are going to stay here and rest," she answered. "Monday's a big day, you know? With school and work starting..."

Bob cast her an annoyed glance. "I was hoping to take you guys out for dinner. I know this really great place."

Laura's heart did a double flip. She knew why he wanted to take them out.

"How about we do that next Saturday? Let's see how things work out with the new job and school first. Then we can celebrate," she said.

Bob finished straightening his jacket while he stared at her.

Laura swallowed.

He's becoming impatient.

Bob picked up his keys and wallet and said, "Right. Saturday it is then." He pressed the button of the penthouse elevator. The doors swung open, and he disappeared inside, without saying goodbye.

Laura let out a long breath of air.

Ben came up behind her. "Mom, but I don't want to stay here. I need to go to the park." He held up his hand; the queen bee rested on it.

She nodded. "I know, so do I," she said. "I just wanted to keep Bob away from the park, now that Mesmo is all over the news. While you take care of Beetrix, I'm going to bring Mesmo some of Bob's clothes and dye his hair; otherwise he's going to stick out like a sore thumb."

* * *

Laura placed a towel over Mesmo's back to prevent the hair colour from staining his clothes. She checked that the creamy substance was spread out evenly over his hair, then nodded satisfactorily to herself as she sat beside him.

The warm afternoon had attracted crowds to the park, forcing them to search for a more secluded area near the lake. They had found a spot behind some boulders and a patch of sand long enough that they could sit with their legs stretched out.

She observed the alien closely and found his skin to be a healthier olive tan. The sun on his face was going to help a great deal, too. But it was clear he had lost a lot of weight while in captivity. Her stomach tightened at the idea he had been cooped up for so long inside four walls—something his people could not cope with, he had said.

He must have realized she was staring at him because he turned his honey-brown eyes her way.

"How are you holding up?" she asked, trying not to blush.

He smiled, laughter lines creasing at the corner of his eyes. She realized he must have been a fundamentally cheerful person before his troubles began. “Better, thanks to you,” he replied.

She smiled back. “So, what’s going to happen now?” she asked softly.

He didn’t let go of her eyes.

Feeling giddy, she had to force herself not to look away.

“Now, Laura Archer,” he said. “You will go on your way, and I will go on with mine.”

She swallowed and was unable to speak for a while. “What about Ben’s skill?” she asked finally, pretending not to be affected by his words.

“What about it? It is Ben’s, now. He can use it as he pleases.”

Laura frowned. “You don’t want it anymore, then?”

“It was never mine to want. Ben provided the information I needed, that is all.”

“Yes, he told me. The animals are sick and at risk of dying out.” She stared at the ground uneasily, afraid to analyze the thought. “That night, when we saw the Northern Lights, you said, something. You said ‘We cannot invade what is already ours.’ Does the Earth belong to the Toreq?” She knew her voice was coming out a little too anxious, but she couldn’t help it; the idea that aliens were secretly running the planet gave her goosebumps.

His smile did not reflect her concern. He picked up a twig and planted it in the sand. “Your species has a strange habit. You believe that, when you plant a stick with a flag into the ground, the surrounding land suddenly belongs to you.” He drew a wide circle in the sand around the twig.

“You create borders that only exist in your mind, as if physical walls were separating one country from another, as if a flowing river, a passing rabbit or a branch from a tree belonged to one place or another, depending which side of the wall it was on. These borders change over time, depending on where you place the stick with a flag. It is a strange concept that makes no sense to me, considering that you are one and the same species living on one and the same planet."

He placed another twig on the circle and drew another circle around it—knocking down the first twig.

"If the Toreq were to apply this theory, then yes, you could say that the Earth belongs to us, because we were the first civilized beings to 'plant a flag' into your soil, before the era of the great giants."

"Before the dinosaurs...?" Laura gasped.

Mesmo nodded. "Fortunately, the Toreq do not abide by your old-fashioned flag theory. And besides," he smiled, "the Earth is a pebble with limited resources, lost in the confines of space, isolated from any cluster of civilized planets. There is nothing of interest to the Toreq here."

Laura shuddered, her arms and legs feeling woozy at the idea that humans were stuck on a lonely speck of rock in the great void of space. "And yet, here you are..."

He wiped away the sandy circles with his hand and nodded. "And yet, here I am." His eyes bore into hers, and her mouth went dry. "We simply like to keep track of the development of advanced species."

Laura bent her knees and wrapped her arms around them, shivering in spite of the sun on her skin. "Maybe that's why you always make me and Ben feel safe," she said, thinking out loud.

Mesmo frowned. "What do you mean?"

Laura shrugged. "I guess it feels good to know we're not the only ones out there. Plus, you know all these things. It's as if you could predict our future and give us a heads-up warning before we strayed too much. If only you could stay and help."

She felt him tense ever so slightly, so she changed the subject quickly. "Then, there's my asthma and Ben's panic attacks. They seem to have evaporated since we met you. I wonder why that is?"

Mesmo smiled. "You never really suffered from them," he said. "It is your mind that is convincing you that you suffer from these illnesses. But when you feel secure, you forget that you are supposed to show the symptoms. The Toreq have long learned to suppress certain illnesses with their minds. It will be a while yet before you learn to do the same. But I guess you and Ben are unconsciously following the right path already."

Laura cocked her head, unsure she believed him, but she said, "If only there were time, to get to know your people better, under friendlier circumstances. You have so much to teach, and we, so much to learn."

* * *

An hour later, Laura and Mesmo ventured out in the open among picnicking families in the park.

She checked on the alien regularly, trying to decide whether he was fit to walk among humans, and found that his now dark-brown hair, jeans and matching brown sweater with a three buttoned mock neck was more than satisfactory, even if—she had to admit—Bob's clothes were a bit small for his tall stature.

She led him to the spot where Ben had found the hive. They made their way through the thick shrubs which had grown around the unused, rundown pedestrian bridge.

Reaching the clearing, Laura gaped at the sight before her.

Ben stood in the centre of the open space, at the foot of the bridge. Sunlight seeped through the trees, illuminating him. But what made Laura start was the dense swarm of bees that circled around him, while he held out glowing blue hands to them.

Laura stayed glued to the spot, mesmerized by this surreal vision of her son. He seemed oblivious to their presence, in what appeared to be a deep conversation, until the intense buzzing dissipated, and she realized the insect frenzy was dying down.

The glow around Ben's hands diminished, the sun dipped further behind the trees and the bees zoomed by Laura's ears, away from the clearing.

Ben dropped his hands to his side, and his eyes lost their glaze as if he were once more becoming conscious of his surroundings. He turned to face Laura and Mesmo and said, "They say there is only silence."

By *they*, Laura figured he was talking about the bees. She approached him. "What do you mean?" Ben looked different, she thought. More determined, less overwhelmed by using his new skill.

I'm the one who has to get used to it now, she realized.

Ben held out his hand, and Beetrix landed on it. "They are able to communicate with other hives over great distances," he continued. "Their senses are so developed that they can capture the vibrations produced by other bee colonies located miles away. But they say now there is only silence. They feel lost and alone. Beetrix says this common web of vibrations is like life itself to them. Without it, they become confused and depressed."

Laura stared at the peanut-sized bee in Ben's hand. "What can we do?" she breathed.

"It's worse, actually," Ben said. "Beetrix says her hive is poisoned. She has lost many bees already. She's afraid other hives may have suffered the same fate."

"Poisoned?" Laura repeated, a heavy realization seeping into her mind.

Ben nodded. "...by the flowers they feed on. She thinks the very thing they need to survive on is the one that is slowly killing them. How can that be?"

Laura rubbed at her brow. "Beetrix is right," she said, feeling ashamed to be the one telling Ben the news. "I've read about it. Apparently, millions of hives are disappearing across the globe because of something called Colony Collapse Disorder. Worker bees in a colony have been disappearing, leaving behind their queen. There is no explanation for it, but it's thought that it has to do with the pesticides we use and the loss of bee habitat from our sprawling cities." She paused.

"The problem is serious, Ben. You see, bees pollinate all types of flowers from which fruits and vegetables emerge. That's food that humans depend on."

Ben's mouth fell open. "You mean, no bees... no food...?"

Laura nodded. "Pretty much. You wouldn't think such a tiny animal could have such a big impact. But entire crops have been lost because there were no bees to pollinate them."

Ben stared at Beetrix, who buzzed her wings while remaining on his hand. "Beetrix' hive is not yet lost. Her worker bees are still here. She can be saved." He kept his eyes on the queen bee and said determinedly, "I'll save you."

Laura put her arm around his shoulders. "We can Google local beekeepers and ask for their advice. But right now, it's getting late. Let's go home."

She glanced at Mesmo as they walked by. He had been standing silently behind her the whole time. There was something in his eyes, something she couldn't quite put her finger on. Was it sadness? Or a longing for hope?

It only took them two minutes to return to the bustling side of the park, where parents were gathering their picnic boxes and their children. It wasn't summer yet, and the spring air tended to cool down by early evening.

"I thought you guys were staying home?" a voice said behind them.

Laura whirled to find Bob walking up to them. She caught him casting a sullen look Mesmo's way. He stopped before them, the muscles on his neck twitching tightly.

There was no way around this, so Laura cleared her throat. "Oh, hi, Bob. I'd like you to meet our friend, Mesmo. Mesmo, this is Bob. He's..." she trailed off.

"He's my uncle," Ben jumped in.

Bob scowled at Mesmo, then reached out to shake his hand. "Mesmo, huh?" he said with a slight edge in his voice. "I hear you're visiting?"

Laura bit her lip as she exchanged a glance with Ben.

Mesmo nodded, staying eye-level with Bob. "Yes, and I'll be on my way again, soon."

Suddenly Ben wrapped his arms around the tall man. "Don't go yet," he said. "Please."

Mesmo tipped his head to the side, then placed his hand on Ben's shoulder. "No," he said gently. "Not just yet." His eyes fell on Laura, who felt heat rising to her cheeks.

"Come on, Ben," she said quickly. "I'm sure Mesmo has things to do. And you have school to prepare for."

I need to break this up, pronto!

Addressing Bob, she said, "Shall we go?" She slipped her arm under Bob's own and led him away, waving at Mesmo.

Eager to pull Bob's attention away from the alien, Laura chit-chatted lightly, pretending not to notice that he was brooding. "Well, that was perfect timing. We were hoping to bump into you."

Bob scoffed. "Bump into me? Or bump into *him*?"

She forced a smiled and squeezed his arm. "There's no

need to be jealous."

He didn't answer right away but frowned at the ground while they walked. Then, he stopped and looked at her directly in the eyes. "Listen, baby, I don't want to see you get hurt. I know you'll always see me as the irresponsible teenager I was. But can you believe me when I tell you I have you and Ben's best interest at heart?"

She returned his gaze. She liked this honest side in him. It was a fair question that required a truthful answer. "Of course, Bob. I believe you."

His shoulders relaxed and they continued walking. "It's just that, sometimes I feel like I'm not the only one who's making bad decisions." He glanced at her meaningfully. "Just watch out for yourself, okay?"

Laura avoided his eyes.

What's he getting at, exactly?

She shrugged. "Sure, Bob."

He offered her a smile. "We're bursting with secrets, aren't we?"

Laura returned his smile. "I guess so. Maybe I'll tell you all about them, one day."

They reached the pedestrian crossing.

In a teasing tone, Bob asked, "So, your Mesmo guy is from out of town?"

"Oh yes," she replied casually. "Light years."

CHAPTER 12 *The Lie*

Hao studied Victor Hayward from behind the one-way mirror. The man was slumped on a chair in the interrogation room, his green eyes empty. Only when the police officer sitting opposite him pushed back his chair, did the former businessman jolt, his eyes darting.

The police officer exited the bare room and met Hao on the other side.

"Well?" Hao said.

The officer shook his head. "He's lost it—he's spooked out of his wits. There's nothing to pull out of him."

Hao rotated his body on his crutches and hopped to the door. "I'm expected in the High Inspector's office. Keep me posted if there's any change."

"Yes, Sir."

Hao headed down the plain corridor to the big, metal elevator that would take him to the first floor, which was located just below the surface. As he reached for the elevator button, one of his crutches slipped from his hand and fell with a clatter.

Hao grunted irritably. Man, how he hated these crutches!

He couldn't run or defend himself, and everything took double the time to get done.

But I'll get them done—eventually, he promised himself as the elevator rose to his destination.

The doors slid open and he headed for his boss's office. His crutches clicked on the concrete floor, irritating him. He could bet on it that the High Inspector' assistant was watching him struggle all the way to her desk.

He had almost reached her when the office door swung open and Connelly stepped out.

Both men stiffened at the same time.

Connelly closed the door slowly, never taking his eyes off of Hao, then took a few steps in his direction. He pointed at the crutches. "Not planning on using those on me, are you?" he smirked.

Showtime! Hao told himself, but he merely shook his head.

Connelly glared at him for a bit, then said, "You're late. The meeting was moved to 8:00 am. Didn't you get the memo?"

How could I, if no one sent it to me? Hao fought to keep his inner fire contained. *He's deliberately keeping me out of the loop,* Hao realized. As normal as possible, he answered, "Nope. Must've missed it."

Connelly nodded without smiling. "Well, seeing as you are currently..." he pointed at Hao's broken leg, "...indisposed, High Inspector Tremblay has made it official that I take over the case. I will be answering to him, now."

There you have it! Hao pressed his lips into a fine line. "I see," he said.

The bald man studied him for a bit longer, then passed him by without another word.

"Hey, Theodore!" Hao called after him.

Connelly stopped and turned around.

Hao braced himself, fully expecting to receive a punch in the face. But there was no reaction, so Hao said, "Look, I owe you an apology, you know, for the way I acted the other day in the infirmary. I don't know what got into me." He shuffled on his crutches. "I gotta tell you, I thought I was living my final hours under that avalanche. I even hallucinated. I... I guess fear got the better of me and I took it out on you. It was very unprofessional on my part, and I apologize."

Connelly nodded without a hint of emotion.

Hao wanted to break his nose. "So," he continued instead. "Well done on your raise." He lifted one of the crutches off the ground. "And you're right, of course, it's not like I can do much right now."

Connelly offered him the tiniest of smiles, making Hao's insides twist. Was it a smile of acceptance? A smile of glee? A smile of victory? Hao had no clue.

The men turned their backs to one another after a minimal salute, but then Hao stopped and called after him once more, "Oh, and one last thing."

Connelly cast him a furious look, which Hao thoroughly enjoyed.

"What now?" the bald man snapped.

"Give my best wishes to Kyle."

"To who... *What?"*

Hao frowned. "Today is April second, isn't it?"

"Yeah, so?"

"So," Hao continued. "It's your son's birthday today, isn't it?"

Connelly's eyes narrowed, but only for a fraction of a second.

Jeez, he's good, Hao thought in wonder.

"Right," Connelly said without intonation.

"Sooo," Hao repeated. "Wish him a happy birthday for me when you call him."

Connelly's mouth shut tight, his fingers twitching at his side. He nodded, then spun around and distanced himself from Hao with large strides.

Hao, his brow knitted, bounced unsteadily on his good leg until he had turned a corner. He sagged against the wall and let out a shaky breath. *For goodness sake, the guy doesn't even know his own son's birthday!* Tamara had told him that Kyle's birthday was on April third. Today was April second. And Connelly hadn't known the difference.

Then there was the *Theodore* issue. Connelly hadn't flinched at hearing the name. Whatever was happening, the Connelly he had just spoken to did not match his wife's description of a loving husband and father.

Hao should have felt elated at having caught his partner in a trap, but he didn't. Something was fundamentally wrong, but what was it, exactly?

He only knew one thing for sure—a thing confirmed by the internal alarms that were screaming at him from his entire body. *There's a traitor at the heart of the CSIS.*

* * *

Ben stepped off the bus and waited patiently for the pedestrian light to turn green. As he crossed the street, he was reminded once more that it was the first time he had returned to school without Tike. His heart weighed so heavily he wondered if he was going to be able to carry it.

He had tried hard to concentrate on his first day back at

school. Mostly for his mom's sake. It was her first day in a new place as well, after all, and he figured it must be as hard for her as it was for him. So he had put on a brave face.

But attempting to make new friends had been beyond him. He couldn't handle it. Not after having made such great friends in Canmore, only to have them taken away from him at the snap of a finger.

New friendships would have to wait.

He pulled open the door to Uncle Bob's bar. The atmosphere was dim and minimalistic, a bit like Uncle Bob's apartment. It was early afternoon, and the place was empty, except for a person vacuuming at the back and two older folk who stared at him as if he wasn't supposed to be there.

"Hi, Ben!" a cheerful voice greeted him. Pearl appeared from under the counter, her hands full of wet glasses. She placed them on the long counter and headed over to him. "Oh my! Look at you!" she exclaimed, holding him at arm's length to admire him better. "Is that a uniform you're wearing?"

Ben's relief at seeing a friendly face was replaced by fire rising to his cheeks. He nodded.

Not long ago, the prospect of wearing a uniform to school would have unchained a monumental confrontation with his mother. But that was the other Ben, the Ben from before *The Cosmic Fall*. This new Ben hadn't given the grey trousers, white shirt and red tie more than a passing thought. His mind was on other things. His mind was on Tike who had died, on Mesmo who was on the point of leaving forever, on Beetrix whose species was in danger of dying out... This new Ben was far removed from the trivialities of the clothes he was wearing. That was, unless Pearl mentioned them.

"I'm so glad you're attending school in the neighbourhood and that your mom's decided to help us,"

Pearl gushed, squeezing his hand, then returning to her position at the counter, where she began to dry a glass with a kitchen towel. "Bobby says you might even settle down in the area."

He thought he glimpsed a tightening under her eyes, but she smiled cheerfully. "We'd love for you to stick around."

Ben nodded again, the theme of where they were going to live a murky question in his mind, then realized he should probably say something. "Thanks. Um, is my mom here?"

"Yes, just head up the stairs to your right. That's the office. Oh, and Ben..." She reached out behind the counter and reemerged with a pile of mail in her hand. "Take these with you, would you? She'll be opening the business mail from now on."

Ben took the envelopes from her.

"And come down when you're done," she added. "I'll teach you to make a mint-orange juice cocktail. You'll see, it's the best in town."

"Okay," Ben said, grinning, then sprinted up the stairs so he could regain control of his burning cheeks. He shoved open the office door, his backpack slipping to his elbow in the process.

He found his mother at a desk with a pile of documents around her.

She placed a pen behind her ear and glued a phone to the other one. She waved at him and signalled for him to wait until she was done. Placing her hand over the speaker, she mouthed, "How was your day?"

Ben gave her a vague thumbs-up. It wasn't as if there was much to say: new buildings, new faces, new teachers. He had waited all day just to be able to join his mother so they could visit Mesmo, for his biggest fear was the alien would take off without saying goodbye.

He dropped his backpack on the floor and rearranged the stack of envelopes from big to small while he waited for Laura to finish her call. Then, he frowned.

Why is the wrong name on the envelopes?

The name printed on them was: ROBERT MANFIELD.

When Laura hung up, he reached out to give her the mail. "That's weird. Dad's name is on all the enve..." he started, before breaking off. His frown deepened, and he pulled back the mail before she could take it.

Wait a minute... This is really strange...

He studied the envelopes again, completely confused. That was his dad's name, all right, followed by the name of the bar he was standing in, then, its address. "Why is Dad's name on the envelopes?" he asked, but as he spoke, something clicked in the back of his mind, something he should have noticed ages ago, but had been too busy to notice.

"Robert..." he said slowly, his mind whirling. "...and Bob. Aren't those names..." His mouth went dry. He looked up and found his mother's face had turned ashen.

A cold shiver travelled up his spine. "Mom?" he croaked, suddenly engulfed in fear. "Is Bob short for Robert?"

His mother seemed to have turned into a marble statue. No sound came out of her mouth.

Ben stared at her. The envelopes slid, forgotten, from his hands. His brain couldn't believe what he said next. "Mom? Is Bob *my dad*?"

Laura faltered as she got up from her chair. "I need you to listen to me, Ben," she said, hanging on the edge of the desk for support.

Ben's eyes bulged. A simple 'No, honey, don't be silly,' would have done the trick.

Why isn't she answering the question?

"Mom?" his voice rose a pitch. "IS BOB MY DAD?"

Her mouth opened, but nothing came out.

Suddenly, Ben didn't want to hear the answer. He couldn't take it.

"Yes," she said.

Ben flinched as if she had just hit him with a bat.

"There's something you need to understand..." she began, reaching out to him.

Ben recoiled. He couldn't comprehend what was happening. "You mean.... You *lied* to me?" His voice was incredulous.

"I didn't mean to," she whispered, breaking apart before his eyes.

"My dad's alive, and you lied to me ALL THIS TIME?" Memories flashed before his eyes—things that hadn't made sense before, but did now; moments that he should have spent with his dad, but hadn't. Years of lies. He backed into the door.

"No, wait, Ben," Laura said. "Don't turn away from me."

He shook his head in disbelief, then whirled, pulled at the door and bolted down the stairs, ignoring his mother's calls.

"Hey, Ben, are you ready for that orange ju..." Pearl's voice came from behind the counter, but he was already through the door of the pub and out into the bustling street.

He ignored shouts of anger as he bumped into pedestrians. He dashed down the street, zigzagging among afternoon shoppers and office people, putting as much distance as he could between himself and his mother, his heart thudding with each step.

The one person I trusted with my life...

His feet took him to the park, and he kept running even

though a stitch nagged at his side. He welcomed the pain. Maybe it would drown his grief. He dropped to the ground at the edge of the lake, sobbing.

Tike! I need you!

He wrapped his arms around his legs and bit into his knee. He shut his eyes tight and screamed into his trouser leg.

Ben rocked back and forth, sobbing his heart out, releasing the pain of Tike's death, trying to make sense of his mother's lie, wondering if he could ever face her or Bob again.

The sun, which reflected a soft orange on the city buildings, did little to warm Ben's insides. He shuddered with thoughts of how his mom had deceived him for years.

A hand touched him on the back. He jumped and laid eyes on Mesmo with relief. The alien sat beside him, and Ben sank his head against his shoulder.

"What happened?" Mesmo asked.

Ben told him.

Mesmo remained silent for a long moment.

When Ben calmed down somewhat, the alien said, "Has your mother told you her reasons? I'm sure there must be an explanation as to why she hid your father from you."

"I don't care. I don't want to hear it."

Mesmo paused, then said, "I've noticed that people sometimes lie to protect their loved ones from painful truths. There is usually a reason behind it. I think you should give her a chance to explain herself."

Ben watched a passing motorboat make ripples on the surface of the lake that slowly trickled to shore, thinking about Mesmo's words. But he felt mentally exhausted and couldn't come up with any reason to listen to his mother. "I want to go with you," he said numbly. "There's nothing left for me here. Grampa, Tike, Kimi, I'll never see any of them again. And now you're going to leave, too." His eyes filled with tears again. "You're the only one left that I can trust."

Mesmo wrung his hands together. "I think you're overreacting right now."

"No, I'm not. I could be your co-pilot. I could learn, you know?" He glanced hopefully at the alien.

Mesmo wrapped his arm around the boy's shoulders and squeezed them without responding. He didn't need to.

Ben's shoulders sagged. "What should I do, then?" he asked, kicking with his heel at the sand.

"Make peace with your mother and father," Mesmo replied. "Bob has offered to help you settle here. You'd be safe here, and you could live close to both your parents. Does that sound so terrible?"

Ben considered it. He had never dared dream of such a thing: to have both a mother and a father in his life. And now it was suddenly a real possibility. But it would be a life without Mesmo. "You stay, then," he shot back. "Teach me how to use the skill! Help me protect the animals! And besides, you love my mom. I saw you kiss her. So, you can't go!"

I sound like a little kid.

"Ben, I..."

"Yes, I know!" Ben interrupted. "The Toreq won't allow you to marry twice or something stupid like that. But you're not on your planet. You're on Earth." He glanced pleadingly at the alien, knowing his reasoning was futile. "What? Does that sound so terrible?" he pressed on anyway.

His words made Mesmo grin. "You are quite a special human being, Benjamin Archer," he said. "And I'm not saying that because of the skill." He fell silent and stared at the lake. When he glanced at Ben again, his smile had faded. "But no, I can't stay."

Ben's head drooped.

"Come," the alien said gently. "I will take you home, to your father. And then I must leave."

They walked side by side through the park, Ben with his hands in his pockets, the red tie of his uniform loose around his neck.

"You know," Mesmo said, "I like it better when you cry from happiness."

Ben smiled sadly and put an arm around the man's waist. "I'm going to miss you," he said.

Mesmo placed his own arm around Ben's shoulders. "I'm going to miss you too, Benjamin Archer."

CHAPTER 13 *Treason*

The elevator to Bob's apartment pinged, and the doors slid open. Ben found his dad pacing beside the kitchen counter with a plastic water bottle in his hand.

"Ben!" he said with some surprise as if he hadn't been expecting him. He stepped forward, but his face fell as soon as Mesmo exited the elevator. Bob licked his lips and drew back.

Ben decided to ignore his father's unwelcome reaction to the alien but felt reluctant to enter the apartment further. His parents' lie loomed like an insurmountable wall before him. "I need to talk to you," he said in a flat voice.

Bob placed the bottle on the counter, then pulled at his collar. "Yes, I need to talk to you, too." His eyes were fixed on Mesmo while avoiding Bens'.

"There's no need. I already know the truth," Ben said glumly. "You're my dad. Mom told me." The words sounded foreign to his ears.

Bob cleared his throat. "I know, she called and told me what happened. She's looking all over for you." He rubbed at the middle of his forehead with his eyes closed. "Look, she made me promise not to say anything. It wasn't supposed to happen this way. We were going to go out, the three of us, have a nice dinner, then talk about it—together. But then, *this* happened." He made a gesture that seemed aimed at Mesmo.

Frustration surged within Ben.

Why's he on Mesmo's back?

Bob's eyes darted across the apartment. He waved the boy over. "Can you come on over here?" he said.

Ben and Mesmo took a step forward.

"Not you," Bob snapped at Mesmo.

Heat flushed through Ben's body. "Will you stop that? Mesmo's my friend. He came to help."

"Just, come on over here, squirt!" Bob demanded irritably, his voice calling for obedience.

Ben approached him, a little apprehensive. He noticed small pearls of sweat on Bob's forehead.

What's up with him?

A reflection on the kitchen fridge moved, making him spin towards the living room. But too late.

From behind a wall, Connelly stepped out with a gun in his hand.

Ben yelped, shrinking into Bob in fright.

"Shh! It's okay! This is a police officer," Bob said, wrapping his arm around the boy's chest.

"No, wait!" Ben shouted, struggling to free himself from Bob's restraining grip.

"Calm down!" Bob urged. "He's here to protect us."

"Are you crazy?"

"Listen to me!" Bob insisted as Ben squirmed. "This Mesmo is a dangerous felon. The police have been chasing him across the country."

"So you went and *called* them?" Ben shouted in disbelief, lunging from Bob's grasp and whirling to face him.

"Relax, will you? I recognized this criminal the minute I laid eyes on him in the park. You can't hang out with people like that! Trust me, I know what I'm talking about. They're dangerous!"

Ben was on the verge of a breakdown. "You have no idea what you did!" His skin crawled at the shapeshifter's proximity. "He's going to kill us!"

"Don't be stupid. Let the man do his jo..."

Connelly bellowed, "THAT'S ENOUGH!"

Ben whimpered.

The shapeshifter hadn't taken his eyes off Mesmo for a second. His enemy stood near the elevator, poised like a prey backed into a corner.

"This show has gone on long enough," Connelly growled. "Time to wrap up."

To Ben's horror, the bald man aimed the gun at him without taking his eyes off of Mesmo. "Let's go," he said, talking to the boy.

"Wait a minute," Bob protested. "Ben's not going with you. And point that thing elsewhere. Somebody could get hurt."

The bald man turned his head and followed the direction of the gun. Even from where he stood, Ben could see his eyes switching from green to honey-brown. "I won't say it again," he hissed.

Ben knew him well enough to realize that they could all be dead in an instant.

But Bob didn't catch on to the threat. "No, no, Ben has nothing to do with this, I told you already..."

"Get down!" Mesmo yelled.

A blue shockwave lashed out of the shapeshifter, knocking them off their feet. Ben hurled back as if flicked aside by a giant finger. He slammed into the kitchen counter and saw stars before his eyes. Fighting to stay conscious, he found Mesmo sprawled on the floor by the elevator, while Bob lay in a heap beside him. His back throbbing, Ben watched in horror as the shapeshifter's body swelled from internal tremors. He reached for Bob and shook him frantically by the shoulder.

Bob lifted his head dizzily and gasped at the sight unfolding before them.

The shapeshifter groaned and bared his teeth, unable to control his metamorphosis from Connelly into Bordock. An eerie blue light emanated from him as he hunched over, the gun forgotten in his hand.

Ben cast a glance at Mesmo, but the alien lay unmoving.

Bob's eyes, on the other hand, bulged in terror. He scrambled on all fours behind the kitchen counter.

Ben wanted to rush after his dad, but instead, he spotted the water bottle that had been knocked to the ground by the blast and had rolled behind a kitchen stool. He reached for it with the tips of his fingers, then shoved it behind his back in a hurry, checking hastily on Bordock.

The shapeshifter straightened his back, his muscles and bones falling into place. His head spun towards the boy, making a jolt of dread scamper up and down his spine.

Bordock tossed the gun aside. "Useless thing," he said. "Don't make me do that again. Let's go."

Ben cringed and glanced at his dad in a silent plea for help.

But Bob cowered behind the counter, peeking out at the shapeshifter. He waved a trembling hand at Ben, indicating he should obey Bordock at once.

His heart shrinking, Ben stood and carefully side-stepped to where Mesmo lay.

The alien groaned as he regained consciousness. Taking in Ben's fearful eyes and Bordock's glowing hands, Mesmo understood they were helpless. He got up with Ben's help and shoved the boy behind him so he could serve as a buffer.

"Get the elevator," Bordock ordered, his eyes burning with anger.

While Ben obeyed, the shapeshifter retrieved a police walkie-talkie from within his suit jacket. He pressed a button and spoke into it, "Coming down with the suspects."

Mesmo reacted swifter than lightning.

Ben had placed the water bottle in his hands seconds after helping him up. A rope of water gushed out of the bottle, lashing at Bordock like a whip. It wrapped itself around the shapeshifter, turning into ice instantly.

Caught off guard, Bordock lost his balance and fell heavily.

"Go!" Mesmo yelled to Ben, who was frantically hitting the elevator button. The doors didn't budge.

Mesmo grabbed him by the arm and reached Bob in two long strides. "Is there another way out of here?"

Bob blinked at him and answered with a trembling voice, "Balcony. Emergency stairs."

Mesmo pulled him up roughly. "Take us there, NOW!"

Bob whimpered but did as he was told.

Ben could already hear the ice rope crackling under Bordock's effort to free himself. He stumbled fearfully after Bob. Behind them, the shapeshifter roared.

For the second time, Mesmo yelled, "Down!"

He threw himself on Ben and covered his head with his arms, just as a massive shockwave burst from the shapeshifter. The invisible onslaught hurtled above their heads, crashing into the large windows as if they were made of paper. The glass rippled, then shattered into a thousand pieces that were cast into the air like ice splinters.

* * *

Laura had combed the park searching for Ben and Mesmo and was heading to Bob's apartment when she heard the explosion.

She watched in terror as the windows in Bob's apartment blew outward. Shards of glass flew down into the street like spears, causing havoc that made cars screech to a halt and pedestrians run for cover.

CHAPTER 14 *Shame*

Mesmo urged Ben and his father to their feet.

Bob hopped on to a ledge which led them across the roof of the building. They sprinted to the other side, then clambered down the emergency stairs at the back of the building.

"Hurry!" Mesmo pressed, as if they needed encouragement.

They had almost reached the bottom when Ben risked a look up and felt a chill run down his spine. Bordock was observing them from the rooftop.

They had barely touched the ground when a police car screeched to a stop at the end of the alley. It backed up and turned to head their way.

The three scrambled the other way.

Ben checked over his shoulder. Bordock was still watching them from the rooftop, giving orders into his walkie-talkie. Ben could tell the outline of the alien was changing; he was shapeshifting into Connelly again.

Mesmo rushed them across a street and into another back alley. They hugged the walls when a helicopter flew overhead.

As soon as it was gone, Ben sprinted on, thinking the

others were following. But instead, he heard someone groan behind him. He whirled in time to see Mesmo keel over and crash to the ground.

"Mesmo!" he yelled, rushing to his side.

The alien's hands flew to his head.

"What's wrong?" Ben said in anguish, searching frantically for the source of Mesmo's pain.

The alien's body went limp for a fraction of a second, then he came to again with a loud gasp of air.

Whirling sirens zipping by at the end of the alley spurted Ben into action. "Help me!" he urged a pale-faced Bob, while he grabbed Mesmo under one armpit.

Bob's eyes were glazed, but he took Mesmo under the other armpit, and together they dragged the alien into an open warehouse which was filled with piles of boxes.

Although half a dozen men were busy carrying cargo into the back of a store at the end of the warehouse, they found a safe spot in the right corner, behind a wall of boxes and scaffolds covered in plastic.

Ben knelt by Mesmo's side, calling his name, trying to help him regain full consciousness while the alien fought a mysterious, inward battle. It took him almost fifteen minutes to control whatever was happening to him and by the time he blinked his eyes open, his face was grey from the effort.

Ben helped him sit and lean against the boxes. "Are you okay?" he asked, beside himself with worry.

Mesmo nodded, wincing.

"What happened?"

Mesmo had to quiet his rasping breath before he was able to answer. "Spirit portal," he managed to utter.

Ben's eyes fell automatically on his wrist. Then he remembered that the last one to have had the watch with the spirit portal was Mesmo. His mind raced as he realized he hadn't seen it since Mesmo's escape from Victor Hayward's clutches. A sinking feeling filled his stomach. "I don't have it anymore. Do you?"

Mesmo shook his head. "No, but someone tried to impose its effect on me. They tried to force my spirit out of my body. I have never experienced anything so powerful! I barely resisted."

Ben and Mesmo's eyes met. They already knew who it was.

"Bordock!" Ben gasped.

Mesmo nodded. "He is desperate. Not a single Toreq in their right mind would consider doing such a vile thing. Where I come from, forcefully separating a spirit from a physical body is punishable by death. The technology was banned eons ago. Only a handful of Toreq still master that technology." He gritted his teeth. "It can only mean one thing. Bordock is backed by some powerful adversaries."

Ben shuddered at the idea that there could be other Bordocks out there pulling strings, giving the shapeshifter orders.

Mesmo must have seen the fear in Ben's eyes because he placed a hand on the boy's shoulder. "You don't need to worry yourself over that. This is a situation that is taking place on my planet. It does not involve you."

Ben nodded.

"But it also means I need to get home at all costs, to warn my people. Give me a moment to gather my strength," Mesmo said. "Then we need to leave."

Ben nodded again and turned to Bob who was sitting on a box with his face buried in his hands. His pale fingers rubbed at his hair as if the back-and-forth movement kept him from falling into insanity.

"Bob?"

The man stared at the ground. "I didn't sign up for this," Ben heard him say.

"Are you okay?" Ben asked.

His father did not respond.

Ben sighed and turned away, but then he heard Bob say in a clear voice, "You were in the car."

Ben whirled.

Bob hid his eyes in his hands so that Ben could only see his mouth and beard. "Back when you were a baby, and I crashed the car..." He lifted his ruffled head and stared at Ben. "...you were in the car with me," he admitted.

For a second, Ben felt the earth open under his feet, threatening to engulf him. He had to lean against a wall of boxes and slide down to a crouching position to steady himself.

Bob's head was in his hands again. "That's why your mom never forgave me," he said. "I... um... I was really proud of becoming a father. The rest of my friends were too young to be thinking about such things. One afternoon, they got together and insisted I come. So I took you with me to show you off. But I stayed a bit too long, and by the time we headed out again it was dark, and I wasn't thinking straight. That's when I crashed the car."

He stared at the floor. "I panicked. My adult life was just beginning, and I was about to lose everything. I fled and..." His shoulders quaked. "...left you in the car."

Ben listened in disbelief. He tried to process this information, considering the man who was sobbing freely before him. After a while, he reached out and placed a reassuring hand on his dad's leg.

"I was young and stupid," Bob whimpered. "I made a mistake."

Mesmo came up beside Ben. "We have to go," he said

softly, but firmly.

Ben forced himself to stand shakily.

His father had his hands to his face again. "I can't do this," he said in a defeated voice.

The boy regarded his father who had the same colour hair and eyes as him. A rebellious mesh stuck out at the back of the man's head, just like Ben, and he knew there was an undeniable blood bond between them.

But Robert Manfield was also numbed by fear, and, although that was a trait Ben knew his mother did not have, he could understand it. How many times had Bordock not had the same effect on him? The difference here was that his dad had a choice to be part of the story, or not. And clearly, he wanted no part of it. Because, whereas Bordock had no interest in his dad, Ben could not say the same. Had Ben been in his dad's position, he probably wouldn't have been up to the task of facing Bordock, either. Few, if any, would accept such a risk. And so, Ben understood.

"Dad," Ben said.

Bob lifted his head.

"I forgive you."

I forgive you for the accident. I forgive you for being too afraid to protect me.

He swallowed a sob.

I forgive you for not wanting to be my dad.

Bob's eyes lit with an inner acceptance of his own weakness. "Then, you are a better man than I ever will be," he said.

Mesmo placed a hand on the boy's shoulder. "Benjamin," he urged. "We can't delay any further."

Ben nodded, reluctant to let go of his father's eyes. "Goodbye, Dad," he whispered as he backed away, but the man had retracted into a shell again.

Boy and alien slipped out of the warehouse, leaving Robert Manfield behind. They sprinted to the end of the back alley, then crouched at the corner to inspect the busy street before them, scanning for police cars.

Ben wiped away the tears that rolled down his cheeks, focusing ahead. He realized they were opposite Berczy Park with its Dog Fountain and wondered if they could make it across without being too obvious.

"Benjamin," Mesmo said, pulling the boy out of his thoughts. Mesmo was observing him curiously.

"What?" he said, sniffing.

"Why did you forgive him?"

Ben stared at the ground, considering the question, trying to ignore a great emptiness growing inside him, and although it hurt, he knew he had done the right thing. He stared at Mesmo and replied, "He made some wrong choices. But at least he tried, and that's good enough for me." He leaned forward again, studying their options, but Mesmo continued to stare at the boy.

Realizing this, Ben frowned. "What is it?"

Mesmo seemed lost in an inner conversation as if he were trying to make up his mind about something. Then he sighed and said, "I think I am beginning to understand something about humans that I didn't understand before."

Ben waited for him to explain himself, but instead, Mesmo said, "You make things very difficult for me, Benjamin Archer."

Ben snorted. "Look who's talking!"

They glanced at each other and grinned.

CHAPTER 15 *Resistance*

Chaos ensued in front of Bob's apartment.

Laura rushed to the scene, her heart thumping, her raincoat flowing behind her as she ran. Police cars halted traffic and surrounded the building entrance. Officers scrambled in and out of the lobby, ambulances whirled to a stop, and first aid crews hurried to check on any injured people who had been unfortunate enough to find themselves under the rain of falling glass.

Laura came to a stop on the other side of the street, desperately trying to figure out what had happened, praying that Ben was not among the wounded.

Then a group of police officers detached themselves from the centre of the commotion and darted down the sidewalk, while a couple of police cars screeched to life, heading the same way. Their sirens wailed down the street.

Laura grasped her handbag tightly. She plunged into the street, oblivious to oncoming traffic, and followed the law enforcement as fast as she could.

* * *

Ben checked the street one more time. "What do you think?" he said.

"We need to keep moving," Mesmo replied.

"There's a bus stop on the other side of the plaza," Ben noted. "We might get lucky. Or we'll come across a taxi."

Mesmo nodded. "Let's go."

They emerged from their hiding spot in the alley and sprinted across the street, forcing a couple of cars to hit their brakes.

They were barely to the other side when the sound of a siren made Ben's blood go cold. He glanced over his shoulder and saw a civilian car bump to a stop on the Berczy Park sidewalk behind him. Two men with bulletproof vests materialized out of the car, one of them barking into a speaker microphone.

"Run!" Mesmo ordered, grabbing him by the back of his shirt collar, almost lifting him up in his hurry to get them going.

Pedestrians froze and looked on in surprise; mothers grabbed their children from the edge of the Dog Fountain and hurried away, while, already, the sound of new sirens approached.

Ben and Mesmo were halfway across the plaza when a helicopter shot over their heads. People shouted and rushed for safety.

"Hold it!" one of the police officers yelled from the civilian car behind them.

"Mesmo!" Ben sobbed, unable to keep up with the alien's long strides. His vision went blurry, and he wiped at his eyes. But the edge of his eyesight began to darken.

What's wrong with me?

"Mesmo!" he called again, his voice sounding far away as if he were crumbling into himself. He couldn't focus or feel the movement of his legs.

Mesmo turned to face him, and Ben vaguely registered the alien's eyes widening in shock. "Benjamin!" he yelled. "Resist!"

Resist what?

That was his last thought before Mesmo's face turned into the granite mosaic paving below him. He did not feel the pain as he hit the ground, however, because already his spirit was plunging through a tunnel of darkness.

* * *

From the opposite side of the street, Laura came to a stop as she watched Ben tumble to the ground. "No!" she yelled in anguish.

Half a dozen police cars rushed to the scene, cutting her off. Two army trucks followed, spewing soldiers, armed to the teeth.

Mesmo stood between Ben and the fountain, frozen in indecision. The soldiers rushed to take position around him, while terrified civilians scrambled in all directions.

Laura looked on in trepidation as the alien hesitated between Ben and his narrowing chance of escape. "Don't leave him!" she begged silently.

Mesmo turned his back on Ben and raced away.

"No!" she breathed, fighting a sudden onset of nausea.

There were yells from the soldiers, who took position to shoot.

In a couple of swift strides, Mesmo's long legs brought him to the fountain. Without pausing, he plunged his glowing hands into the water, and before Laura could open her mouth, a sphere of blue power erupted around the alien, expanding faster than sound towards the soldiers. It was instantly followed by a deafening blast as sound caught up with the expulsed air and an exploding cloud of mist swept across the plaza, knocking over everyone in its path.

Laura toppled as the mixture of air and water shoved her forcefully onto the sidewalk. Shop windows rattled. People lay on the ground, stunned.

Laura picked herself up in a hurry, her head swimming dizzily.

A thick mist emanated from the fountain. The soldiers, who had been hit the hardest, came to their senses and struggled to find their bearings. An eerie silence—only covered by the ringing in Laura's ears and the muffled sound of a helicopter—kept everyone in a daze.

Then people began to scream. They scrambled to their feet, knocking each other over in their haste to escape.

Laura watched dazedly through the running crowds as the mist around the fountain thinned, and Mesmo's outline appeared in its centre. The alien carried Ben in his arms.

* * *

Ben gasped.

He felt as though he had just tumbled down a hill in total darkness and had landed at the bottom, bruised and battered. He figured he must have hit the ground pretty hard and expected pain to engulf him any minute. But the pain didn't come.

Instead, he became aware of muffled silence, cut by screams somewhere far away. He struggled to make sense of sound. His vision focused and he found himself surrounded by metal walls that belonged to the inside of a van. A small window near the front looked out onto an empty driver's seat.

The last thing he remembered was landing face-first on the granite paving. Now, he was in a standing position, inside an unfamiliar vehicle.

How can that be?

He wanted to approach two small, dirt-covered windows on the side of the van but found he couldn't move.

He glanced at his feet and hands, fearfully. There was nothing wrong with them. Yet, when he tried to move, there was resistance. He pressed against the air. An invisible barrier restrained him with force.

Something shone below him. He strained his neck to make out what it was. Blue beams emanated from four hand-sized, black boxes placed in a square formation under his feet. They seemed to determine the limit of his movements.

As if he were stuck in a narrow shaft, Ben managed to bend his knees, grunting as he reached for one of the boxes. He curled his fingers around the object, but his hand passed right through it. Denial seeped into his mind. "No, no, no, no, no." He clung to the word like a life-saving vest.

Unable to fight the horrible, sinking feeling that threatened to engulf him, he stood and stretched his neck to glance out the small windows.

Sounds of screams and running people surrounded the van. He could hear a helicopter hovering overhead. Soldiers gathered before a strange mist which hung to the ground across the street. From it, Ben watched Mesmo emerge, carrying a limp body in his arms.

His body.

"No, no, no, no, no," he repeated. "Mesmo!" He punched at the air that held him prisoner, calling the alien's name desperately. Feeling dizzy with despair, he shut his eyes and puffed his cheeks several times, willing himself to calm down.

Break the connection!

That's what he needed to do.

Take control of your thoughts and break the connection with the spirit portal.

He forced his mind to go blank and willed his spirit back to his body. Instead, a powerful whirlpool of magnetic energy grabbed at him from all sides. He wanted to scream. It was as if he had been swallowed by suffocating quicksand. He didn't know which way was up or down as his spirit stretched in a tug-of-war between his body and the alien trap. Fighting devastating panic, he stopped struggling and let his mind drift. Like a piece of metal drawn to a magnet, his spirit got sucked back into the van.

"Let me out! Help!" he yelled.

Outside the van, chaos drowned his voice.

More police cars arrived at the scene. Ben watched in dismay as his lifeless body was placed on a stretcher and rolled into one of the army trucks. Mesmo was handcuffed and taken into another truck.

The door on the driver's side opened suddenly, and the van dipped as someone took their place in the front seat.

Ben turned in a hurry.

A bald head appeared through the window. "Well, well," Connelly smirked, peeking at him. "I've caught a little mouse." He lifted his arm and tapped on the silver watch that contained the spirit portal. It was safely attached to his wrist. The blue beams below Ben glowed at its proximity.

Ben's voice died in his throat.

Connelly seemed amused. "Don't you just wish I had trapped Mesmo instead of you? His spirit turned out to be too strong, though, and it slipped through my fingers. But then, it occurred to me. Toreq blood now runs through your veins. So, I reactivated my devices and tried again." Connelly clicked his tongue. "I guess my idea paid off."

He turned to face the front, then hesitated and looked back at Ben again, a frown creasing his forehead. "What I didn't expect was Mesmo staying to save you." He shook his head, chuckling. "Or, at least, he made a flimsy attempt to." He raised an eyebrow at Ben's silence. "Lost your voice, little mouse?" He leaned forward and turned on the ignition. The motor roared to life. "Maybe you'll find it again, in the end."

* * *

Laura ran down the sidewalk, bumping into fleeing civilians, trying to approach the group of soldiers who were taking Ben and Mesmo away, while remaining at a safe distance on the opposite side of the street.

A van took off in a cloud of smoke before her, so she stepped onto the parking spot it had left unoccupied. Never once did she take her eyes off Ben's limp body until the back doors of the military truck shut with a clatter, locking him in. The truck sped off without delay, guided by a police car that opened up the way before it, with sirens wailing.

"Ben!" she whispered, weak with worry.

The truck that held Mesmo followed closely behind the first one, and in no time the convoy made their way down central Toronto.

Someone yelled nearby, startling her. A man rushed by, while other people stopped and pointed, commenting loudly. Instead of running away from Berczy Park, she suddenly found civilians heading towards it.

She followed the pointed fingers, and her mouth fell open.

Now that the mist had gone, Dog Fountain was once more visible in the middle of the plaza. Emerging from its top, a thick column of frozen water sparkled in the afternoon sun. The size of it, in itself, was remarkable, but what caught Laura off guard was the shape the icy cylinder had been twisted into. It was a symbol, and the symbol resembled that of a treble clef—just like the one she had strung around her neck.

CHAPTER 16 *The Interrogation*

Laura wandered the streets of Toronto aimlessly, her mind in turmoil. She clutched the object Mesmo had given her for safekeeping several weeks earlier: the one which he had said contained information.

But what kind of information?

Was the frozen symbol at the fountain meant for her? Did Mesmo expect her to uncover a secret message contained in the gadget somehow?

She slipped into a back alley and crouched against the wall behind some garbage bins, then pulled out the object and studied it up close. It was the length of her pinkie and was made from a heavy material. She noted once more that it vaguely resembled the musical symbol commonly placed at the beginning of music partitions. There were tiny indentations and bumps along the surface, but nothing giving the slightest hint as to how it functioned.

Laura leaned back and let out a shaky breath.

What now?

A racket down the alley made her start. She peeked out of her hiding spot behind the garbage bin and saw a form hunch out the garage doors of a warehouse, pushing aside empty boxes that stood in his way. She tensed, preparing to flee. But the man headed in the opposite direction without noticing her.

Is that...?

"Bob?" She got to her feet instantly. "Wait up!"

The bearded man glanced at her, then hastened away.

"Hey!" she yelled, sprinting after him.

Bob broke into a run, but not fast enough that she couldn't catch up with him.

"Stop already!" she panted, grabbing his arm. "Why are you running?" She fell back at the sight of his harried look.

He cringed at her touch.

"What's the matter?"

His eyes darted from side to side. "Danger," he muttered. "Have to go..."

"Wait a minute! What happened? Tell me!"

He wouldn't meet her eyes. "This police officer came to my condo... I thought he was... but his face! His face... Not normal..."

"I know about him already. The police just took Ben away. He's in grave danger! We have to do something!"

Bob rocked on his feet without looking at her.

"Bob!" she yelled, trying to shake him into action. "Come on! We have to save Ben!"

Ben's father remained silent.

Laura lifted her arms in surrender and backed away from him.

Bob scrubbed at his face with his hands. "I... this is not... You never said..."

Laura pressed her hands against her stomach. "I get it," she nodded slowly. "You're doing it again! You're running away!"

Bob dropped his chin to his chest as if she had just slapped him in the face. "No! I... I need to think... I... we could get killed... This is too dangerous... Need to hide..."

She watched him mutter as he distanced himself from her, feeling too numb to retain him. She so needed Bob's help right now, but clearly, Bordock had left a lasting mark on him. Could she blame him?

I'm terrified of Bordock, too.

But turning her back on Ben was out of the question. And with that in mind, she realized there was only one thing left for her to do.

* * *

Connelly drove further and further away from any signs of civilization, with Ben catching glimpses through the small dust-covered windows of the traffic-jammed Toronto streets to hills covered in maple trees that went on and on for as far as the eye could see. Darkness fell, making the whole trip even lonelier.

Where's he taking me?

The longer the drive, the more desperate he became, especially after the van veered on to a bumpy road, away from the main, asphalted highway.

This spirit travelling didn't sit well with him. He yearned to return to the real, physical world and be in charge of his movements. The invisible pressure exerted all around him made it hard for him to concentrate. It was as if an elephant sat on him, making it necessary to focus his every thought on not getting crushed.

Now I know how Mesmo felt all these months.

The van finally came to a stop many hours later, in the pitch of the night. Ben briefly caught sight of a convoy of trucks and soldiers bustling around an open area illuminated by LED floodlights, in the middle of which stood a dull, concrete building.

The van, however, came to a standstill under the shadow of trees, far enough away not to be noticed.

Connelly turned to him. “Don’t try anything funny,” he warned, before getting out and shutting the door.

The shapeshifter’s footsteps faded away, leaving Ben in a crushing silence.

How am I going to get out of this one?

* * *

The heavy Dugout elevator came to a standstill. Three soldiers stepped out of it, flanking the tall alien that Hao had been searching for for a good six months. The Inspector watched, along with a dozen other bystanders, as the subject strode across the hangar dominated by the hovering spacecraft.

Just look at him, Hao thought, observing the man’s traits: wavy, brown hair, high cheekbones, square chin and straight nose. Slightly taller than the average male. Nothing out of the ordinary. *He dyed his hair,* Hao realized suddenly.

He followed the apprehended suspect across the hangar, briefly noticing that he was getting used to his crutches. But while the soldiers took the alien to the interrogation room, Hao split from the group and headed down to the last floor.

There, he found men in protective suits rushing around the safe room containing the three lifeless aliens, and Hao watched as the boy was rolled on a stretcher beside the alien girl.

The medical team shouted orders to each other and Hao had to wobble aside as a heart monitor and other medical equipment were rushed to the boy’s side.

“What’s going on?” Hao asked sharply, addressing a passing

medic. “Is he alive?”

The practitioner lifted his surgical mask. “Barely,” he said, wiping his brow with the back of his arm. “His heart rate is dangerously low. Zero reflex responses. We’re treating it as a coma.”

Hao pressed his lips together.

The practitioner covered his mouth again and adjusted his latex gloves. “It would help if we knew what happened to him. You could consider slipping the question to his alien accomplice.” Without waiting for a response, the practitioner went to join the rest of the medical team.

Hao backed away with dullness in the chest. He did not like it when an investigation went awry. In his mind, if anyone got hurt—be it police, civilian or suspect—it meant unprofessional coordination of the special forces. A successful intervention should occur in a quasi-invisible and swift manner, with as little disturbance to civilians as possible. Hao exhaled air out of his puffed cheeks.

This case is one mess after another, he thought scornfully.

He clambered back up the stairs and headed for the interrogation room. The soldier standing guard moved aside sharply.

Good, Hao thought. *This one still thinks I’m in charge.*

He entered the dark room and observed the alien sitting behind the one-way mirror. A soldier stood guard beside the subject, while another flanked the wall beside Hao.

“Where’s Agent Connelly?” Hao asked the guard.

“He’s debriefing the High Inspector, Sir,” the guard replied. “They’ll be down in a minute.”

Good. Out loud, Hao said, “Well, I don’t have all day. Open up, will you?”

“But Agent Co...”

"...will be down in a minute, you just said. I'm to begin questioning the suspect at once."

The guard shifted, but Hao knew he still exerted enough authority to be obeyed.

Might as well use it while it lasts, he thought bitterly.

"Yes, Sir." The guard straightened and hurried to unlock the door with a code. It buzzed open, and Hao stepped in.

"I'd like to speak to the suspect, alone," he told the guard who stuck by the wall like a poster.

"That is not advisable, S..." the guard began.

"*I'll* determine what *is* and what *isn't* advisable, soldier. You will leave me with the suspect!"

The soldier knocked his army boots together. "Yes, Sir!" He exited the room with quick strides, and the door clicked heavily shut behind him.

Hao paced the room, his crutches clicking on the floor.

The subject sat with his eyes closed, his skin a light shade of grey, his cuffed hands resting on the table before him.

Hao couldn't help but stare in fascination at the extraterrestrial. Had this individual really crashed in one of the alien spaceships that they had recovered on the fields of Chilliwack? Up until this moment, Hao had felt like he had been chasing a phantom. Months of research had only revealed fleeting glimpses of the subject: a lousy image from an airport camera, a grainy picture from a funeral, and a glance of the man fleeing on the Kananaskis Mountains...

Placed next to the other deceased aliens, there was an undeniable similarity. And then there were the hundreds of questions he had about inexplicable whale and crow attacks, the fact that this individual had survived a massive avalanche unscathed, and the many news reports that were surging of the Berczy Park incident with a mysterious, frozen symbol perched on top of its fountain.

Not to mention that there's no trace of him in any official identification system.

Even though he did not have a shred of hard evidence to link this individual to *The Cosmic Fall*, his gut feeling told him that the right suspect had been apprehended—meaning he was once more in the presence of an extraterrestrial being. Hao's stomach felt queasy.

How does one initiate a conversation with an alien? he wondered.

Hao wished he had time to ask the millions of questions that crisscrossed his mind, but they would have to wait. He sat opposite the suspect and said, "My name is Inspector James Hao. My partner, Agent Theodore Connelly, will be joining us soon."

The alien opened his eyes. They were a deep honey-colour. They reflected extreme weariness, yet Hao's heightened senses also perceived the hint of a connection between them.

"How is the boy?" the subject asked.

Hao had hoped for a mutual introduction, but clearly, the alien was testing the ground on which he stood. "Benjamin Archer, you mean?" he replied, deciding to go along with the alien's side of the conversation. "We believe he is in a coma. You can rest assured that he is being closely monitored by our medical team."

The alien gave a single nod.

"Can you tell me what happened to him, so our doctors can treat him, accordingly?" Hao asked.

The alien studied him as if trying to determine how much he should say. "Perhaps you should ask that question to the one you call your partner," he replied finally.

Hao flinched involuntarily. "Why?"

The alien held his gaze with a glint in his eyes but did not answer.

There's that connection again. "What would my partner know, that I don't?" Hao insisted. It bothered him that the subject didn't look away once. *He wants to talk but is cautious.*

Voices came from the other side of the one-way mirror.

Damn! "Talk to me!" Hao urged. "What would my partner know about the boy that I don't? I already know he's not human. My partner took a blood sample from him."

The alien leaned forward, his eyes glued to Hao, and spoke in a low voice, "Did he, really?"

Hao opened his mouth, but just then lights came on in the adjacent room, making the High Inspector and Connelly visible through the smoked glass.

Connelly approached the window to glance at them, then lifted his arm and tapped on his silver wristwatch meaningfully, as if indicating that Hao's time was up.

The door swung open, and the High Inspector stepped in, eyes protruding. "Hao, what do you think you're doing?"

Hao didn't have time to reply.

The alien's reaction was swift. He sprang out of his chair, shoved the High Inspector aside and threw himself at Connelly. The bald man toppled under the attacker's weight.

Chaotic shouts broke out. The two guards rushed to Connelly's aid and tore the alien away from him, then dragged the suspect back into the interrogation room, pinning him down on the chair. The High Inspector and Connelly picked themselves up from the ground, shakily.

Hao gaped from the alien to his colleagues. He grabbed his crutches and hopped out of the room. "Do you have that effect on everyone?" he taunted his partner.

Connelly glowered at him while he straightened his jacket and wiped at the dust on his arms.

Hao turned to his boss. "I take it you don't require my assistance for this interrogation?"

The High Inspector yelled, "Get out of here! I'll deal with you later."

"Yesss, Sssir!"

Just before the door to the interrogation room shut behind him, Hao took due note of the furious stare that the alien was directing at Connelly. *What's up with him?* he wondered.

He stepped into the hangar where he contemplated the spacecraft without really seeing it. *Connelly,* he thought. *Everything always leads back to Connelly.*

His mind whirled. He had told the alien that Connelly had taken a blood sample from the boy and he had replied, "Did he, really?" Why had he said that? And why had the alien attacked Connelly specifically instead of himself, too? Clearly, something was going on between his partner and the suspect. If only he could figure out what it was.

"Inspector?" A woman with a grey skirt and white shirt ran up to him, pulling him out of his thoughts. "Have you seen Agent Connelly?"

Man, our wonder boy truly has made himself indispensable around here, Hao seethed. The Inspector leaned on one of his crutches and pointed behind him. "He's busy right now."

"Oh," the woman said, her shoulders dropping.

"What is it?"

"I have a phone call for him. It's that woman, Laura Archer? She says she wants to turn herself in."

CHAPTER 17 *Fireworks*

What's happening out there?

Not knowing threatened to plunge Ben into an uncontrollable panic. He felt as though he were on the edge of a black hole, looking down. The swirling quicksand inside the hole reached its sticky fingers around his spirit, intent on tearing it apart as it tried to return to his physical body. He dare not try anything for fear he would tip over into the void.

How did Mesmo do it?

How had the alien managed to fight off the spirit portal's powerful tug? He closed his eyes and embraced the despair that swept through his mind.

No hope...

Benjamin Archer?

Something whispered faintly in his ear.

I'm going crazy, he thought.

There was a sound like rushing water, and from somewhere far away, he heard his name being called. He opened his eyes again and felt warmth emanating from his hands. They glowed a transparent blue.

Benjamin Archer?

Beetrix?

He held still with expectation.

Benjamin Archer? Where are you?

Beetrix! His mind burst with relief.

Beetrix buzzed at the edge of his thoughts.

I feared the worst. Your body lies immobile, yet I sensed your presence. How can that be?

I am trapped in the van. Please help me!

The bee's thoughts strengthened in his mind.

You may come.

Ben's eyes rolled back into his head, and suddenly he was floating outside the vehicle, looking back at it. He felt a cool breeze on Beetrix' wings, and leaves from the maple trees swayed above him.

I'm free!

For a split second his mind leapt with elation. But Beetrix' words crushed his hopes.

I feel your spirit weakening. I fear for your life.

Ben felt Bordock's trap tug at him, exerting pressure from all sides. He hadn't been miraculously freed at all.

I'm only using the translation skill.

Mesmo's words echoed in his mind: *The skill is not connected to the body. It is connected to the spirit.* Meaning Beetrix was providing him with a window to the outside, but his situation had not changed.

Beetrix' thoughts reached him.

What is happening, Benjamin Archer! I sense great danger...

But Ben wasn't listening. He had barely connected with Beetrix when he spotted the shapeshifter reach the van, open its back doors and disappear inside. Overcome with panic, he gagged as he disconnected with the queen bee and his thoughts tumbled back into the vehicle. When his sight adjusted, it was to come face to face with Connelly.

"What are you doing?" the shapeshifter growled.

"N-nothing," Ben gasped, wishing he could be anywhere else but here. Beetrix fluttered at the boundary of his mind. He shut her out entirely so his hands wouldn't glow.

Connelly eyed him suspiciously, his irises switching from green to honey-brown.

Ben noted that the shapeshifter was not in a good mood.

"I don't trust you," the bald man said. "Don't try anything funny while I go deal with your Toreq friend."

Fear gripped Ben's mind. "Where's Mesmo? What have you done to him?" he blurted.

Connelly bent on one knee to check on the black boxes. "You can forget about that scum. His hours are counted."

Ben felt the space around him tighten. "Why are you doing this?" he gasped.

The shapeshifter straightened and set cool eyes on him. "There will be time, later, to discuss the reasons for my actions."

Ben's stomach twisted. *I don't want to be here, later.*

He thought frantically. "Killing Mesmo won't change anything. Just leave us alone. What does it matter to you? Once you leave with your spaceship, Mesmo won't be able to follow. Don't you see? Whoever is waiting for you up there won't know the difference."

Connelly cast him a dark look that made him cringe. "*I'll* know the difference," he said. "His remains will be proof that I accomplished my task."

"Proof. For who? I bet even the A'hmun you work for wouldn't accept such foul actions..."

Ben thought he saw a sly smile creep onto the shapeshifter's face.

"Who said anything about working for the A'hmun?"

"What? But you..."

"Enough!" Connelly snapped. "Don't try to delay me any further." He hopped out of the van. His teeth reflected the cold floodlights, and before slamming the doors, he said, "Watch for fireworks."

* * *

Connelly stepped out of the elevator on the bottom floor of the Dugout and smiled. His spacecraft hovered before him, sleek and black, waiting for him. He had longed for this moment for so long. Finally, the pieces of the puzzle were falling into place. Not only would he get rid of Mesmo and his team, but he would return to the Mother Planet with a coveted prize: the translation skill.

These months of hardship, posing as Agent Connelly, had paid off, and he was going to enjoy every moment of the coming hours.

But first, he had to clear the area so he could operate undisturbed. He glanced up at the concrete ceiling, conscious that his means of transport was buried deep under the ground of the Dugout. The several floors built above his spaceship did not worry him, however.

He walked to his vessel, savouring every moment of his imminent victory while soldiers and men in lab coats went about their business around the hangar. He reached for the spacecraft's smooth surface, his fingers tingling with anticipation, and instantly the door mechanism obeyed his touch, sliding open to reveal the inside.

As he hopped on board, he caught sight of a couple of men in lab suits stopping in their tracks, their eyes popping out of their heads.

Connelly chuckled. “Better scamper, cockroaches,” he muttered as he closed the door behind him.

He immersed himself in a regenerative light, recovering his normal traits through waves of pain imposed by his shapeshifting skill.

As soon as he was done, he slipped into the pilot seat, cleared the front window, and began activating the vessel, taking no notice of the cries of alarm from stunned men who gathered in the hangar. The spacecraft vibrated with a low, constant buzz, indicating that an inner mechanism had been brought to life.

Bordock swiped at screens and symbols that materialized before him. The spacecraft huffed and emitted a low, repetitive hum.

The shapeshifter skimmed over symbols that scrolled down in mid-air to make the constant throbs more pronounced. Bluish light left the craft and washed over the hangar, each vibration causing the walls to ripple. Men yelled and scrambled in all directions, their hands pressing against their ears as sirens blared and concrete wall cracked.

Thick slabs detached from the floor above, then crashed to the floor of the hangar, sending soldiers dashing for the stairs like miniature ants.

The blue shockwaves turned orange, then red, rising in intensity, causing destruction as soon as they hit anything in their path. Thick slabs fell from above, some landing with a deep thud on the craft, but Bordock only smiled and increased the destructive power.

One after another, the consecutive floors that imprisoned the spacecraft from above came crashing down on the hangar floor.

* * *

The taxi came to a stop next to a back alley. Hao checked the shadows for signs of life, then, seeing none, paid the taxi driver and clambered out of the vehicle. The driver sped off into the night, leaving Hao on his own.

He checked the time on his phone. It was one o'clock in the morning. Eight hours had passed since the alien had been arrested not far from this Toronto street; three hours since Laura Archer had contacted him and told him to meet her here.

Good thing the High Inspector hadn't confiscated his CSIS badge, yet. Hao had taken a helicopter from the Dugout to Toronto in no time. He needed answers, and he needed them soon before Connelly managed to find a way to kick him out of the Intelligence Services altogether.

Hao tightened his grip on his crutches and made his way down the dark alley, realizing he could very well be walking into a trap with no means to defend himself.

Large garage doors opened onto a dark warehouse filled with boxes. Hao stepped in and placed himself in the centre of the storage place to be visible. His phone buzzed in his inside pocket. He silenced it without even glancing at the screen, focused on scanning the darkness. "Laura Archer!" he called. "I'm Inspector James Hao with the CSIS."

A gust of wind swirled into the warehouse, lifting dust and rippling sheets of plastic that covered scaffolds in the back.

"Ms. Archer?" he repeated.

Only silence greeted him, and for a minute Hao figured he had lost a precious three hours.

He clicked impatiently with the crutches on the ground when a woman's voice spoke from the gloom. "Where are the others?"

Hao squinted and thought he saw a shadow standing by the scaffolds. "What others?"

"I'm turning myself in. Where's your backup?"

Yes, the woman was standing behind the sheets of plastic, Hao confirmed. He shifted to face her better. "It's just me," he said.

Her form cut out against the gloom and stepped towards the exit.

"Wait!" Hao called, realizing she could make a run for it. "I'm unarmed."

The woman slowed down. "I don't trust you," she said.

"Look at me," Hao urged. "My leg's broken. I'm on crutches, for goodness sake! It's not like I can catch up with you."

She studied him from a safe distance. "I turned myself in to be with Ben," she said, then backed away. "I'll find another way."

"Hold on!" Hao called after her. "I understand that you don't trust me. But I came on my own because I need to talk to you about my partner, Agent Connelly."

This made Laura Archer pause.

She knows something! he realized.

Out loud, he said, "I need to understand what's going on. I need you to tell me what you know, one-on-one." Because she seemed to hesitate, he added, "Talk to me, and then I promise I'll take you to see the boy."

Her voice trembled. "Is he alive?"

"He is, but he slipped into a coma."

He heard her sob.

"He's being treated by our best doctors, Ms. Archer, you can count on it," he added quickly.

She stepped forward, a service light illuminating her face. "All right. Stay where you are," she said. "What do you want to know?"

"First off, tell me about Benjamin Archer."

"What about him? He's my son."

"We have his blood sample. It's like nothing we have ever seen before. It's not... human."

She approached him slowly and regarded him with cold eyes. "And that blood sample, who took it?"

"My partner, Agent Co..." Hao broke off, and then it hit him.

She watched his reaction and nodded. "That blood sample didn't come from my son," she said. "Your partner extracted it from himself."

Hao's mouth went dry. The past months flashed before his eyes.

She stood before him now. "The one who calls himself Agent Connelly is not who he says he is. His real name is Bordock. Bordock killed the real Agent Connelly on the night of *The Cosmic Fall* and took on his appearance. He is a shapeshifter."

Hao felt the blood drain from his face. "An alien...?"

Laura nodded.

Hao staggered back a few steps and plopped down on a box. "Agent Connelly..." he whispered, thinking back. "...was the first to arrive at the crash site..."

"Yes, the real Agent Connelly is among Bordock's growing list of victims. You see, Bordock shot down the spaceships that crashed on the night of *The Cosmic Fall*. Only one occupant survived, and Bordock wants him dead. That's why he took on the form of a police officer to infiltrate the CSIS. He's been using your organization to track down his enemy."

"Your alien friend?"

Laura nodded again. "Yes. His name is Mesmo." She bent

on one knee to be level with him, eyes pleading. "Please, you've got to help me. Mesmo and Ben are at Bordock's mercy right now. You've got to take me to them."

Hao rubbed a hand over his face, thinking about what she had said. As crazy as the whole thing sounded, her explanation joined the pieces of the puzzle that were scattered in his mind. He had seen some unbelievable things in the past weeks, but this one topped all of them. Had he really been duped? Connelly's face hovered before his eyes. Instinct told him she was telling the truth, and so he decided to believe her.

"I've been going about this all wrong, haven't I?" he said, half to himself. He tugged at his bottom lip, going over the different events of the past months.

Laura cast him a look of sympathy. "It's not your fault. Bordock had us all fooled."

Yes, but I trained years for this. I should have seen it long ago. Hao cast her a sombre look, trying to process the information. "Don't get me wrong, Ms. Archer. I was only doing my job. I needed to determine whether *The Cosmic Fall* posed any threat to our people, our nation, possibly even to our world. You and your son's constant evasion of the law was highly suspicious."

"We had no choice but to run," she said. "Bordock—your partner—wants to see us dead, too, even though the enmity between Bordock and Mesmo has nothing to do with us. Mesmo is no threat. He just wants to get home alive..."

"But what are they doing here? Are they planning an invasion?" Hao burst out.

To his surprise, Laura gave him a wry smile.

"I asked Mesmo the same thing, not long ago," she said. "But no, his people are no danger to us. He says small teams visit Earth at regular intervals. They do that all over the universe, to observe and gather knowledge, but nothing else."

"What about this shapeshifter? Why would he want to see you dead?"

Laura became even more restrained. "We've been helping Mesmo since he arrived. I guess that hasn't been to Bordock's liking."

"...and yet," Hao pointed out, "It is this Bordock—the very man you have been trying to avoid—that you tried to contact at the CSIS to turn yourself in..."

Laura cast her eyes down. "I figured he'd take me to Ben." She interlaced her fingers and sobbed. "I didn't know what else to do."

Hao stared at her in stunned silence. *She's willing to risk her life to be with her boy...*

His phone buzzed. He reached for it, but just then the sound of a roaring engine filled the warehouse. A black van screeched to a stop in the middle of the exit, its front lights blinding them. Side doors flew open and half a dozen men rushed towards them, threateningly.

"Watch out!" Hao yelled, shoving Laura behind him.

One of the men charged him. He barely had time to react, when the sharp contact of the man's knuckles on his chin knocked him over. Everything went dark.

CHAPTER 18 *The Last Key*

Ben sensed, more than felt, the vibrations that began to shake the ground.

He didn't register them right away because the pressure coming from the four black boxes had become unbearable. His spirit was squeezed too tight, his thoughts scrambled. He knew Beetrix was calling him from somewhere far away, but he couldn't concentrate on connecting with her with all his energy going into surviving the suffocating quicksand that pressed on him from all sides.

The van lurched loudly. His eyes flew open. Through the side windows of the van, Ben caught sight of shadows of running soldiers stretched before the LED floodlights. The vehicle trembled.

What's going on?

His mind felt as though he were suffering from a fever, where everything becomes distorted. The van lurched again, and a rumbling sound came from deep within the ground. Then again. And again.

Ben gasped.

A LED flood light teetered and crashed, the earth shook as

if a superhuman being was hitting it repeatedly with a giant hammer, and to his horror, Ben watched as the concrete building crumbled in on itself and disappeared.

Ben yelled, willing the destruction to stop.

When the earthquakes died down, the rattling walls of the van settled, and the night reclaimed its silence.

A branch thudded onto the roof of the van, making Ben yelp. He strained his neck to glance through the windows. Where once there had been an open area surrounded by trees, now red steam swirled out of a deep wound in the ground resembling the mouth of a seething volcano.

Ben's mind spun with one terrifying thought:

The spacecraft is free to leave!

* * *

"Inspector!" Laura voice came out hushed but frantic, because the bound man lay unresponsive beside her.

"Inspector!"

"It's James, actually," Hao groaned, moving his bruised jaw from side to side. He blinked and forced himself to a sitting position.

Relief washed over her and she realized this government agent had suddenly turned into an ally. "Are you all right?" she whispered, glancing anxiously at the four thugs who stood behind them, waiting. *Waiting, for what?*

Hao opened his mouth to answer, but a persistent sound distracted them. The Inspector's phone lay on top of a pile of boxes five feet away, humming endlessly.

Too far, Laura thought.

Two guards lowered a wheelchair from the van, its headlights bathing them in such a bright light that Laura had to squint. The wheelchair rolled easily toward them, the driver manoevring it with a simple handswitch.

The person stopped before them and turned so that the headlights illuminated his face.

To Laura's surprise, it was an old man. He sported a white goatee and his longish grey-white hair was gathered in a short ponytail at the back of his head. His slanted eyes observed them without a hint of emotion. He waved a hand with long, knobbled fingers at the phone.

In the blink of an eye, one of his men cut the call, then stood on guard once more.

When no one moved, Hao spoke. "I work for the federal secret services. Whatever this is about, you should be dealing with me. Let the woman go."

The old man ignored him and said something Laura understood to be Chinese.

In response, one of the guards grabbed Laura by the arm, making her yell.

"Wait! What are you doing?" Hao shouted.

The guard pulled at something around Laura's neck and it snapped.

The necklace!

"That's mine! Give it back!"

The guard held up the necklace to the old man, who studied it with interest. He spoke slowly, searching for English words. "You must forgive the rough treatment." He gave an order to his men who acted at once.

Laura felt the bonds slip from her wrists.

Hao glanced questioningly at Laura, as he was also freed.

"My name is Su Tai," the old man said. "We had to be sure it was you. We mean you no harm."

Laura saw Hao glare at the guard who had punched him in

the chin and got a cold look in return. "If you mean us no harm, then free the woman," Hao insisted.

"All in good time," Su Tai said. "It is she I have come to talk to."

Laura tensed.

The phone hummed again.

The old man glanced at it, unfazed. "There isn't much time." He turned his attention to Laura. "The Observer has sent us an urgent message. You have been of invaluable assistance to him so far, and you have put yourself in great danger. Yet, I must ask you to continue to do so, for the Observer's mission is at stake."

"What message?" Hao whispered to Laura.

Laura's eyes widened. "The fountain!" she exclaimed to the old man. "You saw the symbol Mesmo created on the fountain!"

Su Tai smiled. He held the small, black object in the palm of his hands. "I came at once and searched for you. But it is the Inspector who led me to you."

Hao twitched beside her, and she was sure he was bursting with questions like she was.

But the old man continued. "The Observer has entrusted you with Angakkuq's life's work."

Angakkuq.

Laura's mind reeled. That was the mysterious woman who had given Mesmo the symbol back in Canmore.

One of the guards approached Su Tai with a box, which he opened. The old man pulled something small from it and placed it in his palm. He now had two identical objects in his hand.

Laura gasped.

"It is highly irregular to trust an outsider with such sensitive information, but the Observer has spoken well of you and, considering the precarious situation in which he now finds himself, I have no choice but to hand over my life's work to you as well."

A guard picked up both objects from Su Tai's palm. He brought them over and placed them in Laura's hands as if they were breakable crystals.

"Laura Archer," Su Tai said. "The Observer never made it to China to meet with me. I have travelled a long way so he could receive this last element. Should you succeed in bringing them both to him, then he will return home a hero, his mission fulfilled."

Laura gaped. "You are one of the Wise Ones!" Mesmo's words flooded her mind: *"I came to assess the planet. My people have been doing so since before the beginning of the Human era, every two hundred Earth years. Seven Wise Ones report to us from different parts of the planet, from places you currently call Bolivia, Australia, Kenya, Polynesia, Norway, China and Northern Canada. I have met with six of them now. My last stop after Bolivia was going to be China, but then I came back here instead and was waylaid..."*

Laura blinked and focused on the old man. He smiled at her and nodded.

"And you..." Su Tai said, turning his attention to Hao. "...you have the access Laura Archer needs to reach the Observer. So, I will ask you, as one compatriot to another, to bring Laura Archer to the Dugout and protect her from the corrupt shapeshifter."

"What?" Hao gasped. "How do you know about the Dugout?"

The old man gestured towards the buzzing phone. "We have eyes and ears everywhere, Inspector James Hao. You have served your organization well, but have made the wrong choices. From now on, you will protect the Observer, the woman, and the boy."

"Is that so?" Hao retorted. "Who do you think you are? I do not serve you. And I am not your compatriot."

"You are right," Su Tai said. "That was a bad choice of words. While we may have come from the same region of this planet, current borders have no meaning to our situation. Those I serve transcend human history. I am here merely to assist the Observer."

Laura burst into the conversation. "You are Toreq?"

Su Tai smiled at her. "Do not mistake the colour of my hair for that of the Toreq. No, I am of A'hmun descent, though I do serve the Toreq. I have served them well. I had hoped that the Observer would concede me a one-way ticket back to the Mother Planet." His smile faded. "But that is no longer to be."

The light on Hao's phone came on, indicating a new incoming call.

"Our shapeshifter is up to something," the old man said, his face becoming gloomy as he glanced at the phone. "You must hurry." He turned his wheelchair around and rolled away from the pair. "I am counting on you, Inspector. And on you, Laura. Forgive me for imposing this burden on you both, but I know that, together, you can free the Observer and send him home. He has already lost his life companion and his daughter, he does not deserve further wrath from the shapeshifter." Su Tai was almost halfway to the van.

The other guards blended into the shadows after him. As they lifted the wheelchair, Laura heard him say, "And if you succeed, I trust he will speak a good word for you, when the time comes."

The van doors rolled shut. The motor roared to life, and the vehicle sped away.

Hao hopped to the pile of boxes and grabbed his ringing

phone, pressing the call button.

Even from her seated position, Laura could hear a man's screaming voice errupt out of it.

"Sir! Where are you? The Dugout is under attack! I repeat, we are under attack!"

CHAPTER 19 *Waking Dragon*

The helicopter landed on a bustling airfield. Hao leaned on Laura's shoulder to clamber out of it. Her hair whipped his face as the rotors continued to turn.

A military jeep stood a few feet away, a soldier ready to lead them into action. LED floodlights illuminated the airstrip, and army trucks passed marching soldiers at high speed.

Hao and Laura took places in the jeep, heading for the source of the commotion. They reached a fence topped with barbed wire and had to come to a halt to avoid running into an armed guard.

"Back away!" the man ordered.

Hao waved his badge. "Inspector Hao. I have clearance."

Laura grabbed his shoulder. He turned to find her leaning forward, staring ahead.

Hao did the same and felt a cold ripple travel up and down his back.

Before them, trees burned and men and women scrambled for safety. Some of them were visibly hurt. But what made Hao's blood turn cold, was an eerie red mist that escaped from an enormous, gaping hole where the Dugout had once been. Hao dropped back into his seat and yelled to the driver, "You! Get out!"

The soldier glanced at him with wide eyes, then hopped out of the vehicle.

"Laura!" Hao barked. "Take the wheel!"

Laura slipped into the driver's seat, pressed the gas pedal and bypassed the guard who was shouting at them to stop.

Hao grasped the side of the car, half to avoid painful jolts to his leg, half from increasing dread as to what they would find ahead.

Laura hit the brakes near the hole. They stepped out, hypnotized by the crater that looked like the mouth of a volcano.

"Ben!" she breathed, breaking into a run.

"Hey!" Hao scrambled to catch up with her and grab her arm just as she was about to loose her footing in her haste to glance over the edge.

Wisps of red, hot water vapour lifted from a dark mass that lay at the bottom, resembling a waking dragon.

Hao and Laura stared at each other as if to give each other strength.

"Ben's down there," she said, eyes pleading.

"This way," he said, ignoring his thumping heart. He had spotted a set of stairs on the outskirt of the hole to their left—only, it was one floor down, and there was no way to get to it.

We'll have to jump, he realized.

Laura glanced at him and drew her eyebrows together.

"I can make it," Hao reassured her.

She nodded and headed to the edge of the hole. Hao watched as she grabbed on to the side, then swung down. He heard a muffled thud and peeked down hurriedly.

Her voice sounded distant. "It's okay," she shouted. "The landing is clear, but you risk falling on your injured leg."

Hao didn't wait to hear more. He dropped his crutches and heard them clatter next to Laura. Sitting on the edge, he lowered himself over the side, copying Laura, then hung on until he had determined how far down the floor was.

"Careful!" Laura warned.

He let himself drop, landing on his good leg, but lost his balance and tumbled into Laura as she tried to break his fall. They landed in a heap on the floor, Hao's broken leg bumping on the concrete. "Ouch!" he yelled, biting back a harsher word.

"Are you okay?" Laura gasped.

Hao shut his eyes. "Never better," he groaned, drawing in a sharp breath. *Damn, this is going to hurt.* He bit his tongue and accepted Laura's help as they stood. She passed him his crutches.

"Where to now?" she asked.

"This way," he said, grimacing. Inwardly, he prayed the emergency stairs were still in one piece all the way to the bottom. At first sight, they seemed to be, but Hao realized he had a bigger problem. "Laura, it's going to take me forever to get down there. If you want to save your son, you're going to have to go on ahead without me."

Fear reflected in her eyes, but she set her jaw and nodded.

She's got guts, this one, he had to admit.

"Listen," he said. "You have to reach the seventh floor, then cross the hangar where the spacecraft is located. You'll find another set of stairs on the other side. It leads to the eighth sub-level. That's where your son is."

She nodded again, wordlessly.

"Be very careful," he cautioned. "We don't know what's down there."

"Be careful, too," she said, before heading away.

"Laura!" Hao hissed, suddenly remembering something. "Check sub-level six. See if the control room is functioning. If security cameras are still active, they might give you an idea as to what's going on down there."

Her eyes widened, but she gestured that she understood, then set off again, with Hao hopping after her at tortoise speed.

* * *

Ben listened to the silence with increasing dread. He expected Bordock's spacecraft to emerge from the hole at any moment. Then the shapeshifter would come for him...

...and that would be the end of me.

He became aware of Beetrix again, anxiously calling his name from nearby. He let the translation skill take over his thoughts and slipped weakly onto the bee's back.

The ground was littered with leaves and broken twigs; the large branch that had landed on the van lay to its side.

He realized that Beetrix wasn't moving, but hovered in one spot. She scanned his mind worriedly, testing his resilience.

Your spirit is frail.

Her statement frightened him because he knew she was right.

Come, she said, lifting upwards into the leaves.

Where are you going?

She didn't answer but used a warm breeze to carry her higher and higher until they reached the summit of the trees.

Beetrix! Where are you going?

* * *

Laura ran down the emergency stairs two steps at a time, swinging around corners with the help of the railing.

Lights flickered on and off. One bulb fizzed just as she rushed by and sparks flew over her head.

She ignored her thumping heart as she wondered what she would find around each corner, then came to a standstill when she spotted a sign that indicated she had reached the sixth floor.

She pushed the door open and glanced down the dark corridor. It was littered with rubble. Not daring to stop for fear she would give in to cowardice, Laura rushed to her right. Not finding anything, she backtracked and headed left.

Double doors, which hung twisted at the hinges, showed promise, and a fallen sign confirmed it was the control room. She hurried inside and found herself in a large room with a broken window to the right and television screens to the left. Wiping away beads of sweat on her forehead, she approached the window slowly, pieces of glass crunching under her feet.

Not far below, the dark form of the humming spacecraft made her skin crawl. She stepped back, willing her mind to focus on what needed to be done.

She turned and glanced at the many screens, half of which showed static. Unstable images scrolled across some other screens. She rushed over to study them, then gasped. A grainy image showed a room with several forms lying next to each other. One of them was Ben.

She touched the screen as if willing herself to pass to the other side, overcome by a mixture of relief at seeing him, but also distressed at the lack of a sign of any life.

She was about to go find her son when a movement caught her eye on another screen. She leaned forward for a better look, then realized the form belonged to Mesmo. The alien lay on the ground, surrounded by rubble. There was a gyrating switch next to the camera, which allowed her to move the camera from left to right. When she did so, a corner of the spacecraft came into view.

Gotcha! she thought to herself, having pinpointed his location, then hurried to find her way down.

She entered the emergency stairs once more but found that the wall had crumbled over the last set of steps. She wasted precious minutes clambering over blocks of concrete and iron poles, coughing her way through the dust that hadn't settled yet.

The final door had burst out of its frame and lay useless on the floor. Slightly disoriented, Laura figured she would find Mesmo to her left, so she avoided the hangar altogether and crept along the wall until she found the spot she had seen on the security screen.

She listened to the muffled silence, her breath coming out too fast. Then she heard a groan.

* * *

Beetrix headed away from the gaping hole and over the treetops, with Ben begging her to turn back.

He fell silent as he became aware of a humming sound from within the branches of a maple tree that towered above the others. It was a comforting, welcoming noise that made him feel safe. He knew before they even reached it that Beetrix was leading him to her hive.

What are you all doing here?

Hadn't he left the hive back at the park?

We followed you and clung on to the roof of the manmade machine that took away your lifeless body. You promised to help us, remember? We couldn't let you come to harm. We needed to know if you were still alive.

Ben felt a wave of agreement from the swarming insects. Although they buzzed around noisily in a chaotic manner, he sensed an inner harmony that allowed them to speak in one voice. He was reminded that Beetrix had told him about an invisible interconnectedness between hives, and the deathly silence that remained when entire colonies disappeared. He couldn't imagine how horrible it would feel if this hive went silent.

He sensed thoughts of wellbeing and encouragement wash over him as if extended family had decided to visit him in hospital at the same time and were wishing him a swift recovery in unison.

I'm not alone.

A gush of gratefulness almost pulled Ben back into the quicksand's arms, and he had to concentrate for several minutes to settle his emotions.

The humming song lulled him, but a persistent thought kept on pushing him to remain present.

I can't let Bordock win.

The idea escaped him, then slipped into the swirling black hole of quicksand that grated beneath him.

Beetrix, don't let that spaceship leave. Get soldiers... to stop... the shapeshifter...

There were gaps in his thoughts, the pressure exerted by Bordock's trap almost too heavy to bear. At the same time, he sensed that Beetrix was reaching some kind of consensus; one he wanted to be part of. So, with superhuman effort, he willed himself back into the centre of the hive and forced himself to concentrate. The queen bee did not involve him, but the determined buzzing suddenly made him aware of what she was doing.

Beetrix! Don't you dare attack Bordock!

The zooming became muted, and Ben understood that the bee colony had already accepted the challenge. His mind did a double take.

Beetrix! I forbid it!

The queen bee turned her attention to him.

My children were born soldiers. They have poison inside of them and will not survive. They know that they are doomed. That is why they are willing to risk their lives for you, so future colonies might survive. It has been decided.

Ben burst in anger with the last mental strength he could muster, *NO! I won't allow it! Don't...*

Something yanked at him.

I... I won't... You... you c-can't...

Benjamin Archer...?

Beetrix's thoughts faded.

Ben fell. His thoughts scattered at the violent tug that sent him reeling into the black hole. He slipped through the dark quicksand so fast he barely had time to open his mouth in shock.

He choked as his spirit collided heavily with something. He opened his eyes, letting out a halted scream. Someone held his wrists tightly, waving his glowing hands before his face.

"I knew it!" Bordock said with an icy voice, his face hovering inches away from Ben's. "You're trying to use the skill on me."

Ben heard something click.

"Not this time," the shapeshifter snarled, and everything went black.

* * *

Clambering over a fallen column, Laura almost stepped headlong into a deep hole. She gasped and pulled back, then spotted a movement to her right.

"Mesmo!" she cried, climbing over the rubble.

She dropped to her knees by his side. His face was deathly pale, dust covered his cheeks and hands, but he was alive. Laura examined his body for injuries and found his legs trapped in a gap between two slabs of concrete..

Mesmo blinked. "Laura," he gasped. "You shouldn't be here."

"Stay still. I'll get you out." She glanced at his legs worriedly.

Mesmo looked down as well and tried to move. "I can feel my legs," he said. "But they're stuck."

Laura exhaled silently, relieved that he was in one piece. All she had to do was remove one of the slabs and free him. *Easier said than done.* She grabbed at both ends of the slab, pulling with all her might. It barely moved an inch.

"I found Ben," she said, trying to sound calm as she grunted under the effort. "He's one floor down, but I think he's unconscious."

Mesmo tried to help her lift the slab. "Bordock has him," he said. "He has the spirit portal and is stopping Ben's spirit from reuniting with his body."

Laura glanced at him with fearful eyes.

He tried to sound reassuring. "We have to weaken Bordock's willpower over Ben. All Ben needs is a fraction of a second to escape."

Laura avoided eye contact. *Is that all?*

Mesmo must have noticed he wasn't helping because he added, "As soon as I'm out of here I'll get my hands on the spirit portal myself."

She nodded and concentrated on the slab with more determination. She groaned under the effort of pulling at its weight. It moved somewhat, but not enough.

Mesmo sank back, panting, then grabbed her by the arm. His attention had turned to a spot higher up.

She whirled around.

The outline of a man dwarfed them from above the fallen column. His hands glowed.

Laura yelled in shock and scampered away.

Bordock hopped down lightly from the column and landed on the very slab they had been trying to move seconds ago. His cold eyes were set on Mesmo.

CHAPTER 20 *Broken Trust*

"Fancy a test of skills?" Bordock sneered, his hands glowing brighter. His mouth curled into a smile. "Ah, but you seem a little *out of your element...*"

"No!" Laura begged, guessing his intentions.

Bordock turned hard eyes on her. "Still confused, are we? But, that's right, Laura Archer. I made you a deal. I promised you this Toreq scum would tell you the truth before I finish him off."

Laura suppressed a whimper.

The shapeshifter stared at Mesmo again. "How about it? She deserves to know, don't you think?"

"Bordock..." Mesmo protested.

"Tell her!" Bordock shouted, his face twisting in anger. "I want to hear you say it! Tell her who you are! Tell her why you're here!"

A thick, threatening silence fell over the two men as they glared at each other.

Laura stared at them, terrified. "Mesmo?" she said in a tiny voice. "Tell me what?"

Mesmo's facial features sagged. He wouldn't meet her eyes.

Finally, he said, "Do you remember, when I told you about the Great War of the Kins?"

Laura nodded stiffly.

"Many eons ago, the Toreq and the A'hmun fought the greatest war in their known history and almost annihilated each other in the process. But the Toreq came out victorious. After much debate, my people decided to banish the surviving enemy." He dropped his chin to his chest. "The Toreq banished the A'hmun to a lost pebble in the confines of space, with limited resources and isolated from any cluster of civilized planets..." His voice drifted off.

Laura crossed her arms over her stomach. She glanced at Bordock, who examined her reaction with glee. She found it harder and harder to breathe.

"Do you get it now?" Bordock said in a low voice. "That lost pebble is Earth. And humans *are* the A'hmun."

Laura shook her head in full denial.

Bordock smirked. "That's right. The human race is all that is left of the Toreq's most feared enemies. You descend from the A'hmun. You were placed on this meaningless planet a million years ago as punishment, your memories wiped clean, and this so-called *friend* of yours is here to determine whether you are still worthy of this rock, or whether you should be exterminated once and for all."

Laura took a step back, almost tripping over her own feet. Her eyes darted from one to the other, hoping for some sort of rebuttal. When none came, she breathed in disbelief, "Mesmo?"

Mesmo looked away. "It's true. The Toreq have kept an eye on Earth for millennia. The Wise Ones keep track of human progress, and every two hundred years, an Observer is sent from the Mother Planet to collect information on them.

"We have never forgotten that, once, the Toreq and the

A'hmun were like brothers, and we have maintained the faint hope that maybe, one day, the A'hmun and their descendants would develop into a wiser, more respectful civilization—one that would allow us to put our differences aside and make peace."

Bordock snorted. "That's never going to happen, of course. Humans are on the brink of space travel. They are already reaching out to other planets in their solar system. Within the next two hundred years, they will have settled on surrounding moons and planets. By the time the next wormhole opens, humans will have the means to cross it."

He grimaced. "The Toreq will never allow it. They can't allow a species that is responsible for the loss of seventy percent of plant and animal life on this planet to spread to other galaxies. Pure greed lives in their blood. It is this greed that sparked the Great War of the Kins. The A'hmun have not changed."

Laura's mouth fell open. She glared at Mesmo. "Is that why you needed Ben's skill? To find out what the animals have to say about us? And he told you they are on the brink of extinction because of us?"

Mesmo nodded.

Bordock gave a hollow laugh. "Your son has doomed the human race. That is..." he hissed, his eyes boring into Mesmo's, "...unless we stop this scum from getting away."

Tears spilled down Laura's cheeks. She couldn't believe the treachery. "You said..." she sobbed. "You said you weren't interested in Earth."

Mesmo set his jaw. "Not Earth, no. But humans, yes."

"I told you, Laura Archer," Bordock quipped. "I told you not to trust him. But you wouldn't listen."

Laura's cheeks burned. "Don't you dare judge me! You are

no better than he is when it comes to deceit. Release Ben at once and show me which side you're on!"

A smile crept on to Bordock's face as if she had just cracked a joke.

"She's right," Mesmo followed. "Which side are you on, Bordock? Are you A'hmun? Or are you Toreq?"

"I am both," he said, sniffing. "My physical appearance has allowed me to blend into the Toreq world, but my A'hmun side has always been a burden. I have lived my life hiding my bloodline from the Toreq. So, when the opportunity presented itself, I volunteered to come to this trivial planet to terminate the Observer's mission, away from Toreq eyes. Because, you see, humans must be saved if they are ever to defeat the Toreq and occupy their rightful place on the Mother Planet."

"Really?" Mesmo spoke sharply. "And who are you *volunteering* for? Who sent you? What did they promise you?" He paused, then gasped. "They promised you legal Toreq status, didn't they?"

Bordock's smile wavered.

Mesmo pressed on. "No Toreq in their right mind would have allowed you to do the vile things you did. And yet you show no fear in returning to the Mother Planet. Someone is protecting you. Whoever sent you must be powerful indeed."

Bordock's face hardened. "This conversation is boring me." His hands began to glow again. "This is as far as you go, Observer."

"Hey! Wonder boy!"

Bordock whirled.

Hao stood behind him. The Inspector swung one of his crutches at Bordock and hit him square in the stomach.

The alien keeled over, losing control of his power. Blue lightning burst out of his hands with a deafening bang, sending

Laura and Hao sprawling.

Laura hit the floor with a humph. Her mind swam toward unconsciousness from the impact, but she forced herself to sit up, fighting the ringing in her ears. Through watery eyes, she registered that Hao was also coming to, though not fast enough.

The shapeshifter had picked himself up. His spikey, white hair disappeared; his neck twisted. By the time he had straightened, Bordock had turned back into the bald Connelly once more.

Hao cringed at the sight.

Connelly smirked. "You got me there, *partner*," he panted, clinging to his stomach. "You should have stayed buried under that avalanche. But no matter, I'd rather finish you off myself." He lunged at Hao, reaching for his neck.

Hao gagged and struggled.

Dazedly, Laura watched Hao and Connelly scuffling dangerously close to the hole that she had narrowly avoided falling into earlier. She could tell Hao was wearing out.

Something small buzzed before her face and landed on her arm.

Mesmo, who continued to pull at his legs to try and free them from under the slab, saw it, too. It was a bee. "It's Ben!" he exclaimed.

Laura's heart leapt. *He's alive!*

Then, following the first bee, an angry hum came closer and closer. Laura lifted her head just in time to see a mass of bees come bearing down on them. She ducked as thousands of them darted by her, heading straight for Connelly. The black tornado drowned the two battling men, who waved their arms in a useless attempt to swipe the insects away.

The shapeshifter screamed.

Then, in a heartstopping moment, one of the men teetered

and slipped off the ledge while the other stumbled to the ground, succumbing to the angry mob of tiny attackers.

A cry stuck in her throat. Laura crawled to the edge and glanced over the side with dread.

Hao hung from the ledge with one hand, groaning under the effort not to let go.

"I've got you!" she yelled, reaching for his wrist. But doubt washed over her as she grabbed his arm and realized she wasn't strong enough to pull him up. She caught sight of sharp concrete blocks in the dark pit below Hao.

She lay down on her stomach and held on with all her might as Hao desperately tried to reach for the ledge with his other hand.

Suddenly, a strong arm lowered beside Laura, took over her grasp of the Inspector, and with one mighty pull, extracted Hao from his precarious plight. The Inspector clambered out of the hole, wincing, and rolled on to his back to see who had saved him.

Both he and Laura stared up at Mesmo, who stood over them. The alien man had managed to push the concrete slab that had pinned his legs to the side.

Bordock lay unmoving in a heap a few feet away. Hao dragged himself up to the shapeshifter and felt for a pulse, then shook his head. "He's gone," he said. "Bees got him good." He checked his hands and face. "I don't have a single bee sting," he noted.

Laura winced at the sight of the shapeshifter's swollen face. A dozen insects rose before her face and buzzed away. She lifted her hand, feeling bumps underneath it, only to realize they belonged to crushed bees. She glanced around as she stood in a hurry and found she was lying on a thin carpet of crumpled insects.

They died protecting us, she realized in horror. *Ben must have sent them!*

She raised her palm with the dead bees cradled inside, her eyes falling on the alien who had once been her friend. Her heart constricted. Fighting anger and grief, she caught her breath and dashed past him.

"Laura, wait!" Mesmo called, his feet thudding after her.

She was no match for his long legs. He grabbed her by the arm.

"Don't touch me!" she yelled, struggling. "I need to find Ben!"

"Ben is fine!" Mesmo said, holding her tightly. "Look." He pointed at Bordock's arm. The silver watch lay with its glass shattered, the tiny spirit portal broken in three pieces, their glimmer gone.

"Bordock's power over Ben's spirit is gone," Mesmo said. "Ben will be waking as we speak."

Just then a massive slab of concrete detached itself from the roof and crashed to the ground not far from them, sending rocks and dust flying. Mesmo rushed to cover her head with his arms, but she pushed him away.

"Leave me alone!" she shouted, her nostrils flaring. "You deceived me! And Ben, oh God, Ben! How could you?"

Mesmo responded, "Did I, really?"

"You lied to us! You used us!" she sobbed. From way up on the surface, she heard soldiers shouting orders, indicating that they were beginning their descent into the Dugout.

"Get away from me!" she yelled angrily. "Go, then!" She was no longer trying to save him. She wanted him out of her sight forever.

He watched her sob, then lowered his eyes and took a step back. He nodded slowly. Walking in a circle around her, he heaved Bordock over his shoulder, glanced at her once more, then turned his back, and left.

She watched him walk away, wiping at her tear-filled cheeks, then bent shakily to help Hao to his feet. They followed the alien from a distance.

Mesmo reached the spaceship, activated its door and dumped Bordock inside.

Laura could hear pounding feet resounding from somewhere high up, and a helicopter's strong light beam swiped past them, its rotor blades causing more red mist to swirl to the surface. Mesmo stood illuminated by the inside of the spacecraft, glancing back at them.

Her heart leapt in her throat. She released Hao beside a column so he could lean on it and stepped forward, but he held her back.

"Don't!" he cautioned.

Oblivious to his warning, she crossed the hangar, clambering over debris, until she was facing Mesmo. Without taking defiant eyes off him, she pulled the two treble clef symbols from her pocket and shoved them into his hand.

Her chin trembling, she said, "Take these, and do with them what you will. If we truly are the terrible species you claim we are, then all my efforts will have been in vain. But at least, I'll know I have nothing to be ashamed of. At least I tried."

Mesmo jerked his head as if she had said something significant. He set his jaw and took her hand. "Come with me," he said firmly. "You and Ben. You have nothing to fear of the Toreq. I will speak a good word for you. You would be welcome on the Mother Planet."

Laura recoiled. "You would save Ben and me, but destroy the rest of the human race—as if we were different from anyone else? How could you think I would ever accept such a thing?"

She could tell her words hurt him. *Good!*

"Who said anything about destroying anything, Laura Archer? Don't let the shapeshifter's words play with your mind." He lifted the side of his shirt and waved at the bare skin with a glowing hand.

Laura gaped as some of his skin became transparent, revealing a hidden row of treble clefs. He pushed the remaining two into place next to the five other ones, and they melted into his skin. "I don't know what these contain. I have not analyzed their data yet. Nothing is set in stone."

He glanced at her. "But one thing is certain: if the Toreq do not hear from me before the wormhole closes, then it is certain that they will send a military fleet to investigate." He paused. "The only way to stop them is for me to return to the Mother Planet."

Laura shut her eyes and shook her head. "And what will you tell them? That an A'hmun shapeshifter killed your wife and daughter, that a human held you captive, that my son told you the animals are sick and dying... How could the Toreq ever forgive us? How could you ever forgive us? We may have sealed our fate, but our fate is our own, and you have no right to meddle with it."

"Yes," he said. "What you say is true. Human greed is destroying the world we entrusted to them. But then, there's you, and there's Ben, your father, Susan, Kimimela... I have met the best and the worst of your species. The Toreq will place all this in the balance."

Laura hung her head, unable to hear more. In a broken voice, she whispered, "You broke my heart."

She heard him catch his breath. His hands went limp by his side, and his voice came out thick and low. "Do you see, now, why I told you I cannot love you?"

Her eyes widened as she met his.

He stared at her, meaningfully. "Now that you know the truth, knowing what you know, could you still love me, Laura Archer?"

Her lips trembled.

Strong flashlights swung past them from above. "Freeze!" voices shouted a couple of floors up.

"Goodbye, Laura," Mesmo said. "Tell Benjamin I'm sorry." He stepped back, his eyes on her the whole time. He entered the spacecraft, faced her and raised his hand.

For a split second, she thought he hesitated, but then he flicked his hand and the door shut between them.

Laura pressed a fist to her mouth as she edged away. "Goodbye," she whispered, tears streaming down her face.

* * *

The door closed behind Mesmo. Sounds became muffled through the ship's thick walls. He activated the front window and found a rain of whizzing bullets pelting the vessel. He caught a last glimpse of Laura as she sought cover.

Turning his attention to the inside of the vessel, Mesmo picked up the shapeshifter and dragged him into a cubicle at the back of the ship, then activated an electrical barrier to lock him in.

He took his place at the front of the ship, his body and hands accommodating automatically to surroundings that were natural to him.

Pressing a couple of commands, he activated the departure mechanism and felt a satisfactory jolt as the spacecraft came to life. Without a sound, the vessel lifted from the ground, making the remaining red mist swirl around it. It fit perfectly through the hole, sending soldiers scrambling to upper levels. The dark ship emerged at the surface and faced a squadron of army trucks, tankers and helicopters.

Unfazed, Mesmo switched to hyperspeed and arrived in a layer of clouds in a matter of milliseconds. Human combat aircraft pursued him for some time but were no match for his speed.

He entered the outer atmosphere and floated there for some time, taking in the curve of the planet, the outline of the continents and the blue of the oceans.

Then, with a heart that suffered as much as when his wife and daughter had died, he checked his trajectory and sped off into the far reaches of space.

* * *

Laura watched from a safe distance as the spacecraft ascended into the night, her throat tight.

Hao hopped over to her. They watched the gaping hole with the red mist swirling upward. "You let him go," he said in awe.

Laura bit her trembling lip. "If not Mesmo, then it will be another Observer. And whether now or in the future, eventually, humans will have to face the Toreq."

Hao squeezed her shoulder. "We will be ready," he vowed.

Laura gave him a small nod, feeling empty inside. "I need to find Ben," she said.

Hao puffed his cheeks. "Let's go, then." He turned and led her to the stairs leading to the last floor, making it down after some painstaking minutes. Hao clearly suffered from multiple injuries, but Laura guessed he wanted to see her through to the end.

"In here," he said, pointing to the sealed room that contained the incubators.

She entered and squinted at the gloom, while emergency lights flickered on and off. The first incubators were empty. "Ben?" she called, rushing to the back, where she had seen him lying on a stretcher on one of the security screens.

The stretcher was there, but not Ben.

She panicked. Mesmo had said he would be awake by now. She glanced around frantically. "Ben? Where are you?"

There wasn't a sound.

A wave of nausea washed over her. "No!" she gasped, cold dread gripping her. "NO!"

She swivelled on her heels, rushed past Hao, and bolted up the stairs two steps at a time. She froze at the center of the gaping hole, lifted her head to the sky and screamed, *"BEN!"*

CHAPTER 21 *Paradox*

The spacecraft skimmed by Earth's Moon, but Mesmo did not see it. He darkened the front window and concentrated on several screens that he had pulled up before him. Different coloured lights flickered, symbols scrolled down the sides, and intricate patterns turned on of their own accord.

He activated the hidden pocket that stuck to his skin. The neat row of seven keys appeared. He stared at them. All the keys were there, yes, but at what cost?

Too many deaths...

He pulled out the first one, examined it, then inserted it into a slot on the dashboard. A waterfall of information gushed before him. Minutes turned into hours, and hours into days, as he analyzed the data on each key, the spacecraft speeding through the darkness towards its inevitable destination.

The equivalent of ten Earth days passed during which time Mesmo scanned six of the keys.

The information contained in them was not good. Once his people were in possession of the data, he knew the Toreq would vote to put an end to the human race before they had time to spread to other galaxies like a cancer. The risk of this species multiplying and then depleting other planets' resources before having learned to respect boundaries was real. The Toreq had seen it before, during the time leading up to the Great War of the Kins, and would not allow it to happen again. Clearly, banishing the A'hmun to Earth a million years ago to give them a last chance to better themselves had not been successful.

The Toreq would vote against the survival of the A'hmun's descendants, they would sacrifice a handful of warships by sending them through the wormhole before it closed, and annihilation would begin.

Mesmo sat back and sighed, only too aware that, not long ago, he would have supported this decision unequivocally.

But that was before he had met Ben and Laura...

He travelled back in his mind to the steps of the Kalasasaya temple in Bolivia. The Wise One called Amaru had delivered a scathing report on humans and yet, when Mesmo had indicated that the Toreq would save him should they attack, Amaru had refused. He preferred to remain on Earth and share the fate of humans.

Mesmo had not understood it then, but he did now.

Amaru had already seen the doubt that clouded Mesmo's judgement from having had too much contact with the A'hmun descendants.

"The Observer is no longer neutral."

With Amaru's words hanging like a dirty smudge in his mind, Mesmo collected the last key and stared at it for a moment, before slipping it into the last slot.

He dozed off while sifting through the data, waking with a start to a crackling sound. A smooth, metallic voice filled the spacecraft. The words were unintelligible to human ears, yet Mesmo's brow relaxed.

"Receiving signal," the placid voice stated. "Identify."

Mesmo let out a shaky breath. "This is Earth Mission. Observer reporting."

There was a long silence, and Mesmo knew he had just unleashed great excitement on the other side.

"Mesmo? Is that you?"

Because his contact had called him by name, Mesmo already knew who it was. "Yes, Torka."

Another silence.

"We feared the worst," Torka's calm voice resonated in the ship. "What happened? I don't recognize your vessel's signature."

Mesmo's face became sombre. "The Earth Mission was attacked by an A'hmun rebel. I lost my two vessels... and my crew." He paused. "Rebel is dead. This is his vessel. I am the sole survivor." He stopped talking, reflecting on the failure of his mission. He had the seven keys, yes, but there had been too many deaths.

This time it took several minutes for Torka to get back to him. Mesmo waited expectantly for the metallic voice that came from his Mother Planet.

"Opening channel to receive data," Torka said. "The Arch Council is ready to debate the fate of the banished A'hmun. Our forces are gathered at the wormhole..."

"I'm not sure *A'hmun* is still the appropriate name for the peoples' of Earth," Mesmo reflected half to himself.

"The Arch Council awaits the keys," the voice interrupted.

Mesmo stared at the seven slots without moving.

"Wormhole closing in four-one units," Torka continued. "Trajectory stable. Confirm transfer of data..." There was a pause, then Torka added, "...and identify the vessel's second occupant."

Mesmo's head shot up at Torka's last words. "Repeat?" he

exclaimed.

The voice came through evenly, yet it turned Mesmo's blood cold. "We are capturing a second heartbeat in your vessel. Identify."

Mesmo whirled. He stared at Bordock, but the shapeshifter had not moved. Yet, Torka maintained there was someone else in the vessel with him. Searching feverishly, his gaze fell on the six, large circles outlined on the back wall of the ship—three above and three below. He jumped to his feet and scanned them with his eyes. Tiny lights scintillated next to each tube. A heartbeat registered in one of them.

The voice insisted behind him, "Identify."

Mesmo touched the flickering light with his fingertip, and a sleep-inducing tube slid out effortlessly before him.

Mesmo gaped at the boy within.

* * *

Ben opened his eyes. The contour of a man's strong features hovered above his own.

"Mesmo!" he gasped. He straightened into a sitting position and threw himself into the alien's arms.

Mesmo almost fell over, but caught himself just in time, then hugged him back. "Benjamin!" he exclaimed. "What are you doing here?"

Ben hiccupped into Mesmo's shoulder. "It was Bordock. He brought our bodies to the spaceship, then broke the connection with the spirit portal. I barely registered slipping back into my body before I lost consciousness. I thought you were... I..." The words wouldn't come as emotion overwhelmed him.

Mesmo pulled him to a standing position, staring at him

with eyebrows drawn together. Ben wondered why his face had turned ashen, but the alien pulled him close and hugged him tightly.

Ben sniffled into the alien's sweater. "I'm so glad to see you!" he said. "I thought I was done for."

"Oh, Benjamin, you have no idea..." Mesmo said, unable to finish the sentence.

They held on a while longer in silence, but then Mesmo let him go and said, "Wait a minute. You said Bordock brought our bodies. Do you mean...?" He broke off and rushed to the other sleep-inducing tubes. He activated them, one after the other, until the six tubes had slid out before them. Two were empty, but three contained lifeless forms.

Ben squinted as both he and Mesmo were drawn to the same tube. It held a young girl with long, white hair. Mesmo grasped the side of the tube, stooping over his daughter.

"Kaia!" he breathed in a broken voice.

Ben stood by him, his throat tight, and observed the delicate features and greyish skin of the one who had given him his skill.

It could have been me.

His legs feeling wobbly, Ben sank to a crouching position. He leaned with his back against the wall of the ship and bent his head in silence while Mesmo spread his arms over Kaia's tube and rested his forehead against the glass.

They remained like that for a long time, until a robotic voice crackled through the craft.

"What's that?" Ben jumped in alarm.

Mesmo slowly released the tube. "Home," he said.

"Wha...?" He stood in a hurry, excitement washing over him. "You can actually communicate with someone on your home planet, on the other side of the wormhole?"

Mesmo nodded grimly and sent the tubes containing their precious cargo back into the wall.

The voice repeated the same thing.

"What's he saying?" Ben whispered in awe.

Mesmo looked at him. "They want to know who's with me."

Ben gulped, suddenly feeling observed. "Oh," was all he could come up with, then spotted a form hunched in a corner. He gasped in fear. "Mesmo! Is that...?"

Mesmo turned and approached the lifeless shapeshifter. He deactivated the electrical barrier, bent to his knees and nudged at the alien with the tips of his fingers. "...Bordock, yes," he confirmed.

"What happened to him?" Ben breathed.

Mesmo turned to him and frowned, but instead of answering, he said, "Ben, your hands!"

Ben lifted them and found that they glowed.

A tired voice entered his mind.

Hello, Benjamin Archer. I am happy to see that you are awake.

"Whoa!" Ben exclaimed as Beetrix lifted from Bordock's form and landed on the palm of his hand.

Beetrix! Am I glad to see you! I was afraid you were going to do something stupid.

The queen bee fluttered her tiny wings without replying.

Beetrix?

She remained silent, and Ben sensed her crushing exhaustion.

"Mesmo, what happened to Bordock?" he asked with fear growing in the pit of his stomach.

Mesmo frowned. "What do you mean? Don't you know?"

"How could I? I was in there." He gestured to the tubes.

Mesmo's eyes narrowed. "You mean, you don't know what happened *at all*?"

Ben shook his head, tears welling in his eyes. "No, but I can already guess. Beetrix sent her hive on Bordock, didn't she?"

"Yes, but why are you sad? Aren't you the one who ordered the attack?"

Ben's nostrils flared. "Of course not!" He turned accusing eyes to the queen bee. "Beetrix, I told you not to do that! Why didn't you listen?" His voice shook as he turned to Mesmo again. "Don't you see? When a bee stings, it dies. It can only sting once. Beetrix sacrificed her hive to save us from Bordock."

"I'm aware of that. But isn't that what you wanted?"

Ben shut his eyes. "Argh! No, no! I told Beetrix not to do that. But she went ahead anyway..."

"Benjamin." Ben opened his eyes and found Mesmo with his head tilted. "If the hive hadn't attacked Bordock, we would probably be dead by now. Are you saying they came of their own, free will?"

Ben was crushed. He stared at Beetrix and nodded.

Mesmo continued, "With the skill you possess, you could have told the bees to save you, even if it meant sacrificing them. You could have imposed your will on them." His voice softened. "But you didn't."

Ben sat and rested his head in his hands. "Of course not. I would never ask that of anyone—or anything—to risk their life for me."

"Even if it meant losing yours..." Mesmo's voice trailed off.

Ben exhaled into his hands.

Benjamin Archer. Those I lost were soldiers who were raised to protect me. They knew that my future hive will only survive if you do, too. I ask you to speak to your kind on my behalf. You must tell them that the connection between bee colonies is broken. We are lost and confused. Our children are sick. My hive is lost, but, with your help, other hives will thrive.

Ben slowly slid his head out of his hands and nodded.

Yes, Beetrix, I promised I would help. And I will.

The insect buzzed.

Then let us get out of this box. I need sunlight.

"What is she saying?" Mesmo asked, observing Ben.

Ben forced a smile. "She says she wants out. Can we get some fresh air?"

The metallic voice burst into the spacecraft, and floating screens went wild with symbols.

"Now what?" Ben exclaimed as he watched the swirling patterns reflecting on the black walls of the ship.

Mesmo remained still as stone, taking no notice of what the spacecraft was telling him. Although the otherworldly voice spoke evenly, its continued repetitions made it clear that something was up.

"Mesmo?" Ben felt pressure mounting. "What's he saying?"

Finally, Mesmo looked him straight in the eyes. "He is saying that we have arrived."

Ben raised an eyebrow. "Arrived... where?"

The alien flicked his hand, and the hovering screens vanished, leaving them in total darkness, but then Ben realized the window had cleared, revealing tiny pinpricks of light on the other side. He bent forward. "Wow! Are those stars?" He glanced at Mesmo, his heart pounding, "Are we *flying*?"

The alien stared at him intensely, and Ben's mouth went dry. "Wait a minute..." he said, staring at the darkness again.

The spacecraft tipped, and a massive planet rose before him, filling the entire window. Brown lines swirled around its yellowish surface while the vessel hurtled under billions of icy rocks that made up row after row of rings that circled it.

Ben's eyes almost rolled out of their sockets. "Is... is th-that...?"

"Saturn."

Ben lost his voice altogether. He pressed his hands and nose against the window, his eyes not big enough to take in the immensity of the view that sprawled before him.

The spacecraft glided to the left, revealing the crackled surface of another globe, this one a beautiful bluish-grey, with wrinkles that resembled rivers.

"And that is Enceladus," Mesmo said, though Ben's ears refused to transfer the unbelievable information to his brain.

The spacecraft slid towards Saturn's moon, and Ben began making out translucent plumes of water vapor emanating from the celestial body. As the ship approached the surface and entered one of the plumes, a gush of tiny ice particles hit the window like glitter, making Ben jump.

The spacecraft emerged from the geyser of ice and headed for another particularly long one that reached out in Saturn's direction, then swirled mid-way and disappeared into nothingness like water going down a drain.

The metallic voice spoke incessantly, with Mesmo answering in a guttural language.

"What did you say?" he asked in awe.

Mesmo did not answer right away. "I told them," he said finally, "that my cold analysis of the data leads me to conclude that the A'hmun deserve to be crushed once and for all, yet my heart aches to embrace each and every one of them individually..."

Ben lifted an eyebrow, not understanding.

Mesmo seemed to have forgotten that he was standing there, and said half to himself, "How does one mend such a paradox?"

Ben opened his mouth to speak, but the alien said, "Approaching wormhole in zero-seven units. Wormhole closure in three-one units."

"Wormhole?" Ben managed, his voice tiny. He could barely stand on his legs. He blinked at the approaching, swirling geyser that was sucked into the pinpoint of a wormhole and forced the words out of his mouth, his heart sinking all the way to his feet as the realization hit him. "You don't have time to take me back to Earth, do you?"

He turned slowly to face Mesmo, who stared at him with intense eyes. The alien's subdued voice sounded far away. "I didn't know you were on the vessel, Benjamin. If I had known..."

Ben closed his eyes as dizziness grasped him. He opened them again and knew instantly that he and Mesmo were sharing the same, overwhelming thought.

One of us is never going home.

CHAPTER 22 *Return*

The doorbell chimed through the dark house. Laura, who lay fully clothed on the sofa where her father had placed an unconscious Mesmo so many months back, pulled herself upright with difficulty. Her hair was in a mess, and dark pockets cradled her green eyes.

She forced herself to the door, pulled the knob and squinted at the sunlight. She hadn't opened the curtains in three weeks.

Inspector Hao stood before her, his car parked in the driveway of her father's house. A black-and-white English Shepherd tugged at its leash, its tongue lolling in excitement. "Sit still, Buddy," Hao said.

The dog sat obediently, grinning at his master.

Hao's eyebrows knitted together as he glanced at Laura.

"Any news?" she blurted, unable to contain herself.

Hao shook his head.

Even though the sun was shining, she pulled her cardigan closer about her and sunk her chin into it so he couldn't see it quiver. She sniffed and moved aside. "Come on in." Her voice sounded tired.

Hao cleared his throat. "Actually, do you mind joining me outside? Buddy has been cooped up in the car far too long. I think he'd like to go for a run."

Laura nodded and stepped outside reluctantly, closing the door behind her.

They walked side-by-side—Hao limping somewhat—until they reached the fields where young corn crops reached shoulder height. The late morning was crisp and clean, and Laura could see across the valley to the mountains on the other side. She swallowed a lump in her throat and almost headed back inside, but Buddy sprang before her, barking excitedly and asking to be patted. Laura obliged. Then, the English Shepherd took off down the fields happily.

"I was at a funeral in Chilliwack this morning," Hao spoke gently. "We combed the Dugout from top to bottom. And we found something... or more accurately... someone," he explained.

Her eyes widened.

Hao sighed. "We found the remains of Agent Theodore Edmond Connelly. The real Connelly. We think Bordock must have kept him in the spaceship all along, then dumped him in the Dugout in the end."

Buddy came back for a pat, then broke away again.

"He was laid to rest this morning with great honours. His wife, Tamara Connelly, will receive government compensation. Hopefully, she will find some peace knowing her husband didn't abandon her, but died a hero."

Laura continued to cover her mouth with her cardigan. She knew he was watching her.

"I'm sorry," he continued. "I wish you could have that kind of closure."

She nodded in thanks, unable to speak, but now tears popped into her eyes.

They watched Buddy for some time, then Hao said, "I have been named Head of the National Aerial Division of the CSIS."

"I heard," Laura managed, sniffing. "They said on the news that the former High Inspector was arrested on money laundering charges. Something to do with Victor Hayward."

Hao nodded.

"Congratulations," Laura said, trying to sound sincere, but her voice sounded hollow instead.

"Thank you. The point is, I came to tell you that my colleagues are convinced only one alien survived *The Cosmic Fall*, and that he took his deceased companions and escaped Earth in the remaining spacecraft. They don't know about Connelly, or what happened to him. They have no clue there was an alien shapeshifter involved."

He paused. "All this to say that I cleared you and your son's name. You won't be bothered by anyone, Laura. Any contact with the CSIS in the future must pass through me."

He glanced at her meaningfully. "There is much to do if we are to prepare for the return of the Toreq. Convincing governments to prepare for a possible alien strike in a distant future is going to be an impossible undertaking—what with governments squabbling and so few people knowing the truth. But I have to try, and I may need your help when you feel up to it."

Laura glanced at the ground.

I don't feel up to it.

"Take your time," Hao said gently. "It's just something for you to consider."

She nodded.

"I... um...," Hao continued. "I also have another request."

Laura glanced at him questioningly.

He gestured toward the dog. "This new position is going to

keep me busy. I'll be travelling a lot. I won't really have time to take care of Buddy. So, I was wondering... you know... would you be willing...?"

The English Shepherd sat beside Laura, gazing up at her lovingly.

She forced a sad smile. "Yes, Inspector, of course. I'll take care of Buddy."

Hao's stance relaxed as if a weight had been removed from his shoulders. "Thank you," he said. "And it's James. None of that Inspector business between us, after what we've been through."

He shifted uncomfortably. "I wanted to apologize, for your son's dog. I would have liked to tell Ben myself, but..."

Laura looked at him in surprise, then said, "It's okay, James. You don't have to apologize. It was Bordock's doing. You were just trying to protect yourself."

Hao nodded grimly. "I'd better get going, then," he said. "I fly back to Toronto tonight." He glanced at her. "Will you be all right?"

No, I won't.

She nodded silently.

They headed back to Hao's car and said their goodbyes.

* * *

Hao glanced in his rearview mirror as he sped off, Laura becoming smaller and smaller. He set his jaw.

How does one get over the loss of a son? he thought sadly.

He didn't think anyone could, including Laura.

Before driving to Ryan Archer's house, he had checked in with NASA for the hundredth time. He had asked the US space program to point their satellites at Saturn and its moons, following Laura's instructions, but the search hadn't turned up anything unusual. A search of the Solar System hadn't revealed any sign of alien life.

He feared the worst for the boy, who, he realized, had become victim to a war no one knew anything about.

Reaching a curb, he slowed down to read a large sign that said FOR SALE. The house behind it was Victor Hayward's. The bankruptcy of the billionaire's airliner was forcing him to sell all his properties.

Hao pressed on the gas pedal, but his motor sputtered. He pushed it again, and the car lurched a few feet, before dying. Turning the key in the ignition several times only strained the motor.

Drat!

Hao hit the wheel in exasperation. Shielding his eyes from the bright sun, he skimmed the area, hoping to find someone who could help, but the hillside was empty of life.

He stepped out of the car, lifted the hood, and checked the motor. At first glance, there was nothing wrong with it. Squinting back the way he had come, he wondered how long it would take him to walk back to the Archer house.

Hao sighed and returned to the driver's seat, then grabbed his mobile phone. The line was dead.

What the heck? He thought as he tugged angrily at his sweaty collar, the sun illuminating his dashboard brightly.

He froze. *Wait a minute, that's not the sun!*

He tensed in his seat, then leaned forward to squint through the front windshield. The fake sun dropped from the sky and glided smoothly towards him in a dazzling display of light.

His jaw dropped as the radiant object dimmed and turned into a black craft that floated soundlessly over his car.

* * *

Laura sat on the steps leading to the kitchen. She watched as Buddy sniffed at the ground in the back yard, then uprooted some yellow dandelions with his paws.

The dog straightened suddenly, his dirty snout sniffing the air, where he remained poised like a statue with one paw lifted.

"What is it, Buddy? Did you smell a rabbit?" Laura said, returning her focus on a dandelion she twirled between her fingers.

She heard the dog bark suddenly from far away.

Laura blinked and stood slowly. "Buddy?" she called, realizing he had dashed off without her noticing.

There was no sign of him.

She left the stairs and glanced at the driveway to check if James had come back, but it was empty of cars.

"Buddy!" she shouted at the fields, stretching her neck.

The dog appeared at the end of the path that cut through the cornfields, running wildly towards her. She cocked her head and then shook it, wondering whether she had made a mistake in accepting a dog that she would have to chase all day.

She was about to turn back when a form appeared behind the dog. The person was walking up toward the house, and it was a boy.

Laura clutched her stomach.

It can't be...

She watched, expecting the illusion to disappear in the time of a blink.

But the boy continued to walk down the path. He saw her and waved. "Mom!" he shouted.

Laura lifted her hand to her mouth, afraid to acknowledge the feeling of extreme happiness surging through her body. She took a step forward, then another, and before she knew it, she had broken into a run, crying "Ben!"

They met in the middle of the path and landed in each other's arms so hard that they fell over, laughing. They hugged tightly, giggling and crying at the same time. Buddy sprang around them, barking. Laura wiped a tear from Ben's cheek, leaving a trail of dust.

He grinned at her. "You'll never guess where I was!"

A shadow fell over them and Laura raised her hand to shield her eyes. Mesmo glanced down at them in amusement.

She took Ben by the hand and pulled him to a standing position, then faced the alien. "You came back!" she said, breathless.

Mesmo smiled. "I had to."

She tilted her head, not understanding.

"You see, you didn't answer my question," he said.

"What question?"

He looked at her with his honey-brown eyes. "Now that you know the truth, knowing what you know, could you still love me, Laura Archer?"

She opened her mouth, but no words came out. *Did he really say that?*

He stood before her, waiting.

The release of a long suppressed hope made her heart bulge. Feeling giddy, she broke into a smile and nodded. "Yes. Yes, I can!" she whispered.

They stared at one another, bewildered at seeing each other in flesh and blood again. Then he pulled her into his arms and she welcomed his embrace.

Before long, Ben latched on to them as well, and the three of them hung onto each other like a single pillar rooted to the earth.

* * *

The giant maple tree spread its branches. Its leaves danced in an afternoon breeze, while the cornfields reflected a setting sun.

Mesmo crouched by his daughter's grave and made delicate flowers of ice flow out of a clay jug. When he was done, he sat on a thick, protruding root, leaned his elbows on his knees and placed his head in his hands.

Ben and Laura bowed their head in silent respect.

Crickets chirped and the first star appeared.

Laura placed her arm around Ben's shoulders, and he intertwined his fingers with hers.

"Mesmo sent Bordock's body, as well as that of his companions through the wormhole," Ben whispered. "But he wanted Kaia to return to Earth with him."

Laura remained silent beside him, then said, "He can never go back, can he?"

Ben shook his head. "I don't think so," he whispered. "It was him or me." He bit his lip. "He chose me."

Laura shut her eyes as she squeezed his shoulders.

They stood together for a long moment, until Laura tugged at his arm, indicating they should head home.

Ben knew she wanted to give Mesmo some space, but he wasn't quite ready to go. "I'll come in a minute," he whispered.

She nodded in understanding and headed back to the house with Buddy in the lead.

Ben stared at Kaia's grave for several minutes, thinking about the past events and about the girl he would have liked to know better. How much could she have taught him about the skill? Now, that knowledge was lost.

His hands glowed, and Beetrix landed in his palm. She fluttered her wings.

I will begin a new hive here. It is a good place. You can count on me for help, Benjamin Archer. You will need it.

She buzzed off and disappeared into the branches of the tree.

Ben sighed and went to sit beside Mesmo without saying a word.

The alien lifted his head from his hands.

"Thank you for bringing me home," Ben said softly, struggling under the weight of knowing what that meant for the alien.

Mesmo remained silent for a minute, then replied, "There is nothing left for me, back there. This is where I belong now."

Ben pursed his lips. "But what did you tell the Toreq? What was on the seven keys?"

"More bad, than good," he said. "But I didn't transfer the data contained in the keys. Without the data, the Toreq Arch Council couldn't draw conclusions." He clasped his hands together. "Thus, making it impossible for them to decide whether or not to send their best military ships through the wormhole before it closed."

Ben blew air out of his puffed cheeks.

"Plus, I told them something you told me," Mesmo continued.

Ben tensed. "R-really?"

Mesmo nodded. "An Observer is not chosen at random. He or she is elected by the Arch Council after much debate and from a large pool of candidates. The one considered the most apt for the mission carries a lot of weight in the decision for, or against, the human race."

He paused. "You said you forgave your father because at

least he had tried to make things right, even if he made bad choices."

Ben raised his eyebrow, trying to get his point.

"So, I, as the appointed Observer, recommended to the Toreq that they should apply the same thought to humans. Humans make bad choices sometimes, but at least they're trying."

Ben stared at the ground.

"Not to mention," Mesmo continued, "that you chose the life of a bee colony over your own..." he broke off, and his voice dropped. "That gives me hope."

Ben blushed and smiled shyly, considering his words as he drew a shape in the dirt with his shoe. How could humans ever come to understand the minds of the Toreq? If ever the A'hmun and the Toreq had once been like brothers, that time had long evaporated from human memory, lost in a blurry prehistory that came to state the human race originated on Earth.

"So, what's going to happen now?"

"Well, I finished analyzing the data contained in the seven keys. I will seek advice from the Wise Ones—some are favourable to the survival of your species, even if the data isn't. Then I will have to convince your leaders that they must act before it is too late. Humans will have to learn to change the way they live, to respect the land and other animal species and to create and nurture, instead of take, and destroy. Only then will the Toreq truly consider pardoning the descendants of the A'hmun." He paused, then added, "It's going to take many years of convincing and a lot of travelling. Two centuries is not as long as you might think."

Ben bit his lower lip and stared at his feet. "That sounds like an awful lot of work," he said.

"It is. But it can be done. I have to try."

Ben pouted and studied a particularly interesting blade of grass.

Mesmo nudged him.

The boy lifted his head and found the alien smiling at him.

"Will you help me?" Mesmo asked.

Ben broke into a grin. "I thought you'd never ask," he said.

EPILOGUE

Day turned into night. Shadows chased each other across the land. City lights came on, mirroring the stars. Coyotes scavenged for prey, hawks settled into their nests, and whales sank deep into the ocean.

The Earth drifted in space, oblivious to the sounds of laughter, conversations and bustling cities that dwelled on it.

Its faithful companion, the Moon, spread its white blanket over the sleeping souls, while beyond, all was silent.

The planets of the Solar System danced around their radiant king, as they had done for billions of years, and all was well in the Universe.

Or was it?

A low humming reverberated in a corner of space. Upon closer inspection, one could pinpoint the origin of the sound to a ghostly moon that belonged to the ringed planet, Saturn. Its unusual proximity to its massive ringed neighbour caused friction deep within its icy surface, resulting in giant geysers of water vapour being ejected into the vacuum of space, feeding Saturn's rings with its material.

It was somewhere in between these two celestial companions, in a blind spot from prying human eyes, that the friction was at its strongest, and water vapour from Enceladus swirled into a pinpoint of nothingness.

This hole, the size of a needle in terms of space measurements, collapsed in on itself, yet not before spewing out five dark spacecraft as it closed.

The impressive ships came to a complete standstill, only visible because their shapes hid the stars behind them.

Crackling sounds like static bounced between them, while sophisticated equipment would have caught the sound of low, metallic voices.

Within the largest spaceship, a tall man with white hair combed to the back and attached in a thin, waist-length braid surveyed the fleet. His small, honey-coloured eyes were hard and his cheekbones, pronounced.

Word spread that the suicidal wormhole crossing had been successfully completed in the nick of time.

But all in all, this event represented a mere ripple in the fabric of the cosmos.

THE ADVENTURE CONTINUES:

Ben Archer

(The Alien Skill Series, Books 4-6)

https://www.amazon.com/dp/1989605281

LEAVE A REVIEW:

If you enjoyed this book, please leave a review in the 'Write a customer review' section:

https://www.amazon.com/dp/1989605036

PREQUEL:

Read the prequel to The Alien Skill Series,

The Great War of the Kins:

www.raeknightly.com

The Alien Skill Series continues!

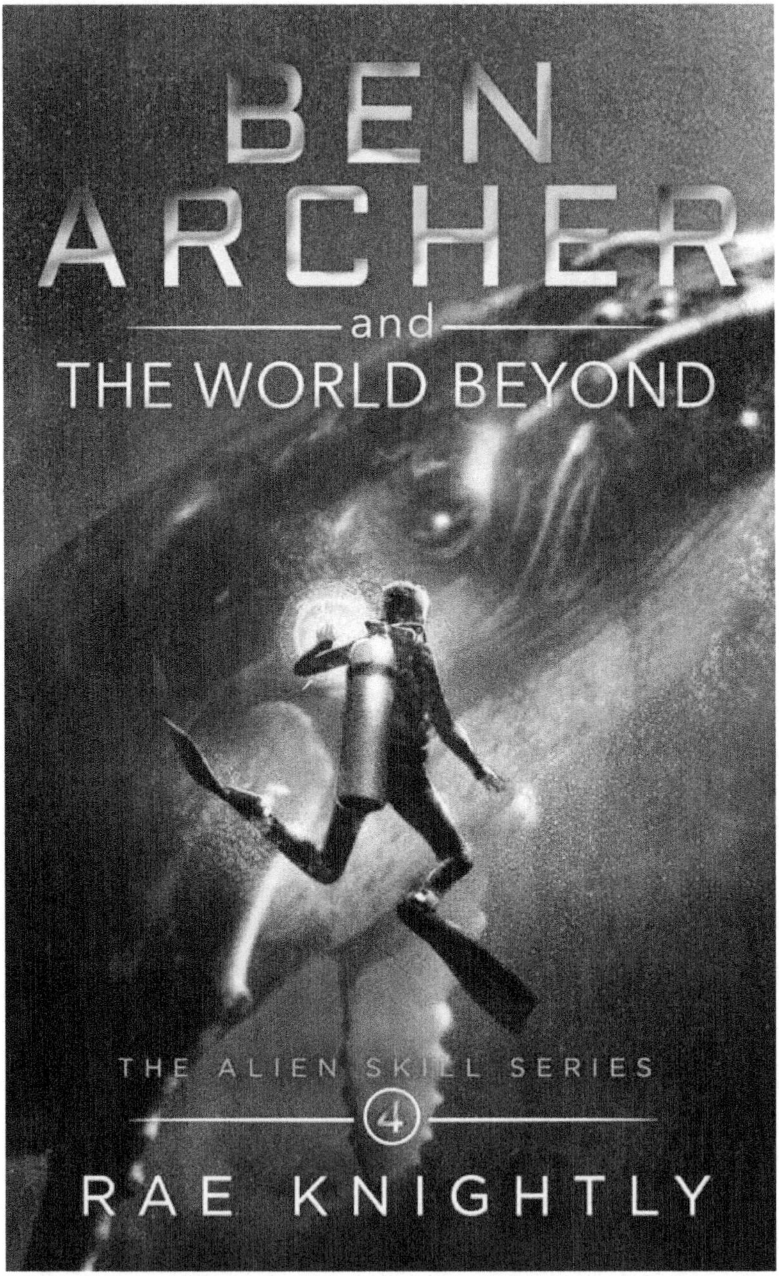

Turn the page and start reading...

CHAPTER 1 *Motu Oné*

Ben Archer pressed his forehead against the window of the spaceship. The crystalline waters of French Polynesia stretched out before him. An uninhabited island curved out of the sea to his right, displaying its sugar-coated beaches, lush bushes and coconut palms.

The alien who sat at the controls by Ben's side brought the spacecraft to a gentle stop, letting it hover above the water without making a sound.

The size of a fighter jet with two sets of wings and just enough room to fit eight people in its hull, the black craft escaped radar detection with ease. Nevertheless, the thirteen-year-old squinted as he scanned the sparkling horizon, confirming that no humans sailed in the vicinity. Cumbersome reports of UFO sightings could complicate their mission and were best avoided at this point.

Ben puffed his cheeks, the hot cabin making him sweaty under his diving suit.

Guess the Toreq forgot to install air conditioning...

"Mesmo, are we going or what?" he said, backing away

from the spacious window and throwing an annoyed look at the humanoid. "Gotta save the world, remember?"

The coral reefs off Motu Oné, one of a string of islands in the remote South Pacific Ocean, had been on Ben's mind for weeks. Yet, now that he was here, at last, Ben had to admit he had gotten up on the wrong side of the bed. Ever since he'd said goodbye to his mother that Sunday morning, a dark cloud had followed him from his pillow to this idyllic place. Mulling over why that could be, he picked up one of his fins and fought to pull the sticky rubber over his foot.

Mesmo didn't answer—too absorbed with his task as he shifted through holographic screens that floated before his face. The shadow of intricate symbols scrolled down the man's high cheekbones and honey-coloured eyes.

Irritated that the alien didn't answer, Ben sighed and crossed the hollow interior of the vessel to activate a switch. It released a metallic door that slid open, letting in a hot breeze that smelled of summer at the beach. He plopped down at the edge of the opening, swung his bare feet outside and dipped his toes into the transparent sea, admiring the pure white sand that lay ten feet below the surface. He reached for one of his fins and squeezed his eyes shut as he tried to pull it over his foot.

"Give me a moment," Mesmo said in a delayed response to Ben's question.

Ben knew he was reviewing the data given to him by one of the Wise Ones, who had last studied the area five years ago. "Jeez! You've gone over that ten times already," he said, grimacing as he struggled to put on the second fin. "Let's get our message out, Mesmo."

"You're right," Mesmo said, tearing his eyes away from the screens and leaning back in the pilot seat. He clapped his hands together. "Let's do this."

Ben watched him from the corner of his eye, becoming seriously offended with the uncooperative fin. "Mom's gonna need to dye your hair brown again," he said, noting that the roots of Mesmo's hair had turned white. Even though he looked like a normal man, the alien's otherwise bleach-white hair and unusual height could stick in people's minds.

"Yes, she told me." The alien tossed his flip-flops aside and removed his Hawaiian t-shirt, revealing his tanned torso. "So, are we going or what?" he poked, before taking three big strides across the egg-shaped interior and executing a perfect dive.

"Show off," Ben muttered, then whooped as his foot slipped into the stupid fin.

Mesmo resurfaced. He turned to face Ben and pointed behind him. "The coral reef's that way. Or we could try our luck farther out. There's a five thousand foot drop nearby—the entrance to the Pacific Ocean. Might be interesting..."

"No, thanks," Ben cut in, slipping his mask over his head and eyes. "I'm not trained for the deep yet. And besides, it would take me hours to decompress." He tapped his pressure gauge with his fingers.

"Come on, Benjamin, you don't need that old diving stuff. You know I can take both of us underwater." Mesmo's hands began to glow as he called up his inner power. The alien's fingers released a blue force that dented the surface of the sea until it reached Ben's feet. A large bubble surged from the water before the boy.

Trying to hide his admiration, Ben strapped the air tank to his back. "Jeez', Mesmo. We've been over this. You know I have to do this on my own. It's not like you're going to be around every time I need your water skill. And this *old diving stuff*—as you say—is the best my backward little civilization has got for now, so deal with it."

"Suit yourself." Mesmo shrugged with a smile. His hands stopped glowing, and the bubble burst, splashing Ben.

"Ha-ha." Ben grimaced, before shoving the snorkel in his mouth and placing his hands at the edge of the door. But his right hand slipped on the wet surface, sending him tumbling out of the spaceship. The side of his head hit the water, shoving liquid into his mask. He tore at it, sending stinging salt water up his nose in the process.

Spluttering and wiping at his face, Ben found Mesmo staring at him with one eyebrow raised. "Are you okay?"

Ben gagged at the sea-salt sliding down his throat. "Don't... you dare... laugh."

"I'm not," Mesmo said innocently, the corner of his mouth curling. "You know me. I'm incapable of humour."

"Yeah, right. But you sure learn fa..." Ben cut short because a familiar rushing sound filled his ears. He raised his hands, already expecting them to shine a clear blue. Ben closed his eyes and felt his own alien skill take over his human blood cells, the way it always did when an animal was nearby.

Trying to ignore his burning nose, Ben searched left and right. For the first time, he noticed how silent the ocean was. Wouldn't he be hearing a mingle of voices from sea creatures by now? He swam to the front of the spaceship and found the source that had activated his translation skill. A shiny black animal flopped around the surface. He reached out to it with his mind.

Hello? Are you in trouble?

Silence.

As he waded towards the creature through shallower water, Ben had to form a mental block to fend off fear that emanated from it.

Sh, it's okay. I'm here to help.

The animal twitched, and suddenly Ben recognized it.

A manta ray!

No bigger than a dinner plate, one of its triangular wings twisted in an awkward manner, deforming its sleek body. Leaning in closer, Ben understood the problem. The remains of a fishing net made from thin, nylon strings was wrapped around the young manta ray's body, pinning one of its wings over its back and hindering its movements.

Mesmo joined him, and they both set to work removing the entangled mesh. When they released the pectoral fin, the manta ray slid away in a hurry.

Ben and Mesmo exchanged a glance.

"It wouldn't even let me talk to it," Ben said, disappointed.

The alien placed a reassuring hand on his shoulder. "It's okay. We'll have better luck at the coral reef. They will listen to you there."

Ben tightened his grip on the nylon strings. "I hope so," he said. "Our lives depend on it."

Continue reading

Ben Archer

(The Alien Skill Series, Books 4-6)

https://www.amazon.com/dp/1989605281

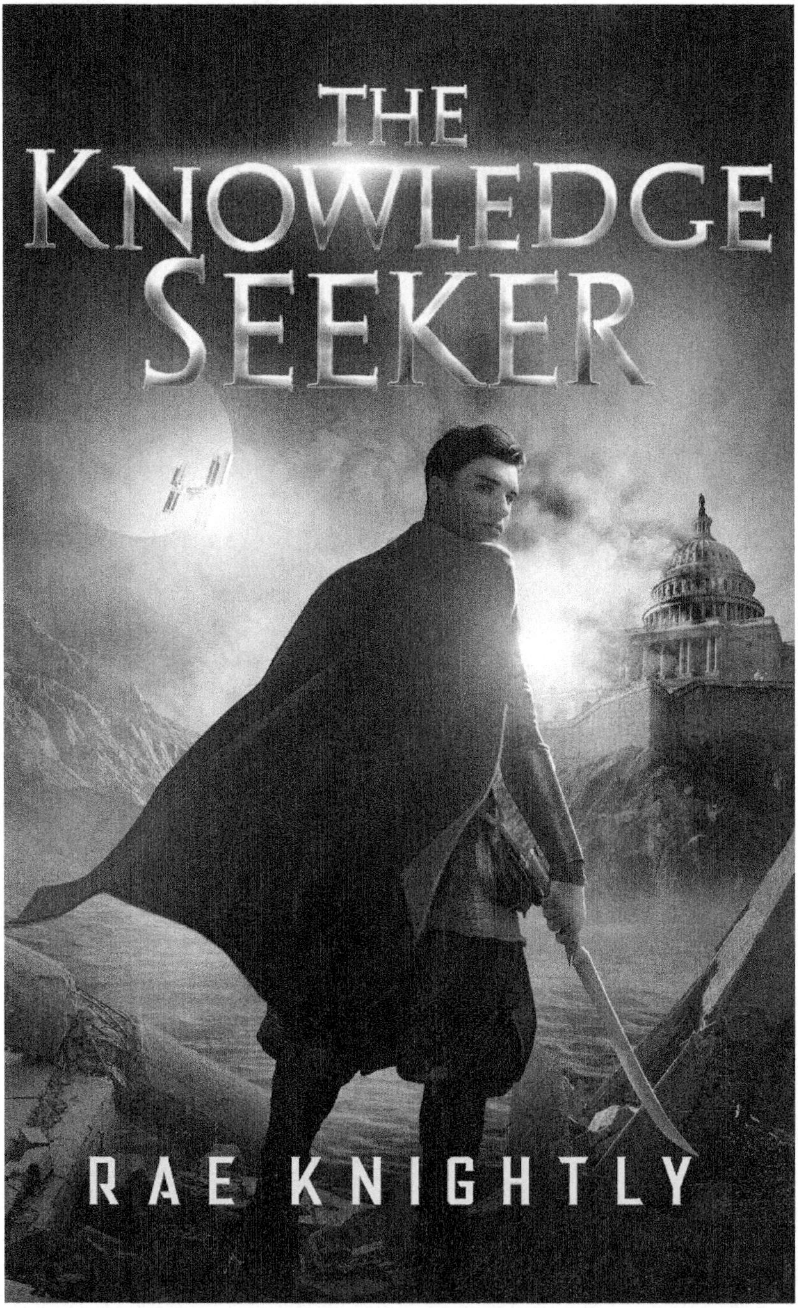

Turn the page and start reading...

CHAPTER 1 *The Coming of Dust*

My heart sinks as I watch the enemy approach. Tens of thousands of marching boots raise thick clouds of dust, obscuring the afternoon sun, which scorches the desert plains. Already, the advance troops are hammering away at the defensive wall, which is all that separates this vengeful invader from the hill on which I stand. Once the Roarim breach the defensive wall and take over the City of Eliadys, there will be little hope for us up on the hill.

A sharp pain shoots from my left hand up my arm. I stifle a wince and rub the place where, six years ago, the Roarim cut off my ring finger. The ghostly jab is like a warning of the suffering to come: the enemy will be upon us within a few hours, sowing death and destruction in their path.

The faint sound of creaking leather makes me glance sideways. Uncle Denesius's hand is clenched so hard around his leather scabbard that his knuckles have turned white. His tall frame towers beside me—stoic and commanding—and his gaze is set on the horizon. A gust of hot wind lifts his burgundy cape, the edge of it brushing against the back of my throbbing hand. The woolen fabric feels rough and used against my skin.

Poor Uncle Denesius! Did he really think the Roarim would lie low after he defeated the head of their army six years ago? Did he not foresee that a new head would take his place? Unless the rumors are true...

I hesitate, but need to know. "Uncle," I say in a low voice, so the soldiers positioned along the fortifications before us do not overhear. "Do you think the Wraith Lord is out there?"

A vein in Uncle Denesius's temple throbs, and I instinctively know I should not have asked that question.

"There are no such things as wraiths, Termite!" he snaps, turning hard eyes toward me. "I already told you that!"

My cheeks burn. His harsh words bother me because I suspect his anger is hiding fear. It is not good for a leader to go into battle like this. But the Grand Protector of the Atheneum fears nothing, or does he?

There are no such things as wraiths...

A troop of Knowledge Seekers rushes to join their companions, lining up along the fortifications that surround the Atheneum. Their burgundy capes flow, and their greatswords gleam in the sharp sunlight. I take comfort in the sight of them. These men will fight to the death to protect the Atheneum and what lies within.

I do not have such a cape, so I close my right hand over the pommel of my curved sword, which is smaller and thinner than the traditional Seeker blades. It is all I have to offer. "We will defeat them again, Uncle," I venture, deciding to ignore his anger. "You led us to victory before, and you will do so again."

Uncle Denesius does not answer right away, but when he does, his words chill me to the bone. "No, boy," he says, his voice cold. "Not this time."

One of the Seekers turns to glance at us, his eyes wide. He is only two years younger than me. I know this because he was Anointed yesterday when he turned fourteen. He received his official name—Odwin Atheneumson—, his own Talisman, his greatsword, and a brand new Seeker cape, which hangs down his stiff back. Its burgundy color is rich and full.

The young orphan glances at Uncle Denesius, perhaps waiting for a comforting gesture or a reassuring word. When he receives none, he pulls the cape closer around his shoulders and turns to face the army swarming beyond the wall.

A torrid wind picks up, bringing with it the sounds of thumping feet, grinding carts, and sharp metal. Battering rams thud against the defensive wall, the violent sound reverberating through the air all the way up the hill, and, each time, I feel as though I am being punched in the gut. Hundreds of our archers fight bravely from atop the defensive wall, sending volleys of arrows at the enemy, but, really, they look like tiny ants facing a storm.

Frantic screams from fleeing citizens rise from the jumble of low structures and narrow, dusty roads of Eliadys. Families and elderly people rush out of their clay homes—homes that had to be rebuilt after the last attack—and their disorganized escape jams the messy streets.

I rub my hand. Is this it, then? Will the City of Eliadys fall? Will the Roarim steal the Knowledge contained in the Atheneum tonight? Silently, I calculate the date according to the calendar of the Enlightened People: today is June 7th, 2613.

Will this be a day of triumph or disaster?

Continue reading

The Knowledge Seeker

https://www.amazon.com/dp/B09HL252JQ

About the Author

Rae Knightly invites the young reader on a journey into the imagination, where science fiction and fantasy blend into the real world. Young heroes are taken on gripping adventures full of discovery and story twists.

Rae Knightly lives in Vancouver with her husband and two children. The breathtaking landscapes of British Columbia have inspired her to write The Alien Skill Series.

Follow Rae Knightly on social media:
Facebook/Instagram/Twitter/Pinterest
E-mail: raeknightly@gmail.com

Acknowledgments

To my husband, for believing in me.
To my parents, for opening my eyes to the world.
To my children, for the stars in their eyes.
To Cristy Watson, for her positive mentorship.

To Giselle Schneider, Cora, Jonathan and Bob for their valuable insights.
To the people behind the scenes without whose guidance this book would not be what it is.

To you, reader, for taking the time to read
Ben Archer (The Alien Skill Series, Books 1-3).

Thank you!
Rae Knightly